The Beginning
of the End

Fredrick Hudgin

Novels
The End of Children Series:
    The Beginning of the End
    The Three-Hour War
    The Emissary
Ghost Ride
School of the Gods
Green Grass
Sulfur Springs
A Rainy Night and other Short Stories
    (My Short Story Collection)

Short stories
A Rainy Night
Ashes on the Ocean
Being Dad
Get Them OFF!
Gina
Green Grass
Nice Day for a Ride
Sowing the Seeds
The Chair
The Last Salute
The Longest Ride
The Mission
The Second Chance
The Wiz
They Don't Have Christmas in Vietnam
When Is a Kiss Not a Kiss

Poetry Collection
Four Winds

Fredrick Hudgin

The Beginning
of the End

Book One of
The End of Children Series

This is a work of fiction. Names, characters, places, and incidents either are the product of the author's imagination or are used fictitiously, and any resemblance to actual persons, living or dead, business establishments, events, or locales are entirely coincidental.

All names, measures of distance, time, temperatures, and math have been converted into their common English equivalents for ease of understanding. There are not English words for many of them and in their native languages, pronunciation would be impossible for human vocal cords.

No aliens were hurt in the production of this book.

The Beginning of the End, Book One of The End of Children

For my friend, Reid Cameron, who said, "You have to write this and, by the way, when is the next chapter going to be ready?"

"The greater the power, the more dangerous the abuse."

Edmund Burke

Chapter 1 – Sowing the Seeds

Fifty Thousand Years Ago

Grock Species Mining Ship GSMS-032 entered real space about half a million kilometers from Earth, the rosy glow of the wormhole portal surrounding its exit like a halo. The ship accelerated into a stable descending orbit that would avoid the planet's moon and give them a better view. It appeared to be everything the drone scan had promised.

Captain Phillium stared at the beautiful world, not really believing his luck had finally changed. From what the octopus could see under the intermittent clouds, liquid water covered at least two-thirds of the surface—not the superheated steam and sulfuric acid he had found on the second planet or the mantel, thousands of kilometers thick, of frozen water and methane that covered the gas giants farther from this sun. This one had huge oceans and massive continents with mountains, deserts, and plains, and, unless he was wrong, those green areas were filled with forests, rivers, lakes, and grasslands. Life—that's what he was looking at. He pinched himself with his primary tentacle to make sure he was not dreaming.

After nine duds on this expedition, this one had huge potential. Corporate would be thrilled. This was where the big money was: raising up intelligent life on living planets. No one had mined out this far before. Permission to go somewhere new was hard to get and even harder to get funding for, but all the deals and bribes he had made to middle-level managers were going to pay off—and this star was only the beginning. This tip of the arm of the galaxy contained thousands more systems just like this one, ripe like a basket of perfect fruit waiting for him to claim.

"It's all about return on investment, Captain. You find a Class 1 planet and we'll invest in you with better equipment."—The frigging accountants ran the galaxy!

The crew knew the drill and went about their jobs enthusiastically. So many species on board—each one chosen for their particular talents. Almost all species types in the galaxy had been found on multiple worlds.

Octopuses, with their eight-lobed brains, were normally the navigators, perfect for managing both ends of a four-dimensional wormhole jump. Med-techs were primarily arachnids because they could use the front four of their eight legs asynchronously. Felines and heavy-worlders made up Security—felines because they were so ferocious and cunning, heavy-worlders for their massive strength from living in two or more G's most of their lives. Because of their devious nature, primates were most often used in Analysis. Of course, based on individual talents, there were many exceptions. One of the captain's many functions was to keep everyone working together and minimize any inter-species friction.

The crew could see this world had more potential than any claim they had ever found; the bonuses paid to the captain would trickle down to them as well. They also looked forward to the "recreational" time, while everyone waited for the raise-up virus to incubate. During rec-time, they would have a chance to actually visit the surface of this beautiful planet and explore the other planets in this solar system. But they wouldn't get rec-time unless the Galactic Species Control Board (the GSCB) accepted their claim, and the crew had a lot of investigation to complete before they could submit it. The air on GSMS-032 practically crackled with anticipation.

While the company registered their claim, the crew hurried to their stations, preparing to examine the world. There would be plenty of time for play, after the work was done.

As soon as the Drone Control Center was manned, the technicians there released the marker drones. To begin their scan, the drones descended almost to the surface. Sites where intelligent life might reside had to be examined carefully. Was there any sign of crop cultivation? Had paths or roads been built? Did any population centers exist—villages, towns, cities? If they found technology, how advanced was it?

Each time a likely site was observed, the operators would have their drone release a marker pod—a sphere about ten centimeters across—which would descend the rest of the way to the surface. Each pod had a sophisticated internal AI to guide it and, based on the terrain, the device would configure itself appropriately: on a savannah, its legs could extend up to three meters; in a forest, it could hang from a tree limb; in water, it could float or descend as needed; in a canyon, it could hover; and if a particular configuration didn't work, it could change to a different one that worked better.

Once the pods were in place, they began executing hundreds of tests: atmosphere analysis, soil analysis, water analysis, radio wave detection, radioactive isotope detection, and a hologram high-def photo scan of the surrounding area in fifteen different wavelength ranges. The team gave special attention to the identification and classification of any life forms they encountered.

Two of the pods had to be replaced soon after they were deployed—two large, furry pachyderms crushed one as they mated and a huge grazing herbivore decided another looked good enough to eat.

"Captain to the bridge." The call came through his personal communicator.

"What's happening?" he asked as he arrived.

"Another starship just arrived. We think its beginning its own species examination."

"Who the hell is it? Are they pirates?"

"I asked. They say they are registered to Quyshargo."

"The Mer-people? What the hell are they doing here? How did they find this system? We're out in the middle of nowhere!"

"They said they found this system months ago and are getting approval to raise up one of the air-breathing aquatic mammals. They said *we* are claim jumpers and to leave immediately."

Quyshargo was the only world accepted into the Ur with indigenous water-breathing aquatic mammals. The Ur was the loose government of the sentient species of the galaxy that controlled all commercial interaction between member worlds. It was no secret that Quyshargo's king mentored aquatic species of all kinds into galactic citizenship, but no one thought they would stoop to piracy to achieve it.

"Open up a comm link to them. I want to talk to their captain."

A floating female Mer-person appeared in the hologram in front of him. A three-inch thick layer of water surrounded her, supported by the antigrav unit underneath. Her long blonde hair swayed in front of her breasts as the water rippled around her slim, muscular body. They stared at each other without saying anything for a moment.

"You must leave immediately," the being said. "This is our claim." Her voice was almost musical.

"We have registered this claim with the GSCB. It is you who must leave."

"We have also registered this claim. Leave or we will be forced to remove you."

"Not gonna happen, you overgrown fish egg. Go steal someone else's claim."

The Mer-person's eyes grew hard. "Leave now, or ..."

"They've opened a wormhole!" the exec shouted and hit the emergency jump button all navigators kept ready. In space, there were many reasons you would want to be somewhere else within seconds and every navigator built at least three safe, jump-away coordinates upon arriving anywhere.

The emergency wormhole they had used to escape was still open when the torpedo exploded, and shrapnel peppered the hull of GSMS-032. While most of it had been deflected by the asteroid shields every starship left active while parked in orbit, a few pieces got through, and hull penetration alarms began screaming all over the ship.

"That daughter of a monkrus!" Captain Phillium screamed. "Send a torpedo back at her."

"They've already jumped, sir. I don't know where they are."

"Engineering?" the captain called into his comm unit.

"Yes, sir. Almost done." He paused. "Two penetrations remain unrepaired, sir. One jump coil was damaged. Other than that, nothing vital was hurt. Emergency sealing should be completed within four minutes; permanent repairs will take longer."

"After the breaches are sealed, send me a report of the damages and repair estimates."

The Beginning of the End

The captain turned to Major Ang, his exec, "Twermy, will that jump coil hurt our ability to move?"

"Well, yes, if we jump in a direction that requires using that coil. I'll make sure we don't until it's fixed."

Captain Phillium pondered what to do for several moments. "I want you to move this ship in random directions at random intervals. Do it now—do it often. I don't want to be anywhere more than twenty minutes at a time. Outside of linked-hore communications with the pods, maintain emission silence." Major Ang nodded and began planning his next jump. Phillium pressed his comm button. "Analysis?"

"Yes, sir."

"Find them."

"Yes, sir. Working on it, sir."

He pressed the comm button again. "Communications?"

"Yes, sir."

"Tell Grock Central what's going on—and send them the electronic signature of that Mer-ship."

"Yes, sir."

He pressed the comm button one more time. "Sergeant at arms, report to the bridge."

"I'm here, Captain." Lieutenant Yawl Ohmel, a heavy-world primate with four arms, weighing in at over two hundred kilos, stood behind him. After the emergency jump, he'd figured the captain would need him.

"Yawl, wormholes work both ways; if they open another at us, send one of our torpedoes up theirs. Twermy, turn up our shields to emergency power. If Yawl launches a torpedo, jump somewhere else instantly—you don't need my permission. If we launch, you jump. Understand?"

"Yes, sir."

"Do either of you have any other ideas? Beyond waiting for them to send another torpedo, how can we hit them back? I'm not going to let those Mer-people wriggle out of jumping our claim."

Yawl had been working out how to protect the starship since he arrived on the bridge. He answered without hesitation, "I'll send listening posts with linked-hore transmitters into various orbits around the planet. As soon as they detect the fish ship's electronic signature, they'll alert us."

Then an idea occurred to him. "Twerny, can you move us perpendicular to the wormhole exit as soon as we go through—to avoid the blast path?"

"Yes, but things are gonna get broken. This isn't a military cruiser—it's not made for that type of maneuver. They know we have their ship's signature and will assume we sent it to Corporate. Why don't you remind them of that? And where the hell *is* Corporate? Why haven't they dispatched a security detail to protect us?"

"Give me a minute." The captain floated into his secure voice cube on the side of the bridge. Everyone could hear him shouting but not exactly what was being said. The door opened and he floated out, and by the look on his face, they already knew what the answer was. "All the security teams are busy somewhere else. It looks like we'll have to protect ourselves."

Everyone knew the real reason: they weren't a Class 1 ship at Grock—those ships got the first of everything. But unless the Mer-people took this claim away from them, they would *become* a Class 1 ship, when they left this planet.

Now the analysis of the life forms became a race against time—billions of huz and all of their bonuses depended on it. The GSCB would award the permit to perform the raise-up to whoever completed their package first, but first all the data had to be bundled according to the guidelines in the Galactic Species Proliferation Act.

... ...

The crew became so used to the sound of a jump warning alert that, beyond clasping a jump anchor nearby, most of them didn't pay any attention to it at all. Sleeping crew didn't awaken. Eating crew simply held on to their meals and tightened their containment belts a little.

The Analysis Center began examining the data as soon as the first of it flowed into the ship's computers from the pods. They ruled out the presence of advanced technology pretty early on—no radio emissions of any kind, no dams on the rivers, no visible roads, no radioisotopes, and no pollution. Some primitive, stick-wielding primates were found, clustered around a water-filled basin on the largest continent about thirty degrees up from the equator and several air-breathing aquatic life-forms, both had intelligence potential.

Grock Corporation had filed a complaint about the Quyshargo ship jumping their claim. The Mer-ship had done the same thing. Data collection pods placed by GSMS-032 kept disappearing or becoming nonfunctional. The Mer-ship denied any knowledge of the disappearances and damage, of course, but the Mer-pods began disappearing also. No one had the slightest idea where they had gone. Each time a Grock pod disappeared, the Drone Control Center had to send a new pod down and start its scans over. The end result was that data collection was taking far too long for everyone.

Finally, the Grock ship completed their scan. Admin filled out the electronic forms to accompany the collected data and sent the package to the GSCB. The captain got on the shipwide PA system. "The analysis package is being sent. Thank you for your hard work in finishing up in spite of the interference. As a way of saying thank you, even though we haven't yet received approval for our claim, I am declaring a Captain's Holiday.

"Medical has approved visiting the surface; oxygen-breathers desiring it may descend to relax or explore. You must wear your nano sterile suits while you are away from your lander. I know they feel like you are wearing nothing, but trust them. They will float you to the ground if you fall and protect you against anything this side of a nuke, including biological agents and predators, and still let you feel the wind, waves, and sand.

"Use the waste cabinets in the landers for your bodily functions—we don't want to infect this world any more than we want it to infect you. Always stay in groups of two or more. Bring freeze guns to protect yourselves. And remember to stay away from the possible raise-up species.

"Most important, stay away from the Mer-people's examination areas. Don't let them see you, don't interact with them, if they approach you, return to the ship without delay—don't let them near you. And no souvenirs! We don't know what germs this world has and we certainly don't want theirs onboard. Other than that, have fun. You've earned it."

The anticipation was over. It was finally here: REC-TIME!

Only a combat crew remained on the ship to continue moving it from spot to spot and keep their claim secure. The Mer-people's ship was still an unknown and other pirates could show up at any time.

... ...

The raise-up permit status remained pending—the Quyshargo ship had submitted their application within seconds of the Grock filing, and the GSCB had escalated resolution to the emperor's office. There was nothing to do but wait.

The crew had the traditional lottery going as to which species the GSCB would chose for the raise-up, and animated discussions and analyses filled every off-duty place of relaxation. Most crew members chose one of the air-breathing, aquatic mammals or the primates, but some members thought neither species was ready.

After another three days, the GSCB announced the claim was being awarded to Grock Corporation and the selected species was the primates. They instructed Grock to begin its raise-up.

All the winning tickets from the crew members who'd bet on the primates were put into a box. The captain put on a blindfold and chose one to receive the collected money. It was a popular ceremony that everyone enjoyed. "Six-fifty-nine," he announced into the shipwide PA. Two decks below, a female medical technician squealed in excitement and ran all the way to bridge; she arrived out of breath and almost stumbled. "Do you have six-fifty-nine, Greeha?"

"Yes, I do, sir. It's right here." The arachnid held out the ticket.

The Beginning of the End

He checked the numbers and announced: "Med-Tech Greeha has won the prize and the right to collect the DNA from this species' Eve. Congratulations, Greeha!"

If her smile had been any bigger, her face would have popped. She had never won a species-picking contest before. She tucked her orange hair behind her green antennae and hoped her mother wouldn't notice how much it needed a trim.

The ship's photographer circled around the two of them, making a hologram for the Grock Corporation Community Relations Department.

The captain continued, "As soon as the collection is complete, the DNA from the Eve will be inserted into the SIV-2 for incubation." The SIV-2 was the Species Inoculation Virus. It was the vehicle that delivered the DNA modification to the selected species during the raise-up process. "In a week we will release the virus and start these primates on their way to galactic citizenship; then we can move on to the next wonderful world waiting to make us rich!"

A combat team and another medic accompanied Greeha to the surface in case things got out of hand. Primitive animals, especially primates, were sometimes violent and always unpredictable. The team landed near a settlement of the primates and began a careful approach. Greeha, armed with a freeze gun, was in the middle of the team so they could protect her from interference by the other members of the clan.

While the team was on the ground, the Genetics Lab prepared multiple copies of the SIV-2 virus for the coming DNA; if one virus failed, a backup would succeed. The primates' intelligence would double with vastly increased cognitive powers and brain mass. At least as important, their manual dexterity and use of opposable thumbs would increase by the same amount— intelligence without the ability to make and use tools hardly ever led to an admissible species.

The ground team encountered a group of primates eating in a berry patch, not far from their cave. "Remember to select a female for your Eve," the team commander whispered. "Female primates will have teats on their chests."

She chuckled. "You think a med-tech wouldn't know the difference between a male and female primate?"

He ignored her. "Juveniles are the best candidates, and aim at her chest—it won't hurt her a bit. The Eve will collapse where she is, unconscious. Make sure she's somewhere where she won't be injured by the fall."

Greeha sighted the weapon easily with her front four legs—it was a little heavy for just her front two, which the arachnid used for fine detail work when performing medical procedures Her other four kept her body stable. The moment before Greeha pulled the trigger, the juvenile female she had targeted turned to look directly at her. Instead of panicking, the female cocked her head and studied the arachnid. She had no fear in her expression, just intense curiosity. Greeha pulled the trigger; the weapon emitted a slight buzz, but no recoil, and the female primate dropped, unconscious.

The other members of the female's family fled to their cave nearby. Greeha opened the primate's mouth and pressed the DNA collector against her inner cheek. The green light on the side of the collector turned red, indicating a successful collection, and a confirmation beep issued from the unit.

"Why do they always call the DNA donor Eve?" Greeha asked the team commander as they made their way back to the lander.

"Don't know where the term came from," he said gruffly, "but everyone uses it."

"I know where it came from," the backup medic whispered to her from behind.

"Where?" Greeha whispered over her shoulder, intrigued.

"Eve was supposed to be the first mother of the first species. Legend gives her lots of different names around the galaxy. Eve is the most common."

"That's just an old myth," Greeha laughed, dismissing the whole thing. "Something mothers tell their babies on rainy nights. Nobody knows what really happened."

The old medic shrugged. "Many legends have some basis in fact. Is there really any difference between birthing a new species or being the person who selects the members to be included—all of them belong because of her."

... ...

Genetics did a cursory scan of the collected DNA and saw nothing out of the ordinary. They saw what changes were necessary for the raise-up and quickly built the instructions into the virus. They inserted the Eve's DNA into the SIV-2s and started their incubations. Since many different species on a developing planet had a similar genetic makeup, the virus used the DNA from the Eve to identify the exact group of organisms to be modified. Before the SIV-2 accepted any individual for modification, a 99.5% or higher match between the Eve's DNA and the target organism was necessary. Once a candidate passed the identification threshold, the Eve's DNA was discarded and the rest of the virus took over to perform the actual modifications on the candidate's own DNA. This allowed the genetic diversity of the species to be preserved, which further increased the chances of the raise-up being successful in the long term.

Creation of enough virus to disseminate it across the surface required a full five more rotations of the planet. Even then, only half of the primates would actually be raised up—there were just too many isolated colonies of the animals to depend on the virus being carried to the entire population by air or personal contact. All uninfected members of the species would continue on their original genetic path. The raised-up members of their species would eventually overwhelm them—it had happened too consistently for any other outcome to be expected. Modified members would begin to appear within a year as the infected individuals reproduced.

As everyone on the starship waited for the virus to incubate, the captain began to rotate the crew down to the surface. Genetics released the virus to the sergeant at arms after five days of incubation. The distribution vehicle left the ship and traveled halfway to the planet, where it split into sixteen separate modules which descended into the atmosphere. Those sixteen devices flew preassigned patterns as they emptied their reservoirs into the air over the known areas of the primates.

"Captain to the bridge." Phillium rolled his eyes. *What now?*

His exec was waiting for him. "I think the Mer-people just released a raise-up of their own?"

"WHAT?"

"They just sent this on its way to the surface." He pointed to his navigation hologram in front of him and both of them watched something moving on a trajectory toward the largest ocean.

"Evacuate it into a stable orbit! I don't care what it is—this is our planet now and they can't touch it!"

His exec had expected this reaction; in anticipation, he had readied the evacuation device. Moments later, he sent the evacuator, via wormhole, to intercept whatever the Quyshargo ship had released. The item disappeared from the hologram.

"Send a robot to examine the device in orbit. I don't want anyone near it until we find out what it is."

"Yes, sir. Do you think it was a raise-up?"

"We have to find out before we start screaming foul. If that daughter of a monkrus ..."

"Yes, sir." His exec left without hearing the rest of the captain's tirade.

After the robot examined the device and found it did not contain any explosives, they passed it to Engineering, who disassembled it and passed the payload to Genetics.

The head of Genetics called his communicator an hour later. "Captain?"

"Yes, Palno. What did you find?"

"As you expected, the device was a virus distribution vehicle. It wasn't a raise-up, though, it was an elimination virus."

"Elimination? That doesn't make any sense." A light went on in the captain's head. "They were trying to eliminate the *primates!*"

"No, sir," his exec added hastily. "The DNA doesn't belong to any of the species down below—we crosschecked all of them. I checked the DNA profiles of the species onboard, though, and ... Captain, the virus was targeted at you—your species, I mean."

"*ME?* Son of a monkrus!" A wave of anger coursed through Captain Phillium. Now it was personal! "How did they get my DNA?"

The Beginning of the End

"It wasn't your DNA, sir—it was from a female—but, as I'm sure you know, any member of your species would have worked, sir. Many starships have an octopus navigator."

The captain still couldn't believe the Mer-captain had done it. She knew he would not allow it to deploy the device—that he would retrieve and examine it. If he had opened the device outside of the sterile containment in Genetics, he would have carried the virus back to his home without even knowing it. It would have made his race of octopuses sterile and, over the course of his lifetime, died off. No one had ever found a cure for an elimination virus, and that was kind of the point: why would you have an elimination virus with a cure?

He brought up a real-time hologram of the beautiful blue orb slowly spinning below them. "We will meet again, Mer-monkrus. Somewhere, someday, we will meet again and settle this one-on-one." He made a pirate's rune and spit into his shadow on the deck.

Analysis could detect no trace of them in this solar system—the Quyshargo ship had apparently disappeared into a wormhole as soon as it released the device. Grock Corporation filed a complaint against the Mer-people. Their king responded, saying he had no knowledge of any species mining ship or species elimination virus.

Before they could move on to the next star, the crew had to put in place the wormhole detectors on the planet's moon and register them with the galactic government via a special initial broadcast. These detectors would do two things: alert the galaxy when this raised-up species opened their first wormhole, assuming they ever did, and protect this world from any other unauthorized intruders while the raised-up primates matured.

Some modified species failed to thrive and disappeared without a trace. The few species that did make the cut, however, recouped the expense of all the failed ones. The money to be made from a new galactic member was massive; the mining company got twenty-five percent of all profits from the sale of goods from around the galaxy to the new member and twenty-five percent of all profits from the sale of any new technology and products from that member to the rest of the galaxy.

The GSCB acknowledged the registration of the wormhole detectors. Phillium congratulated the crew on a job well done and then alerted them that they were about to jump to the next potential star. When everything was ready, he reached for the jump button and pressed it with one of his tentacles.

… … … … … … … … …

After the rosy glow around the portal from the departing Grock starship faded, a small, non-reflective, non-emitting device, appearing to be an asteroid on the scans, left a low orbit and descended into the atmosphere over the largest ocean. It made its way in a crisscross pattern, leaving a powdery residue in its wake that settled gently on the waves. After its reservoir was empty, it accelerated out of the atmosphere and began its long descending orbit into the oblivion of the nearby star's nuclear holocaust.

This was the first of many genetic nudges for the dolphins. Captain Anemone preferred to use incremental changes instead of the massive single mods that Grock Corporation procedures dictated. Her technique was more expensive and took longer, but the end result was far better. The species had a chance to adjust to its newfound intelligence and capabilities without all of the wars Grock's technique seemed to precipitate.

The wormhole she had opened after releasing the elimination device had been a dummy. She hadn't turned on the thrusters to enter it and remained in the same orbit as the Grock vessel, on the other side of the planet, and all detectable emissions had ceased while they waited for Grock to leave.

Using conventional propulsion, the Mer-captain began moving her starship toward an intersection with the moon. If she had used a wormhole, the detectors Grock had placed there would report her presence. A week from now, when they arrived on the moon, Engineering would modify those buried detectors to turn off for a one-day window on each rotation of this planet around its sun. This would allow her to return to check on the progress of *her* raised-up species, and no one would ever know. With her little periodic pushes, Captain Anemone had no doubt which species

The Beginning of the End

would succeed. She settled into her sleep cell; non-jump travel, even for the small distances around a planetary orbit, took a while.

... ...

The first non-detection window for a wormhole departure would begin in just a few moments. The timer on the captain's clock gave its alert—the window for a wormhole departure without the detectors sending alert was open. She reached out of the water bubble surrounding her and pressed the jump alert. Seconds later, her starship disappeared into a rosy halo. It was time to get paid.

Chapter 2 – The World Will Never Be the Same

December 10 in the near future

Lily approached Doug and Kevin after Dr. Johnson's particle physics lecture. The rest of the students swarmed around them in the hallway, on their way to their next class or back to the dorms to study. The expression on her face was what caught their attention first. Usually her soft Asian features and dark brown eyes showed amused disbelief at the brainless conversations swirling around the hallways at Stanford University. Today she appeared perplexed.

"You guys feel like helping me build something a little weird?"

"How weird?" Kevin smirked, tossing his head to move his slightly greasy hair from in front of his face. "Thrown-in-jail weird or just physics-department weird?"

"Physics-department weird," she said tentatively. "An idea came to me in a dream last night and, for some reason, I can't get it out of my mind."

"Let me get this straight," Doug said, shifting his overloaded backpack to his other thin shoulder. "You got an idea in a dream and now you want to try to build it? Really?"

Lily wasn't sure what to do. The whole thing sounded even crazier now than when she'd gotten up in the middle of the night to draw the schematic. These two were the only friends she'd made since she began the graduate physics program two years earlier— she had nowhere else to turn.

"I had a dream like that once." Kevin's corpulent face became serious, a rare occurrence. He frowned a little and his voice lowered to a conspiratorial whisper as he leaned in closer. "I even wrote down the words. They were the solution to world peace— they were going to end all conflict around the globe, save millions of lives, usher in a new millennium of harmony and growth ... I went back to sleep, happy I had saved humanity. When I woke up, the first thing I did was grab that piece of paper and read it. You know what I had written?" Both of them shook their heads. "The effing paper said, and I quote, 'Say please.'" Lily and Doug didn't understand. "No shit. I got up in the middle of the night to write 'Say please' on a piece of paper." He snorted and rolled his eyes. They were alone in the hallway now; the next classes had begun.

Doug was curious. Lily never asked for help. "So, what do you want to build?"

"I think it's a transmitter."

"What does it transmit? Radio waves?"

"I don't know. I'm still trying to figure that out." She flipped the stubborn lock of hair off her forehead in exasperation. "The dream said 'Build it and it will change the world.'"

"What do we need?" he asked, a rare twinkle in his eyes. "Plutonium's going to be a tough sell to Dr. Johnson."

"No, nothing like that. As far as I can tell right now, we can get everything on the schematic from the physics, engineering, and chemistry labs."

… … … … … … … … …

The first time the aura appeared, it scared the shit out of them. Knowing nothing in the transmitter was radioactive had helped a little. As long as they kept the coils chilled with liquid nitrogen and the frequency constant, the glow continued. If they let the coils warm, even a couple of degrees, the aura disappeared. If they varied the frequency of the oscillation up or down more than a tenth of one percent, the aura disappeared. They tested it with Geiger counters, infrared heat cameras—anything they could think of.

The aura appeared to be visible light, generated by the transmitter and harmless to humans, but it was not visible light or at least what caused the visible aura was not light. The aura passed right through anything they held up to it: lead, steel, and plastic. They noticed another strange thing, too: it cast no shadow. Kevin crawled under the lab bench and announced the aura was also underneath the transmitter, passing right through the solid soapstone.

The transmitter itself looked like a basketball wrapped in aluminum foil. The aluminum surrounded high-density foam insulation, which cut down on heat intrusion into the circuit board and nitrogen tank.

They lowered the curtains over the windows and turned off all the lights, making the lab as dark as possible. The glow of the aura from the transmitter became visible much farther out than the six inches or so they had seen in the well-lit laboratory, slowly fading to nothing about three feet from the transmitter. The aura wouldn't photograph, either—all their cell phone cameras showed was the aluminum foil-covered transmitter sitting on the bench, not a glimmer of the rosy aura.

They began to experiment with it. They tried light reflectors—no effect. Sound reflectors—no effect. Heat reflectors—no effect. It was a fan that caused the first noticeable change; as soon as they turned it on, the aura leaned away from it.

"How can light be sensitive to air movement?" Doug questioned, as he moved the fan around the transmitter. "This doesn't make any sense."

Kevin took the fan from him and turned it off. He folded a piece of paper into a fan and began waving it at the transmitter—the aura didn't budge. He turned on the electric fan again and the aura retreated, same as before. After picking up the small soldering gun they had used to create the circuit board, he held it next to the transmitter and the aura didn't move. When he pulled the trigger on the gun, the rosy glow jumped away from it.

"It's not air movement, Doug. I think it's the magnetic field from the coils in the soldering gun and the motor of the fan."

Once they found out was sensitive to magnetic manipulation, Doug came up with the idea of trying to focus it. They built a parabolic mirror lined with magnets and turned off the lights in the lab again, so the mirror's effect on the aura would show more clearly. They quickly discovered the magnetic field from the alloy magnets they were using was not powerful enough and switched to electromagnets. By changing the current entering the various electromagnets that made up the mirror, they were able to change the shape of the magnetic field. After experimentation, they created a field that focused the aura into a narrow beam that stretched all the way to the wall.

The Beginning of the End

Lily stepped into the hallway to see the faint rosy aura, though fainter and fainter, went right through the wall of the lab. It continued across the hallway and into the lab on the other side.

With surprise, she noticed the hallway was empty and dark. She pulled out her cell phone, and the display showed "12:37." Past midnight? They had worked for almost eighteen hours straight, not even stopping to eat.

"It's like visible radio waves," she muttered to herself. "How strange." Lily stuck her head back into the lab. "It went through the wall into the next lab."

Kevin came out to watch the beam with her. "I wonder if it keeps going through the outside wall?"

Suddenly they were racing to be the first outside. They ran to the stairway, leaping down the steps three at a time, and then arrived at the outside landing together, laughing, flushed, and out of breath. The light from the streetlight next to the lab masked any aura that might have been visible.

Kevin put his hands on his knees while he caught his breath. "Crap. I was sure we'd be able to see it."

An idea occurred to Lily. "Go back up to the lab and turn the mirror, so the aura goes out the other side of the building. There aren't any street lights over there."

"Give me a second," he gasped. Kevin was six feet tall and carrying at least an extra hundred pounds. The run down the steps had winded him. He walked slowly back into the building and Lily followed the shrubs around the corner and continued to the dark side of the physics building. No aura was visible. Disappointed, she was about to leave when the glow appeared—faint and rosy as a straight, pale pink garden hose. The aura faded into invisibility about five feet beyond the wall. With her eyes, she followed its line across the grassy central mall of the campus; the aura pointed directly at the administration building.

Kevin came back down and stared at the pink line with her. The aura disappeared, and then reappeared a few seconds later.

"Why did it do that?" he wondered as they started back inside.

Doug was laughing silently when they opened the door to the lab.

"What's going on?" Kevin asked.

Their friend frantically held up a finger to his mouth. "There's more to this than we thought!" He scribbled on a piece of paper he held up to them.

The sound of voices came into the lab from the magnetic mirror; it was like the people speaking were in the lab with them.

"Oh, Jason, do you think it's safe?" a woman's voice asked. "I thought I heard someone talking."

"Of course it's safe—this is the president's office. The cleaning staff is gone; I think you're imagining voices. It's just us and that wonderful couch. You're not going to chicken out now, are you?"

"Well, let's do it and get out of here," the woman's voice said a little shakily as they could hear the sound of clothing being removed.

"Is that why you turned off the transmitter?" Lily whispered to Doug.

He nodded. "I thought it was picking up a radio or TV show, but now I'm not sure. Where did the aura beam go when it left the building?"

"It was pointing at the admin building."

"Come on, you guys," Kevin said conspiratorially. "Let's see if what I think is happening really is."

All three ran out of the lab and down to the street, where they continued on to the administration building a quarter mile away. As they walked around the outside, they found one unlocked door. Kevin opened it and the three of them climbed the broad stairs to the second floor and then into the president's secretary's office. A light was on inside the president's office and the door was open a crack. The sounds coming from inside were unmistakably two people having sex.

Kevin raised an eyebrow and got a smirk on his face. Lily had never seen anything good come from that expression. "Remember that scene in *M.A.S.H.*," he whispered, "when Hawkeye put the microphone under the bed as Hot Lips and Major Burns were getting it on?"

Doug gasped in alarm. "No, Kevin! That's too cruel!"

The Beginning of the End

He walked over to the cabinet beside the secretary's desk and opened the door. The campus-wide PA system came into view. He flipped on the power switch, turned up the volume, and activated the microphone on the president's desk. Into the silence of the late-night Stanford University campus, the sounds in the president's office began broadcasting loudly over the PA system in every dorm, building, and parking lot. Lily, Doug, and Kevin fled and watched from beside the physics building. Within minutes, lights came on all over the campus and every security car on the force converged on the administration building with blue lights flashing. Soon after, they led the couple who had been using the president's sofa out of the building and put them in the back of a campus security car. The PA system shut off with a pop.

... ...

They walked back into the lab together. "What do you think will happen to them?" Lily wondered out loud.

Kevin was still grinning from ear to ear, proud he had pulled off the coup of the century. "Who cares? You take a chance and you pay the price."

Doug was deep in thought, his forehead wrinkled all the way up to his red crewcut. "You guys, I'm a lot more concerned about *how* we heard them speak than what'll happen to the people we heard. How could we hear them at all? We were at least a quarter of a mile away with two solid stone walls between us."

Lily and Kevin both came to the same observation simultaneously. "We heard them like they were in the room with us."

"And I think she heard us. How could that happen?" Doug asked.

Lily took a seat on the bench next to the device with a puzzled expression. "The Rosy Transmitter must have allowed us to hear them."

Kevin glanced out the windows of the lab. "How far is the campus security office from here?

"About the same distance as the admin building, only in that direction," Doug pointed.

Kevin swung the Rosy Transmitter around so it aimed at the campus security office and flipped the power-on switch. The familiar glow from the transmitter made his ruddy face appear flushed—almost demonic. After five seconds, they heard a few steps in what sounded like gravel, a car door close, and then the sound of a car starting.

Lily went to the window. "A patrol car is leaving the parking lot to the right of the security building." She walked to the transmitter and moved it a couple of degrees counterclockwise on the lab bench.

"We need more distance," Kevin said. "What do you think would happen if we turned up the power a smidge?"

She was irritated. "What do you mean? The circuits might fry if we add more amperage."

"Only one way to tell, Lily, my dear. Check the nitrogen, will you please."

"Nitrogen's fine."

Kevin reached for the knob labeled *Gain* and turned it clockwise a tiny amount. The voice of a man flowed into the lab like the students were in the same room and then faded as Kevin turned the knob farther. He turned it back. The voice got louder, like a microphone was moving around in the room.

"... a babe," a voice said. "What's a babe like that doing with a creep like him?"

"You mean besides doin' the dirty deed?" a second voice chimed in, laughing. "I'll bet President Jourey will have some choice words for them tomorrow." The first voice joined the second in laugher.

Lily reached over and turned off the transmitter. Kevin was just staring at it as he let his breath out in a rush. "Holy shit! What is this thing? Sound waves travel through the transmission path like there's no distance between us and them."

She was staring at it, too. "If sound waves can travel through the rosy path, could something else? A laser?"

"Should be easy enough to test," Doug said thoughtfully. "Now that we know how, we can aim the rosy path anywhere we want."

The Beginning of the End

"And if it produces a rosy path, that makes this a Rosy Transmitter." Lily added, giving the device a name.

Doug and Kevin nodded in agreement.

... ...

Lily twirled a strand of her black hair rapidly around her index finger—a habit she had manifested since she was a child. The faster she twirled the strand, the harder she was thinking. "You know what this means, don't you?" She tried to hide the disbelief in her voice.

The rest of the team kept swinging their eyes back and forth between the two timers. They were displaying different values— that was the problem; they shouldn't be. According to their engineering friends who had set up the locations of the senders and receivers, they were exactly one thousand meters apart. One timer showed 3.4 millionths of a second, as expected. That was the time a laser beam took to go one thousand meters through clear air. The second timer showed the elapsed time of the same laser beam through the Rosy Transmitter aura to the second pickup. That timer showed zero, making the travel across the campus apparently instantaneous, which, according to the known laws of the universe, was impossible.

Kevin wasn't ready to believe it. "Something's wrong. The timer, the pickups, the ..." He paused to lick his lips. "Something *must* be malfunctioning. We're only talking about three millionths of a second. That could be resistance in a soldered connection."

"We've swapped the senders and receivers three times," Lily said, in almost a whisper. Both Doug and Kevin glanced at her cautiously. A whisper was not one of her comfy sounds—it usually preceded and explosion, like the calm before a storm.

She continued, "Each timer display is a composite average of a thousand separate samples taken over two seconds. When a set is used with clear air, the laser gets there in 3.4 millionths of a second. When we send the same laser signal through those same sender and receivers along the Rosy path, it gets there instantaneously, no matter how far apart we put them. We got the same results at a hundred meters, remember? That's why we did the thousand meter test."

"Well, we have to have made a mistake somewhere," Kevin said nervously. "You can't go faster than the speed of light—it's a universal constant. The whole of modern math and physics collapses without that to depend on, not to mention the laugh Dr. Johnson will have at our expense when we tell him we can send a signal faster than the speed of light." Dr. Johnson, their advisor, was renowned for his sarcastic criticism of the graduate students assigned to him for mentoring. He made even Kevin's scathing comments seem innocuous.

They stood in silence, pondering the glow from the Rosy Transmitter. The soft rose-colored aura sparkled as you moved your head, like a laser beam did when it hit something solid.

Lily pursed her lips as she pondered what to do next. "I think you're right. We need to go farther The short distances we're traveling could be explained by environmental or test equipment discrepancies. We need a big, dramatic test that can demonstrate once and for all that Rosy can provide instantaneous signals over any distance—something no one can dispute."

"We're a little limited here by something called Earth," Kevin observed. "We might be able to send it a hundred miles by standing on top of Mt. Whitney, but beyond that, we're stuck—unless you can convince NASA to launch a Rosy Transmitter into space." He laughed at the thought of big, arrogant NASA acknowledging three graduate physics students even existed.

"You're still thinking about clear air," Doug said. "From what I see, solid obstructions have no effect on the Rosy aura. We could try to send it through Earth—the diameter at the equator is a little less than eight thousand miles. Of course, we'd have to figure out a better way to focus it. Beam distortion, negligible at a thousand meters, would be significant at eight thousand miles."

Lily twirled a strand of her hair as she stood at the window. "Actually, something different occurred to me. We've been focusing on sending lasers and sound through the Rosy aura. Why can't we send something more solid?"

The Beginning of the End

"Waves are one thing, but particles are another," Doug said gently.

"Not according to Einstein. He got his Nobel by proposing light consisted of protons, not waves—radical thinking for the early twentieth century."

"Light is a delicate subject, Lily," Kevin said. "You know that. Light can be either particles or waves, depending on how you test it."

"It ought to be easy enough to test." Doug scratched his chin and held up the pencil he had been using to record what they had accomplished so far in his lab notes. He set it on the bench. "Let's try to send this pencil across the room."

Kevin inserted a plastic straw, large enough in circumference to slide the pencil through, into the back of the mirror. Lily aimed the transmitter at a trash can Doug had placed upside down on another lab bench across the room. When she powered up the transmitter, it began emitting its familiar rosy glow. Doug tapped the top of the trash can while Lily adjusted the gain until the sound came through clearly, like the can was right next to it.

Kevin taped a rubber band to the end of the straw to launch the pencil into the Rosy field in the same direction as the trashcan. He pulled back the rubber band and prepared to launch the pencil into the aura, but before he released it, he paused. "If this works, mankind will change forever. This could be a Nobel for us."

"And if it doesn't," Lily said, rubbing her arms, "we're still graduate students with a class in six hours. Let go of the pencil, Kevin." His words had inexplicably chilled her. They sounded just like the words from her dream.

He released the pencil. The rubber band snapped forward pushing the pencil down the tube. It entered the Rosy aura and ... disappeared. In the same moment, they heard a metallic *thunk* from the trashcan, like someone had pounded on it, but no one was near. He turned off the transmitter.

Doug walked over to the trashcan and picked it up. "Nothing—it's not here."

"The pencil's still in the mirror," Kevin announced, picking it up and handing it to Lily.

"And the tip is broken off," she said.

Doug studied the inside of the can. "There's a dent in the side of the can. It looks like someone shot a pencil at it." On the lab bench where the trash can had been upside down was a small, pointed bit of pencil graphite. "Here's the tip."

Chapter 3 – Prize Cheeses

January 8

The encrypted, interstellar, linked-hore receiver crackled to life. "Grock Species Mining Ship, GSMS-77, this is Grock Central. Acknowledge."

Lieutenant Nussi, the on-duty communications officer, spilled the breakfast beverage she had just retrieved from the canteen all over her lap as she reached to answer the call. "This is GSMS-77." This channel was used only for the most important messages. The receiver was always on and always monitored.

"GSMS-77, you were sent a top priority message five minutes ago. Receipt of that message has not been acknowledged. It should be in your message queue. Read the message back to me and acknowledge receipt."

The message light flashing was flashing on the device. "It must have come in while I was getting my breakfast drink," she muttered in frustration. She brought up a hologram of the email queue. The new message was flashing in red. She selected it and the text appeared in midair in front of her.

She read it out loud. "Grock Central has received a wormhole activation warning from the Grock-inoculated planet circling star EB-31-21-98. Immediately alter your mission and jump to that planet. Determine if the warning was valid and contact Grock Central on this channel with your determination."

"GSMS-77, that is the correct message. Identify yourself and acknowledge receipt of that message."

"This is GSMS-77, Lieutenant Nola Nussi, communications officer, employee number 234-447-844. I acknowledge message receipt."

The channel went dead. Nola cringed, sighed, and then reluctantly called the captain's quarters. He was with his concubine and he wouldn't like being disturbed.

"WHAT?" his voice screamed into her earpiece.

"Captain Xanny, this is Lieutenant Nussi. We've received orders from Grock Central to alter our mission and investigate a

Fredrick Hudgin

wormhole activation alert on a planet about three hundred lightyears from here."

There was a long pause before he muttered faintly, "Shit! Why me? Somebody at Central is laughing his ass off." After another pause, the faint sound of two voices came through. She strained to hear what was being said but couldn't quite make it out. The captain's voice suddenly came clearly through her earpiece and made her jump.

"Gimme a second."

The comm link popped closed.

… … … … … … … … …

GSMS-77 appeared in real space about a million kilometers from Earth. If the alert was real, these primates were probably already using chemical rockets to investigate their moon and other nearby planets in their solar system.

Traveling three hundred lightyears took a while—not the actual jumps, of course—once the portal was open, the starship needed only three seconds to pass through, whether the wormhole spanned a hundred feet or a hundred lightyears. What took the time was figuring out where to jump next. At three hundred lightyears, the difference between landing in a star, an asteroid belt, or empty space was the tiniest fraction of a degree or volt— and who knew what had changed in the three hundred years that had passed while light traveled from your destination to where you were now? So, instead of jumping three hundred lightyears at once, you made many smaller jumps. You wanted to be sure the end of the wormhole was not going to be inside something that would ruin your day.

In the time between the jumps, Captain Xanny carefully studied the company status reports of visitations, starting with the first visit 50,000 years ago, which included documentation on the confrontation with the Mer-people. Since inoculation, there had been no surprises—typical primate stuff: wars, wars, more wars, resource depletion, wars, barely restrained capitalism, wars, kleptocracies, subjugation of almost everyone for the benefit of the few super-rich, and unrestrained population growth.

He chuckled a little when he read the report about an incident some four thousand years ago when an employee doing a status visit had decided to stay on-planet to fraternize with the indigenous primates. He'd created a town and named it Ur, and one of his confidants had gone on to create a religion that still existed in the modern world. Status visitors were well paid and trained to prevent exactly what happened, but they could fall prey to any manner of misfortunes.

Twenty years later, Grock followed up with an investigation team to see what had happened, expecting to find that he had been killed somehow. When the investigators arrived, they quickly found the missing person. He told them he had entered the atmosphere too quickly and his landing craft had been damaged, but when the lander was examined, the team discovered that the craft had been sabotaged after landing. Management figured the guy had wanted to be the big fish in the little pond for a few years—all *highly* unauthorized, of course—and the errant status visitor had been fined and fired because of it. The second ship hadn't had room to bring the disabled lander with them, so it was buried to protect it from curious natives and left for later retrieval.

"Why do they waste their time with these violent species?" Xanny grumbled. "Surely another could have been raised up."

It had been a lot easier when he was an unregistered miner, before he was recruited by Grock Corporation to captain one of their legitimate mining ships. There'd been fewer rules and a lot less overhead, but the penalties for getting caught as an unlicensed miner were enormous. Still, the captain reminisced on those dark, early days of his career rather fondly: quick money, no questions, hiding from the storm troopers sent to investigate rumors of unregistered mining, and selling the unregistered claims in smoky bars on fringe planets to agents of mining corporations who didn't ask any questions and paid in cash.

Memories filled his mind of loose women, cheap drink, and quick death. Free and easy was the life of a pirate—except, of course, when it was not. There had been plenty of good times and those were the ones Captain Xanny liked to remember. There had been a lot more of the other kind, though: when he held a friend as she died, when he was broke and hungry, when a claim he had stolen fair and square was stolen by someone else, and when he spent time in prison because a covert buyer turned out to be an Ur agent.

Sometimes, in quiet moments, he wondered what had happened to the people he had known then. His friends and partners in crime had gone to the six winds when Xanny decided to go straight; he had wished them well and made sure they had traveling money. But his enemies? Now those were beings he hoped he would meet again—maybe in a dark alley with a knife.

Knives were a very personal way to kill someone; you couldn't do it from across the room. With a knife, you looked someone in the eyes when you killed them. You felt them die and they knew it was you who did it.

Of all the life forms he loved to hate, one name stood out— one person he would do almost anything to find. Fey Pey, captain of the *Easy Wind*. Fey Pey had killed Xanny's family after raping Xanny's mate, and the only reason was because he hated Xanny as much as Xanny hated him.

"Now *he* I would like to meet again!" The captain made a pirate's rune and spit, sealing the covenant.

He sighed, rubbing the scar that went from his ear to his chin—his only scar from those early days—and then turned his attention to what was happening on his ship. High above the planet, GSMS-77 was bustling with activity. He slipped into his anti-grav pack, stretching his eight legs. Grock seemed to be fond of octopuses as their captains and overlooked his less-than-stellar past because of how successful he had been in finding Class 1 planets.

His black pirate tattoos were plainly visible on his mottled gray and green skin, but only a few members of his crew knew what they meant. Some were the logos of hated enemies he had killed, some in memory of fallen friends, and some just whimsy. He floated out of his chamber and moved toward the bridge.

The scan teams sent him the data they had collected since they emerged next to Earth, thousands of satellites in orbit around

The Beginning of the End

the beautiful, water-covered world. The radioisotope signature of many fusion nuclear explosions was in the atmosphere, although the last one, based on the ratio of the various isotopes, had occurred at least fifty years ago. Some fission explosions were much more recent. Air, water, and land pollution were rampant throughout the world, overpopulation was everywhere. The remains of three fission reactor meltdowns were obvious. A lot had happened since the last scheduled status visit two hundred years ago.

The wormhole detector warning was legitimate—these bastards had opened eight, so far, with a ninth opening occurring as the data collection took place. Once they figured out how to send the originating transmitter along with the rest of the transmitted mass, the door would be wide open to the rest of the galaxy. The ninth opening allowed them to get exact coordinates on the origin of the wormholes.

After he passed all the scans to Grock Central, he sighed and sat back in his chair. "It's just a matter of time now." In one month, this place would be crawling with every bullshit bureaucrat in this arm of the galaxy—then the flies and maggots would really come out of the walls for the feeding frenzy.

The first ones who showed up were the New Species Evaluation Team from the GSCB, or "Team" for short. Captain Xanny sent them all the data his ship had collected since it arrived and the status reports from 50,000 years of bicentennial visits. The Team was followed by the "new world" herd of interested parties, but he didn't give them any of his data—the Team had strict rules about that.

"Do your own scans, assholes!" he muttered half-heartedly.

After two hours and some bribery, the newcomers would have everything he had sent to the Team. That was the real reason they wouldn't let the miners share their data with anyone else: they wanted the bribery money for themselves.

This gathering was normal and expected, as it happened with each potential new member, no matter how unauthorized and illegal the new world armada was, and the fêtes and celebrations began almost immediately. Many corporations apparently had a financial interest in humanity, both for the assimilation of this planet into the Ur and for the rejection of it. The lobbyists paid by those corporations, both registered and unregistered, began to bring the pressure of their particular point of view to bear on the Team members—especially the leader. Sex, drugs, money, property, and power—all were pawns in this very expensive game of cat and mouse, with Earth and humanity the prized cheeses.

Chapter 4 – What Would Happen If ...

January 9

"Let's try sending a ball bearing through," Lily suggested. "We can test it lots of ways before we send it and then do the same tests afterward—see if there's any physical differences."

They turned the trash can over so it caught the things they sent through and calibrated the gain knob into a reliable distance predictor. They found no changes in anything they sent through.

Doug figured out the aura beam they had been using was not a particularly good one. Magnetically, their "mirror" resembled a bowl full of rocks more than the polished surface they envisioned and that yielded a distorted beam. While the mirror worked for small distances, it was useless with anything beyond 1,000 meters. Another thing they noticed was the effect other magnetic fields had on the aura. The farther the aura got from the Rosy Transmitter the less another magnetic field affected it. Beyond ten meters, even a strong field did not alter the direction or distance of the beam.

Doug got his computer science friends together with his electrical engineering friends to figure out a way to use a computer to focus the mirror. The solution took two all-night design sessions and three cases of beer before they successfully created a computer-controlled magnetic mirror that could be focused electronically. The hardest parts ended up being the creation of a USB interface and LINUX driver for the mirror. Once they finished debugging the software, the aura became much easier to manipulate.

Word was beginning to spread around the campus that the three had discovered something very unusual. While they learned about the properties of the aura and its capabilities, Kevin, Lily, and Doug tried to keep the transmitter under wraps by saying the device was their master's project.

When they put the new, computer-managed magnetic mirror in place, Kevin sent a peanut through to the trash can. He picked up the nut and popped it into his mouth. "Tender and nutritious—tastes like a peanut. Hey, do you guys think something alive could go through?"

"Alive like a plant, or alive like an animal?" Lily asked him.

"Alive like a lab rat."

"Well"—she paused to consider it—"yeah, I think it could go through, but it may come out like this on the other end!" She held up her arm and pretended it came out the top of her head.

"I could get one from the psych building," Doug said. "I know where they keep the test mice."

"Cool. Go get one," Kevin said in a raspy whisper, rubbing his hands together. "While you're gone, I'll put in a bigger delivery tube." He began laughing like a mad scientist.

When Doug returned with the mouse, Lily held the tiny rodent up to her face. "I name you Kirk, going where no mouse has gone before." Kevin began whistling the theme song to *Star Trek*.

Doug had a grin on his face as he turned on the transmitter. "You guys ever notice the aura takes about five seconds to appear?"

"And lasts about five seconds after you turn it off," Lily said.

Kevin walked to the trash can to watch for the mouse's arrival as she put its head into the opening of the enlarged tube. The mouse resisted entering, but after a few moments, its natural curiosity overcame its reluctance and it ran down the tube to the end and stopped, testing the air with its nose. Doug leaned past Lily, put his mouth around the end of the tube, and blew a mighty puff of air; the mouse disappeared into the aura.

"Oh, YUCK!" Kevin called out from the trash can, clasping a hand over his mouth, wide-eyed. His friends hurried over to see what had happened. A normal-looking mouse stared back at them, sniffed the air, and then began examining the trash can for a way out.

"You asshole!" Lily hit Kevin's arm.

He laughed. "Made you look!"

… … … … … … … …

"What do you think would happen if we created a beam into space?" Doug asked them one afternoon as they were testing a new, more refined magnetic mirror control program. They had upgraded the computer to a much faster model to keep up with the calculations. "What do you think about sending it, say, 100,000 kilometers out?"

"Well, it's a vacuum," Lily said. "I don't think we'll hear anything." She glanced at Kevin and rolled her eyes. He had his raised-eyebrow/smirk plastered all over his face which morphed into a grin as he turned the mirror so it pointed straight up. He flipped on the power switch. Five seconds later, the rosy glow appeared. He reached for the gain knob, turning it up to 100,000 meters, way past what they had used up to that point.

There was a massive whoosh and the transmitter, power supply, magnetic mirror, and laptop disappeared into the aura as the door to the hallway slammed open into the wall of the lab, smashing its glass. Kevin grabbed Lily as she lost her balance and fell toward the rosy glow. Everything not tied down on the lab bench blew into the aura. Doug tried to grab his glasses as they shot off his face, but instead snatched his lab notebook out of midair as it flew past him. The only thing left on the bench was the power cord to the laptop, still plugged into the outlet under the workbench. It stretched tight into the aura as the air from the hallway blew past them into the rosy glow. The aura disappeared. The power cord plopped back down on the bench—three feet of black wire ending in a clean cut.

Dr. Johnson walked into the lab, stepping over the remains of the door. The three students were staring in shock at the empty lab bench. "Okay, kids, tell me about it. What're you working on and why don't I know anything about your master's project. I'm your bloody advisor."

Chapter 5 – We Can't Take That Chance

January 20

"Has anyone been down there yet?" Envoy Gart-Disp asked Captain Xanny telepathically.

"Not since the last status report two hundred years ago."

The envoy was leader of the Team. He had asked for a face-to-face meeting with Captain Xanny. Gart-Disp was an aquatic, air-breathing mammal, looking much like a dolphin on Earth, with a two-inch-thick cocoon of water around himself. No one dared call him a fish—the term *fish*, when used to describe an aquatic mammal, was considered demeaning and profane. Straps held his anti-grav device underneath him like a reverse backpack, supporting both him and the water cocoon. He moved by swimming through the air—the anti-grav device picked up his movements and provided the locomotion. The only part of him not immersed in water was his breathing orifice.

The captain lifted his hot beverage to his mouth with his favored tentacle. Humans were mostly left-handed or right-handed, and so were octopuses—only a little different. Within the favored four tentacles were a favored two and within the favored two was the favored one, which Captain Xanny used primarily for things requiring manual dexterity.

The envoy continued, "Given the rate of technology expansion noted during the last visit, why did the Grock Corporation wait two hundred years for another visit?"

Xanny had been expecting the question; so had Grock and he had been told what to say. "No one knows why. The scan team recommended the next visit be in one hundred years, as noted in the report. Apparently a clerk didn't notice."

"Grock Corporation will be fined accordingly. This whole issue might have been avoided with a little more warning. What else is at the location of the wormhole origination?"

"It appears to be a university. We suspect scientists at the university discovered how to generate a Hore field and are experimenting with it. Until this morning, nothing substantial had been sent through—the largest mass noted was about one hundred grams."

"What happened this morning? Why was I not told about it?"

"We wanted to do some initial investigation before we made it public. This transmission was very different from the previous wormholes." Captain Xanny signaled Lieutenant Nussi, who rolled a cart into the room. On it were the students' transmitter, computer, power supply, and magnetic mirror. "This is what we found at the end of the transmission aura, spread out over three kilometers."

The envoy stared at the equipment, slightly irritated, more than slightly bored. He was not a technician and had no interest in technology, as long as it worked. "What is this?"

The captain shrugged. "It's a fully functional Hore field generator with a focusing mirror driven by a primitive computer. We think the scientists focused the device into the vacuum of space and the equipment they used to generate the field was blown into space before the field collapsed."

Gart-Disp quivered a little. "Do you think they understood the significance of the event?"

Xanny wondered at his reaction—excitement or disgust? It was hard to tell with a fish. "No way to know. It could have been someone who said 'Hey, let's send an aura straight up and see what happens.'"

"We can't take that chance. Bring them here. We have to know what they know."

Chapter 6 – Two Cases

January 21

Dr. Johnson was examining Doug's lab notebook. He was a balding, short, middle-aged man, a little overweight with a small potbelly, and clean shaven with mutton chop sideburns. The trash can with the pencil dent was beside him. "And you think you can make another one of these Rosy Transmitters?"

"I'm sure we can," Lily answered.

"We'll need another laptop for the mirror." Doug watched the clouds through the window while he built a mental list. "I made a backup of the aiming software yesterday before we started playing with it. Other than the tweaks we made yesterday, it should be current. I made notes about what we changed. I should be able to reproduce them."

"I can get you another laptop. How can we prevent what happened before from happening again?"

"The laptop has to be fast," Doug continued. "Don't bring me a four-year-old loaner from the department storeroom—it won't be able to keep up with the calculations. And it has to be running Linux; I don't do Windows."

"How about floors? Do you do floors?" Dr. Johnson laughed at his own joke.

Doug couldn't believe the man was making light of his missing laptop. When his old one couldn't keep up with the calculations, he had taken out a loan he couldn't afford to buy a new one. It was the fastest, most wonderful laptop he had ever owned—not even old enough for the "new" to wear off. Doug continued to stare out the window into the courtyard. Dr. Johnson was an asshole.

"How can we prevent what happened yesterday from happening again?" their advisor asked again.

Doug's face was red, his lips were pursed, and his eyes were hard and hostile. *Please, shut up, Doug*, Kevin pleaded silently to his friend. To Dr. Johnson he said, "Well, we could totally mount the equipment in a rack we could fix to the floor—put the mirror and the transmitter on a secure pivot on the top of the rack."

Oblivious to Doug's anger, their advisor made a decision. "Go ahead and build it. I'll get a rack from electrical engineering, but let me be clear about this: *don't turn the transmitter on.* I want to be here when it's turned on for the first time." He made eye contact with each of the three students, saying each word slowly, distinctly. "I ... mean ... it. ... Don't ... turn ... it ... on. Understand?" They nodded, and he got up. "I'll go find a laptop that will work. You guys get to work on the transmitter. How long do you think it will take?"

"Give us the rest of the week," Lily said. It was Tuesday.

"Let's get back together on Thursday afternoon to see how everything's going."

"When will you get the laptop?" Doug asked, finally breaking his silence.

"Should be back with it this afternoon. Is that soon enough?"

"Sure." He still wouldn't meet the man's eyes. After Dr. Johnson left, Doug asked, "How does a guy who dresses like *that* get to be a professor at Stanford?" Their advisor was famous for his cheap, worn-out suits with shirts and ties that didn't match.

"Must be his bloody British accent," Kevin snickered, trying to imitate how Dr. Johnson talked.

Lily asked the question she'd been holding back. "Doug, can you get your engineering friends to build us another magnetic mirror?"

He took a deep breath, trying to calm down, and then smiled at her. "Sure, they'd love to stop what they're doing and build us another mirror. I'm sure nothing else in the world would be more important to them."

Kevin cracked up. "Was that sarcasm? My god, there's hope for you yet!" He turned to Lily. "How long do you think it will really take to get a second transmitter up and running?"

"If his friends can come through with a new mirror, we can have it running tonight."

Doug pulled out his wallet and laid a twenty on the lab bench. "How much money do you two have on you?"

Kevin didn't know where Doug was going with this but he reached for his wallet. He pulled out a twenty as Lily dug her wallet out of her backpack and did the same. Doug reached for his cell phone and dialed his friend's number. Anything that would piss off their advisor was all right with him and certainly worth twenty bucks each.

"Hi, Kiran. Doug. Hey, do you remember that magnetic mirror you made us last week? ... Yeah, that one.... Yeah, it worked great. Thanks again. Uh, we need another one just like it." Kiran's voice went up two octaves and fifty decibels. Doug let him rant for a full minute before he broke in and added, "I'll buy you *two* six packs of Stone Ruination IPA."

Kiran's was silent for a moment."FINE! Tomorrow!"

"We need it this afternoon."

"This *evening* will be costing you a CASE, asshole! There's no way I can finish sooner—I have a class this afternoon and I'll have to break a date with my girlfriend."

"The case will be here when you bring it over, my friend. Say hi to Patti for me."

... ...

The three male primates on Captain Xanny's ship were not an exact match to the primates on this planet but would have to do.

The captain floated back and forth in front of them as they stood at attention. "You three understand I *don't* want you to kill the scientists, whoever they are, don't you?"

"Yes, *sir!*" Corporal Mneemus said. He was small by human male standards—maybe fifty kilograms and his arms were longer than what humans thought of as normal. This was his first big chance to show the captain what he was made of.

"I want to talk to them and find out what they know about the Hore field, how they discovered it, and what they plan to do with it. I can't do *any* of those things if you kill them. Am I understood?"

"Yes, *sir!*" Corporal Mneemus said, his back ramrod straight and his bald head slightly redder than it had been.

The Beginning of the End

Captain Xanny turned to the one combat veteran on the team. "Private Flug, do you understand what I want?" Flug was as much bigger from the average human normal as Mneemus was smaller. He had a military crew cut and a perpetual smile, like he found his life amusing.

"I sure do, Captain," Private Flug rolled his eyes at Mneemus's posturing. "We'll bring 'em back alive and well for you to talk to."

The captain wasn't sure about including Flug in the operation. He had been a senior sergeant in the combat corps before he was demoted to private and asked to find another line of work—something about disobeying an officer's order to kill a native on a developing planet. The order had been ultimately judged to be illegal, but Flug had still been run out of the combat corps; they had a problem with sergeants who disobeyed their officers, no matter the reason.

Captain Xanny addressed the third member of the team. "Private Litu, do you also understand?"

"I do, Captain." He was of medium, human-sized build with symmetrical ridges running from his forehead to the back of his neck, like a freshly plowed field. His beige eyebrows went straight across his forehead, with no break between them, and then down in front of his ears, across his chin, and up to his bottom lip. It was his coal-black skin and orange eyes, however, that were his most prominent features.

"You will wear clothes based on our understanding of what natives on this planet wear. Do any of you have any deadly-force weapons?"

"No, Captain, only freeze guns"—Corporal Mneemus hesitated—"and an engineering laser, in case we need to cut through something."

"Do *not* use the laser on the natives or I will use it on *you* when you get back." The captain's voice was very quiet. "Go complete your mission. Amaze me."

… … … … … … … … …

The trip down to the surface was uneventful. They jumped to the area over the planet containing the lowest satellite congestion, the North Pole. The lander entered the atmosphere without incident, invisible to the multiple radar batteries that swept the sky through which it passed. The lander was preprogrammed to set down at the university in an unpopulated rectangular amphitheater near the building from which the Hore transmissions originated. The white stripes on the close-to-the-ground synthetic vegetation were intriguing to the team until they became unnerved by all the empty seats lining the amphitheater; it was like they were filled with the spirits of the natives of this world, guarding it from those who didn't belong.

Corporal Mneemus carried a satellite drone picture of the campus—the target building was seven hundred meters from the amphitheater. He oriented his map. "It's this way," he said and headed off.

The two followed him, watching and listening for danger, their freeze guns at the ready. It took them half an hour to find their way out of the football stadium; they ended up using the laser to cut through a chain link fence as all the exit gates were tightly locked.

… … … … … … … … …

Kiran showed up with his girlfriend, Patti, around ten o'clock to deliver the magnetic mirror. They opened some of the beers and everyone had a cold one before Doug helped carry the rest out to Kiran's car.

"What's the hurry on the mirror, Doug?" his friend asked as he closed his trunk.

"Dr. Johnson got wind of our project—he wants to muscle in. We're trying to finish and publish before he can claim the whole thing as his and leave us out in the cold."

"He *is* such an asshole!" Kiran agreed. "Thanks for the beer."

"Thanks for delivering on such a short notice."

"Glad I could help, Doug. Try not to lose this one."

The Beginning of the End

"I won't. Thanks again. See ya, Patti." He gave her a quick hug and then stepped back and waved while they drove out of the physics building parking lot.

When he got back to the lab, Kevin had already set up the mirror. Lily positioned it for the transmission, connected it to the department laptop, and filled the nitrogen reservoir. The Rosy glow appeared after about five seconds after she powered up the transmitter.

The door opened and three people entered the lab dressed like actors in *The Matrix*—overcoats, sunglasses, and fedoras.

"Who are you guys?" Kevin asked. "Is there a costume party somewhere?"

The short guy in the lead held up what appeared to be a pistol and aimed it at Lily. Kevin jumped between her and the gun. There was no sound, but he fell to the floor, motionless. Doug dove behind a lab bench as Lily launched herself at the intruders. Her foot caught the pistol-wielder on the side of the head, dropping him like a stone. She spun around to kick the big guy next to him, but he had his own pistol out and dropped her instead. When they found Doug hiding under the desk at the front of the room, he came out with his hands up and they froze him like his friends.

Flug contacted the ship and gave them the status.

"Is Mneemus dead?" Captain Xanny asked.

"Nope—unconscious."

"Can you and Litu get him and the scientists back to the lander without being seen?"

"Shouldn't be a problem—there aren't too many natives around, and it's dark—but we'll need to make two trips. The gravity here is half of what my home world has."

"Transfer them to the lander. What freeze loads are you using?"

Private Flug checked. "Number twos."

"Good. Freeze anyone who sees you; those loads will wear off in an hour."

Private Flug and Litu made the trips to the lander, each carrying one person. On the second trip, they had to freeze a couple walking hand-in-hand toward another building on the same path that led to the football field.

As they finished securing the unconscious scientists inside the lander, the lights came on in the stadium. Private Flug activated the console and pressed the *Return to Ship* button on the pilot's hologram. The lander lifted off the football field and accelerated up and out of sight over the edge of the stadium.

Jerry Fagan, the guard who'd turned on the lights, recorded the whole thing on his cell phone camera. "Goddamned aliens!" he screamed, shaking his fist at the black sky. "I knew I'd get a picture a you sonsabitches sooner or later!"

He hobbled down to the field as fast as his arthritis allowed, forgetting for once how old he had become. He took pictures of the depressions where the lander's circular support feet had crushed the AstroTurf. Jerry had kept the *National Enquirer*'s submission number in his cell phone's speed dial directory for years, awaiting this opportunity. In two more minutes, the video and pictures arrived at the *Enquirer*'s server.

Chapter 7 – The Cusp

January 22

Kevin woke up first. He was in a room with no furniture and no windows. Lily was on one side of him, and Doug was on the other. He studied the walls more closely—no doors either—at least none he could see. The ceiling glowed, but beyond that, there was no other illumination. The temperature was warm, but not too warm.

Doug stirred, put his hand to his face, and then suddenly sat up straight. "What the *hell?*"

That woke up Lily. She twisted around, shouted "Ha-yaaa!", and swung her foot at Doug, catching him on the knee. He yelped and rolled away.

"Lily!" Kevin shouted, moving out of range. "It's okay. It's just us."

She got to her feet, like a ballerina rising gracefully from the floor. "Where the hell are we? Where are the idiots with the guns?"

"No idea," said Kevin, "to either question."

Doug limped to one of the walls where he ran his hands over it. "Smooth, possibly plastic." He tapped on the wall—a dull thump. He continued to tap all the way around the room, but there was not much change in the sound. He did the same with the floor and found it seemed more solid than the walls.

A hologram appeared in the middle of the room where Lily stood. She moved out of it to stand beside Doug and Kevin. A vaguely human computer-generated face coalesced in the middle of the hologram.

"Hello, scientists. I am Captain Xanny, captain of this vessel. We came to your planet because an alert sounded when you opened your first wormhole. I need to know how you invented the Hore-field generator you used to open the wormhole." The mouth movements of the hologram didn't match the words it was saying—like watching a foreign movie poorly dubbed in English.

"Bullshit!" Kevin spat, starting to laugh. "Who's doing this? Jeffery? I'm gonna kick your ass! Nice touch with the hologram and CG face."

The walls disappeared and the artificial gravity with them. They were floating weightlessly in clear space a million kilometers from earth, about three times the distance from Earth to its moon. All three students began moving randomly in the weightlessness. Kevin fought back a desire to puke. Doug put out his hand to where the wall used to be and ran into the force field keeping the atmosphere contained. Lily studied the astral panorama surrounding them.

Earth was in full view, half illuminated by the sun to their left. The moon was to the right and would appear full to the people on the ground. The space above, below, and around them was filled with unblinking stars. They were about forty-five degrees up from the equatorial plane with Central Asia, going through dawn, directly below them.

The hologram spoke again. "I need to know how you opened the wormhole and how you invented the Hore-field generator."

"What's a wormhole?" Doug asked.

"What's a Hore-field generator?" Kevin asked.

"Where the hell are we?" Lily asked.

… … … … … … … … …

"I hate full moons!" Officer Swingle swung his substantial bulk around in his desk chair to face his fellow night-security officer.

The couple had just left after coming into Campus Security with some wild story about meeting two people dressed like *The Matrix* actors on the path to the stadium right after midnight. The actor-people were carrying two other people who seemed to be unconscious, and the couple had somehow been knocked out without anyone or anything touching them. By the time the couple had awoken, the *Matrix* guys and the people they were carrying had disappeared.

The Beginning of the End

Officer Swingle ticked off on his fingers the items that he'd discovered during his investigation. "No physical trauma beyond a skinned elbow. No evidence of a scuffle. No one witnesses. No sexual assault."

"Maybe we'll get more complaints during the day shift," Officer Ping suggested. "Maybe this is the just tip of the iceberg."

The two security officers didn't know it, but Laurel and Hardy was what they were called by the students, named after the famous comedy duo of the 1930s and 40s. Ping was the Stan Laurel to Swingle's Oliver Hardy—slim and lithe versus overweight and ponderous.

"I think they just got stoned and stumbled." Swingle winked at Ping and laughed, causing his triple chin to wiggle. "That happened to me once. I didn't inhale, of course."

Ping shook his head. "The next thing we'll hear about is aliens landing at Walmart on the other side of campus."

"It's always the fat chick who gets the anal probe!" Swingle laughed even harder, his chin jiggling like a bowl of Jell-O.

The guard from the stadium walked into Campus Security. "Hey, Jerry," Ping greeted him. "How's the stadium?"

"I got them sonsabitches!" he said proudly.

"Got who, Jerry?" Swingle asked, wiping a tear from his eye.

"Aliens!" Jerry said vehemently.

The two officers glanced at each other surreptitiously and then burst out laughing again.

Jerry started to get pissed off. "Okay. Laugh at this, you two." He pulled his cell phone out of his pocket, brought up the movie of the lander departing from the football field, and shoved it in front of Ping. The date/time stamp at the bottom of the picture showed "12:45 A.M." that morning—about two hours ago. They both watched the movie three times.

Swingle touched the screen in amazement. "How did you get it to look so real?"

"It *is* real, you moron!" Jerry screamed at him, in his raspy out-of-breath voice. "Them sonsabitches was on the football field less than two hours ago! Here's pictures of where the spaceship was sitting on the forty-yard line." Jerry brought up his pictures of the circular lander pad marks.

"And these are still there?" Ping asked.

"Damn right they are!"

"I think I should go over and see what Jerry's talking about."

"Sure, go check it out," Swingle said with a twinkle in his eye. "I'll hold down the fort, in case more aliens show up." He walked over to the firearms locker, pulled out a shotgun, and cranked a shell into the chamber with the characteristic *shick-shack*. "I will protect and defend!" He stood at attention in mock military fashion, his face rigid with barely contained mirth.

Ping stood, ignoring Swingle. "Come on, Jerry. Show me what you got." He picked up the security office digital camera as they walked out the door together.

… … … … … … … … …

"Those depressions were really there," Ping said when he returned. "I don't see how Jerry could have made them. There were three of them about ten feet apart, each one a good three feet in diameter. They sunk into the AstroTurf at least two inches—whatever made them must've weighed tons. And, get this: there weren't any tracks leading up to them or going away. Any machine that heavy would have made tracks."

"Did you take pictures?"

"Of course. Here, see for yourself." Ping passed the camera over to him.

Swingle hooked the camera up to his laptop and transferred the pictures; the resolution was much greater than the display on the back of the camera. The two security officers studied the pictures; Ping had even taken some from high in the grandstand, showing the undisturbed turf all around the depressions including footprints in the dew from people going to and from them. "I'll be damned. I wonder how he made them. Turf's gonna have to be replaced. I'll bet he loses his job for doing it."

The phone rang. "Stanford Campus Security, Officer Ping speaking."

"This is Gene Ariel from the *National Enquirer*. We've had a report of aliens landing on your football field this evening. Have there been any reports of odd happenings or unexplainable things?"

Ping checked the caller ID: Las Vegas. He decided it was a prank call, but this night couldn't get any weirder, so he played along. "You mean, besides the security guard at the football field saying a spaceship landed on the forty-yard line and a couple saying they were knocked out by a ray gun?"

"First I've heard about a couple being knocked out. Can you give me their names? Was there an anal probe incident?"

Ping hung up the phone.

... ...

The captain turned off the display of the area outside the ship and turned on the artificial gravity again; the students fell to the floor with a thump, back in the small room where they had woken up. A hologram of their original Rosy Transmitter, magnetic mirror, and laptop appeared in front of them. "This is the Hore-field generator I believe you created. We found it floating near your planet one rotation ago. I need to know how you invented this device. What led to your discovery?"

"Holy crap! It worked! " Doug crowed. "We really did send it a hundred-thousand kilometers out."

"Then you did create this device?"

"Yes, we did," Lily told the voice. "Why is this so important to you? Who are you? We're just some students at a university."

There was a pause, and then the voice continued. "I need to know how you invented this device. What led to your discovery?"

"I want my laptop back," Doug demanded. "I bought it a week ago—it's brand new."

"Where are we really?" Kevin asked. "Anyone could have generated those pictures of Earth and space and projected them onto the walls. For all we know, you guys are Chinese and we're in Mongolia somewhere."

"I'm not Chinese, whatever that is. Are you sure you would like to see my real image?"

Kevin glanced at Lily and Doug, who nodded. "Yes."

The CG human face vanished, and in a moment the image of a floating, gray-green, tattooed octopus replaced it. It made some unintelligible sounds, followed by some static, and then, "I'll bet this isn't what you expected."

None of Earthlings said a word. They were feeling pretty alien.

"Is everyone on this ship an octopus?" Doug managed to ask.

"No. There are nineteen different species onboard. Grock Corporation hires from all species based on the attributes needed for a job."

"An equal opportunity employer!" Kevin commented sarcastically. "Won't the Department of Commerce be thrilled?"

... ...

"You got the idea of how to build the Hore-field generator from a dream?" *This was not good.*

"Yes, and the dream said humanity would never be the same," Lily said.

"Had any of your classes laid the groundwork for how you designed it? Could this device have been a natural extension of someone else's research?"

Doug chimed in next. "Nope. No one, to my knowledge, has even postulated this was possible, let alone begun research on how it might be done."

"Well, that's not entirely true," Kevin said. "Science-fiction writers have been talking about portals and wormholes for a hundred years. Some of our most important discoveries began with someone saying 'What if something is true? What else would be true?' Einstein created his famous theory of relativity using that technique. He said, if the speed of light is constant, time has to slow as you approach it."

Xanny chuckled, "That's true in real space, but not with wormholes."

"Actually, the signal through the wormhole is not going faster than the speed of light," Lily said. "The wormhole is simply bypassing the distance between the two points. The signal is still traveling at the speed of light through the wormhole."

The captain tried to get them back on subject. "How far did you get with your research on wormholes?"

Doug answered for the group. "Well, we started out with sound waves, and then found it worked with lasers, as well. After that, we sent small items from one place to another, including a small mammal. We wanted to see what would happen if we opened a wormhole into space." He shook his head with chagrin. "Our whole apparatus got blown into the vacuum."

Captain Xanny's wrinkled his face, like he had eaten something spoiled, which stretched reality even further for Earthlings; until that moment, none of them had supposed an octopus could have *any* expression, let alone a *pained* one. "And what did you learn from that?"

Lily got it first. "That we can send the generator through the same wormhole the generator creates!" Her friends stared at her in astonishment.

"Yes," the captain agreed, "and what would that allow you to do?"

"Transport a ship containing the generator anywhere we could aim the generator," Doug said in a whisper, the implications slowly sinking in.

"Yes," Xanny said sadly, "that's what it means. What would *that* allow you to do?"

Kevin's eyes became wide as the octopus's insinuations became clear. "*That* would allow us to start exploring the rest of the galaxy!"

"You are correct," the captain said, and then quietly, almost to himself, "and that will, most probably, not be allowed." There was a long silence. Finally the captain spoke again, "Who else knows about your research? Did you show it to anyone?"

"Our advisor, Dr. Johnson," Lily said.

"Does he have a copy of your notes? Could he build a Horefield generator with them?"

"We left a functioning generator on the lab bench when we were taken—he wouldn't even have to build one."

The octopus was amazed. "You created another generator in less than one day?"

"It was a team effort, but yeah," Doug said.

"A team with whom?"

"Doug's Double-E friend—he made the magnetic mirror," Kevin said.

"What is *Double-E*?"

"Electrical Engineering."

"Who programmed the computer to control the magnetic field?"

"I did most of the work," Doug said. "I got some help from some friends to create the computer interface."

Xanny changed the subject. "Tell me about the dream. Did you get any image of who or what gave you the information?"

Lily paused a moment, struggling to remember the details. She'd had the dream over a month ago. "No. As I remember, it was a floating marker, drawing the components of the transmitter on a virtual whiteboard—that and the phrase 'It will change the world.' That's all I remember."

"Was there a voice—one you could recognize?"

Lily tried again to remember the dream. "It wasn't a voice ... more like a memory I knew I'd never had, if that makes any sense. I could remember the words, but I knew no one had never said them. Are we almost done? I need to pee."

"Yes. We are done. I will have you transported back to your planet. Thank you for your help."

Doug raised his hand. "What about my computer? Can I have it back?"

The captain considered his request for a moment and then shrugged. "Yes. I don't see how you having it will change anything."

The hologram disappeared, and all three students were silent, overwhelmed by the enormity of what they had seen and heard.

After a few minutes, a door opened in one of the walls with an almost silent whirring. Doug watched it opened in disbelief; no door had been there before. The three humanoids who had entered the lab were outside the door, their freeze pistols at the ready.

The Beginning of the End

They motioned the students to come with them. The smaller humanoid—the one Lily knocked out—led. He had a large bruise on the side of his face. The other two followed.

They walked a short way through what appeared to be a pretty normal hallway, through a hatch, and into a spherical room, maybe twenty feet in diameter. In the middle of the sphere, suspended between six cables to keep the ball centered, was a smaller sphere, about two feet across. Around the outside of the room were seats. They sat where the humanoids indicated and strapped in. Doug's laptop was on one of the seats. He picked it up and hugged it to his chest like a long lost puppy that had returned at last.

The three aliens took seats across from the students. The one with the bruise touched a panel and a hologram appeared in front of him. He pressed some buttons on the hologram, the hatch to the ship closed, and they broke free. All three students studied the mother ship through the viewing portals, spellbound, as the lander moved away. It was nothing like the starships of Earth's science fiction or the chemical rockets of Earth's current space technology. The ship was a sphere.

"The transmitter must be in the middle somewhere," Doug said in awe.

"Those drum-looking things must be the electromagnets to focus it," Kevin said.

"What are those huge cones?" Lily wondered aloud.

Doug answered, "I'll bet they're thrusters. You'd need them to move into the aura."

"Hard to believe they're powerful enough to accelerate the mass of that ship through the aura in five seconds," Kevin said. "It must weigh thousands of tons!"

The lander followed the same path to the university it had used previously. As they jumped to the area over the North Pole, the inside filled with a Rosy aura. The jump through the aura was over in two seconds. The students were glued to the windows of the lander as it transited Earth in a great circle route, from the frozen wastelands of the artic to Stanford University. Once they began their descent into the atmosphere, it took thirty minutes to arrive at Stanford, with none of the flame and fury the space capsules of humanity experienced. The lander set down with a soft bump on the football field and the hatch opened. Bruised-guy indicated the students should exit.

From the outside, the lander was a smaller version of the mother ship. The bottom thrusters doubled as landing pads, giving it the appearance of a flying ball with legs. The hatch closed, and the lander lifted off the gridiron, rising out of the stadium. It oriented toward the mother ship, accelerated, and disappeared in a twinkling rosy glow across the dawn of a new day.

... ...

Envoy Gart-Disp was unmoved by Captain Xanny's explanation of the origin of the student's Hore-field generator. He had watched the hologram of the interview with the students four times.

"The plans for the Hore-field generator were planted in her subconscious by an agent—that much is obvious. We don't *know* who, why, or how, although I'm sure everyone who's seen this hologram has their own suspicions. What was done to this species is reprehensible—they aren't ready for intragalactic commerce. Now we will have to evaluate them, and I think everyone knows what the verdict will be. Whoever inserted those plans in her subconscious wanted this to happen." He frowned his distaste over the situation. "Which corporations would stand to benefit most greatly from the non-acceptance of this species?"

Xanny had also been thinking about this. "We haven't finished the scan of what technology they have that could be marketed to the rest of the galaxy. I suspect we should focus on what competing technologies they have developed from which the current owners are making significant profits. As you know, when the Ur admits a new member with technology already being marketed by another species, the profit from that technology is equally divided between the two species going forward. This cuts in half the profit the originally owning species was receiving."

"Yes. Quite. Please let me know when the technology scan is complete. Do you have an expected delivery date?"

The Beginning of the End

"I expect it to be complete in twenty more rotations of this planet."

"I need it in ten—and that's pushing our required decision date. Is there anything I can provide that would expedite your scan?"

"I don't see what would. We are currently at our maximum data transfer capacity. My teams are working in shifts to analyze it." The captain was silent a moment, trying to find a discreet way to ask his next question. He decided to just throw it out there instead. "Is there any chance this investigation could migrate from a new-species scan to a criminal scan?"

The envoy *was* authorized to do such a thing. It had never happened before, in Xanny's limited experience, but he had also never seen such a blatant violation of the rules of new species administration and development. Even in his time as an unlicensed miner, he never would have considered sabotaging an entire species like this.

The envoy sighed. The same thought had occurred to him. "Not yet. We have no evidence other than a student's recounting of a dream." He raised his flipper as the octopus began to object. "Don't misunderstand, Captain Xanny. If you can uncover who has planted this technology, I *will* prosecute them. Even if you don't uncover the actual person, if you can find any hard evidence, I will file an Unknown Perpetrator charge."

"You actually have *two* abnormal things. The dream *and* the creation of a technology, which has no preceding basis in their existing science—technology created by an easily-impressionable, young mind and which would cause the species to be evaluated before they would have the opportunity to mature enough for acceptance. These beings are still fighting the coming-of-age problems every new species has to solve. Give them a few hundred more cycles around their sun and I have no doubt they'll sort it all out."

"Unfortunately, we don't have the luxury of allowing them that time. Even if we could prove the species was molested, nothing would change in the near-term. They *have* created a Hore-field generator, they *have* made wormholes with it, and most important, they *have* sent the generator through the wormhole it created.

Within a year, they will be leaving this solar system. It has happened too many times to doubt the outcome. They will have to be evaluated—the law gives us no leeway in that."

Both of them were silent. Finally the envoy added, "You have ten rotations of their planet, Captain Xanny. Find out what you can. My team's decision will be made on your and others' observations."

Ten minutes later, the captain watched Gart-Disp's shuttle leave his ship and wink out of sight. He pressed the ship-wide comm button on his anti-grav pack and called for his second-in-command. "Commander Chirra, please attend me in my quarters."

Several minutes later, Xanny's exec floated through his door. "You wished to speak to me, sir?" Like Xanny, Chirra was an octopus but he was one of the rare members of his species who was ambidextrous. This attribute, combined with his eight-lobed brain, allowed him to manipulate eight different parts of the navigational hologram simultaneously and independently, making their jumps much safer.

"Yes, I did, Yidee. The envoy just left. We have ten rotations of this planet to finish our technology survey. Can you do it?"

"What's the hurry? We usually have at least twenty."

"He's concerned about the proliferation of Hore-drive technology throughout the species. If that happens, they could have a functional interstellar vessel within a year. Even if he selects them for elimination, it could take months before they realize it has happened. If they create a Hore-drive vessel before they figure out they're dying, I believe he will call in the storm troopers—it will be a bloodbath."

"I didn't know they were that close. Most species take several years from the preliminary dabbling before they figure out they can send the generator through the same wormhole they created with it. How would they power the Hore-drive vessel? We've seen no evidence of cold fusion, let alone a Hore energy portal. I've never seen a species develop a Hore-field before they made cold fusion work."

"They'll power the Hore-drive vessel the same way they now power their primitive nuclear reactors: fission," Xanny said with distaste.

The Beginning of the End

"So, they're going to be sending unstable, dirty reactors around the galaxy, searching for habitable planets. It's just a matter of time until an accident occurs. They've already had three meltdowns. Who's going to pay for the cleanup?"

"Don't know. Maybe we'll be lucky and it won't happen where the radiation will hurt anything else. Maybe we'll be able to send the whole mess into a star." The captain stared at his hologram of Earth. "Well, now you know why he's in such a hurry." He explained his theory: that the Hore-field generator plans were planted in the female's dream so she would discover worm holes before the species was ready to be evaluated. "The envoy agrees with me incidentally, but he can't do anything about it unless we find some proof beyond the female's dream. We need to find the proverbial smoking laser.

"The only reason I can see for someone to take such a chance would be if this species had developed technology someone else is or is about to make a bundle on. We've found nothing even close—this species is still cracking atoms to see what's inside. The stuff we've found has been invented thousands of times before, all of it long out of license range."

"Why would he hesitate to open a criminal investigation? I've never seen anything so blatant."

"I don't know, but I'm not going to call him on it. Envoys are one step below the emperor."

"There has to be something the dream planters left when they exited the planet or something here that would make the gamble worth the risk," Chirra said, pondering where to examine next. "Maybe we're looking in the wrong places. We've been focusing on published work through their computer network; I think we need to get inside individual researchers' computers."

The captain was puzzled for a moment and then smiled broadly. "Terrific idea, Yidee! Go do it. And I just had a thought, too. If someone visited this planet to plant a dream, there would have to have been a record of their visit in the wormhole detectors. The last authorized visit was almost two hundred years ago, but we didn't get wormhole notifications of any visits since then. Could the wormhole detectors have been tampered with? Did you send someone to physically check them?"

"I only examined them remotely—they appeared to be unmolested from my scan. I will send a team to retrieve them immediately."

"I can take care of that. Go back to your scan teams and see if you can find anything in the various individual computers at the research centers around the world. Start as soon as you can and let me know if you find anything of interest. There has to be a reason someone wants to kill this species."

Chapter 8 – We'll Be Back

January 23

The three students watched the aura fade from the sky over the silent stadium where they had attended countless football and soccer games with the rest of their classmates and alumni, trying to draw normalcy from a world that would never be normal again.

"I wonder where the starship is," Kevin said, studying the stars spread across the sky.

Lily pointed to a spot about thirty degrees up from the horizon. "Up there somewhere, maybe a million kilometers out. Let's find a bathroom—I've got to pee."

They started across the field toward the main concourse.

"What do you think the captain meant when he said 'That will, most probably, not be allowed'?" Lily wondered. "Do you think humanity will not be allowed to explore the galaxy?"

Kevin laughed disparagingly. "Would you want humanity showing up on your doorstep? We can't even get along with ourselves. When I was a kid, I lived next to a couple who were always fighting—McMahon was their name. They would duke it out in the front yard, and two or three nights a week, the cops were knocking on their door. One night, my dad tried to calm them down and *they* attacked *him*. He got a black eye and a bloody nose for his trouble. On a hot night in the middle of summer when I was about twelve, old lady McMahon killed her husband with his hunting rifle—blew his brains out all over their living room wall. The bullet went right through our house and missed my mom's head by inches—scared the crap out of all of us. I hope that crazy woman is still in jail."

After all three used the restrooms, they walked around the inside of the concourse, trying to find a way out. All the exits were locked.

"Do you think they'll just shut down our Rosy generator project or do you think they'll do something more?" Lily asked again. They didn't know what the aliens could or would do—that was the scariest thing of all. Images from all the alien movies they'd seen came to the surface.

"Maybe they've been coming for thousands of years, like *Predator*—drop in with their buds for a weekend of hunting, and then home to the kids," Kevin suggested in mock seriousness.

"I think *Men in Black* might be more like it," Doug joined in. "I wonder what other kinds of aliens were on that ship."

"Or would it be like *Mars Attacks!* or even *Independence Day* or," Lily stopped. "Oh, shit!" The chain link fence they had been following had a gaping hole, melted around the edges. Droplets of solidified metal littered the ground.

"I'll bet there's a story here," Kevin said, examining the hole and then stepping through.

"Hold it right there," Jerry commanded, stepping out of the shadows, his nightstick held high. The students froze. "I figured them alien sonsabitches was dropping off some a their compatriots to infiltrate Earth. Where're you from? What're you doing on Earth? You work for the Russians?"

"No, you don't understand—we aren't aliens," Lily tried to explain, desperation creeping into her voice. This day kept getting weirder and it just wouldn't end. She wanted to crawl into her bed in the dorm and pull the covers up to hide from octopus captains and starship abductions. "We're students here at the university. We got kidnapped by aliens. That was their lander leaving—you must have seen it. Let me reach in my pocket and I can show you my student ID."

"Kidnapped, huh? I don't think so. I think they just dropped you off like them sonsabitches earlier tonight. Everyone knows aliens can produce any kinda ID whenever they want." Jerry was not going to be taken in by some slick-talking aliens.

"He figured it out, Heechee—he discovered us." Kevin said to Doug in a raspy, falsetto voice. "Protocol 15-169 is needed."

Jerry hesitated, not knowing what to expect. Kevin grabbed the guard's nightstick out of his hands and, in a flash, was behind him, holding the stick across the old man's throat. "Did you bring the anal probe, Heechee?"

The Beginning of the End

Doug couldn't believe this was happening. When would this night end? He shook his head and said doubtfully, in a scratchy voice, "Yeah, it's right here." He reached into the pocket of his sweatshirt. The old man's eyes got wide, but Doug's hand came out empty, and he shrugged. "I must have left them on the lander."

Lily decided to play along, hoping it would be enough to keep anyone from getting hurt. She reached up and put her palm gently on Jerry's face, her eyes crossed. "This your lucky day, old Earthling. Let him go. He won't spread alarm. If he do, we come back. We try new probe on him, one with electric shocks that go in front instead of back."

Jerry's eyes grew even wider and he began to hyperventilate. Kevin released him, gave him back his nightstick, and the students walked away, keeping in step and swinging their arms like they were one mind and body.

When they got out of sight of the stadium, Kevin let a tiny chuckle escape. Once he did, the laughter tsunami blasted through the three of them and they laughed until they lay gasping on the ground. It felt so good to let the tension and stress of the night go into the brightening sky.

High above them, one of the dots of light was the starship. Captain Xanny watched Earth turn, hoping he could find a way to prevent what he knew was coming.

... ...

Lily, Doug, and Kevin missed all their classes that day. They had returned to their respective dorm rooms and collapsed into bed. Nothing—not even the excitement of the events of the last twenty-four hours—could have kept them awake one second longer than it took to rest their heads on their pillows.

... ...

Dr. Johnson came into the lab before his first morning class. The Rosy Transmitter was still on, but the liquid nitrogen had boiled away long ago. No aura surrounded the transmitter—the circuits were much too warm. He played with it for a few minutes, moving the mirror, turning the gain and frequency knobs all the way down and all the way up, powering it off and on with no effect. No rosy glow appeared.

"Goddamned graduate student bullshit artists!" he snarled in his UK accent. "Faster than light, my bollocks! They're probably down at the IHOP having breakfast and laughing their asses off. I'll just hold onto this laptop, thank you very much. They'll have some explaining to do before I give it back to them. You don't leave pilferable equipment sitting around unsecured."

He disconnected the cable from the laptop to the mirror, set the laptop aside with its AC adapter, and moved the rest of the equipment into the storage room. He made sure the door locked when it closed.

His first class, Intro to Physics 105, started in half an hour. He could still make it to his office and grab a cup of tea before wasting yet another hour trying to explain Planck's constant to freshmen who couldn't care less. Dr. Johnson left the lab with the laptop and AC adapter tucked safely under his arm.

… … … … … … … … …

After she woke up in late afternoon, Lily lay in bed, thinking about what had happened yesterday. Kevin had tried to save her life when the guy from the starship pulled out his ray gun or whatever it was. No one had ever tried to protect her from anything before—not even her parents when her uncle had come calling. The memories of those nights still made her skin crawl. Somehow, Kevin's actions eclipsed everything else that happened to them yesterday, which was quite a statement considering she was kidnapped by aliens and help prisoner in a starship, been inside a Rosy jump and had her first ride in space, spoke to an octopus starship commander, and pretended to be an alien to the guard at the stadium.

She went into the bathroom as her body woke up. As she let her nightgown drop to the floor, she eyed herself critically in the full-length mirror on the door. Her Chinese roots showed clearly in the image, along with all the years of martial arts and physical fitness training her parents had forced upon her: almond-shaped eyes, off-white skin, a flat stomach, clear muscle definition, and firm breasts. She was pleased with her body.

Her parents had been so sure Chairman Mao and his communist regime would collapse and the resistance would rise into the void. Now they were gone to a labor camp, maybe lying dead in a ditch somewhere. Their only legacy to her had been a one-way passage out of China in the middle of the night when she was seventeen; the next day the state police had arrested her parents. Lily had survived alone in the US for six years, earning a BS from UCLA, magna cum laude, and now she was pursuing a PhD in physics from Stanford. The US government had paid for her baccalaureate, but she had used loans to pay what Stanford's tuition assistance did not.

Did she want Kevin as a lover or friend? Did she dare let him inside her carefully maintained Chinese bitch persona? It was her lifetime goal to rescue her parents and would continue to be until they were by her side or she had proof they had been killed. Would having a lover interfere with that?

The image of Kevin jumping between her and the alien with the ray gun kept returning to her. Every time she remembered it, she got a warm lump in her chest that filled her with feelings she had never experienced before. Was there room for both Kevin and rescuing her parents in her life? What if there was? What if there wasn't?

She forced herself to see the image in the mirror as Kevin would. She had always liked him—how he made her laugh and always went out of his way to do nice things for her. She realized in that moment she had passed "like" a long time ago.

Her stomach got her attention—she had not eaten since lunch yesterday. She pulled on a T-shirt and jeans, ran a brush through her hair, and began to pull it back into her standard ponytail. The face in the mirror made her pause. Instead of a ponytail, she let her hair hang around her face. It extended past her shoulders.

I have beautiful hair, she thought. It glowed and glittered in the light from above the mirror, black as a star-flecked night. *I think*

I'll leave it down. She added a touch of blush, a little mascara, and that new lipstick she'd bought on a whim a week ago.

There was a knock on her door. When she opened it, she found Doug standing in the hallway with his laptop under his arm. "We have a problem. The transmitter's gone."

"What do you mean?" she asked, astonished. "It's not in the physics lab?"

"Nope. I was there ten minutes ago."

"Have you talked to Kevin? Does he know what happened to it?"

"Nope. I mean I haven't talked to him yet. I was going there next."

"Let me get my jacket and backpack."

… … … … … … … … …

Kevin answered the door, dripping wet with a towel around his waist. He saw Lily was with Doug, gasped, and slid behind the door with his head sticking out. They filled him in on the missing transmitter and his face grew red.

"I'll bet Dr. Johnson took it. That asshole's going to claim our work as his!"

"Let's find out what happened before we start making accusations," Lily suggested.

"Yeah, that's good advice," Doug agreed. "And, Kevin? Maybe you should get dressed first?"

He laughed a little self-consciously, looking down. "Yeah, give me a minute."

… … … … … … … … …

When they arrived at the physics lab, the last class of the day was letting out. The grad student in charge of the lab session nodded at them as they came in.

"Hi, Helga," Doug said. "Have you seen our master's project? We left it in here yesterday evening."

The Beginning of the End

"The aluminum foil ball? Nope. It was on the lab bench last night when I stopped by to get some papers. Could Dr. Johnson have put it in the storage room? Did you check?"

"Of course not," Kevin said, shaking his head. "Why would we do that? It makes too much sense." Doug reached for the door; it was locked.

"I have a key here somewhere." Helga searched through her backpack. "Here it is." She unlocked the door. Inside was the transmitter without the department laptop.

"Okay, I'm beginning to understand," Doug said thoughtfully. "I'll bet Dr. Johnson moved it there when he found it out on the lab bench this morning. I'll have to tell him how much I appreciate him doing that the next time I see him."

"Thanks, Helga. You're a life saver." Lily gave her a quick hug.

"Glad I could help. Close the door when you're done—it will lock automatically."

"Will do. Thanks again."

After Helga left, Kevin turned to them. "What should we do about last night?"

Doug didn't understand. "What do you mean?"

"We were kidnapped by aliens because we built Rosy and they're still in orbit around Earth. Don't we need to tell someone?"

"Who would we tell?" Lily asked. "People would say we made it up or are wacko— just like *we* say when those alien pictures show up on the front page of the *National Enquirer*. That guard *saw* the lander and *he* didn't believe us."

"So we ignore that the whole thing happened?"

The three sat quietly for a while.

Kevin spoke first. "I have an idea about how we can demonstrate Rosy—how we can make the world understand what we discovered."

"I'm not sure we should demonstrate anything, Kevin." Doug was trying to sort out his mixed feelings about the whole Rosy project. "After last night, maybe we should just forget about the transmitter—pretend none of this happened, and that we never invented Rosy."

"I'm not forgetting about anything or being intimidated by some asshole alien octopus. We're scientists—this is what we do. Rosy is the biggest discovery since the wheel. Free transportation! No more carbon emissions from trucks and boats! No more oil dependence! We can put anything we want into orbit without having to use billion-dollar rockets that fill the air with toxic chemicals. I want to shout about it from the treetops! We've discovered something that will change the world. How could we even consider not telling everyone about it?"

Lily glanced at Doug to see if he agreed with them. He shrugged and nodded. "Well, then what's next, you guys?"

"I want to build a remote-controlled transmitter we will send into orbit, say a million miles out. Once the satellite is out there, it orients on Earth and opens a laser channel to us. We leave the Rosy beam open and send the satellite a signal, and the satellite sends it back to us through real space. We record the time the signal goes out and when it gets back. A one-way trip from a million miles out takes ..." Kevin keyed some numbers into his cell phone calculator. "5.3, 5.4 seconds, depending on how close we get to a million. If the transmission between us and the satellite is not instantaneous, the delay will be longer."

"We'll need some help from the MEs and Kiran again," Doug pointed out, referring to their mechanical engineering friends.

"I think I can front a couple cases of beer," Lily said, "but we have to send the satellite from a vacuum or risk losing the transmitter again."

"Let's cross that bridge when we come to it," Kevin said. "Until then, there's a lot of work to do to get everything ready."

"You guys have fun. I've got a choir practice at the church in an hour," Doug said, getting up.

"I didn't know you could sing," Kevin said.

"I can't, but I croak as well as the rest of them."

"I didn't know you went to church," Lily said. Doug kept surprising her.

"All of us have things we keep private, Lily. After last night, I want to spend some time in the chapel and ask Him what He thinks about this. See ya."

The Beginning of the End

"Bye, Doug," they both said together.

After he'd left, Lily said, "I need to eat something before we start working on this." Kevin didn't understand. He was ready to get to work. She rolled her eyes. "You know? Food? The stuff our bodies run on? I haven't eaten since yesterday at lunch. I can't keep working unless I get some food."

Kevin realized he was hungry, too. "I suppose the universe and its alien octopuses can wait for another hour." He put a piece of tape across the door latch to the supply room, so it wouldn't lock again. "The dining hall is closed. Mickey D's or Jack in the Box?"

"Tough choice." She sighed. Neither one sounded like something she wanted to eat, but they both lived on student budgets. "Let's walk around and see what's open."

… … … … … … … … …

They found a bagel place on California Avenue that made a pretty decent sandwich, but after eating, they were both a little ill at ease. Kevin didn't know if they should go back to the lab and start laying out the satellite or take a break for an evening. It had been an intense couple of days. Lily had never allowed him to relate to her on a personal level, so he decided to test the water.

"Would you like to go out?" he asked. He then realized what he had said and blushed to his ears. "I mean go out for some real food? I could pay for dinner if you're broke."

In that moment, Lily came to a decision. She was tired of being alone and she would make sure having a relationship with Kevin didn't interfere with rescuing her parents.

"I'd love to go out, but after the culinary masterpiece we just ate, I feel more in the mood for a beer than a meal. Is that all right?"

"Beer works for me," he breathed in relief. His checking account wouldn't get cleaned out tonight.

They went to O'Hanrahans where they drank Irish beer, laughed together a lot, and danced until the bar closed. It was more fun than Lily had allowed herself in the six years since she had left China and her parents. Kevin had pulled her out on the dance floor for every slow dance the DJ played, and Lily had pulled him out for the fast ones.

As they walked back to the dorms, he held her hand and told her about his dreams after graduate school. He wanted to work at JPL, NASA's Jet Propulsion Laboratory in Pasadena, beside his dad and was scared to death that he wasn't good enough to make the cut.

They stopped in front of the entrance to her dorm. He hesitated and then bent to kiss her; she was ready and kissed him back, running her hands through his hair. He pulled her into his arms and kissed her deeply.

Kevin was having a little trouble believing this was happening to *him*—the overweight, goofball, physics nerd. He loved Lily, her full lips, graceful movements, and brilliant mind. He had longed for her since the first day they met. He pulled her close and kissed her again and again, and she kissed him back just as hard. Tonight, they had each other. Tonight, the rest of the universe and its octopus captains could go to hell.

Chapter 9 – The Beginning of the End

February 8

The wormhole detectors *had* been tampered with; someone or something had reprogrammed them to allow one planetary rotation window of non-detection for every revolution around the sun. How this had been done was unclear. The ground around the devices had not been disturbed for thousands—perhaps tens of thousands—of years. Captain Xanny figured the reprogrammer must have found an electronic backdoor into the detectors. Remotely, they appeared identical to the original programming. Xanny told Lieutenant Nussi to relay this information to Grock Central, and he recommended examining the detectors on all Grock-inoculated planets to see if they had been altered, as well.

During that one day a year, anyone could jump into the solar system, manipulate the species, and jump out without leaving so much as a vapor trail behind and the latest non-detection window had been one week before Lily's dream. He realized with dismay that the detector recovery had only proven a species manipulation *could* have taken place without knowing of their entry or exit—not that one actually *had* taken place. They still didn't know who was behind it.

Suddenly, something clicked. There was no time delay on subliminal dream plants; once the plant was made, the dream would start with the next REM sleep. "They must have come in during the window the week before the dream was planted! The week delay must have been because they were searching for a suitable candidate ... and if no record exists of them leaving before we arrived, they are still here waiting for us to go home, so they can sneak away! If they are here, I will find them!" He made a pirate's rune and spit into his shadow.

Since the first wormhole alert had been issued, hundreds of jumps into this system had been recorded but very few of anyone leaving. He pressed his comm button. "Lieutenant Nussi, please attend me in my quarters." When she came in, he explained what he wanted and why.

"I will examine the jump history log," she promised. "Give me an hour."

... ...

The captain retreated to the only place on the ship where no one would disturb him—his private waste disposal room. He considered what to do next. Commander Chirra's technology scan had not turned up anything of significance. Many of the computers his teams had examined contained encrypted files, which caused much excitement and speculation. Xanny instructed Analysis to pass the files to Envoy Gart-Disp, who passed them to the much larger capacity computers at Galactic Central. After they were unencrypted, most of the files were found to contain images of unclothed primates in various stages of sexual coupling; the remainder were messages to active or potential sexual partners. Of the research observed on the computers, there was nothing amazing or extraordinary. This species was plodding down the same discovery paths countless others had already followed—except for the Hore field generator.

Nothing Analysis had found laid any of the foundations necessary for discovery of the Hore field. They had not detected the resonance of the Girf particle near absolute zero, they had not built virtual transistors, no one had yet found the speed of light anomaly surrounding magnetized argon ions, and of course, no one had created a cold fusion generator in a working form.

Of all the missing technology, cold fusion was the one nearest fruition. It would help this species to accomplish the five basic milestones all new members were required to satisfy before the GSCB would allow them to leave their solar system. Of course, cold fusion could also make their problems worse. Cheap energy was not a cure-all by itself—it simply took the pressure off the other problems so these primates *could* solve them, if they had the inclination.

For a species to leave their home system and begin to intermingle with the others, peacefully living and trading around the galaxy, the law specified two nonnegotiable milestones that must be fully achieved: regulated capitalism and peaceful coexistence. Three slightly less important and therefore slightly more negotiable milestones also existed: overcome pollution, overpopulation, and resource depletion. For the GSCB to give probationary membership into the galactic confederation to a new species, those last three could be in progress but not achieved. If they offered probationary membership, the envoy would specify the changes that would have to be put into place and a timetable for the species to implement them. The repercussions of turning loose a violent, greedy species with no interest in sustainable life on the galaxy were well documented, and allowing it was absolutely forbidden. It was after a particularly bloody purge of a vicious species that the Ur created the GSCB; they were the cops that enforced the warlike species prohibition.

A gentle knock sounded on the door. "Antatay?" his concubine asked, using the affectionate nickname she had given him. "Are you all right? Do you need anything?"

Captain Xanny sighed. "No, my love. I'll be right out." There was nothing he could do unless Nussi found an unidentified departure or Chirra's team turned up something unexpected. He had to get them searching for the signature of a Hore energy portal—a portal where none should have been.

Chapter 10 – A Rare Sign of Respect

February 18

On day ten of the technology scan, Envoy Gart-Disp floated in Captain Xanny's conference room.

"Have you discovered any proof of manipulation of the species, Captain Xanny?"

For ten days Commander Chirra's team had crawled into every computer they could find, searching for proof of the manipulation or the reason behind it. They found nothing. They had also not found any unexplained jumps out of the solar system or the perpetrators who had made the plant. Either the perps had left the solar system somehow, without leaving a telltale jump signature or they were still here but not using Hore energy portals to power their ship.

"No, sir, I have not. The evidence is entirely circumstantial. I have no doubt a manipulation has occurred, but as to who did it or why, we have discovered nothing." The captain told him about the altered wormhole detectors and the search for the beings who did the plant.

"Captain Xanny, your efforts have been exemplary, but without something more concrete than circumstantial evidence, I have no alternative but to fail this species. They have partially achieved only one of the nonnegotiable milestones. Regulated capitalism is important, but far more important is peaceful coexistence. The other three are also underway, but no one could say they are even close to a solution on any of them." He paused, looking at the hologram of Earth on the wall, and then read from the virtual document he had just signed.

"This species has not met any of the milestones and, as far as we can tell, does not have any interest in changing. The evaluation of this species has resulted in a rating of 'Failure.' Species elimination is authorized and required."

The Beginning of the End

Grock Corporation had come to the same conclusion. They were anxious to cut their losses and establish a new dominant species on the planet.

"I understand, sir. Given the circumstances with their having a Hore-drive starship in reach, would you like me to use a SEV-1, SEV-2 or SEV-3?"

A Species Elimination Virus was the preferred way of cleansing a world of a binary species—one with two genders. The GSCB considered it a gentle and painless way to eliminate a failed species and was much more cost-effective than sending the storm troopers to kill everyone. Plus, the removal did not damage the world itself.

The Ur had approved three viruses for an elimination. A SEV-1 caused a massive die-off. A SEV-3 caused species-wide consciousness-alteration (insanity). Of the three, envoys most commonly chose a SEV-2. It stopped the target species from producing offspring by altering the chemistry of the gametes (sperm and eggs) of both genders rendering them unable to fertilize each other.

In several thousand revolutions around their sun, the world would be cleansed of most of the artifacts and pollution they would leave behind and a new species could be raised up. For a species mining corporation, two or three thousand years was just part of doing business. Grock Corporation normally had several thousand of these mining operations running simultaneously.

The envoy considered which SEV would be appropriate for the primates. "My inclination is to use SEV-1, given how close they are to a functioning Hore-drive vessel." He sighed. "Maybe I'm getting too old for this job. Use a SEV-2. Once they figure out what's going on, my hope is they will forget all about building a starship and will concentrate on finding a cure."

"I hope you are correct, sir."

"I hope so as well, Captain." He held out a flipper which penetrated the water cocoon and extended toward the octopus. It was a rare sign of respect and admiration—water mammals hardly ever let another species physically touch them. "I have enjoyed working with you, Captain Xanny. My report will reflect how hard you struggled to find a solution to this difficult issue."

"Thank you, sir." The captain grasped the flipper gently with his tentacle.

After the envoy left, Xanny summoned Commander Chirra.

"Yidee, have the genetic team prepare the SEV-2. I want it ready for release in twenty rotations. Use the DNA sample we collected from the female scientist."

"Yes, sir." Chirra floated out of the room.

Like a species inoculation virus, the SEV used the sample DNA to identify which organisms were to be infected. Even close genetic cousins would be bypassed. Genes that caused minor differences, like hair color and body mass, were ignored, but the 99.9% of the DNA the members of one species had in common were used to verify an exact match. Once the virus identified a member of the target group, the rest of the virus went to work.

Chapter 11 – See You on Saturday

March 7

The three of them were proud of the mechanism sitting on the lab bench in front of them; it had taken six weeks of hard work for the students and their friends to put it together. It consisted of a compressed gas tank with six small computer-managed thrusters to control its movement in all three dimensions. The device would use those thrusters, along with the six cameras, to aim a laser back at Stanford from a million miles out. The satellite also contained a laser receiver and, of course, a small microprocessor and battery. The microprocessor would stabilize the device, home in on the laser sent from the top of the physics building, receive the signal from the wormhole, and then send an acknowledging laser back to Palo Alto. To launch the satellite, they had also made their transmitter and mirror proportionally larger.

"We still don't have a vacuum room," Doug said.

Kevin smiled like Mona Lisa. His friend was developing a burgeoning talent for stating the obvious. "I have an idea about that. Let's see what you guys think. My dad works for NASA's Jet Propulsion Laboratory in Pasadena. I bet he would be willing to let us use their vacuum room on a weekend. It's where they verify their satellites don't have leaks and can function in space. He will probably be able to make some suggestions for the refinement of our unit—that's what he does for JPL." He pulled out his cell phone and started dialing his dad.

Lily interrupted him. "Wait a minute, Kevin. Before you call, let's talk about this for a few minutes. What are you going to say to him? Did you tell him about the starship and the octopus?"

Kevin sniggered. "Of course not—he'd have thought I was a looney or doing serious drugs—but I see what you mean. Our request does sound a little crazy. 'Hi, Dad. We built a transmitter that sends things faster than the speed of light. We want to use the JPL vacuum room to test it by sending something a million miles out.' He'd call for the guys in the white coats."

They discussed what to say for over an hour. Finally, Kevin reached for his cell phone again and selected his dad's number from the speed dial list. He explained what they wanted and why. There was a long pause on the other end of the phone line. "This is a joke, right?"

His father was not reacting as they had hoped. "No, Dad. We think we've found a way to launch a satellite into space without a rocket. We need to do it from a vacuum, though; otherwise, the launch mechanism will get blown into space, along with the device."

"How about your advisor, son? What does he say?"

"We haven't told him yet," Kevin lied. "We're afraid he'll claim the whole thing as his and we'll be left out in the cold."

Dr. Langly, Kevin's father, considered how to proceed. He didn't want to crush his son's creativity by refusing to help. On the other hand, what his son was proposing was so far out in left field, he would be a laughing stock at JPL if anyone else found out. He decided to play along for the moment. "How about I fly up there for the weekend and you guys can show me what you've come up with? If I think it's warranted, I'll try to get permission to use the room."

Kevin gave a thumbs-up to Lily and Doug. This was the best outcome from the many possibilities they had contemplated.

"Hey, could you send me any notes you have about what you've done so far? Circuit designs? Test results? I'd like to hit the ground running when I get up there."

"Sure, Dad. I'll shoot them to you right away. Check your inbox in a couple of minutes." They already had the email ready to go.

Chapter 12 – The End

March 9

The sixteen virus distribution vehicles left Grock Species Mining Ship, GSMS-77, right on schedule. Captain Xanny watched them go as each jumped to its respective entry point over Earth.

A much greater volume of virus was required to kill a species than to raise them up. A fifty-percent infection rate was adequate for a raise-up; the uninfected members would die off eventually as the altered portion of the population pushed them progressively farther from the good hunting and farming lands. Species elimination, on the other hand, required every member of the species to be infected within a week of release—before anyone figured out the virus had even been released—before any population segment could be protected. The SEV didn't die after a month, as the SIV was programmed to do during a raise-up. These primates would never reproduce on this world again.

Halfway down to the surface, the sixteen distribution vehicles would split into two, each targeted at a separate section of the planet. In half of the remaining distance, they would split again, then again, and then again. When they quit dividing, there would be five hundred twelve distributors. They would enter the atmosphere, covering 256 separate overlapping areas, emitting the SEV-2 as they went back and forth over their assigned section. The devices would blanket the planet twice over with a virus that produced no side effects other than to stop the fertilization of the primates' eggs. No one would develop fevers, coughs, or joint pains, and no other species would be affected. No one would even know they *were* infected until someone realized women weren't getting pregnant anymore.

The Earth rotated slowly in the hologram in front of the captain's chair on the bridge. He imagined the billions of primates that were going about their daily lives, oblivious to the doom descending through their atmosphere. After the distributors finished emptying their reservoirs, Armament had programmed them to jump into the nearby star.

The virus would take about a week to infect the entire primate population. The eight billion primates on this planet would die over the next one hundred revolutions of this world around its sun, exactly like they would if the SEV had not been released. The only difference was that no new children would be born to replace them. The end of children. The end to a species. The end to the hopes and dreams, to the art, to the poetry, to the lessons learned and mistakes made. The end to the good guys *and* the bad guys. The end of everyone.

The new-world armada had dispersed as soon as Envoy Gart-Disp made his decision public. GSMS-77 was the only vessel remaining within a hundred lightyears of Earth; they could not return to their mining mission until verification was received of the success of the infestation, which normally took about two months. Until then, they would wait, play games, and see if there was anything else of interest in this solar system. A couple of the moons around the gas giants had captured the attention of several crew members; apparently, those moons already had some flourishing primitive life-forms.

Chapter 13 – Pet Gorillas

March 12

On Friday evening, Kevin's phone rang. He checked the caller-id. "Hi, Dad. What's up? I thought you'd be in bed by now."

"Kevin, who else knows about this?"

"You mean the transmitter? Just the three of us, Dad."

"And there are no other copies of your notes?"

"No, just what we sent you."

"Well, I built it yesterday and it works as you described it. I believe this is the most important discovery since the theory of relativity. I showed it to the management at JPL this afternoon; they have classified it top secret and clamped down an airtight umbrella of national security over it. The FBI is about to knock on your door and confiscate your notes, devices, and computers. Give them what they want and go with them. They will bring you here and we will continue to work on this together."

A knock sounded on his door. When he opened it, a guy in a blue FBI windbreaker and sunglasses stood there, flanked by four FBI storm troopers with full SWAT gear, visors, and automatic weapons. Kevin had never had a gun pointed at him; he decided he didn't like it.

The guy in front spoke up. "Are you Kevin Langly?"

"Yep."

"I am Special Agent Courapo of the FBI. I have a FISA arrest and search warrant for you and notes, devices, and paraphernalia associated with a 'rosy' transmitter. Please turn around." The agent took Kevin's phone and wallet, ended the call, and then zipped plastic handcuffs on his wrists. He powered Kevin's phone completely off and put it in a ziplock bag with the wallet. Six other people in matching blue FBI windbreakers streamed into his room and they began to pack everything into boxes labeled "FBI Evidence."

"Mr. Langly, anything you say may be used against you in a court of law ..."

After the guy finished reading the Miranda rights, Kevin was bewildered. "Agent Courapo, do you have any idea what a Rosy Transmitter looks like?"

Courapo wore a noncommittal semi-smile. "Just let us do our job." None of the rest of the team said a word to Kevin as his room's contents disappeared into the boxes labeled "FBI Evidence"—bedding, books, notes, clothes, laptop, condoms, pens, pencils, a picture of him and his dad on a camping trip, and even the Jim Morrison poster over his bed. One person pulled a small bag of pot from Kevin's nightstand, opened it, and sniffed. He *almost* smiled and then glanced out of the corner of his eyes to see if anyone had noticed. The rest of the team was busy with their own tasks. Satisfied, he put his professional frown back on, and the pot went into the box with the rest of Kevin's stuff.

"Be careful with that clock radio," Kevin told the agent who was wrapping the cord around it. "It's really a Rosy Transmitter," he whispered. "We camouflaged it, but couldn't hide the color of the dial."

She looked at Courapo for guidance—he indicated the radio should go in the box with everything else.

As students walked by in the hallway, peering in, Kevin pursed his lips and hung his head, not believing this was happening. Officer Ping appeared in the doorway. "What's going on here? Who are you people? What are you doing in this student's room?"

Agent Courapo got Ping's name from his nametag. "We are the FBI, Officer Ping. Kevin Langly is under arrest on a FISA warrant. Please stand clear of this room."

"Where is the warrant?"

"The warrant is classified. I can't show it to you."

"Then I need to see your ID. This should have been cleared through our Security Office first."

Courapo pulled out his FBI credentials and let Ping photograph them. "Here's my business card—your head of security can call my office tomorrow. We picked up two other students, as well." He checked his clipboard. "A Lily Yuan and Douglas Medder."

The Beginning of the End

Officer Ping looked back and forth between the agent, Kevin, the business card, and the other people packing the room. "Okay, this sucks. Have you not heard of the Sixth Amendment to our Constitution? It states you can't arrest someone without telling them what they are charged with and who is charging them."

Courapo ignored him, so Ping turned to Kevin. "Do you know why you are being arrested? Has anyone told you what you are being charged with? Or who charged you?"

Kevin shook his head. "Nope, no idea. Agent Gestapo and his pet gorillas showed up, cuffed me, and started packin' my shit."

Agent Courapo finally lost patience. "Officer Ping, you must leave this area or I will arrest you, also. *Your* charge will be interfering with a federal investigation."

Ping turned on his heel and walked away. He pulled out his radio and started talking, explaining what was happening to Officer Swingle.

"Do you have a car?" Courapo asked.

"Yes."

"I'll need the keys and where it's parked."

Kevin was wondering where this would end. "And if I don't give them to you?"

"We'll find it and tow it. It could be damaged. The government would incur no liability for the damage."

With his hands still cuffed behind his back, Kevin awkwardly tried to stretch around into his front right pants pocket. The agent reached in and pulled the keys out. "It's in the parking lot outside—a black Toyota Camry." One of the blue jackets accompanied Kevin to a white panel truck where Lily and Doug were waiting inside, also handcuffed behind their backs. He climbed in awkwardly and sat down next to Lily as the door closed. Their only illumination was from the little light on the ceiling.

"Dad called me just before the Nazis showed up. He said he built a transmitter yesterday from our plans and it worked. He did a demo for his management this morning: they declared it top secret and sent Agent Gestapo to round us up."

"Are we really under arrest?" Doug had never gotten even a parking ticket his whole life. "I have classes tomorrow."

"I think so. They told Laurel, AKA Officer Ping, they had a classified FISA warrant to arrest us and clean out our rooms. They even packed the pot I just bought from that new store on Washington. At least they emptied out my bong before they put it in the box." After a couple of minutes of silence, he continued, "You'd have been proud of Laurel—he read them the riot act about the Sixth Amendment. They had to threaten *him* with arrest before he went away."

"Laurel did *that*?" Lily was amazed. "Who would have thought he would stand up for *us*? I thought all he was good for was handing out parking tickets and getting in the way at football games."

They were quiet for a while.

"Did they take away your phones?" Kevin asked.

"Yep." "Sure did." Doug and Lily answered in unison.

"Damn. I was gonna call Dad."

All three were quiet while they tried to puzzle out what would happen next. The front door of the truck opened and closed, the motor started, and then the back door opened and one of the FBI guys got in with them, pulling the door closed behind him. Someone outside locked it.

"I have to put on your seatbelts—we're about to move." He reached behind each of them and snapped on their seatbelts with their hands still cuffed behind them. He slapped the front wall twice and the truck began to move.

After an hour of driving around, the truck stopped with a squeaking and shuddering of the brakes. The front door opened and closed again. The back door swung open onto a brightly lit tarmac and the roar of a plane taking off. They were in the Bizjet area of San Francisco Airport—an unmarked private jet next to them with its engines whining. Their chaperone followed them onboard, waved at Courapo, and then departed. The steps folded into the airplane door and the door closed. The only others onboard were Agent Courapo and the pilots.

"Would you like your handcuffs off?" the agent asked. All three students turned around, presenting their wrists. As he cut off their cuffs, the plane started rolling toward the runway. "Buckle up. Next stop is Burbank."

"Are we under arrest?" Lily asked. "We haven't done anything."

"To be decided. About an hour before we showed up at your rooms, our office got a semi-hysterical call from the director who had just gotten off the phone with the attorney general, who had been called by the president. The director said to pick you three up, keep you incommunicado, and ship you to JPL in Pasadena. Kevin's father is waiting for you there, along with a gaggle of JPL PhDs."

The tower gave them clearance to take off on runway 28L. The little jet turned onto the runway ahead of a monstrous Japan Airlines 787, also waiting its turn to depart. They accelerated and lifted off smoothly into the night sky above South San Francisco Bay, and the landing gear retracted with a thump. San Jose passed under the plane shortly afterward.

"Are there, like, fine wines and booze on this plane?" Kevin asked. "Cute flight attendants with short skirts?"

"Only when the director uses it," the agent chuckled. "They pull all that stuff out when us peons get to ride. I think there might be some coffee, though. As far as the cute flight attendants, I guess that's me. Sorry about the pants."

"Was that humor? My god, I thought you guys had your sense of humor surgically removed at the academy."

Courapo rolled his eyes. "Sometimes this job gets to be too much. Come on. Let's see what they gave us." Kevin followed him to the back of the cabin, where they found coffee, Coke, cranberry juice, bottled water, small bags of chips, and tuna fish sandwiches.

"It could be worse," Doug observed, removing the plastic wrap. "Southwest doesn't even give you sandwiches."

Kevin sat down beside Lily and handed her a sandwich and a glass of cranberry juice. She smiled at him, squeezed his hand, and went back to watching the coastline below them. He kissed her on the neck and dug into his snack.

Doug was surprised at their intimate interactions, and then a big grin spread across on his face. *It's about time,* he thought.

The lights of the California coast passed under them as the plane headed south toward Los Angeles.

... ...

They got to JPL around midnight. The guard at the gate waved them through after Courapo flashed his FBI ID; apparently they were expected. As the black Suburban pulled up to the admin building, a balding man in a lab coat and jeans walked out to greet them. He introduced himself after they got out of the car.

"Hi, kids, I'm Kevin's dad, Dr. Langly." He shook their hands and gave Kevin a hug. "Welcome to the Jet Propulsion Laboratory. Sorry for the way they brought you here. The director of NASA gets a little crazy sometimes."

"Dr. Langly, I am Special Agent Courapo of the FBI. May I see your ID, please?" Langly pulled out his plastic ID badge and handed it to Courapo. The agent photographed it. He held out his clipboard. "Please sign here." Dr. Langly signed it. "Thank you, sir. These three are in your hands now." He turned to the students. "Take care, kids. Sorry it was so rough at the beginning." He shook their hands, got into the Suburban, and the driver put the car in gear and drove away. Next to the curb were three black duffle bags the driver had taken out of the back.

Lily studied Dr. Langly. He had the same square jawline as Kevin and the same rotund body shape but a little shorter. They had the same hazel eyes, too, but his hair was short and brown—different from Kevin's longish strawberry blond. She yawned and checked out JPL. It was huge. White box buildings with black windows filled the campus. Beyond the fences, guard towers, and buildings, some mountains were sprinkled with lights that were probably houses. Kevin held her hand; she liked that he did it in front of his father. "Why are we here, Dr. Langly?" she asked.

"You three have discovered something no one in the history of humanity has discovered before. It's so huge, the POTUS himself declared you a national treasure! He said to bring you here and figure out how to use your Rosy Transmitter with our development team. You are to be housed in our visiting VIP quarters for the duration of the project."

"POTUS?" Lily didn't listen to the news.

The Beginning of the End

"The president of the United States."

"What about our classes?" Doug wanted to know. "I have classes tomorrow—all of us do."

"Your classes are suspended for the time being. Stanford's President Jourey will get a call from the Health and Human Services secretary this morning. From what I understand, those two are old friends. The secretary will explain that NASA needs you three on a sabbatical to work on a critical project of national security. We don't expect much resistance."

"Dad, none of us brought any clothes. We don't have anything but what we're wearing. I don't even have a toothbrush."

"The FBI packed what they thought you would need from your rooms. The rest of your belongings should show up tomorrow. Each of you belongs to one of those bags; grab yours and come with me."

All of Kevin's underwear had been in the dirty clothes hamper—laundry day was tomorrow. He couldn't wait to find out what the FBI thought he needed. *Maybe that pot made it through,* he thought hopefully. *Hey, it's legal now!* His subconscious snickered, *Yeah, right! They're the FBI, idiot!*

Dr. Langly led them into the admin building and had the guard issue them visitor badges. "We'll start tomorrow at 8 A.M. I'll show you where you'll be staying. Collect you around seven o'clock for breakfast?"

"Sure. See you then, Dad."

Three military trucks arrived at the front gate and unloaded a platoon of marines in full combat gear with automatic weapons and bomb-sniffing dogs. They began augmenting the civilian security throughout the campus. JPL was now on full lockdown— no one could enter or exit without explicit approval from the Lab director.

… … … … … … … … …

When he got to his room, the first thing Kevin looked for was the pot. It was not in the duffle. "Probably in that agent's pocket," he grumbled. The bag had most of the stuff from his bathroom and the clean clothes from his dresser but not a single pair of underwear.

"Guess the shorts I'm wearing will just get used twice." He shrugged and then had an idea. "Or maybe I'll do no shorts at all." Somehow, the thought of being in a room with all those stick-up-their-asses NASA PhDs while he was free-balling was irreverent enough to make him laugh. A knock sounded on his door; Lily was outside.

"Want some company?"

He opened the door wide and she came in with her arms crossed protectively in front of her, peering into the shadows of Kevin's room as though someone would jump out at her from under the bed. He had never seen her scared before. "What did they pack for you?" he asked, trying to put her at ease.

"Things from my bathroom and dresser," she replied distantly.

"Yeah, me too." There was an awkward silence.

"Kevin, are there cameras in these rooms?"

He studied the ceiling and walls but he didn't see anything that resembled a lens or camera bubble. "I don't think so. Why?"

"I feel like we're being watched."

Kevin walked up to the mirror on the wall over the dresser and lifted it off its hooks; a blank wall was behind it. He got a chair and closely examined the overhead light fixture—just a lamp. He got down from the chair, undid his pants, and bared his bottom to all four walls.

"What are you doing?" Lily asked in surprise.

He laughed as he zipped up. "Well, if they *are* watching, I thought I'd give them something to see."

Something seemed to thaw in Lily after that. She put her arms around him and hugged him tightly. "The last time I had anything to do with the state police, I was still in China." Her voice trembled a little. "It didn't end well."

"What happened? What did they do?" She didn't reply for a while. He held her gently, figuring that was what she needed.

"I was seventeen. They killed my father and mother—at least, I think they did. My parents delivered me to a safe house the night before they disappeared, and I was smuggled out of China through Tibet and Nepal. When I got to Kathmandu, The US Embassy put me on a plane to the United States, where I was given asylum. I never heard from my parents again. Someone returned the letters I sent to our old address with 'No Such Person' stamped on them. My whole family is gone—uncles, aunts, cousins, grandparents, everyone—like they never existed."

Kevin was beginning to appreciate the steel inside Lily. He wondered how well he would have fared after leaving behind everything familiar in the middle of the night, losing his entire family, and then being dropped into a country with no friends or family when he didn't speak the language or understand the customs. "Part of me is really glad that happened to you," he said softly into her ear. "If you hadn't come to the US, I never would have met you—I never would have loved you. I know that's selfish, but I can't imagine not having you beside me."

She squeezed him back even harder. "Cameras be damned!" she whispered. "Let's go to bed."

"I don't have any condoms, Lily," he whispered back, kicking himself for saying it.

"Maybe we'll be lucky. Tonight, I don't care."

Chapter 14 – Aliens!

March 13

The next morning a knock came on Kevin's door. His dad's face was visible through the security lens, so he opened the door a crack.

"Rise and shine, Son—breakfast in half an hour."

"Yeah, okay, Dad. Gimme a couple of minutes."

"Doug's up. Lily didn't answer."

"Lily's in here—she's up."

"You guys get dressed. I'll be back in half an hour."

Lily pulled on her clothes and walked across the hall to her room to take a shower and dress for the day. Half an hour later, Dr. Langly returned and accompanied the three to the cafeteria. The food was surprisingly good, and Kevin's dad paid for their meals.

"Did you get everything you needed from that bag, Doug?" Kevin asked as he munched on some breakfast yogurt over granola.

"Well, yeah, I guess." He tried to find a way to say this. "They didn't pack my Bible. I read it before I go to sleep. It was on the nightstand by my bed in the dorm. There wasn't even a Gideon Bible in my room here."

"I'll see if I can't rustle up one for you today, Doug," Kevin's father said gently. "Those aren't motel rooms. To my knowledge, no one has ever asked for a Bible while they stayed here."

"So NASA scientists don't believe in God?" he asked, a little hostilely.

"It's not so much that; it's simply exhaustion. By the time most people use those rooms, they're so tired that reading is the last thing on their minds. A day or two of straight work preceded the few times I've spent a night there. I didn't even take my clothes off." He shook his head at the memory and continued, "As far as believing in God, there are certainly many scientists here who claim to be either agnostic or atheist, but there are also many others who see God every day in the things we do. We see Him in the stars and planets and beauty of the universe. We see Him in the symmetry of the equations we use. You get the feeling that all that has happened to us and our solar system has happened countless times before and will happen countless times again. There's a lot of peace in that perspective."

Lily approved of the diplomatic way he handled Doug's request. "Dr. Langly, I think there's a poet hiding somewhere inside you."

He smiled at her and then at his son. They were obviously in love. Lily was bright and beautiful, and he couldn't imagine a more perfect companion for Kevin. Dr. Langly had no words to describe how proud he was of his son—one of the three people who'd discovered the way to the future for humanity, and now the two of them would be able to work together at last.

"If only your mother were alive to be here for this moment." His chin trembled a little. "I'm going to the cemetery tonight to tell her about it."

Lily was surprised. Kevin had never mentioned his mother. Until that moment, she had thought his parents were divorced. "Your mother is dead, Kevin? How did she die?"

"Breast cancer, about five years ago."

Everyone's plate was empty, so Dr. Langly decided to change the subject. "Are you guys ready to meet the rest of the staff? We should be going."

They dropped their trays off at the collection belt and walked into the central corridor of the building. The elevator stopped at the fourth floor, and he led them to a conference room. Eleven men and women waited for them, arrayed around a conference table. Several gave a professional nod, several frowned, and the rest were busy on their iPads. Kevin's father motioned them into the three chairs beside him. Everyone waited for the man at the end of the table to start the meeting; when he finished an email on his iPad, he smiled at the students.

"Hi, I'm Dr. Samuel Lowell, the director of JPL. Thanks for coming on such short notice." Kevin coughed. Lily kicked him under the table. "How were your rooms last night?"

Lily spoke first. "Dr. Lowell, why are we here? You yanked us out of our dormitories and classes in the middle of the night like criminals to come down here with an FBI 'escort.' Please dispense with the banal trivialities and get to the point."

"Well said, Lily," he responded with a chuckle. Several of the people around the table tried very hard not to laugh out loud. "Dr. Langly got an amazing email from his son, Kevin, three days ago. Kevin's email allowed his father to build your transmitter, and it is everything Kevin said in the email and more. We feel this device could revolutionize life as we know it—instantaneous communications and moving mass from one point to another without huge expenditures in energy. We want to know how you came to invent it and who else knows about it. The three of you invented it, am I correct?"

"Yes, you are correct," Lily said. "We built it after I had a dream that told me how to do it. In the dream were the words 'Build it and it will change the world.'" Lily gave them the same story she had given Captain Xanny, only these people obviously didn't believe her.

"You're Chinese, aren't you?" an Asian woman across the table asked Lily. Her nametag said "Dr. Xiau Wei."

Lily responded in perfect Mandarin. "Yes. I was born in China in a little town near Chengdu. The state arrested my parents about seven years ago—both were dissidents and I haven't heard from them since. They were probably executed while the underground dissident network smuggled me out of the country. The United States gave me amnesty and allowed me to go to college. What does that have to do with anything?"

"Was this technology known you or your parents while you in China?" she asked in stilted English.

Lily decided she didn't like the woman or her implication that she had somehow stolen the Rosy Transmitter design from China. She replied in perfect English without any Chinese accent, "No, that would have been impossible since I had the dream in December and left China seven years ago. I would have thought someone with a PhD in physics would understand basic arithmetic. Are you Chinese also?"

"I am from Republic of China," she said with disdain.

The Beginning of the End

"Ah," Lily said with just as much disdain, "the people who ran away." They stared at each other coldly, neither blinking. The non-Communist people in mainland China had never forgiven Chiang Kai-shek for abandoning them when he fled to Taiwan and established the Republic of China. The director watched their interaction with interest, but after thirty seconds of silence, he interrupted their confrontation.

"Lily, could you please describe in your own words what you three found in your experimentation?" He nodded to Doug and Kevin. "You two jump in whenever you think you can add anything of interest."

She walked to the whiteboard, took a deep breath and picked up the marker. She started drawing the schematic of the Rosy Transmitter and explained the steps in its development and how they discovered it was sensitive to a magnetic field. Kevin explained the development of the magnetic mirror through its various incarnations. Doug described how he and his friends created the interface and how he programmed the computer to control the mirror. All three would periodically interject with pertinent facts.

"The pencil," Dr. Lowell said to her. "Tell me about the pencil."

"We figured out the pencil had run into the side of the trash can and bounced back into the mirror. That's when we realized the aura opened a wormhole—a way to go from one place in our universe to another without having to travel the real space distance or fight the real space forces, like gravity. If something solid was at the other end of the aura, it would be like running into it at whatever velocity you sent the item into the aura relative to the velocity of what you ran into."

To say the assembled scientists were skeptical would have been quite an understatement. "Please continue," Dr. Lowell instructed.

She told them about losing the transmitter when they sent the aura into space and, how they used another laptop from their advisor to build their second transmitter.

"A second transmitter?" Sam sat up. "You built a second transmitter?"

She nodded. "Yes."

"How did you build the mirror? You had help on the first one, didn't you?"

Doug coughed a little. "Uh, we didn't actually build the mirror either time. A friend built both—it cost us a case of beer."

Everyone in the room cracked up. When the laughing stopped, a guy at the other end of the table said loudly, "Sam, you should hire them immediately. When was the last time anyone built anything around here for less than a million dollars?" Everyone laughed again.

"Where is this second transmitter?" Dr. Lowell asked.

"We left it in the storage room in the physics lab," Lily said. "I'm sure it's still there."

"So you left a functioning transmitter in the physics lab?" He pulled his iPad toward him.

"Yes," Kevin said a little bitterly. "We didn't feel much like helping the FBI while they were arresting us and confiscating everything we owned."

"But it doesn't function without my laptop," Doug added, "and my laptop was packed with the rest of my stuff from my room."

"Unless Dr. Johnson's department laptop was used," Lily interjected. "It would still work well enough to focus the transmitter mirror for short distances. That is, assuming he didn't erase everything from the hard drive after he took it back."

The director was no longer listening as he sent a second email. Afterward, he put his bland almost-smile back on his face. "Please continue. How did Doug's laptop return after it disappeared? You said Dr. Johnson took back the department laptop and that Doug used his own laptop to make the new transmitter mirror function but before that you said his laptop was blown out into space. How did he get it back? Or did he buy a new one?"

The three students glanced at each other covertly and were silent. Kevin sighed, wishing he had talked about the starship visit with his father before now. He shrugged and said, "You aren't going to believe us. I'm not sure we believe what happened."

The Beginning of the End

"Try me. After what's been said in this meeting, my disbelief quotient is at an all-time low."

"Aliens!" Doug said to the group.

Everyone in the room stared at him for a good five seconds, expressionless. Dr. Lowell cocked his head slowly to one side. "Okay, Doug, you've got my attention. Please explain yourself."

He began the whole story of their abduction, questioning, and return with Kevin and Lily changing and adding bits and pieces to his story. After they finished, Sam was deep in thought.

"Would you draw a picture of the starship and the shuttle, please?" a man across the table requested.

"Sure." He got up and drew what he could remember. Doug and Lily made small corrections to his drawing. Kevin added the thrusters and Doug added the electromagnet array. "The lander was just a smaller version of the starship with landing pads underneath," Lily said.

The room was silent as everyone studied the first drawing ever seen on Earth of an actual alien starship.

"Do any of you have any questions for these three wayward strangers?" the director asked the assembled group of scientists. "If Dr. Langly hadn't built and demonstrated their Rosy Transmitter, I would have shown them the door, but he has and it works as they said it would. If our preliminary testing holds true for scale, we will be able to send satellites, people, supplies, and parts into orbit for essentially free. We could build a starship capable of traveling wherever we chose within a year."

"Do you have shred proof any this?" Dr. Wei asked disparagingly. "Pictures, anyone sighting them, radar contact, radio contact, cell phone picture, police report? Anything make us believe flying basketball exist?"

"You mean besides the transmitter working as described?" Lily laughed like the woman was stupid.

Doug snapped his fingers. "Jerry!" No one understood. "Jerry is the guard at the stadium—an old man who does night security. He caught us as we returned. He must have seen the shuttle!"

Kevin raised his hand.

"Do you have something to add?" Dr. Lowell asked.

"You could probably still see the depressions from the landing pads of the shuttle—it had to weigh tons. They should still be there in the AstroTurf. There were three of them, about a meter across. We landed on the forty yard line."

Another idea occurred to Lily. "When we were on the ship, the orientation of Earth, the moon, and sun was clear. From what I could tell, the ship was three times farther out than the moon's orbit—about 900,000 to a million kilometers out from Earth. We were about forty-five degrees up from the equatorial plane, orbiting Earth from east to west. You should be able to see the starship with Hubble or the Thirty Meter Telescope at Mauna Kea, unless the ship's already gone. Based on the size of the shuttle when they released us, I would estimate it to be four hundred to six hundred meters in diameter.

Dr. Lowell was typing on his iPad again. He sent several messages and then looked up, surprised everyone was still in the room. "Does anyone have anything else?" The people around the table pushed their chairs back and began to leave. Lowell turned to Kevin, Lily, and Doug. "Thank you for your help. We'll need you to stay at JPL for a while." To Kevin's father, he said, "Dr. Langly, please give them the big tour and show them what we've already done with their ideas." He left without a backward glance.

Kevin was blown away by Lily speaking Chinese to Dr. Wei. She had never spoken anything but English while they were together. They walked back to the cafeteria for some coffee. "Why you don't have an accent, like Dr. Wei?"

Lily was quiet for a moment. "When I arrived in the United States and was given amnesty, I was overwhelmed. I spoke the horrible English I had learned in high school and no one could understand me. All the Chinese people I met spoke Mandarin when they were away from the Americans. Their English was worse than mine, and Americans treated them with distain. I promised myself I wouldn't sound like them, so I took classes in reading and speaking English. I used to practice saying the words I heard on TV into a tape recorder, saying them over and over until I said them the same way. I started with soap operas and then graduated to newscasts. I bought audio-books with matching written books and practiced them, as well. It took me a year before I was ready to attend college. I worked in a Chinese restaurant for that year, practicing on my customers and translating for the other workers."

"You do it so effortlessly, going back and forth between Chinese and English. It's amazing to hear. Do you think I could learn Chinese?"

She laughed. "First of all, it isn't Chinese. I speak Mandarin. There are hundreds of dialects in China—Mandarin's just one of them. Second, why would you want to? English is the language of technology."

It was Kevin's turn to be quiet. "Because it's part of you, and the only other language I know is the little bit of French I learned in high school. I don't want to be the ugly American, expecting everyone else to speak English. If you learned English in a year, I should be able to learn Mandarin in, say, four or five. Will you help?"

She took his hand and squeezed it. "Of course, Kevin. We'll start tonight."

Chapter 15 – A Hundred Bucks

March 15

Agent Courapo's desk phone rang. "Courapo."

"Lou, could you come in here for a minute?"

"Sure." He hung up the phone and walked into the office of Bill O'Connor, the Northern California FBI station director. "Hi, Bill. What's up?"

"I've got another special assignment for you down at Stanford."

"More students to kidnap?" Lou asked innocently. "I could use another trip to LA in the jet—maybe they'll leave the booze and flight attendants on this time."

His boss laughed a little uneasily, took a deep breath, and let it out. "Not this time, Lou. I need you to go down there to check out a story about an alien spaceship delivering those three students to the football field and anything else unusual that happened last Tuesday night."

Courapo didn't know how to react. "You're kidding, right?"

"Nope. This came straight from the attorney general."

The agent had trouble believing this conversation was taking place. "And this is more important than the meth distribution center bust I've got scheduled for tomorrow morning with the DEA?"

"I told Ainsman to take over that one for you."

"Look, Bill, anyone could do this—it's basic cop 101. Put one of the newbies on it."

"The director requested you by name, Lou. Until I got this post, I don't think he even *knew* my name."

Agent Courapo took a deep breath and looked out the window at the Transamerica Pyramid in downtown San Francisco for a few moments. He pursed his lips and asked, "Anything else you can tell me? Anything to go on? Leads? Witnesses? Police reports? Why you're asking me to do this?"

The Beginning of the End

"The only witness we have is the guard at the stadium who was supposed to have witnessed those kids you took to JPL getting out of a spaceship. Go find out what you can. It's gotta be complete BS, but spend the night down there. Tomorrow, you can fill me in on anything you turn up. I'll email you what I got from the director."

Lou walked back to his desk. "This just keeps getting weirder."

... ...

"Jerry doesn't come in 'til around eight o'clock at night," the voice at the end of the line said. "Before that, you can almost always find him over at the Mayfield Cafe on El Camino Real having breakfast."

"Okay, thanks." After he hung up the phone, he got the number for Campus Security from the Stanford website.

"Hello, Stanford University Campus Security, Sergeant Cooper, speaking."

"Hello, Sergeant Cooper. This is Special Agent Courapo of the FBI. I am investigating a report of aliens landing on your football field last Tuesday night. Can you tell me anything about it?"

There was a long pause. "Let me transfer you to the chief," the voice said. The phone clicked and he was suddenly listening to a Mozart piano concerto. A moment later the line clicked again. "Hello. This is Chief Swartz. Can I help you?"

"Hello, Chief Swartz. This is Special Agent Courapo of the FBI. I am investigating a report of aliens landing on your football field last Tuesday night. Can you tell me anything about it?"

"What's your office switchboard number? I'll call you back in a few minutes."

"415-555-1353"

"Frisco, huh?"

"I'll be waiting for your call." Lou put his feet up on his desk, trying to decide what the odds were that Swartz would call back. If someone had said those words to him, he wasn't sure *he* would call back. "I'll wait five minutes before I go to plan B." His phone rang in two. "Courapo."

"Well, I'll be damned," Chief Swartz said into the phone. "I'd have lost a hundred bucks. Agent Courapo, what can I do for ya?"

"I escorted some of your students down to NASA's Jet Propulsion Lab last Friday. They gave the people down there some song and dance about aliens giving them a ride in their spaceship. The director wants me to check out their story. Did you get any reports last Tuesday night of strange events or alien sightings?"

"So you're the guy my nighttime officers were raising hell about. Something about a classified FISA warrant. How are those kids?"

"They're fine. I left them at JPL; they're still there I think. Part of some super-secret project—should look great on their resumes. How about last Tuesday? Did you hear about anything strange happening?"

"I am assuming that when you say *aliens* you aren't referring to our southern neighbors."

"That is correct. I'm talking about the kind that arrive in a spaceship."

There was a pause, and then Swartz said, "Well, the short answer is *yes*." He gave Lou the thumbnail on the couple who reported being knocked out by guys from *The Matrix* and the night guard at the stadium raising hell about aliens on the football field.

"Do you still have the pictures of the circles in the grass?"

"Don't know. I expect so—no one throws anything away around here."

"How about the cell phone movie of the spaceship taking off that your night officers saw? Did anyone save a copy of that?"

"Don't know that either, I'll ask 'em when they come in. We wrote the whole thing off as a prank."

"I'll be down in about two hours. When your night officers come into work, I'd like to talk to them—and I'd like a copy of their report on the couple who got knocked out. Think you could line them up for me to talk to?"

"Officer Ping and Officer Swingle come in 'round six P.M. As far as the couple goes, I wouldn't get your hopes up. Spring break started on Monday, and students can be kinda hard to track down until classes start again. No promises, but we'll give 'er a try—always willing to help the FBI."

Agent Courapo groaned at Ping's name. He was the guy who had confronted him when he was cleaning out Kevin Langly's room. Courapo didn't expect to get much help from him.

... ...

Officer Ping didn't disappoint him.

"Are you going to arrest more students on a bullshit FISA warrant?"

"Nope. My boss sent me down here to find out what really happened last Tuesday night. The JPL people who needed the help of the students now want to know about that, as well."

"What's the JPL?" Swingle asked.

"NASA's Jet Propulsion Lab in Pasadena."

"Is that where you took the kids?" Ping asked hostilely. His face was red and his lips were pursed.

"I suspect I shouldn't have told you, but yeah, that's where I took them. What happened with the two people who were knocked out?"

"We never did figure it out," Swingle said. "They came in here raising hell about some guys dressed like actors from *The Matrix*. There was no trauma, no sexual assault, no evidence of a scuffle, and no witnesses. We figured they had just gotten stoned and passed out."

"I'd like to talk to them if I could."

"Well, let's go see if we can find 'em. As I remember, they live in separate dorms." Swingle pivoted his massive weight out of the chair and stood. He picked up the report Agent Courapo had just copied and checked the students' addresses. "The dorms aren't far."

... ...

Neither student was in their room. Courapo checked his watch: 7:30 P.M. "Feel like some dinner? I'm thinking Mayfield Cafe."

Fredrick Hudgin

"If you're buyin', I'm eatin'." Swingle said, licking his lips.

As they walked into the restaurant, the night stadium guard was just leaving. "Hi, Jerry," the officer said to the old man. "Seen any aliens lately?"

"Check this out, Mr. Officer Doubt-My-Story Swingle!" He held up a copy of the *National Enquirer*. "I told ya I seen them sonsabitches." On the cover was a picture of the lander lifting off the football field with Stanford's name on the score display right under the ship. The headline said "Aliens Land on Stanford's Football Field!"

Agent Courapo spoke up. "Jerry, I'd like to buy you a cup of coffee. Would you mind telling me what you saw?" The old man wavered, trying to decide if Courapo was making fun of him. "I saw some aliens in New Mexico once. No one believed me either," the agent said. It was a complete lie, but Lou figured Jerry would like some support and he would open up if he got it.

"Well, I *would* like another cup, but maybe we should drink it alone." He stared hostilely at Swingle.

"I'll see you back at the Security Office later, Officer Swingle. Thanks for the lift." The agent indicated to the hostess that he needed a table for two. Swingle left in a huff without the pancakes he had longed for.

… … … … … … … … …

"So you're telling me you took the pictures that are on the cover of the *National Enquirer*?"

"Yep, I got them sonsabitches."

"Do you still have the cell phone movie and pictures on your phone?"

"Yep."

"Could you send them to me? I have some friends who would love to see 'em. I'll give you twenty bucks for them."

"Twenty bucks ain't shit for something this good. The *Enquirer* give me a hundred."

"A hundred bucks it is if you send them right now."

"Mister, you just bought some pictures."

The Beginning of the End

He sent them to Courapo's phone. They watched the movie and pictures together, he gave Jerry five twenty-dollar bills, and wrote out a receipt, which Jerry signed.

"Where can I get a copy of that *National Enquirer*?"

"Next door at the Safeway, but you better hurry. They only had five copies left when I bought this one. Every student at Stanford is buying one."

"One more question. Did you happen to see any students getting out of the spaceship?"

He jerked his head around and stared at Courapo. "Who did you say you was? Who the hell told you about them kids?" He realized he had said too much. "I gotta go. I'm late for my shift." He got up and almost ran out the door.

Now what was that all about? The agent wondered. *He acted like he was terrified of those kids.* Well, if he needed to ask more questions, he knew where Jerry worked. No need to push the old man.

He settled the tab with the cashier, walked next door to the Safeway, and bought their last copy of the *Enquirer*. He began the walk back to Campus Security, paused, and then went back into Mayfield Cafe. Fifteen minutes later he walked across the road toward Campus Security carrying a bag with two to-go boxes of pancakes, scrambled eggs and bacon—one for Swingle *and* one for Ping.

They're cops, for god's sake. We're on the same team.

... ...

Dr. Johnson answered the knock on the door to his home. Courapo and four other people in suits stood outside. "Dr. Albee Johnson?"

"Yep. What can I do for you?"

"I am Special Agent Courapo of the FBI. I have a warrant to search for and confiscate all copies of the research notes and Rosy Transmitter devices created by three of your students: Lily Yuan, Douglas Medder, and Kevin Langly."

"May I see the warrant?"

"Here it is." He handed the document to Johnson. "Please stand back while we search your house." A federal judge signed the warrant two hours ago.

Marijuana smoke was thick in the air as the agents entered Johnson's house and began their hunt. The agents boxed everything resembling a research note, which was most of the piles of papers and files filling the professor's small house. He watched a lifetime of research papers disappear into their boxes.

"Could you leave those, please?" he asked the agent about to put a stack of papers into a box. "Those are the exams my Intro to Physics students took on Friday—I haven't graded them yet."

The agent glanced at Courapo for guidance; Courapo held out his hand for the papers and studied them—they were indeed exam papers dated Friday. He handed them back to Dr. Johnson without a word.

Three hours later, the agents left with at least half of the clutter that had filled Johnson's house. They also took his computers, his hard drive backups, software that dated back to Windows 3.0, and printouts from his first computer programming course at Rutgers University. They even took his last box of computer punch cards he had been saving to make Christmas wreaths.

Courapo gave Dr. Johnson a receipt for the boxes of papers they had confiscated. "Do you know the location of the Rosy Transmitter that was in the storage room in the physics lab?"

"No, I don't. I haven't been in the physics lab all week. I assume you have asked Lily, Kevin, and Doug."

"Goodbye, Dr. Johnson. Thank you for your cooperation." The FBI agent got back into his black government sedan, and the taillights disappeared down the street, turning toward the freeway access ramp.

Yesterday, President Jourey had proudly announced at a staff meeting that the three students were on a sabbatical to NASA: "Another feather in Stanford's academic hat." Now the FBI showed up searching for what the students had left behind, and the feds were so interested in it that they had cleaned out his house. The students' silly project about faster-than-light travel had suddenly developed massive credibility. Johnson was glad again that he had given the notes and transmitter from the students' project to Shao Nasheem in electrical engineering to play with. Now he figured there had to be a lot more to this transmitter than he had believed. If the feds were that interested, he made a bet the Chinese would be even more interested. This could be his retirement.

Chapter 16 – When Donkeys Fly

March 22

"These guys are amazing!"

"I think Doug may have finally found true love," Kevin chuckled, watching his skinny friend's Adam's apple bounce up and down in awe as he swallowed.

Lily didn't say a word.

The three students were studying the satellite the JPL machinists, engineers, and physicists had built in ten days for the communication test. It was ready to launch into space a million miles out from Earth. The Rosy Transmitter JPL had built to launch the satellite was so far beyond the one the three of them created, they just stared at it in awe.

The scientists had already launched a reflective balloon with the same mass as the satellite. The balloon inflated to a hundred meters in diameter as soon as they sent it through and Hubble took a picture as it appeared a million miles out. The total energy consumption for the transmission had been 4.31 watts for thirty seconds—not nearly enough power to illuminate a single household light bulb. Everyone at JPL was ecstatic.

Kevin and his dad were working twelve hours a day since he had shown up at JPL with Lily and Doug. For the first time in his life, Kevin was living his dream, of working side by side with his father—the dream he had clung to since he was a little boy and his dad and he had built their first rocket together. His father was as excited about it as he was.

The scientists could now engineer satellites for function without having to worry about the constant trade-off between function, weight, and cost. They could use common steel and aluminum instead of the stronger, lighter, and much more expensive titanium. They no longer had to worry about making satellites strong enough to survive the launch on a chemical rocket or small enough to fit in the delivery capsule on top.

The Beginning of the End

The communications people had found a way to link two transmitters together and create an absolutely secure transmission path, undetectable and untappable. Interested government agencies were starting to show up at JPL from all over the country. The NSA and CIA were both on-site, working with the JPL engineers to create secure spy technology. The spooks had realized they were able listen to anyone, anywhere, without the person of interest having the slightest idea they were being overheard. Once they had working prototypes, they carried their research back to their respective development centers. They worked as hard at finding a way to break into the transmission as they did to make it more secure; so far, nothing even detected that the channel was open, let alone allowed them to tap in. Several of the scientists, however, thought they could build a detector for the frequency the transmitter used.

The Department of Defense showed up for the satellite launch. The number of shoulder stars and gold-braided sleeves eating next to them in the cafeteria seriously intimidated Lily and Doug. There were generals and admirals with chests full of ribbons everywhere.

"I don't know why you guys are impressed by those guys in the monkey suits," Kevin snorted. "They get up in the morning and use the bathroom, just like we do. My brother is a captain in the Army—I guarantee *he's* nothing special."

This was the first Lily had heard about any siblings. "How many brothers and sisters do you have, Kevin?"

"Three: two brothers and a sister. They don't talk to me, and that's fine." He left out the part about the reason they didn't talk to him—about being arrested twice for selling pot in high school and once for rolling his dad's car, drunk as hell. Luckily, he was only sixteen when this had gone down, so his arrest record hadn't followed him into adult life.

At the table next to them were two graying generals eating breakfast. Doug strained to hear what the female general was saying. "You realize if this works, we can throw away our entire arsenal of rockets, artillery, and bombers. We can just turn a dial and say 'Put the bomb there.' There's no defense to worry about, no time to take cover, and no planes being shot down over enemy territory."

"*If* this works," the other general said ominously. "That's the key word. This wouldn't be the first time these guys promised us steak and gave us tofu."

Doug got a chill down his spine. A weapon—they were going to use Rosy as a weapons delivery system. It was bad enough when the spooks invented a way to use Rosy as a spy tool, but now the Department of Defense was going to use it to kill people. He was surprised he was even surprised.

What will happen when the Chinese or the Russians or Al-Qaeda get this same technology? he wondered. *Because they will—the Rosenbergs and the Manhattan Project proved that. You can't keep something this big a secret—it can't be done. Would this mean World War III? Would it mean IEDs going off in all the major cities in the United States? If you wouldn't be able to defend yourself next year, would you attack while you still could?* The little boy inside him screamed, *No! You put down all your weapons and learn to walk together in peace!*

"Yeah, right," Doug muttered grimly out loud. "When donkeys fly!"

Both Lily and Kevin raised their eyebrows at him, concerned.

… … … … … … … …

The cell phone movie ended for the tenth time. Every time Dr. Lowell watched, the hairs on his neck stood up. Anti-grav drive—it had to be. How did they power it? There were no turbines or propellers, no exhaust gases—nothing chemical—and surely not batteries. Lily had estimated the lander weighed tons; based on the indentations the pads made on the football field, she was right.

He studied the pictures Hubble took of the starship. He had not known where to search until now; if it was where Lily described on January 22, the ship certainly was not there on March 13 when she met with the group of scientists at JPL. It would have been in orbit around Earth, but they didn't know which orbit. With

The Beginning of the End

only one known point, it could have gone in any direction on the compass. The orbital period of a satellite in a circular trajectory one million kilometers above Earth, was one hundred eighteen days. That was the time a satellite takes to do a full revolution around Earth. If the orbit was not circular, there was no way of predicting when the starship would come back, or even if it would.

Betting on a circular orbit, they could have waited until the starship made a full revolution and returned to the same place where it had been when the three students were onboard—May 18. Instead, the scientists had waited half the orbital period and aimed Hubble at the only other predictable place in every circular orbit. They drew a straight line from the location Lily described through the center of Earth to a location one million kilometers from the other side of the planet.

Today was March 22—fifty-nine days after the students' abduction—and Dr. Lowell made sure Hubble was waiting. It took two wide-angle pictures of the area in question, five minutes apart. The astronomers at JPL had compared the two wide-angles and found the starship by seeing a point of light moving at the expected velocity of six hundred and thirty meters per second. Once they had detected the moving point of light, Hubble zoomed in for a close-up; and the starship was there.

As the students said, it was a bigger version of the landing shuttle without landing pads—a sphere four hundred meters in diameter. The sun lit it perfectly for a photograph with a background of brilliant stars, almost as if it were posing; the thrusters and electromagnet array showed in perfect detail.

Dr. Lowell had waited his whole life for this moment. Humanity was not alone, anymore.

Chapter 17 – Thank You for Coming

March 25

"Dr. Johnson, so nice to see you." The attaché to the Chinese consulate in San Francisco stood to greet him. "My daughter says you are one of the shining stars at Stanford University."

Johnson enjoyed the compliment. "I believe your daughter is the shining star, Mr. Chan. I wish I could have her in all my classes."

There was a moment of silence between them, and Dr. Johnson decided to just throw out the reason for his visit. "I have discovered something I believe the People's Republic of China would be interested in."

Chan smiled. "We are always trying to find new ways to expand the friendship between our countries."

Johnson described in general terms what the three students had said the transmitter would do.

"And you have built one of these transmitters? It performs as your students say?"

Since the feds had demonstrated their interest so clearly, Johnson took a chance on the lie. The thing must have worked or they wouldn't have sent the FBI to kidnap the kids and steal their notes. "I have and it does."

"I would like to examine this transmitter and your notes. Where is it located?"

"It is in a safe place."

Chan was silent for a few moments. "Dr. Johnson, has the United States government indicated they are not interested in this device?"

Johnson thought about how to answer that one. He decided to use the biggest worm in his tackle box. "They are interested—so interested they sent the FBI to kidnap the students, clean out their dorm rooms, and take twenty years of papers from my house."

"Where did they take the students?"

"JPL."

The Beginning of the End

That more than anything else caught Chan's attention. Covert services all over the world had noticed the militarization of JPL. No one knew what they were working on or why it was suddenly a matter of national security. China was very interested in finding out what was behind the electrified chain link fences, dogs, and marines that now guarded JPL. That this plum would drop out of the sky into his lap was beyond belief. It became obvious why Dr. Johnson had come.

"I assume you would like some reimbursement for your research. I suspect your country has confiscated your invention and paid you nothing."

"That is correct, Mr. Chan."

"How much do you think this device, assuming it works as you describe, would be worth?"

"I want ten million dollars."

"We would want to examine it."

"I expect that can be arranged, but the device is not for sale—only the design."

"I will let you know what Beijing says. Thank you for coming. I will accompany you out."

After Chan escorted him past the guards at the front gate, Johnson walked down the street with a spring in his step toward where he had parked his car. His appointment with the Russians was in half an hour.

Chan waved to a man smoking a cigarette as he leaned on a street pole near the gate. The man walked over. "Follow him," he whispered in Mandarin, indicating Dr. Johnson as he went around the corner at the end of the block. The man alerted his team via encrypted text on his secure cell phone. Thirty seconds later, an eight-year-old gray Impala rolled out of the consulate and turned in the direction Johnson had gone. The man by the lamppost got into the front passenger seat, and the car continued around the corner, out of sight.

After walking back inside the consulate building, Chan dispatched another team to Johnson's house and office. If the device existed, they would find it. He closed the door of his soundproof office and called Beijing on the secure voice line even the NSA could not decrypt. This could make his career.

Chapter 18 – Here in Spirit

April 10

"You're pregnant," the general practice doctor for the JPL told Lily, watching her carefully as he said it.

She had expected the doctor to say those words, as she was experiencing nausea, sore breasts, and seemingly constant urination—plus her last period was six weeks ago. Before that, they were so regular you could set a calendar by them. When Lily didn't grow excited, the doc said, "I take it this wasn't a planned pregnancy?"

"No—but nothing's changed. All babies are a gift from God."

The doc grinned at that, deciding his professional detachment was not going to be necessary this time. "They are, indeed, Lily. So, I guess I don't need to talk to you about the options you have? Adoption? The abortion pill? A classical abortion?"

"No, Doctor. I'm going to have this baby, and I'm going to keep it."

"Good. I'm so glad to hear that. I'm going to refer you to an OB, unless you have one you'd like to use."

"No, I don't know anyone here—I'm from Palo Alto. I'd appreciate a referral."

"I'd like you to see Dr. Linda Plumber at The Baby Center in Pasadena. Here's the number. They only do babies—not gynecology. Is that all right?"

"Sure. An OB would be perfect."

… … … … … … … …

The Baby Center was able to fit Lily in the next week. Two FBI agents accompanied her and then sat outside the door to the exam room. Lily instantly liked Dr. Plumber. After the doc finished the initial exam and took some blood samples, she checked Lily's chart.

The Beginning of the End

"Your conception date was March 10, based on two weeks after your last period. That makes your due date December 2. We're going to set you up for monthly visits until we get into the last trimester. As of now, everything is normal. You are young and healthy. You have a blood pressure and pulse rate most of my patients would kill for, and you don't smoke or drink in excess. I'm sure your blood work will be just as wonderful.

"Here's a prescription for prenatal vitamins. If your nausea doesn't stop, you can drink some of the ginger and peppermint tea they sell at Herbal Lifetime. It's a mile down the street, at the Colorado Boulevard intersection. Tell them I sent you. No sugar, though."

Even the thought of sweet tea made Lily gag.

"Let's see if we can find the baby." Dr. Plumber hooked up the ultrasound pickup, smeared the end with goo, and pressed it against Lily's abdomen. She studied the monitor as she moved the pickup back and forth. "There it is." She pointed to a white dot the size of a peanut. "Right in your uterus where it's supposed to be."

"How about exercise?" she asked. "Can I still do yoga and run?"

"Yoga—absolutely. I wish more of my patients would. Stay away from the more energetic stuff. What type of running? A morning jog or a marathon?"

"Just jogging, something around five miles a day."

"First trimester—sure. Second trimester maybe. Your pelvis will start loosening up to get ready for the baby's birth. Listen to your body—it will tell you when to stop. Here's a Happy Pregnancy present from me to you."

The doctor handed her a copy of *What to Expect When You're Expecting*. "This book saves me so much time answering questions that I give each new mom a copy when they come in for their first appointment. Read it. If you still have questions, ask them at your next visit. Here's my card—the office number is right there. If you have any problems, call this emergency number." She wrote it on the back of the card. "The on-call nurse will answer 24-7, and, if they feel it's necessary, they will call me and I will call you back." The doctor got up. "That's it for today. Go ahead and get dressed.

The people at the front desk will set up your next visit. Congratulations!"

After the doctor left, Lily was feeling more than a little overwhelmed. She desperately wanted her mother to be here for this. She knew exactly when she conceived: March 12, the one time she had made love to Kevin without a condom. She allowed herself a few minutes of tears for the baby her mother would never hold, and then Lily steeled herself for the job she had accepted. She would do this, and it would be wonderful!

She dried her eyes and put her clothes back on. The baby would be named after either her mother or her father—if they couldn't be here in person, they would be here in spirit. As the FBI agents drove her back to JPL, she pondered how she would tell Kevin. She had no idea how he felt about children or being a father.

The Beginning of the End
Chapter 19 – Perfect

April 21

The nurse practitioner at The Baby Center, Jenny Mi, was examining their patient database. "Dr. Plumber, have you noticed the number of start-finish appointments have been steadily declining for the past month? We haven't had *any* in the last week."

The doctor was taking a moment to drink a coveted cup of coffee in one of those rare unassigned time slots between patients. A start-finish appointment was when a newly pregnant woman began her 40-week journey to the delivery of her baby. During the first visit, they established the mother's conception date and, from that, what her expected delivery date would be, hence the name.

At Dr. Plumber's obstetrics clinic, people normally filled the waiting room. Today, people were waiting, but some empty chairs had begun to appear. The doctor shrugged, checking at her schedule on an iPad. "Nobody has figured out they made a baby last month, Jenny. Next week they'll be beating down the door. One thing you can count on in this business is that you never run out of customers."

The nurse paged down through the client list on her computer monitor. "Another weird thing I noticed is we haven't had any conception dates after March 15—not one."

"Beware the Ides of March," Dr. Plumber said ominously, laughing at her poor paraphrasing of Shakespeare. She poured out what was left of her coffee into the break room sink, and then walked down the hallway to her next patient, rubbing sanitizer on her hands.

... ...

Geoffry Rama got to his desk late. He had stayed at a bar until closing time last night; three ibuprofen and a cup of strong coffee later, the fog began to lift. Maybe the cute redhead he had bought drinks for until she left would call.

His message light was blinking on his phone as he hung up his coat and sat down. Geoff picked up the handset and listened to the voicemail. "Hello, hello, hello. Mr. Rama, if you're there, please pick up ... Damn. ... Do you know why no one is having babies anymore? There are no new conceptions after March 15. What's going on?" There was no call-back number and no name—a waste of time. He was about to push the delete key but then hesitated. *What the hell. A couple of phone calls. What's the harm? Maybe a story was in it somewhere.*

Geoffry was a reporter for the *Ithaca Journal* in Ithaca, New York. His paper was usually filled with Cornell this and Cornell that, as the university was the largest employer in Ithaca. He always investigated any non-Cornell story—it put you above the herd. He brought up a browser and Googled "obstetric clinics Ithaca," picked up his phone, and started calling them. He got the same story from each one: no conceptions after March 15 and the number of pregnant women coming in for start-finish appointments had fallen dramatically in the past month.

He changed his search phrase to "obstetric clinics new york city." Hundreds appeared. He randomly selected five and called them, receiving the same results as in Syracuse. He queried and then called in Boston, Los Angeles, Chicago, Philly, Atlanta, and Dallas. Everywhere, the news was uniformly awful.

"This is amazing. Why haven't the wires broken this story?" He changed his query to "no more babies" and got lots of hits on vasectomy sites but no news about reduced conceptions. He searched for "birthrate reduction" and got a bunch of stories on how India's birthrate had dropped to near-US levels and China's one-baby policy reversal. "Conception rate reduction" resulted in lots of articles on how to increase your conception rate and how the number of teenagers getting pregnant was at an all-time low.

The CDC's website was next, but it had nothing about a reduction in conception rate. He called the CDC's number from the contact tab and was told, "I'm sorry, sir. We have no information to provide about a reduction in conception rates across the US."

The Beginning of the End

He wrote a story about his research, the questions he had asked, and the most important question of all: Why was this happening? He titled the article "Where Have All the Babies Gone?"

Fifteen minutes after he submitted it, his phone rang. "Get in here." The phone went dead. Geoffry walked into his editor's office.

"What is this shit?" He pushed the hard copy of his story across his desk. "Where is the article on women's hockey I assigned to you on Monday?"

"I'll have it to you this afternoon. I have all the pictures and text done—I just need to paste it together."

"So, what is this?" He indicated the birth rate story.

"A voicemail from an anonymous caller was on my phone when I got in this morning. It asked why there were no new conceptions after March 15. I made some phone calls to local clinics and then to clinics in population centers all over the nation. Country-wide, none of the fifty clinics I called had any conceptions after March 15. I called the CDC and they said they didn't know anything about it. Seemed like a pretty big story. I checked all the wire services, but they had nothing about it."

"You don't really expect me to run a story like this, do you? We can't be the first people to notice this across the country. If this were real, people would be screaming about it from the top of the Empire State Building."

"Well, the clinics I called sure thought it was real. They were wondering the same thing—why no one else was wondering."

"Get out of here. I won't make this paper a bigger laughing stock than it already is."

"Or you could put us on the map for being the first paper with the balls to break such a big story."

His boss hesitated. "I'll run it on page two, and I want the hockey story in one hour!"

"You'll have it, Chief." Geoffry walked back to his desk. It was going to be a good day!

Chapter 20 – Dumbasses

April 22

The paper hit the streets of Ithaca at 5 A.M. Geoffry Rama sat by his phone waiting for it to ring; surely someone would read the article and want to know more. Maybe even one of the wire services would want to pick it up. He connected to the *Journal* website and found the story. His editor had run it verbatim from the copy Geoff gave him. He waited all day, skipping lunch so he wouldn't miss the call. By 5 P.M., the phone had rung twice—once from his editor asking for a progress report on the article about drug usage by the fraternities at Cornell and once from a telemarketer trying to sell him a water treatment system.

Geoffry walked across the street to the same bar he had visited two nights ago—maybe the redhead would be there again. Two hours later, he was sitting by himself, drinking his fifth scotch.

… … … … … … … … …

"I need to show this to Captain Xanny," the tech said to her supervisor. "I think this is what we're waiting for." She displayed a translation hologram of the article from the *Ithaca Journal* website.

The supervisor read it quickly. "Yeah, he would want to see this."

The captain read the text. "Great! Now maybe we can get out of this shithole and start earning a living again. Forward the article to the GSCB—it may satisfy them that the virus worked."

An hour later, they sent back their reply. "They want more?" Xanny fumed. "What the hell else could they want?"

"They said they want a national or international news source, not a second page article from a backwater newspaper."

"Dammit! That means we wait." He brought up the real-time hologram of Earth and stared at the slowly-spinning world in irritation. Greenland was going through dawn and a huge storm filled the North Sea, covering most of Great Britain and Ireland. "Don't you guys know you're dead yet? Let's go—figure it out! I've got better things to do than sit around up here waiting on you idiots to discover you aren't having babies anymore."

Tempers were wearing thin. This was the hardest part to ending a species—waiting for them to die and knowing you killed them. GSMS-77 was normally in the raise-up business; the put-down role was new to them, and no one on the ship was happy about it.

Chapter 21 – There Has to Be an Answer

May 5

The decline Jenny had noticed was unchanged. The only start-finish appointments The Baby Center booked were women who had been in denial they were pregnant for several months. There were not very many of those. Dr. Plumber reached for her phone and called another OB in the area. They had been friends since medical school.

"Hi, Tom. This is Linda. Got time for a strange question?"

"Got lots of time for my favorite OB. What's up, Linda?"

"Have the number of your start-finish appointments been dropping lately? Say, over the past six weeks?"

"You mean you're seeing it too?"

"I'll take that as a yes." She was concerned.

"Yes," Tom replied in a low voice, like he was afraid of being overheard. "No one here wants to talk about it. Everyone is convinced one of us has offended the preggy population, although no one knows what we did. No one thought to ask any other clinics if they were experiencing a decline also."

"Could you call around and see what the other clinics on your side of town are seeing? I'll do the same over here."

"Will do. What do you think is going on?"

"I have no idea. We haven't had a single start-finish conception date after March 15. It's like someone drew a line in the sand."

... ...

"Every clinic and hospital in the north end of L.A. County has experienced the same decline."

"I think it's time we raised a flag. I'm going to call the County Department of Public Health—maybe they know what's going on."

The Beginning of the End

Fifteen minutes later she called her friend back. "Tom, you're not going to believe what they told me."

"Okay. I won't believe it," he laughed. "What did they say?"

"I talked to a guy named Dr. Blessing. He said he's been getting the same type of questions from clinics all over the county. He's raised the alarm to the California State Department of Health, and they told him the decline is statewide. The state alerted both the CDC and the US Surgeon General's Office. Apparently, the CDC is aware of it and, get this, the decrease is not just happening in California. As of yesterday, the decline was being seen across the United States, and an hour ago, the CDC issued a worldwide alert. This is happening in every country in the world."

"Well, I would have loved to know it was going on. What the hell could cause this, do you think? How could women across the world stop making babies simultaneously?"

"I don't know. This is crazy." The hair on the back of Linda's neck stood straight up. Worldwide non-conception was just too biblical. "Why haven't the media started screaming?"

"Why should they interrupt their harassment of the president to report real news?"

Linda snorted. Neither of them had any use for the news industry and its biased reporting.

... ...

For the first time in his life, James Klavel, president of the United States, didn't know what to do. Surgeon General Dr. Robert McConnell sat across from him in the Oval Office. His subordinates at the Public Health Service were screaming for a response to give to the medical and news communities.

"I think we need more information," the president told him, shifting his bulk behind his desk in the oval office. "I want you to set up an emergency summit in conjunction with the secretary-general of the UN. Invite your peers from countries around the world. Focus on our allies, but invite everyone with a GDP of over five hundred billion. You have three days to set up the conference. I need answers to what's going on. An opportunity like this doesn't come along more than once in a lifetime; I want to be viewed as the guy who started the solution. We're talking *motherhood*, here. There's *nothing* more important to Americans than motherhood."

"Where do you want the summit to be?" McConnell asked without much enthusiasm. The world didn't need another conference—he needed money to fund the research to find out what was happening and why.

"Camp David. It's big enough, secure enough and has a high enough profile worldwide."

"Yes, sir." The surgeon general rose to leave. This was just another distraction from him coordinating the research effort.

"Dr. McConnell, I want updates on your progress twice a day—who's coming, and what they say. Tell everyone to keep their mouth shut until we figure out what's going on—the rumor mill will start as soon as you ask them to come. I'm going to assign my chief of staff to you to help make the conference a success."

"Yes, sir."

After McConnell left, President Klavel pressed the button for his office manager. "Get me Mitch, NOW! And I want to talk to Gloria." His chief of staff, Mitch Donner, walked into his office two minutes later. The president filled him in and told him to jump on the logistics for the meeting at Camp David—catering had to be arranged, security augmented, Dulles and Reagan Airports alerted, DC police notified, support staff arranged, and the CIA and FBI had to be on site. "And, Mitch?"

"Yes, sir?"

"I told McConnell you work for him for the duration of this conference."

"Okay?" Mitch was confused.

"That's bullshit and you know it—you work for me and only me, but I'm counting on you to be my eyes and ears. Bob's never done something this high profile before. Don't let him do anything stupid. I have a feeling he's not a hundred percent on board with putting on the summit. I can't afford for him to screw this up."

"I understand, sir. This conference will go off without a hitch."

The Beginning of the End

"Perfect. I want to give the opening remarks and I want them televised nationally, internationally to any country that will agree. Understand?"

"Crystal."

"Great. Go do it—get outta here."

The phone rang. "I have the secretary of state on the line."

"Great! Next I want the head of the CDC." There was a click. "Hi, Gloria. I've got a project for you to help with." He filled her in on what he'd told the surgeon general to do.

There was silence on the other end while she absorbed what he had said. "My god! I had no idea this was world-wide. How can the state department help?"

"I need the people who can make decisions to come to this summit. Make sure the invited governments send the right people. We don't need puppets who want to make speeches—we need people who make things happen. Offer jet rides, limos while they're here, hookers if you have to, but make sure the right people are at the conference."

"I'm on it, boss." The line went dead.

His secretary broke in, "I have Dr. Hehsa from the CDC waiting."

"Put him on." The line clicked. "Hi, Sridhar. Have you made any progress?"

"No, sir. We have no cause at this time for what is causing the infertility."

That was not what the president wanted to hear. "Who's working on the problem?"

"A more correct way to ask would be: who is not?" Sridhar said nervously. "We have suspended all other research to investigate what happened and how to fix it."

"Good. Keep working on a solution. There has to be an answer somewhere."

"Yes, sir."

Chapter 22 – I Want to Go Home

May 8

"How long do you think they'll keep us locked up here?" Doug asked Lily and Kevin as they ate lunch one day. "We've been here eight weeks!"

"Your guess is as good as mine," Lily said. "Those marines at the gate and walking around outside the fence have real guns with real bullets. Nothing goes in or out without being searched."

"I tried to pet one of their dogs when I was taking a walk around the inside of the fence," Kevin snickered. "I thought the effing dog was going to take my hand off. The corporal yelled at me for doing it—he actually yelled at me!" He was still amazed. "Then he pointed his rifle at my chest and told me to back away. His dog was still going nuts. Those guys have some *big* teeth!"

"What are you guys working on now?" Doug asked.

"Dad has us doing research in the library, trying to find some historical basis for Rosy. They won't let us anywhere near a computer with internet access. It's pretty much a waste of time—Rosy has no historical basis. Everything we did started with Lily's dream."

"They're putting me through dream analysis by a team of shrinks." She shook her head. "I still can't believe it. They think they can psychoanalyze where the dream came from. Thank God they assigned me to the basic research team on Rosy fields; if I didn't have that, I would be insane by now." She turned to Doug. "What are you working on now? Are you still helping out in the assembly plant?"

"I gave up." He pursed his lips. "I was embarrassed that I was slowing them down. They were polite, but you could see they wanted to be left alone."

"Did you hear what the CIA has done with Rosy?" Kevin was bursting to share his secret.

"What now?" Doug braced himself.

The Beginning of the End

"They put a transmitter on a computer-controlled rifle, so it can use Rosy to find and kill enemies. It blew up a coconut *inside* a secure bunker at a *thousand meters*. They wired the coconut with a little speaker that simulated someone talking. The rifle's computer searched the area for voices using a Rosy mirror and a microphone, and if it found a voice where none should be, it pulled the trigger. Goodbye, target. No one knows where the bullet came from, there'd be no return fire, it's completely automatic, it doesn't sleep, and you can't hide from it. They're going to try the same thing with a low-velocity grenade launcher. Put a seven-second delay on the fuse in the grenade, launch the grenade through the aura, kill the aura, and the grenade explodes without blasting back through the wormhole."

"Great!" Doug said in disgust. "Rosy has allowed the United States to kill people more efficiently. The next thing will be conventional and atomic bombs. There's no defense—no warning. Just death on a massive scale."

All three students were quiet, remembering what they had overheard when the generals were brainstorming in the cafeteria.

"We could resist," Lily said quietly. "We could refuse to help our government develop weapons that use Rosy."

"Like that would do any good," Doug said bitterly. "We're just in the way now. Resisting would do nothing but *help* them."

"Or we could resist a little more actively," she suggested.

Kevin snorted. "How? Sabotage? And get charged with terrorism when we get caught."

"Only *if* we get caught."

Doug was curious. "Three months ago, both of you were excited about Rosy. Kevin you said, 'How could we even consider not telling everyone about it?' Would you guys still build it now, knowing what our country has done and is going to do with Rosy?"

Neither of them answered, and that was answer enough.

... ...

Doug returned to his room at the end of the day's non-work. The satellite was being launched tomorrow—not that they needed him around to launch it. The scientists at JPL had left the students in the dust as they ran with Rosy and what it could do. Now, the three were just observers. The scientists tolerated their questions, but he could see they were up to their eyeballs in theoretical physics and didn't want to be disturbed.

He wanted to forget everything about the Rosy Transmitter and how his government had taken such a wonderful invention and changed it into something so evil that nothing in the history of mankind was even close—not the gas chambers of the Third Reich, not the purges of Stalin and Chairman Mao, and not even the atomic bombs the United States had dropped on Japan. He had been instrumental in the creation of this evil thing. He felt dirty for even being a part of it. He had committed a sin. He had soiled his soul. He had listened to Satan without even realizing he was doing it.

When he wasn't beating himself up for being part of Rosy, he was lonely. Kevin and Lily had each other, and everyone else they worked with went home to their wives, husbands, girlfriends, and boyfriends. Every night he returned to an empty motel room and his Bible. No matter how many glowing words they used to describe these "Visiting VIP" rooms at the JPL, they were still just motel rooms. Doug wanted to be in Palo Alto. He wanted to finish his PhD. and get a job *improving* the world. He missed his friends at church and he missed the peace he got from singing with them every Wednesday and Sunday. He especially missed one particular woman in the choir.

Clara and Doug had been in a relationship for two years, although neither had made their relationship public. Many of their friends would disapprove of them sleeping together without being married—a sin to the primitive Christianity their church practiced. He had asked her many times to marry him, but she'd turned him down each time. Before she met Doug, Clara had been married to a nice guy. He'd died in a car wreck three years earlier, and she said she was still married to him—that they would meet again in Heaven as husband and wife.

Since the FBI had escorted Doug to JPL, he had not been allowed any contact with Clara or his friends. He had no other family. One lonely evening, Doug came to a decision. He wanted nothing more to do with JPL, Southern California, or the Rosy Transmitter, so he packed his duffle. The next morning he walked to Dr. Lowell's office and sat in the waiting room for two hours before Lowell's secretary showed him in.

Dr. Lowell was noncommittal. "Hi, Doug. What can I do for you? Sit down, relax."

"I'm ready to go back to school." He ignored the offered chair and began pacing back and forth. "I'm not doing anything here. I miss my friends. I want to go home. I want to get back to work on my PhD."

"I can't let you leave, Doug. This is too important to the United States."

"But I'm not doing anything here. How can my camping in a motel room at JPL be important to the United States?"

"You know how to make a Rosy Transmitter. We can't take a chance on that knowledge escaping to our enemies."

"I won't say a word—I promise. I just want to go home. I want to be with my friends."

"We can't take that chance, Doug."

"Am I charged with anything?"

"No, of course not."

"Then you can't keep me here against my will!" he shouted. "That's the Sixth Amendment to the Constitution of the United States. I don't think being here is more important than that."

"Calm down, Doug. Can't we find something you'd like to do around here? JPL is a pretty amazing place to be."

"I'm not qualified to empty the trash cans here," he said angrily. "You know that. I want to go home."

"Doug, this is a matter of national security. You know too much about Rosy—you could be kidnapped by one of the United States' enemies. You know enough to tell them how to build their own Rosy Transmitter."

"Protecting our constitution is also a matter of national security," he said loudly. "Unless you charge me with something, you can't keep me here."

"Doug, if you try to leave, I *will* have you arrested."

"And charged with what? Walking without a license?"

"Terrorism against the United States."

"Terrorism?" he whispered incredulously. "First I'm a national treasure and now I'm a terrorist?"

"If you try to leave here, you *will* be arrested."

"And you'll ship me to some covert prison with all the other 'terrorists' who have been there for years without being charged or tried? So much for the land of the free and home of the brave! Why the hell do you think so many people hate the United States?" Dr. Lowell took a deep breath and considered how to respond. "So, the three of us are prisoners here?" Doug spat.

"I wouldn't view it that way. I would treat this time as a sacrifice could make to help your country overcome its enemies around the world—like Nathan Hale, George Washington, Abraham Lincoln, and John Glenn did before you."

"They didn't help the United States create the most dangerous weapon since the beginning of time," he said slowly, enunciating each word. "The hydrogen bomb is nothing compared to what you have perverted Rosy into!"

"Now that is a terrorist speaking."

"One person's terrorist is another person's hero," he replied darkly.

"That's the type of statement that *gets* people sent to those prisons. It makes me glad you are here and will stay here where it's safe."

Doug walked out of the director's office without saying another word, slamming the door behind him. Dr. Lowell stared at the door for several minutes, considering his options, before he picked up his iPad and started typing.

Chapter 23 – Half an Hour

May 11

"Hi, Miss Travis. I am Dr. Poppalov. I will be performing the procedure."

Mindy nodded at the doctor. She was on her back on the operating table, draped and shaved with her feet in the stirrups.

"The state makes me ask you some questions and have you sign a release before I can continue. Is that all right with you?"

She nodded again.

"I need you to say your answer audibly—we are recording this as well."

"Yeah. It fine wid me. Ask away."

"Do you know you are pregnant?"

She rolled her eyes. "Yeah."

"Have you asked this clinic to perform an abortion to end your pregnancy?"

"Yeah."

"Do you understand this will kill the living fetus growing inside of you?"

"Yeah—that kinda the idea, Doc."

"Have you considered other alternatives to this abortion? Giving the baby up for adoption or raising it yourself? You can get help financially, if you need it."

"Yeah. I thought about dem."

"And you want to go ahead with the abortion?"

"Yeah."

"Well, that's all the questions. I apologize for having to do that. I understand how tough they are to answer."

"Can we jus' get on wid it?"

"Sure. Sign right here."

Mindy scrawled her name.

Dr. Poppalov considered her signature and wondered if she knew about the issue with conception that had just surfaced world-wide. He decided he had to ask. "Mindy, have you heard about the problem people are having getting pregnant? My clinic hasn't had any new pregnancies in almost two months. Are you sure you want to do this? What if you can't get pregnant again when you're ready to have a child?"

She studied him for a moment. "Is that part a the script, Doc? A guilt trip on top a everything else?"

"Nope—that was from me to you. I guess you've made up your mind."

"What you tellin' me is you got a bunch a rich, white women who wanna get pregnant and for some reason they cain't." She took a deep breath and then spoke to him in a deadpan monotone, no emotion. "Doc, I'm nineteen years old. I been fucked by every man in my life since I was eight. I got a fifth-grade education. My pimp give me two days off to get this abortion or he gonna give me one hisself. In two days, I gotta go back to work. The last thing this world need is another mulatto, crack-addicted baby with no father and a junkie mother on welfare with a revolving door to her bedroom. I could be dead the day after it born. If she a girl, then what happen to her? If she live to be my age, she be doin' the same thing I do. I don't wish that on nobody—especially my baby girl. If he a boy, he be dead before he make fifteen, selling drugs or robbin' people. You say them white women wanna get pregnant? Maybe they should keep they husbands outta my bedroom. But they might change they tune if'n they live my life for jus' one day. Me? I'm thinkin' this fertil'ty thing is god's way a shuttin' down a world what makes people like me live like I do."

Mindy let a bitter smile creep onto her face. "I do believe I could give an amen to that."

"If I could get you into rehab—get you out of the situation you're in—would you reconsider? I have a friend who runs a ranch in Big Sur. She takes in people just like you, straightens them out, and helps them start a new life. She called me yesterday to say she has an opening for someone new. Her last 'client' had her baby and is starting classes to get her GED."

Mindy didn't respond for a few moments. Her mind was in turmoil. The hit of crack she took before she walked into the clinic was wearing off, and the familiar hunger was waking up. Her whole life, she'd had bullshit government programs thrown at her. They'd

The Beginning of the End

started with the same type of big words the doc used and then stopped before they changed anything—or they made it worse.

Jonah, her pimp, would come find her in two days. If she was trying to start a new life, he would kill her and laugh while she died—every girl in his "house" knew that. The words the doctor said kept echoing inside her head. Was there really a new start for her? Did the god who had abandoned her still care enough to offer her another chance? Did the possibility of another life even exist in her short future?

She put her hands over her stomach. Something new was there—something she'd never felt before. It was called hope. It scared the shit out of her. When you were hopeless, nothing could hurt you.

"Tell me about the place, Doc. Tell me about the woman who wanna save a worthless ho like me. She white, ain't she? I had my fill a self-righteous white women with a god-stick up they ass."

"She's black, actually, and she does it because she was right where you are about thirty years ago. She worked in Oakland and she was a heroin addict. She got a helping hand from another woman who had managed to break free all by herself. They run the ranch together. She's put herself through high school, college, and just finished her masters in American history. They've acquired a lot of friends who make sure they stay in business without one dime of public money."

Mindy was silent again, deep in thought. Finally, she shrugged. What difference did it make? If these people wanted to do their salvation thing, it had to be better than dying in an alley with a needle in her arm. She wouldn't let herself hope, though— hope was for white people. All she had was today, tomorrow, and yesterday.

"Call her up. Tell her you got another pregnant, junkie ho. If she still say yes, then so do I."

Chapter 24 – This Is All My fault

May 15

"This network is interrupting its normal programming to bring you the following special announcement from the president of the United States." The seal of the president came on the screen and stayed there silently for about fifteen seconds before President Klavel's familiar clean-shaven face appeared, framed by his signature comb-over of blond hair and double chin. He was not smiling.

"Good evening. This broadcast is going out worldwide to all countries, regardless of religious or sectarian orientation, whether they consider themselves a friend or foe of the United States. I am speaking to you from Camp David, outside of Washington, DC, where we have convened a special summit of the surgeon generals from countries all over the world.

"Three days ago, some incredible and terrible news was brought to my attention by the surgeon general of the United States. This news is unparalleled in the history of the human species." The president looked directly into the camera. "Across the world in every country and territory, from the North Pole to the South Pole, women have stopped becoming pregnant." The president paused again and took a deep breath.

"Whatever happened—and at this time, we have no idea what *did* happen—it apparently took place on March 15 of this year. Since March 15, two months ago, there is no record of any woman anywhere in this world conceiving through normal man-woman relations." President Klavel paused to take a sip of water. "United Nations Secretary-General Bassar and I have convened this summit so the physicians and scientists of the world can begin to find the cause of this terrible thing. We will find out why this has happened, and we will find a way to reverse it.

"I have committed the vast resources of the United States of America to this effort, and I would like to encourage all other countries and scientific research facilities of the world to join us. Only through working together on a worldwide scale can we hope to uncover why and how this happened. The alternative to working together is to allow humanity to perish in one hundred years. I, for one, will not allow that to happen. Good night."

Every reporter in the audience was on their feet, shouting questions. The president walked off the podium and out of the room without acknowledging them.

... ...

Lily sat between Kevin and Doug, watching the president's address conclude. None of them said anything for a full minute. The talking heads were on the screen, discussing the pregnancy issue, postulating how it began, how to fix it, and who was now working on it.

"Holy shit!" Kevin finally whispered.

"You don't think this has anything to do with Rosy, do you?" Doug asked.

Lily spoke in a whisper, "I keep remembering the octopus's words: 'That will, most probably, not be allowed.' I kept expecting them to come down and confiscate everything."

"Like that would have done any good," Kevin said. "We built another transmitter in a day after we lost the first one, and now they are experimenting with it in at least five different labs of the federal government. The octopus knew they could never keep us from using it—it was just too big a discovery."

"And they knew what would happen when we started using Rosy—that it would become a weapon." She started crying. "So, they shut down the human race. I can see they had no alternative. We're a stone's throw away from escaping the solar system and spreading our violence into the rest of the galaxy." She stopped for a moment, trying to regain some semblance of composure and failing—the tears wouldn't stop. "But the bottom line is: this is all my fault. I am responsible for the death of humanity."

"We have no proof of any of that, Lily," Kevin told her, putting his arm around her shoulders.

"What will become of us?" she asked, trying to hold on to her self-control by her fingernails.

He handed her a tissue. "Someone will find a way to beat this, whatever it is. So, some women don't get pregnant for a while—so what? There're too many babies anyway. It'll trim the population a bit—a few less mouths to feed in Sudan."

Lily didn't answer him. Instead she gazed out the window at the guard towers around JPL and then at the mountains around Pasadena. When he gave them the tour, Dr. Langly told them they were the San Gabriel Mountains. She suddenly bolted for the bathroom. The noise of her vomiting was clear through the door.

Doug had not said a word. After the President's address was finished, someone had killed the news feed on their TV again. The screen displayed a uniform blue, but he was not watching.

… … … … … … … … …

"Captain Xanny," Lieutenant Nussi alerted him. "You need to see this." The captain watched President Klavel's address with the rest of his staff on the bridge. He sighed and turned to his communications officer.

"Lieutenant Nussi, please send a message to Grock Central and the GSCB that we have received confirmation the virus was effective. Attach the clip we just saw. Tell them the person in the clip is the leader of the country with the largest economy in the world."

"Yes, sir." She turned to her console to prepare the message.

An hour later, the GSCB acknowledged the virus had done its job. They released Grock Corporation from enforcing the quarantine

"Commander Chirra," the captain called out to his second in command.

"Yes, sir?"

"Return us to our mining mission."

Five minutes later, the jump alarm sounded throughout the starship. GSMS-77 oriented toward Aries, accelerated, and disappeared into the rosy twinkle.

The Beginning of the End

... ...

Byteen pressed the comm button next to his station. "They've gone, Captain."

"Excellent!" Fey Pey was ecstatic. Even through the comm link, the exec could hear his captain's excitement. He understood Captain Pey's moods well after being his executive officer for so many years. "Now all we have to do is wait around on this rock for another seven months until our wormhole window opens again, and then it's payday!" The captain's comm link popped shut.

Byteen sighed. Another seven months inside *Easy Wind* with no exploring and no mingling with the natives. At least they could go out hunting, as long as they stayed underwater. Bored, he glanced at the observation panel. It showed a shark swimming by in the murky water. Since they'd settled into the mud at the bottom of the bay, the most exciting thing that had happened was a fisherman's anchor dropping on top of them and sliding off the hull.

He checked the chart he had downloaded from this planet's commerce network. This area was known as South San Francisco Bay. The witch had selected it because of its close proximity to the female she had chosen for the dream plant. For five months, they had remained here, buried in mud, running on cold fusion at minimal output, and not daring to start their Dark Energy Portal. There was no talking to anyone at home and barely enough power to stay warm. At least no one from the Ur had any idea they were here, though, and it was going to stay that way—Grock's last ship had departed a few minutes ago.

The end of his shift was coming shortly. He had intercepted a movie from the primates' data sharing network. It was about machines taking over the world with one male and one female primate standing in the way. The machines of the future sent a killer robot to kill the female so she couldn't mate. Sometimes the translator program had trouble with the dialogue—there were so many languages, dialects, and accents on this planet—but it should be a fun movie. Maybe Uta would want to watch it with him. She got so hot when natives started killing each other.

Chapter 25 – Paying the Price

May 18

Four different teams searched Dr. Johnson's home and office. The Israeli team came closest to finding the transmitter as they walked and probed around his backyard fence, but didn't go quite far enough. The professor had hidden the device, Doug's notes on its development, and Lily's schematic in his neighbor's abandoned tree fort, where their kids had played long ago.

The searchers were frustrated, angry, and finally entertained by the non-clues Johnson *had* left in many of the places they examined. "Not here," became a standing joke among them.

The Russians contacted him first. A small man with slicked-back hair and a hatchet face covered with smallpox scars knocked on his door. "Dr. Johnson, we should like to meet with you and your device."

"We can do that. First, deposit the money into this offshore account." He gave him the account and bank numbers, written on a small piece of paper.

"No money will change hands until we verify the device works," the man told him, pocketing the paper.

"Well, that requires a level of trust we obviously don't have." Johnson smiled, thoroughly enjoying himself.

The man pulled out a silenced pistol and pointed it at the professor's knee. "Where is the device?"

"Pull that trigger and both the Israelis and Chinese get the design, but sadly, Mother Russia will not. Your choice."

The man put away his gun, pulled out his phone, and read the numbers on the paper into it. Five minutes later, he got a call. "Check your balance, Dr. Johnson."

He pulled out his phone and connected to his bank. A huge smile grew on his face. "Thank you, Russia."

"You have your money. Where is the design?"

The Beginning of the End

"It will be delivered to your consulate in San Francisco tomorrow morning by courier."

"I hope it does not appear"—the man studied Johnson's face coldly, like an artist surveying a blank canvas—"Or at least does not work. I have volunteered to kill you very slowly. This is something at which I have become quite skilled during my career. Sometimes it can take weeks. I would consider it an honor to demonstrate my skills for you." He turned on his heel and left without saying another word.

… … … … … … … … …

As hard as it was to believe, the Israelis were the best mannered of the bunch. The Chinese were the most creative in their promise of life-ending events. All three ended up paying the price and getting a full set of the plans and notes. The professor kept the transmitter; he figured it should be in the Smithsonian someday, and he wanted to have his name on the donation tag. He spent a few hours composing his resignation letter to President Jourey, made a first-class reservation to the Cayman Islands, and went to bed a happy man.

Chapter 26 – Shootin' the Curl

May 30

Doug made sure they understood. "When I'm gone, don't forget to rotate the transmitter."

"Are you sure you want to do this?" Lily asked. She had very mixed feelings about Doug's escape plan. What if he was committing suicide? "Humans haven't gone through our aura yet."

"One way or another, I have to get out of here," he said grimly. "We went through the aliens' aura in the shuttle, and Kirk went through ours at Stanford. I'll be fine."

She *did* remember Kirk, the mouse they had used in their first tests. He had been healthy and active. "Please be careful, Doug. If you're going, you'd better go. We'll turn the launcher after you're gone." She gave him a hug, and Kevin shook his hand and hugged him. Being locked up at JPL was wearing thin on all of them.

The guard would be on his rounds in five more minutes—now was the time. Doug stripped down to his shorts and put his clothes in a large ziplock plastic bag. He had a second bag with a towel in it. He tied the two bags together with a piece of twine, and then the other end around his waist.

Kevin turned on the transmitter that JPL had built for the satellite test. The satellite had weighed a little under one ton; there was no reason for it to weigh so much—the scientists had filled it with steel blocks. The realization then came to Kevin that they had been seeing if it would accurately transmit such mass. One ton, coincidentally, happened to be the same mass as a nuke. That was the last straw for Doug. He wanted nothing more to do with JPL or his government ever again.

The rosy glow came on in five seconds. Doug pointed the mirror to the southwest of JPL. After two minutes of adjusting the gain and angle, the sounds of the surf came through clearly and a clean-smelling ocean breeze came out of the aura. Doug climbed into the launch bucket and nodded. Kevin pressed the release lever, launching his friend like a stone out of a slingshot into the aura.

Kevin moved the dish, so it aimed at a hilltop nearby, and left the transmitter on. Lily and he escaped out a window on which they had disabled the alarm earlier in the day. The guard came by on his rounds two minutes later and reported the transmitter was on. In fifteen minutes, the building was crawling with security and scientists. Dr. Lowell appeared half an hour after that. Ten minutes later, marines were combing the hillside with orders of shoot to kill.

… … … … … … … … …

"So, you don't know where Doug might have gotten to?" Dr. Lowell asked Lily and Kevin later that night.

"You didn't find him up in the hills?" she asked innocently.

"Now why do you think we were looking for him up there?"

"Gee, I don't know. Maybe it was the headlights, helicopters, and rifle shots we heard. It was just a guess. I'm curious, though. Why *did* you search up there? I would have thought Doug would have gone *toward* civilization, not *away* from it."

"I guess he's long gone by now," Kevin said with wide-eyed innocence.

"Oh, we'll find him. You two should consider yourselves under house arrest until we do."

Kevin laughed at that. "You mean more than we already are?"

… … … … … … … … …

Doug appeared in the air about forty feet above the combers coming into Manhattan Beach. The glow from Los Angeles filled the sky to the east of him. The momentum from the launch sent him in a graceful arc into the ocean, where he did a perfect belly flop onto a wave just curling. He came up gasping from the impact and floated on his back while he regained his breath. The ziplock bags with his clothes inside floated nearby, still tied to his waist.

He swam the quarter mile to shore, dragging the bags behind him. No one noticed the almost-naked young man walk out of the surf in the dark. It *was* Manhattan Beach, after all—many things stranger than Doug had come out of those waves. In fact, a young man in his underwear was actually pretty normal.

Doug had jumped the twenty-seven miles from JPL to the ocean in less than a second. Now he had to find a way back to his friends in Palo Alto. He dried off using the towel and dressed in the clothes from the bag. He dumped the bags and towel in a trash can and walked out to California Highway 1, more lovingly known as the Pacific Coast Highway. Memorial Day weekend was in full swing, and there was lots of traffic from the bar crowd, going in both directions. Doug stuck out his thumb on the northbound side.

A VW microbus, with a surfboard on top and a peace sign in front where the VW emblem used to be, pulled over. The dreadlocked black driver leaned out the window. "I'm going up to Big Sur, dude. Would that help you out? I could sure use the company."

"Big Sur would help a lot—on my way to Palo Alto."

"I can dig it, brother. Hop in. Let's beat feet."

... ...

The VW pulled into a ranch with a breathtaking view of the Pacific Ocean. A herd of horses ran down to the fence line to inspect the bus as it entered the gravel and dirt road that wound up the hill from the highway. The horses escorted them until the driveway ended at a cabin next to an old barn. The on-shore winds blew the smoke from the chimney east into the mountains.

The ride had taken eight hours. They'd encountered almost no traffic after passing through Malibu, stopped for coffee in Santa Barbara at an all-night diner, and were greeted by the dawn as San Luis Obispo disappeared behind them.

"Stick around a couple days, Doug, and I'll run you up to Palo Alto, no problem. I told my mom I'd fix her barn roof. Gotta do that first."

The Beginning of the End

"I could help you with the roof, John. I did a lot of construction with my dad when I was in high school."

"Far out! Offer accepted—but first we eat. Mom said she would feed us and when my mom cooks, the world stops. After breakfast, I should catch some Zs before we start—don't wanna be crawling around on a tin roof when I'm sleepy. I figure we'll begin this afternoon and finish tomorrow." The door to the cabin banged open, and a stocky black woman with salt and pepper hair ran out with a shout of glee. He was a head taller than her, and he picked her up and spun around. When he set her down, he said, "Doug, this is my mom."

"Hi, Doug. I'm Mona." She gave him a big hug, and then stepped back and studied his face for a moment. He felt like she could see right through him, as though every secret he'd ever had was laid bare for her. She patted his arm in approval. "Welcome to Sunshine Ranch."

Chapter 27 – Impenetration

June 2

"Sridhar, what can you tell me?"

There was a pause on the other end of the phone line. Pauses were never good—especially when the other end was the head of the CDC, Dr. Sridhar Hehsa. President Klavel was getting a lot of pressure from all over the country to commit much more federal money to the infertility issue. Constituents in their home districts were raising hell, and Congress had opened the funding floodgates.

This was not a small minority that could be politely ignored or thrown some political bone—this was middle-class America, the largest voting bloc in the country. Liberals, conservatives, Christians, Jews, Muslims—it included everyone not super rich or dirt poor, and they were not happy. They wanted answers and none were forthcoming. Scientists worldwide were studying the problem and trying all manner of things to diagnose and fix it, but no one was making any progress.

"We think we have discovered something going wrong with the fertilization process," Dr. Hehsa announced. "We don't know what caused it yet, or if this is the only thing wrong." He took a breath and considered how technical to get. "There is a process in fertilization that takes place when the egg is still in the fallopian tube called the acrosome reaction. This starts when the sperm has fused with the secondary oocyte. The sperm must penetrate the corona radiata of the oocyte for fertilization to complete. This is caused by the sperm releasing hyaluronidase from the acrosome. The hyaluronidase digests the cumulus cells surrounding the oocyte and exposes the acrosin, which is stored in its precursor form, proacrosin—"

"English, Sridhar," the president snapped impatiently. "I have to be able to explain this to people who don't have a PhD in medicine."

Page 140

The Beginning of the End

He tried again. "When a healthy sperm fuses with a healthy egg, a chemical reaction takes place immediately after the fusion, making the egg impenetrable to other sperm cells. This is normal and necessary to prevent multiple fertilizations of a single egg. Since March 15, however, this impenetration process now occurs upon contact with the *first* sperm, preventing even it from penetrating the outer layers of the egg. If the sperm cannot penetrate the egg and release its DNA package into it, fertilization cannot take place and both the egg and sperm die within two days."

"I need what you just said in writing, so I can say it correctly in a press conference."

"Yes, sir. I will send it to you when we finish this call."

"How about the drug companies? Have any of them signed up for the research?"

Sridhar took a moment to check a report. "Merck, Sanofi, and Pfizer are organizing the other drug companies into a united research effort. Roche and Novartis are resisting—they want to be the ones who find the cure."

"And make the money from selling it, too!" Klavel grumbled bitterly and made a note. The world was falling apart and those bastards were trying to profit from it. "Let me talk to the president of the Swiss Confederation. Let's see if he can help convince Roche and Novartis to join the other companies. It all comes down to money, and we have a lot of it to spend. Research grants are available into eight and nine figures—that can be pretty convincing. What are the universities doing?"

"A lot of them are starting their own programs," he continued. "The University of California has encouraged everyone to talk together. They want to establish a clearinghouse for the information each discovers. Even within the UC domain, though, Berkeley wants to do it their way. The universities in Canada and Mexico have agreed to join and share."

"You might as well try to herd cats as make those guys in Bezerkeley work *with* anyone else. Let me talk to the chancellor of UC Berkeley. Maybe this time, he will see the benefit of being part of the solution for once." An idea occurred to President Klavel. "I think the surgeon general is a Berkeley graduate. I'll talk to Dr. McConnell. Maybe the chancellor can be made coordinator of the universities' research—that should soothe Berkeley's radical effing feathers a little." He made a note to call the surgeon general. "How about the UN? I want to make sure all our researchers are talking to their researchers. Make that clear to everyone. Even if the information is all send and no receive, we share, whether or not everyone else does."

"The EU has created their team; Great Britain, Switzerland, and Norway have joined them. Russia and China are doing their own thing. India wants to join the EU effort and, I'm sure, will be allowed to do so."

"Where's the goddamned secretary-general of the UN? Isn't he supposed to be coordinating this?"

"Secretary-General Bassar has met with all the teams and offered funding. They want the money but won't promise to share."

"Why should those bastards change just because everyone's going to die?" the president shook his head in disgust. "On another note, if this was caused by a contagion, shouldn't there be islands of people who were not infected?"

Dr. Hehsa hesitated. He had been wondering the same thing. "Well, at this time, we don't have any idea what the vector is. We believe the only way a contagion could have been distributed worldwide is via an airborne microbe. Water, food, or passing person-to-person via contact would have taken much longer. That said, the only people who would be uninfected would have to have been in enclosed environments since March 15, over two months. If the vector is a virus, the air would have to have been filtered to twenty nanometers."

"Thanks for the update, Sridhar. You have your job to do. Let me do mine. If I can help in any way, call me."

"Yes, sir." The line went dead.

What he hadn't told the president was something his staff had pointed out this morning. The sperm they had collected since March 15 was not even trying to penetrate the egg. They still sensed the egg and turned to it but, as the sperm cells approached the egg, they went through something called a spontaneous acrosome reaction. It was like they *thought* they were attached to the outside of the egg and released their DNA packets without *being* attached to the egg, leaving the DNA floating near the unfertilized egg but not inside where it would cause fertilization and mitosis.

Even if the egg *would* allow the sperm to penetrate its outer layer, the sperm cells *couldn't* do the job. Neither Dr. Hehsa nor his staff had any idea why this was happening or how to reverse it—they just didn't understand enough about the chemical triggers that made the process function. Explaining what happened when it worked was hard enough; trying to figure out why it used to work and what changed was beginning to seem impossible.

The only eggs they had found that allowed fertilization were ones harvested before March 15, and the only sperm that still worked were also from sperm banks, collected before March 15. Suddenly the future of humanity was tied to a very finite collection of human gametes stored in labs, egg banks, and sperm banks around the world.

None of this made sense. The rules of epidemiology did not seemed to apply to this pandemic—there had been no primary infection. When a new infection took place, it could always be traced back to a primary individual or area. Ebola began on a single mountain in Africa. With this outbreak, however, the whole world seemed to have been infected simultaneously. No one could figure out how that was even possible with no one seeing anything out of the ordinary. Rockets, planes, drones, a meteor—someone would have seen something.

Sridhar was frustrated with their lack of progress. They didn't know what they were looking for—a virus, chemical, bacteria, spoor, or radiation. They had not found the cause or the vector—the method of transmission. It could be air-borne, water-borne, food-borne, passed by contact, an insect, or something else never encountered before. That was the most frustrating thing—all they really knew was women had gotten pregnant before March 15 but not after March 15.

... ...

President Klavel paused for a moment after he had ended the call with the CDC. He pressed the intercom button. "Maggie, get me Melvin."

A moment later, she answered. "The secretary of defense is on the line."

"What's up, Jim?" Melvin Burger, his sec def, asked.

"Do we have any subs that have been underwater since before March 15?"

"Don't know. I'll find out."

"If we have, make sure they stay that way. We have women serving on nuke subs now, right?"

"Yeah, we have something around two hundred female submariners across the fleet. Females serving on subs started in 2016 under Obama. I'll find out how many have been on patrol since this started."

"Well, at least we'll have plenty of uninfected sperm."

Melvin chuckled. "If I know anything about submariners, I'm sure they'll be happy to provide all you need." He had been a retired admiral when James Klavel asked him to become his secretary of defense.

"How about nuke silos? Don't they filter their air?"

"Yeah, but only during an alert—same as Cheyenne Mountain. Most of the time they take it from outside."

"Can you think of anywhere else we keep a sterile environment and have since March 15, two months ago?"

"Not offhand. Let me check around."

"One more thing. I want you to find a sterile place or one you can make sterile, capable of housing hundreds at first and then thousands of people over time. It has to be secure and able to support itself off the grid—food, water, energy, healthcare. If we don't have one, build one. Start yesterday."

"What kind of budget are we talking about?"

"It's a 'you need it, you've got it' kind of budget."

Secretary Burger grinned. Those budgets were the best kind.

Chapter 28 – A Wonderful Morning

June 4

"This is god's will," Pastor Williams ranted. "We have failed God for the last time. It began with Eve and the snake. It continued as the Hebrews made their golden calf and lost their homeland, as God's own son, Jesus, was betrayed and murdered, as the Crusaders failed to return Christianity to the Holy Land, as the spread of apostasy was not halted, and as we allowed abortions to be used as birth control, as we have allowed heathen religions to spread around the globe. We have failed God since the beginning of time and He has finally stopped forgiving us for our failures.

"Our loving god has turned His back on His sinful children as we have turned our back on Him. This was foretold in Revelation. The next time it storms, listen to the rain on your roof—you can hear the hoofbeats of the Four Horsemen in it. They are coming for us, and Satan is leading them. How many second chances can we expect? How many would you give your own children? Not as many as God has given us, I guarantee! Now we will pay the price for our failures. Soon, no children will join us in prayer as we thank the Lord for the things He has given us. Mary and Tommy Farrah were married last week in this very church. Stand up, Mary and Tommy.

The couple stood, self-conscious.

"Take a good look, everyone," Pastor Williams commanded. "These two, who have been joined together by God, will never experience the joys of parenthood—of seeing the love of god looking back at them through their newborn's eyes. There will be no joyous cries of children from their backyard as they play and rejoice in the beauty of God's world.

Mary turned her face into Tommy's chest and began sobbing. He put his arm around her shoulders and pulled her back into their seats.

"Our world will grow quieter and quieter as our grandparents and then our parents go to their reward. Imagine city parks with no children on the swings. Imagine schools standing empty. Imagine Walmart without a baby aisle! These things are coming. This isn't a pulp science fiction novel—this is as real as your father's heart attack and just as deadly.

"Join me now and pray for forgiveness. Together, let us lift up our combined voices to God. Let Him hear our prayers and lamentations. Pray to Lord God Almighty that He will return children to us. Pray that He will forgive us, the unworthy sinners we are. We must pray together since anything else is to give in to Satan.

"Join me as we say the twenty-third Psalm together—for we *have* entered the Valley of Death on March 15. We have never needed His rod and staff more than we do right now! Brothers and sisters, reach deep inside yourselves to that most private and personal part of your heart and pray our Lord, the Lord of our fathers and mothers, hears us!"

The pastor paused with a stern expression that *dared* dissent. He slowly raised his arms toward the ceiling of the church, tilted his face up, as though he could see God listening to them, and with a deep bass voice trained from thirty-three years of delivering hellfire and brimstone Baptist sermons, he began, "The Lord is my shepherd ..."

Sunday morning at the First Baptist Church of Sulfur Springs, Arkansas, was in full swing. Brother Williams had not let anyone down with his sermon. He had raised the hair on everyone's neck at least ten times—a new record. The sermon had lasted a full two hours as they had prayed, sang, feared Satan, and felt the love of God. It was a truly wonderful day.

Chapter 29 – Federal Crime Scene

June 5

"Dr. Johnson's dead." Agent McGregor's voice was on the other end of the phone line.

Courapo was shocked. "Damn! When did it happen?"

"No idea. We hadn't seen him for a couple of days. He missed his plane reservation yesterday for the Cayman Islands, but we figured that was just a decoy. I was sure he had snuck out of the country, possibly on a freighter leaving the Port of San Francisco. With all that money in his Cayman Island account, he could hire a boat and pilot to take him anywhere. So, I sent Gerald up to his house to see what he could through the windows. They were all covered. He went in through the back door and found the doc in the bedroom, lying on the floor—looks like whoever did it worked him over pretty good before they killed him. Once we saw he was dead, I called the Palo Alto PD. The coroner's on his way. The police have the whole street taped off."

"Did you go through the house?"

"Yeah. It was turned upside down. I'm sending you the pictures now. I didn't want to disturb it too much. Whoever killed him got his wallet and cell phone, too. You want us to intervene with the local police and make it a federal crime site?"

"Could it have been a simple robbery?"

"Well, someone went to a lot of trouble to make it appear that way. But they left the 60-inch flat screen TV, Blu-ray player, microwave, the diamond ring on Johnson's pinkie, and they missed the ten thousand bucks in cash he had in his suitcase on the bed, plus the 9mm hole in the middle of the doc's forehead and the two through his kneecaps don't really fit the MO of a cat burglar. Why would a robber kill him if he was tied to a chair with some duct tape over his mouth?"

Agent Courapo reached for his phone as it beeped at him. "I just got the pics. Yeah, you're right. Make it a federal crime scene. I'll notify the search team. Maybe we'll get lucky."

"Okay, hold on. I'll send Gerald over to tell them." Some talking in the background came through the phone and then the sound of a car door closing. "I'm back. Gerald's on his way to alert the PD."

"Did anyone come or go in the last forty-eight hours?"

"No one went through the front door. We got license plate data on a shitload of cars and trucks that passed the house. Maybe the alley or house-side cameras got something—I'll go through their footage after we hang up. This smells like a pro to me. None of us on surveillance heard or saw anything, and we were right across the street."

"Protect the crime scene until the team gets there."

"Roger that."

He hung up the phone. "Freda!" Freda Bines, the newest agent in the office, walked over to him. "Run Dr. Johnson's phones again—cell and home line for the past week. Try to access the cell phone GPS for a location, and run his credit cards, email, Facebook, Twitter, and LinkedIn accounts again. We're looking for activity in the last week."

She turned to her computer and started keying.

… … … … … … … … …

Samantha Gomez of *The Daily News* parked her car down the street from the collection of blue and red lights in front of a small white house. The tip from the coroner's office hadn't been bullshit. She approached an officer standing nearby. "What's going on?"

"Don't know. Some professor got killed. The feds took over the investigation."

"What was the professor's name?"

"Don't know that, either." The officer laughed. "Probably 'forgot' to pay someone for some drugs. From what I hear, he's a mess."

"Who's running the scene?"

"That guy over there," he said, pointing at a balding guy in a black windbreaker with FBI on the back in big, yellow letters.

The Beginning of the End

She walked over to him. "Excuse me, sir. I am Samantha Gomez from *The Daily News*. Can you tell me what's going on here?"

The man glanced up at her from his clipboard and frowned. "Who let this civilian in here? This is a federal crime scene—get her out!" As he walked away, two other men appeared, one on each side of Samantha, and led her back to the other side of the yellow crime scene tape.

Samantha wrote down the address. Tomorrow, she would come back and interview all the neighbors. A quick Google search of the address turned up Dr. Albee Johnson, and a second search listed him as a member of Stanford's physics department. LinkedIn showed him as retired two days ago, and his Facebook had a picture of a beach and an iced drink with a little umbrella sticking out the top. Maybe he *had* been trying to skip town on a debt—stranger things had happened—but why would the feds be so interested? At minimum, she was going to alert the obituary section that they needed to announce his death.

Chapter 30 – Food First

June 7

"Doug! Praise God you're all right." Pastor Evans was surprised he had knocked at the back door to his house. He reached out and gave him a huge hug. In his heart, Doug was the son who'd been returned to him after his own son was killed in Iraq. "Where have you been?"

"It's a long story," Doug said, wondering how to explain the last seven weeks to the white-haired old man who had treated him so well during his time at Stanford. The familiar smell of his lavender aftershave almost made him cry. Doug didn't have many people he loved. Since he had moved to Palo Alto, Pastor Evans had been his surrogate father.

"Why are you at my back door? No one ever uses my back door."

"Because the FBI is watching your front door."

That made the pastor pause. "Are you in some kind of trouble?"

"In a way of thinking, yes, I am—but I've done nothing wrong. I'm trying to find Clara. I went to her apartment, but someone else lives there now."

"Sister Clara had a personal issue that made her return to her family in Montana. She left about six weeks ago. She tried to call you, but you never answered—your phone number just rolled over to voicemail. I think she finally gave up."

"What personal issue?"

"She didn't tell any of us. It was very mysterious." He looked at Doug over his half glasses, perched on the end of his nose. "Do you have time to come in for dinner? You could fill me in on what's going on with the FBI. Maybe I can help."

"The less you know, the better. In fact, I'd better go now, before they figure out I'm here. I'm the reason they're watching

The Beginning of the End

your front door. If you can keep my visit a secret, I would appreciate it."

"Count on it, Doug." The old man clearly wanted to say more.

Doug was torn. He wanted to explain himself and his disappearance but he didn't want to get Pastor Evans in any deeper than he already was. Just knowing Doug put him in danger. This old man was the closest thing he had ever had to a father. He wanted to say something, but what?

Finally he stammered, "My friends and I discovered something ... something so big and so important that the government wants it all for themselves. They've turned our wonderful idea into a weapon so evil that I can't be part of it anymore."

"Imagine that—our government being the bad guys." The pastor shook his head. "I can see why you can't say more. If they're hunting for you, you'd better go. God be with you, my son." Doug started to turn away, but Pastor Evans scanned his backyard quickly and then put his hand on Doug's shoulder, pulling him back to whisper into his ear. "Wait a minute." His voice was full of concern. "Do you need clothes? Some food? Money?"

Doug had never borrowed or begged for anything. He started to say no, but realized he had no money, ID, cell phone, credit cards—nothing. Even if he could access the little money that had been in his checking account, he was sure the FBI had frozen the funds. "If you could loan me some money, I will pay you back as soon as I can."

"Of course." The old man led him back into his house and reached for his wallet. He pulled out all the cash, folded it twice, and put it in Doug's hand. "You don't have to pay me back." The pastor stepped away and appraised the young man. "You are almost the same size and shape as Gregory before he left for Iraq. Wait here, just for a moment."

Doug shoved the wad of money into his pocket as the pastor's cat, Delilah, pushed up against his legs, purring. He picked her up and scratched behind her ears; she closed her eyes, and her purr-engine went into full volume. Five minutes later, Pastor Evans returned with a backpack full of clothes and a sleeping bag.

"I put some bathroom stuff in the bottom compartment—I figured you would want to shave and brush your teeth—but here is what I went upstairs for." He handed Doug a wallet.

"What's this?" he asked, turning the wallet over in his hands.

"Gregory left all his personal identification behind when he went to Iraq four years ago. You could be his brother. This has his driver's license and credit cards—I couldn't bring myself to cancel any of them, so they should still work. I would charge something on them every so often, just to keep getting mail with Gregory's name on it. I renewed the license two months ago. I thought they would have realized he was dead by now, but that one showed up with his old picture on it—California only makes you get a new picture every other renewal. Now I know why the Lord moved me to do that. It was so I could give them to you."

Doug was at a loss for words. He steeled himself for his departure. "If the police ever ask you how I got this stuff, tell them I stole it from you—that I came to you for help and you turned me away. Tell them I threatened you and tied you up."

"If they believe that, they're even bigger fools than I thought. You would never hurt me or steal from me. Here's Gregory's cell phone. He is still on my family plan. It's not a fancy phone, but it works; the charger is in with the shaving stuff. And this is Clara's phone number in Montana. I don't have an address for her."

Doug pulled the old man into another hug, trying to remember every smell and texture of what it felt like to be loved.

"If you can, send a message to me when you're safe," the pastor whispered. "The whole congregation will pray for you."

Without saying another word, Doug turned and left the same way he came in: over the corner of the fence into the neighbor's yard and into the alley, staying next to the bushes and pausing over the trash cans like he was scavenging for dinner. The old jacket and knit cap he had found in the homeless hideout under the freeway ramp helped with the image.

The backpack made a comforting bulk on his back. He couldn't return to his student dorm room, but even if he did, there was not anything left inside anyway, courtesy of the FBI. Both his parents had died in a car wreck when he was a child. His grandparents, who were long dead, had raised him. He didn't have any brothers, sisters, uncles, aunts, or cousins—there was no one to turn to and nowhere to go.

The lights of a McDonald's glinted through the trees ahead of him as he walked back toward the freeway. "Food first!" his grandmother had told him countless times. "You can't make good decisions on an empty stomach." It still sounded like good advice, so he walked up the driveway of the restaurant.

Chapter 31 – Glowing Cows

June 11

"Lemme get this straight," the old rancher told the man standing in front of him. "You want me to sell you my ranch, lock, stock, and barrel? You want the horses, cattle, and even the frigging chickens? You want me and my wife to just get in my truck and leave?"

"Yes, Mr. Wysnewski, that's correct—and the US government will pay you twice what this property is worth."

"You cain't have my dog, and I expect the cat'll have'ta come, too, or you're gonna fight my wife." The man smiled at the imagined scene. "You'll lose."

"You can take the dog and the cat. Do we have a deal? I have a US Treasury check here for twelve million dollars. It's made out to you." The government agent pulled it out of his notebook and handed it to the old man.

Wysnewski turned the check over a couple of times while he considered the offer. His wife had been whining at him to sell the place and move into town for years. Her health was declining, and she needed medical care that wasn't available out here in farm country. Last winter, he had lost forty percent of his herd in a freak snowstorm that had caught the entire state off guard. He had contemplated changing from ranching to farming, but the amount of work to convert the pastures into plowable farmland where he could grow wheat was incredible—too much for an old man. Two thousand acres for twelve million dollars meant he was getting six thousand an acre. That was a damn sight better than the price his neighbor had offered last year.

"I got roots that go deep inta this land—my family's lived here for four generations. Any chance you could go up a little on your offer?" The old man figured, if the government was offering such a fine amount up front, maybe they would make it even finer if he questioned it a little. There was a reason they weren't trying to low-ball him with some bullshit like eminent domain.

"We feel this amount is very generous. If you don't want to sell, I'm going to your neighbor, Mr. Wilson, next. What's it going to be, Mr. Wysnewski?"

"We got lots a pictures and personal whatnots. My wife ain't gonna leave without 'em."

"You can take all that you want, but leave the farm equipment."

"Some of it ain't paid off."

"That's fine—we'll pay off the balance."

The old man studied the check again and then took off his worn-out Kubota ball cap with the dark sweat stain that went all the way around the hatband. He ran his hand through his sparse white hair, put his hat back on, and slowly turned in a circle, studying the land that had filled his life since he was born. His parents, grandparents, great-grandparents, and youngest son were buried on the little hill behind the house. He felt the spirits of them standing beside him as he reminisced, gazing at the ancient mountains that surrounded his property.

Ranching in Montana was a hard life. The spirits knew it, too. They had sweated and bled to wring a living out of this land, just as he had. It was too damned hot in the summer and too damned cold in the winter. Between the bugs, droughts, floods, and snowstorms, he was just scraping by. His arthritis was becoming more of a problem, and none of his kids wanted anything to do with this place other than a random visit every couple of years.

Still, the ranch was so much a part of him, that he might as well have been selling his right foot. On the other hand, for twelve million dollars, he could buy a new right foot—and he would put that new foot on the beach in Sarasota, Florida, far from the cold and snow! His wife would receive the medical care she needed, and he could get that new RV bus they had seen in Billings.

He had always wanted to live in Sarasota, ever since he'd seen a poster of the beach at that travel agency in Butte. The poster still hung on the back of the door to his bathroom and it was a standing joke among his kids when they came home from college for Christmas—college paid for by this ranch and his hard work. If he lived in Sarasota with his house on one of the most beautiful beaches in the world, maybe those same ungrateful kids would visit more often, and he would be more than just a name to his grandkids.

"Son, you just bought yourself a ranch. Where do I sign?"

"Right here, Mr. Wysnewski," the man said, indicating the line on the bill of sale with his pen. "The US Government appreciates your sacrifice."

"What're ya gonna do with it?" the old man asked, handing back the paper and pen. "Raise cows that glow in the dark? Dump radioactive waste from that Hanford place in Washington State?"

"That's classified, Mr. Wysnewski. When can you leave?"

"It'll take the rest of the week to pack the crap my wife's sure to want to drag along. Depending on how many migrants we can find to help out packin' and loadin', we should be gone by Saturday."

"That'll be fine. Call this number when you're done." He handed the old man a business card that said "Thomas Shelton, United States Heritage Protection Services, Department of Homeland Security" and a phone number with a 202 area code.

... ...

"Another broken cable?"

"Two," the tech said.

"Dammit, how is this happening? We did a full test of that transmitter yesterday. This is beyond normal. What's this, five – six this week?"

"Seven."

"It's like someone is doing this on purpose. I think it's time to escalate."

Chapter 32 – The Search for a Cure

June 13

"Sridhar, what can you tell me?"

President Klavel's familiar phone greeting filled the director of the CDC with anxiety—mostly because he had nothing new to say about what had happened to make the male and female gametes incompatible with each other. It was like they were now separate species. The receptors in the RNA that facilitated the insertion of the DNA from the sperm into the egg were just not firing. This was exactly what happened if you used gorilla sperm and human eggs—the two just couldn't make music together. Dr. Hehsa had told all of this to the president before. No one had yet figured out what had changed or how it had happened.

"Russia and the UK are remapping the post-infection human DNA, so they can compare it to the mapping done at the end of the twentieth century. The CDC doesn't think the problem is in the DNA, but we are following their research with interest. A researcher at Oregon Health & Sciences University thinks the problem is with the interference RNA and how it relates to the messenger RNA. We think he might be onto something, and have given him funding to continue his line of research.

"We have made great progress in the cloning of primates. We are making our mistakes with one our closest genetic cousins, chimpanzees. We feel if we can reliably clone a chimp, and then we can clone a human—their DNA is ninety-six percent identical to ours. You must understand, however, the cloning process isn't like stamping out flawless copies of the donor.

"From a technical perspective, cloning humans and other primates is more difficult than in other mammals. The big reason is something known as spindle proteins, which are essential to cell division and located very close to the chromosomes in primate eggs. Consequently, the removal of the original nucleus in a primate's egg also removes the spindle proteins. In other mammals, such as cats, rabbits, and mice, the spindle proteins are spread throughout the egg, so removal of the nucleus does not result in their loss. Another problem is the dyes and ultraviolet light we use to remove the egg's original nucleus can also damage the egg cell and prevent it from growing. In primates, we haven't yet found a reliable way of removing the original nucleus without harming or removing the spindle proteins along with it.

"Even if we can overcome these issues, we may only create one viable clone from a hundred attempts, and that clone may be deformed, retarded, or insane. There are many things besides DNA affecting who or what the clone develops into. Nature has an elimination process that keeps substandard fertilized eggs from developing into substandard babies, but cloning bypasses most of that natural culling. We may get lucky with a few of the eggs that survive cloning, but you can count on most of them being someone or something you wouldn't want to be living next door to you or playing with your kids.

"Besides the cloning process itself, the major problem is B15 (before March 15) human eggs are in such limited supply. We are hesitant to use any more, since Habitats A and B are using them to create the populations for their sterile environments. Those fertilized B15 eggs are being implanted in rigorously cleansed chimps, bonobos, and orangutans in sterile environments."

"Aren't chimps our closest genetic ancestors?"

"These three apes are equally close to humans genetically. We don't know which surrogate will work out best. So we are trying all three." Dr. Hehsa took a deep breath and continued. "The A15 (after March 15) eggs we have used reject implantation of a replacement nucleus; we have tried putting A15 human DNA into a chimp egg, and it lives for about fifteen days before it dies. We tried the same thing with B15 human DNA and five percent of the embryos are still alive and dividing after twenty days. While those embryos will soon die without an actual placenta to nourish them, we are about to try the same thing with a new batch of fertilized chimp eggs and implant them into the same chimp mothers the eggs were harvested from. This technique doesn't use B15 eggs or sperm—we are extracting the genetic material from B15 blood. We have lots of it around."

The Beginning of the End

"Have you tried to implant a chimp egg with a human nucleus into a human?"

"Not yet." Dr. Hehsa hesitated. "Some members of our team have an ethical problem with creating human life based on a monkey egg."

"Can you replace those team members with people less squeamish about saving the human species?"

"I suppose I can, but you would have to find a new director of the CDC."

"I see," the president said, pausing a moment as the implications sank in. "Can you implant a fertilized B15 egg into an A15 woman?"

"Yes, and we have done that several hundred times. There is a limited supply of fertilized eggs women have placed in cryogenic storage. Usually, this was done when their husbands were going into harm's way or the women were having something like chemotherapy to treat cancer, which could damage their eggs or render them sterile. We are keeping the pregnant women in Habitat A-prime until Habitat A is ready for occupancy, but we believe the offspring will be infertile, as well. Time will tell.

"Our work at creating an artificial placenta is progressing better than expected. The Chinese have produced a viable artificial endometrium wall. It passes nutrition one way and wastes the other. The Norwegians, under the administration of Dr. Skilling, are trying to develop a replacement amniotic fluid that would function with the Chinese endometrium. The Swiss have created version one of a uterus that should work with the Chinese endometrium and Norwegian amniotic fluid. A team from Merck is working on nanotechnology to manage the changing requirements of the amniotic fluid as the embryo matures into a fetus and then a baby."

"Besides our eighteen female submariners, we have been able to find only one human female who was not exposed to whatever happened on March 15."

"Who did you find?" President Klavel was intrigued. "Where has she been?"

"She is Rebeka Valov, one of the scientists on the International Space Station."

"The Ukrainian?"

"Actually she's Bulgarian. Everything is sterilized before it is sent to the ISS—even the resupply oxygen is chemically pure. We did this to prevent our microbes from infecting any new life we might encounter in space. If the cause of the sterility was a contagion—a virus or bacteria—she should be free of it."

"How about the team at the drilling station in Antarctica? Weren't there a couple of women on the team?"

"Yes, sir. They have been checked and are infertile, as well."

"How the hell did *they* get infected?" the president fumed. "They've been completely isolated since March 15. It's the middle of the winter down there!"

"We don't know, sir."

"Thank you, Dr. Hehsa."

Chapter 33 – The Spotlight

June 14

Doug made his way back to Big Sur over the course of a week, sleeping by the side of the road with homeless people. He met a gay couple who had become wanderers, living off day jobs that paid in cash without taxes being withheld to support a government that had betrayed them. Around a campfire, he told them about Rosy and how the US government had perverted the invention.

After a week of traveling together, the three walked up the gravel driveway to Sunshine Ranch. Mona came out to greet them.

"Hi, Mona!" Doug called out to her. "I've brought you two more wandering souls."

She gave each of them a hug. "Welcome to Sunshine Ranch. All God's family is welcome here."

"This is Craig and this is Bruce." He gestured to each of them in turn. "I met them as I was walking back from Palo Alto."

Mona studied them, taking their hands in hers and peering into their faces. She wasn't sure about either one. "I take it you didn't find Clara?"

"Clara left for Montana soon after I was kidnapped by the FBI. Pastor Evans gave me a number he said would reach her in Montana. It rolled over to a voice message recorder. I left a message, but she hasn't returned my call."

"Don't give up on her yet, Doug. I suspect there's more to Clara than meets the eye. From everything you've told me, the girl's got steel inside. I would count on it that she hasn't forgotten you, either."

"I hope you're right." He missed so many things about Clara and their quiet nights together. She was the first woman he had known who wondered and talked about God's plan for them and the world. Her faith in God was as unshakable as his. Together, they had examined scriptures, discussed their hidden meanings, and tried to unravel the metaphors in the Old and New Testaments. Her mind was amazing in its ability to tease out new facets he had never considered. His love for Clara had the same simplicity with which he viewed life: This was God's plan, and He was presenting it to him for his growth and well-being.

"Have you had any contact from your friends down at JPL?"

"No. I worry about them, but I can't think of any way to help them escape. The marines have that place locked down tight. I'm sure the transmitter I used is on 24-hour surveillance now."

"If you're interested, I may have an idea about who *could* help."

He was confused. "What do you mean? How could anyone get them out?"

"Doug, Sunshine Ranch is one of many places people who have decided our government is out of control meet and plan how to resist further erosion of the freedoms guaranteed by our inspired constitution. For over two hundred, years people like us have kept presidents, congressmen, and governmental institutions from canceling the guarantees promised in that document. I have told them about how the three of you were kidnapped by the FBI and held incommunicado for six weeks for doing nothing more than being students investigating the limits of the universe. They want to help Lily and Kevin escape from confinement at JPL."

"How would they do that? JPL has marines, guard dogs, and electrified fences. How could you sneak them out past all of that?"

"*Sneaking* isn't how these guys operate. In fact, what they do is the opposite of *sneak*. They shine a great big spotlight into the dark little holes our government tries to keep hidden. They've been waiting for you to return. Come with me now. I will introduce you to some people. They are prepared to take the US Government to court to *force* the release of Lily and Kevin from JPL."

She turned to Craig and Bruce, having come to a decision about them. "You guys are welcome to stay as long as you want. You can get food and showers in the house. If you're hungry, Mindy's in the kitchen fixing dinner. She'll get you something to eat, and the loft of my barn has been home to many who wander and are not lost. Throw out your bedrolls up there."

Mona walked into her barn and got in her ten-year-old Prius. Doug followed along behind her, put his backpack into the back seat, and belted into the passenger seat, unsure of what was going to happen next. She handed him a knit cap, sunglasses, and a newspaper. "Put the hat and glasses on now; pull the hat down low, so it covers most of your head and that red crew cut. When we approach the Bay Bridge, put the newspaper over your face and lean your seat back—pretend you're sleeping. They have facial recognition scanners in every lane."

"Facial recognition scanners? Really?"

"It's a new millennium. Don't underestimate our government. The scanners are everywhere—airports, bus stations, train stations, the rapid transit, football and baseball stadiums. Everywhere people congregate, there are little cameras, trying to find people who don't want to be found. Those cameras feed underground server farms in the desert in Nevada that examine every face that goes by every camera—over a billion faces a day— and those faces are compared to the digitized faces in their database. I have no doubt yours is on file there, too."

... ...

"Doug, this is Dr. Mark Livingston," Mona nodded to one of the men in the room. "He's one of us. He teaches in the physics department at Berkeley. This is Dr. Roberta Jones, professor of electrical engineering, and this is Dr. Binh Nguyen-Tan, professor of computer science."

Doug shook each of their hands. They were in a small conference room on the Berkeley campus. Classes were over for the day, so the rest of the building was silent. "I know of you, Dr. Livingston. My advisor, Dr. Johnson, was pretty impressed. He said you were one of the most brilliant physicists on the West Coast."

"Thank you, Doug," the professor said, blushing a little. "Johnson was always saying stuff like that. I guess you heard about him?"

"What do you mean?"

"He's dead, Doug. He was murdered in his house a couple of weeks ago."

Doug was quiet for a minute. "I wondered why he didn't answer his phone. He had a full set of my research notes and a copy of Lily's schematic for the first Rosy Transmitter we made."

"Then Rosy has gone offshore," Livingston said. "That explains why the FBI took over the investigation from the Palo Alto police."

The implications of hostile countries having Rosy technology took a while to sink in for all three of them. Doug was terrified. "They will have the ability to send bombs here! IEDs will be an everyday occurrence!"

"Do you think you could create a Rosy Transmitter here?" Livingston asked. "Maybe we can find a way to detect, circumvent, or disable it."

He closed his eyes, took a breath, and brought up the schematic mentally. It was all there. "Yeah, I'm sure I could."

"How long would you need?" Nguyen-Tan asked.

"The mirror is the hard part. It's controlled by a computer— we might need someone in mechanical engineering for that bit— and it means you need an interface from the computer to mirror. We built a USB interface with a driver for it. I'll need a computer— the fastest one you have, running Linux with the Java Development Kit installed."

"I'll have it for you in an hour. Anything else?"

He paused, trying to decide if he wanted to take a chance on FBI arresting him again. The memories of the FBI getting him out of bed and ransacking his room at Stanford and of having to escape from JPL were still vivid to him. "Assuming it works, what will become of whatever we build?"

Livingston glanced at Mona and then back at Doug. "We have to find a way to identify where a transmission began. If no one can send a bomb without everyone else knowing they did it, anonymous bombing won't happen. Without the ability to identify who sent a bomb, however, everyone will start throwing them without fear of retaliation."

All four of the people nodded in agreement. They had obviously thought this through as a group.

The Beginning of the End

Doug paused while he considered the scientist's words and pondered what to do. "If we build a detector, the only way this works for me is if we give away the technology for free to everyone in the world when we're done—whether they are friends or enemies of the United States. The objective is to prevent Rosy from being used by anyone to kill anonymously, not to make money or give the United Stated an edge over everyone else. If Rosy can't be used as an anonymous offensive weapon by anyone, and then maybe it will be used as Lily, Kevin, and I intended—for purely peaceful purposes." They all nodded again in agreement, and then he asked the most important question. "The transmitter we use to develop this detector and all notes about the transmitter's creation will be destroyed once we finish, right?"

All three of the scientists stared at Doug without moving. He was asking them to break the cardinal rule of research—to prevent anyone from reproducing their efforts.

"If anyone finds out you were involved with this, your lives and the lives of the people you love will be in extreme danger. At least one person has already been killed because of Rosy, and I don't want anyone else to die. We have to keep this project completely secret. You can't tell your wives, husbands, girlfriends, boyfriends—not even your priest what we are doing."

One by one, each of the scientists nodded, realizing this was the temptation that had gotten Dr. Johnson killed, that none of them would be safe if anyone knew they were able to make a Rosy Transmitter.

Livingston cleared his throat. "I think I can speak for everyone. We understand the danger inherent in this project. We also understand how important this is to the future of humanity. We're on your side. This may not save the human race—the governments of the world continue to be awash in stupidity—but without the Rosy detector, we don't stand a chance."

"Then count me in," Doug said, deciding he had no choice but to trust them. "I think we can have a transmitter going in a couple of days."

"I've built many USB drivers and interfaces," Nguyen-Tan said. "Let me take that part."

"Talk to Sam McNulty," Doug said. "He's a computer science grad student at Stanford—he created the last one for us. He works nights at the McDonald's on El Camino Real in Palo Alto."

"I'll do the hardware for the interface," Jones said. "Binh and I have done this before."

"I'll need your help on the motherboard for the transmitter, also," Doug said.

Livingston spoke up. "Can you give me some specs people here could use to build what you need without them knowing what they're building?"

He thought for a moment. "I'm sure I can. And Dr. Jones, you will save yourself a bunch of time by visiting Kiran Janalagana at Stanford. He's an electrical engineering grad student, and he built all of our magnetic mirrors. But be warned—he may require a case of beer before he'll show you what he did. I think he's working at the Googleplex in Mountainview for the summer as an intern."

She was impressed. "Lucky guy. What kind of beer?"

"His favorite is Stone Ruination IPA."

"I'll find a case of it somewhere."

Chapter 34 – The Writ

June 16

"You must turn your vehicles around and leave the premises!" the marine corporal shouted at the collection of vans, pickups, and cars that showed up at the main gate to JPL at 8 AM.

"I demand to see Dr. Samuel Lowell," the man in the lead car told the guard as he got out of the vehicle. The television cameras behind him were recording and sending the live feed to both local and national news services.

"Sir, this is your last warning! Get back in your vehicle, turn it around, and leave the premises."

"I will not. I am unarmed and have a federal writ of habeas corpus issued by the Ninth Circuit Court demanding Lily Yuan and Kevin Langly either be released from confinement or charged with a crime." The lawyer from the American Civil Liberties Union held a document over his head for the cameras, and then presented it to the marine guard. The judge had resisted issuing the writ until the ACLU lawyers demonstrated that the two students were being held incommunicado on a federal reservation being guarded by federal troops. State jurisdiction did not apply.

The lawyer turned sideways, so the cameras would have a good profile shot of him haranguing the marine corporal with the huge metal gate behind him while the corporal and other guards pointed their rifles at him. He was milking the moment for all it was worth—you couldn't pay for this kind of press coverage.

"Habeas corpus is a right guaranteed in the US Constitution," he announced to the corporal standing face to face with him. "The *same* US Constitution you swore to uphold and defend when you became a marine. Is Dr. Lowell on his way? This writ must be served to him personally."

The marine lieutenant in the guard station was on the phone, gesturing frantically while he talked to the person on the other end.

Chapter 35 – Out of the Bag

June 19

Lily was having trouble fitting into her jeans. Her second appointment at The Baby Center was at 10 A.M. today. The FBI would accompany her and bring her back, as they had the first time. A big commotion was going on at the front gate, however, and until it was cleared, no one could get in or out. TV cameras and news vans were everywhere with their satellite dishes extended toward the sky.

Kevin didn't answer her knock on his door, so she decided to walk down to see if whatever was happening would delay the departure for her appointment. A line of picketers walked around in a circle in front of the main gate, chanting something she couldn't quite make out. Members of the Los Angeles Police Department riot squad stood shoulder to shoulder across the entrance to JPL in full riot gear, shields, and batons at the ready. The picketers chanted one slogan after another, but all she could hear was the noise. As Lily walked closer, the words they were saying became clear. She stopped with her mouth open in disbelief.

"STOP THE ROSY TRANSMITTER!"

"STOP THE INVASION OF OUR PRIVACY!"

"STOP THE EVIL WEAPON!"

Some of the demonstrators began new phrase that shocked her even more. "FREE KEVIN AND LILY! FREE KEVIN AND LILY!" The rest of the picketers picked up the chant.

"Pretty cool, huh?" Kevin said from behind her.

She spun around to face him. "How do they know about Rosy? How do they know about us?"

"Three guesses," he laughed, "and those guesses are Doug, Doug, and ... *Doug*! He found the Mounties, Lily. The cat is *officially* out of the bag! I wonder if we could sneak through the side gate while everyone is distracted by what's going on here."

The Beginning of the End

She studied the marine guards with their fixed bayonets and full combat gear, the three rows of twenty-foot-high chain link fence with razor wire on top, the gate itself, which would be a challenge for a tank to get through, and the solid line of LAPD riot control officers. "Maybe this isn't the best time to consider sneaking out, Kevin."

"THERE THEY ARE! ARE YOU KEVIN LANGLY? ARE YOU LILY YUAN?" The news team from channel 2 had pointed their big sound pickup dish at them. They were speaking to them via loudspeaker, over the noise of the demonstration.

"Yes, we are!" Kevin shouted toward the dish. "Can you hear me?"

"YES, WE CAN HEAR YOU. ARE YOU BEING HELD AGAINST YOUR WILL?"

"Yes—we cannot leave! If we try to leave, Dr. Lowell said we will be shot or arrested and sent to Guantanamo!"

"HOW LONG HAVE YOU BEEN HELD HERE?"

The marines began running toward them from the front gate.

"We have been held here three months! We were kidnapped by the FBI from Stanford University where we are graduate students!"

"Help us!" Lily shouted as the marines reached them and began pulling them back toward the administration building. "I'm pregnant! I need to see a doctor!"

Shock played across Kevin's face that changed into rage in the same heartbeat. He threw off the arm of the guy who'd been pulling him and then hit the guard who was pulling Lily. A third marine smashed him in the face with the butt of his rifle. Kevin fell to the ground, holding his head, as blood ran through his fingers from his broken nose. He reached out toward the news cameras with his bloody hand and collapsed.

Lily screamed and fell to her knees, pulling Kevin's bloody head to her chest. "You've *KILLED* him, you *BASTARDS!*"

Three Humvees pulled up and made a cordon around the two students. Two minutes later, an ambulance pulled up with a screech of tires, its lights flashing and siren wailing. The students were loaded into the back, and the ambulance disappeared around the corner of the administration building.

... ...

Nothing makes quite as good prime time news feed as American troops beating young Americans bloody. The image of a bleeding Kevin reaching out toward the cameras on the other side of the chain link fences was on CNN's website within sixty seconds of him hitting the ground. Reuters, Al Jazeera, the BBC, AP, UPI, Xinhua, and RT all picked up the story minutes later. What had been a local demonstration at an obscure federal campus in Los Angeles was suddenly catapulted into an international incident, and Rosy was carried right along with it.

An hour after Kevin had collapsed, a van pulled up to the demonstrators and began distributing white T-shirts with two-color printing on them. They showed a bleeding, reaching, Kevin behind a chain link fence. Some of the shirts had the words "Free Kevin and Lily from JPL-tanamo" above the picture. Some said "Freedom? What freedom?" Some said "4th, 5th, 6th Amendments—null and void!" On all three T-shirts, the red of the blood stood in stark contrast to the black printing and image of Kevin.

... ...

"You mean that's all there is to it? It's that easy?" Dr. Livingston was amazed.

"Yep, seems to be," Doug said, just as surprised. They had accomplished in five days what the CIA and NSA had not been able to in months. The Rosy detector they built detected both the beginning and ending of the portals they generated all over the San Francisco Bay Area. By triangulation from the three pickups, the detector gave the coordinates of the portal—both the originating and ending sites—how long the portal was open, and based on the strength of the signature, how big the portal was.

The Beginning of the End

They would have been done sooner, but the system kept detecting Rosy transmissions that couldn't have possibly been happening. The team thought what the detector was picking up was noise and concentrated on finding a way to filter it out. While he was taking a shower, Doug realized these other signals actually *were* Rosy transmissions and taking place not only in five different places around the US, but also in several places in Israel, China, Russia, Lebanon, Libya, Indonesia, Afghanistan, and Iran. Rosy had broken free of the US and was proliferating, just as he'd known it would.

Once he explained what they were seeing, the team knew they were done. All three scientists stood and applauded Doug. He had never received an accolade before—especially from three world-renowned professors. He had no idea how to respond, so he smiled, swung his backpack onto one shoulder, and walked out of the room. After one more side errand, he could start his trip to Montana.

Chapter 36 – Do You Have a Warrant?

June 20

"Good evening. This is Bradley Smythe on KALX, the student-run radio station of UC Berkeley. This evening, we have a special treat for you anti-government people. In the studio with me is Douglas Medder, one of the most sought-after people in the history of the United States. Doug is on the FBI's Ten Most Wanted list—but, unlike the rest of the people on the list, he didn't murder anyone, steal from anyone, molest a child, smuggle drugs, or support terrorism. He was just a graduate student in physics at our neighbor across the bay, Stanford University. Together with Lily Yuan and Kevin Langly, Doug invented the infamous Rosy Transmitter. Welcome, Doug."

"Hi, Bradley. Thanks for letting me on your show."

"So, Doug, what can you tell us about the device you three invented? What is a Rosy Transmitter?"

"A Rosy Transmitter opens a portal—some people call the portal a wormhole. It goes from one point in our universe to another, bypassing everything between the two points, including the distance. Portals allow near-instantaneous transfer of almost anything between the two points. When we first started, we thought all a portal could transfer was energy—sound waves, radio waves, a laser beam. Then we tried to send a pencil. It went through the portal the same as the lasers had, so we tried a lab mouse next. It also went through unharmed."

"How much energy do you need to send a mouse through a portal?"

"The energy to open the portal is proportional to the diameter of the portal. It has nothing to do with what you send through and very little to do with how far you send it. The bigger the portal, the larger the energy requirements. To answer your question, we sent the mouse across the physics lab. The energy required to do that was less than what you'd need to power a flashlight bulb for one second."

"And you could just as easily have sent that mouse to the moon?"

"Yep—only the moon is surrounded by a vacuum. We found that, when you open a portal into a vacuum, it's like opening a hatch on the International Space Station: everything that isn't nailed down gets blown into the vacuum, along with whatever you're trying to send."

"What would happen if the other end of the portal were inside something solid? Like a rock?"

"Whatever you sent through would hit that solid thing and bounce back. The faster you launch an object into the portal, the harder the object hits. We did that with a pencil at the beginning of our research. The pencil bounced off the side of the trash can we were using to catch what we sent through, and we found it back in the transmitter dish with a broken point."

Bradley wanted to mention the rest of Doug's team's incarceration. "Lily and Kevin are still being held at NASA's Jet Propulsion Laboratory in Pasadena, California, one of the most heavily-guarded installations in the world. How did you manage to escape?"

"The JPL scientists built and used a Rosy Transmitter to send a satellite into orbit; I used their transmitter to send me into the air above the L.A. harbor. I swam ashore to Manhattan Beach."

"How far above the harbor did you come out? Ten feet would have been exciting—a hundred feet would have been a different story."

"It must have been forty or fifty feet," Doug said, remembering the fall with a grimace. "I did a pretty amazing belly flop."

"A belly flop from fifty feet. Ouch!"

"You have no idea."

"Nothing you've told us sounds dangerous to our country. Why did the government lock you three up?"

"Our government took what Lily, Kevin, and I discovered and is building a whole new class of weapons around this technology. Instead of being satisfied with a discovery that allows us to send materials into orbit for almost free and have instantaneous, secure communications, they have developed an eavesdropping system capable of listening to conversations anywhere in the world without people having any idea they are being overheard. They have built a secure communications system that is untappable. They have created a rifle that can open a portal to someone's head a hundred miles away and blow their brains out. They have built a bomb delivery system that can send anything from a hand grenade to a nuke anywhere in the world with no warning and no chance at defense."

The implications of what Doug had said were so overwhelming that Bradley sat with his mouth open without any idea what to ask next. Finally he snapped out of his silence. "Who else has this technology, Doug? Is the United States the only country working on it?"

"We've detected Rosy transmissions from the US, Russia, China, Israel, Iran, Afghanistan, Libya, and Indonesia. The FBI confiscated all our research notes, transmitter designs, and computers, but we gave a copy of our notes and first transmitter design to our graduate school advisor, Dr. Albee Johnson. Two weeks ago, *The Daily News* website in Palo Alto reported that Dr. Johnson had been murdered and the FBI had taken over the investigation."

"Are you saying you think Dr. Johnson's death was related to him having your research notes?"

"No, I'm not. All I know is Dr. Johnson is dead and he had a copy of our notes. As far as why the FBI is investigating his murder, you'll have to ask them."

"How did you three come up with the idea for the Rosy Transmitter?"

Doug knew this question was coming. He sighed, wishing he had a better answer. "Lily had a dream. In her dream, she was told how to build it. The dream also told her 'It will change the world.' It turned out, the prophecy came true, but not exactly in the way we had expected."

"Lily had a dream? When was that?"

The Beginning of the End

"It was right before everyone at Stanford left for Christmas break."

"When did you guys get the first transmitter working?"

"The first weekend in January. We had four days to work on it, undisturbed, before everyone came back from break."

"Why do you call it the 'Rosy Transmitter'?"

Doug laughed. "That was Lily's idea. The transmitter gives off a rose-colored glow when it's active."

"How do you aim a Rosy Transmitter? How do you say, 'I want to open a portal from here to there, wherever *there* is?"

He described how they discovered Rosy was sensitive to magnetic fields and built their first magnetic mirror. Bradley got a chuckle about campus security leading the semi-dressed couple out of Stanford's president's office in handcuffs. Doug breathed deep and steeled himself for what he was about to say next. The world didn't know it yet, but it was about to pass through a cusp from which there was no return. He had rehearsed this part many times with Mona and Dr. Livingston.

"As I said before, Rosy is being developed by our government and many other governments around the world as an anonymous weapons delivery system. Anyone with this technology can send a bomb, bullet, biological weapon, or chemical weapon anywhere in the world without their sending location being detected. This makes retaliation impossible. It's the ultimate roadside bomb—anonymous and deadly. No one will be safe or immune. This technology will get into the hands of the terrorists of the world, and they will be able to bomb the Super Bowl, the World Cup—any large gathering of people. If they blew up the State of the Union Address by the president of the United States, they would get both houses of Congress, the president and his whole cabinet, the Joint Chiefs, and the Supreme Court."

He took another deep breath that failed to calm the butterflies ramming into the walls of his stomach. "I have created a way for anyone to track the origin and destination of a Rosy transmission; I call it the Rosy Detector. I have posted the plans to make the detector on the WikiLeaks website—they are available for free to everyone. I decided the only way to prevent Rosy technology from being used to send bombs was to give everyone the technology to detect that a transmission had taken place, where it came from, and where it went. If a bomb is no longer anonymous, I believe it won't be used."

For the second time in the interview, Bradley sat in shocked silence. This was going to make him famous!

Doug continued, "I expected that if WikiLeaks was the sole source for the plans, they would be shut down by the NSA in short order, so I've also posted the plans on eleven different Craigslist sites, YouTube, Facebook, Amazon's Kindle site in e-book form, and twenty different offshore anarchy sites. Do a search for 'Doug's Rosy Detector' and you'll find one. The hardware without the software would be worthless, so I posted the Rosy Detector source on all the websites, as well."

"Give me a list of the websites. I will post it on ours also."

"I'd hoped you would say that. Here is the list."

Bradley scanned it, intrigued. "What do I need to build one?"

"The Rosy Detector is much less complicated than the transmitter itself. We designed the detector so you can make the hardware parts from stuff you'd find in any scientific supply house and a computer. I found both ends of the portal have a magnetic resonance, unique and detectable from thousands of miles away. The software uses three pickups to triangulate on the portal ends. The larger the portal, the easier it is to detect. Rosy Detector tells you when and where the portals begin and end, the direction and distance from the center of the pickup triangle to both the beginning and ending of the portal, and how long the portal was open. It even estimates how large the portal was. I've only tested the code on a Linux machine, but it's in Java, so the program should be portable to an Apple, Windows, tablet, or mainframe computer. A smartphone app should be pretty easy to develop."

"Do the plans on these websites also allow me to build a Rosy Transmitter? Could I use them to open wormholes of my own?"

"Nope, sorry," Doug said, chuckling a little. "These plans only allow you to see where someone else has opened a wormhole and where it went."

The Beginning of the End

Bradley decided to ask the rest of his preplanned questions. "Is there any connection between your Rosy Transmitter and the fact that no women are getting pregnant? Both of them happened around the same time."

Doug cocked his head at that question. He couldn't tell the world about being abducted by aliens. "I don't understand how there could be any connection. Lily was exposed to Rosy from the first day, and she's pregnant."

Suddenly, the door to the radio station burst open and a flood of Berkeley police in SWAT gear came through, red laser spots from their rifles dancing all over the walls. The photographer from Berkeley's student newspaper had heard them coming up the stairs, and he had his high-def news camera recording their entry and search as they swept through the empty offices and studio.

After they discovered the cameraman was the only person on the premises, the lieutenant in charge screamed at him, "WHERE ARE THEY?"

"I don't know. I've never met either one," he said, trying not to laugh. "The whole show was pre-recorded. I got a call an hour ago to come up here and wait for you guys to show up. The first time I heard the interview was while I sat here, waiting for you." He panned in for a close-up of the lieutenant's furious face. "Do you have a warrant?"

Chapter 37—A Lot of Nos

June 21

Freda handed Agent Courapo an inch-thick envelope. "The results are back from Dr. Johnson's house."

"Did they find anything?"

"Yeah, they found a lot," she said in disgust. "A lot of porn, a lot of dirty underwear, and a lot of trash that hadn't been taken out for a couple of weeks. Nothing that would tell us who killed him, though. They found the three fragmented bullets, one from each knee and the one that went through his head. The bone impact had shattered the bullets and we couldn't match the fragments to anything in the database—9mm hollow point—as if that helps. There were a lot of no's—no unexpected fibers, no unexpected fingerprints, no bodily fluids beside Johnson's, no witnesses, no footprints, no escape route, and no forced entry.

"The generic duct tape that was used to restrain him could be purchased in ten stores within five miles of the crime scene and was probably bought by Johnson himself at some point in the past. We found the rest of the roll—more was gone than the perp used to secure Johnson to the chair. The time of death was approximately three days prior to when we found him. Whoever killed him was good—they didn't leave *any* clues. They never hit him with their fist. Based on the signature and note Ken Griffey put on the baseball bat they used, it belonged to Johnson, and there was nothing but traces of latex on the handle. The only surprise is they didn't torch the place after they killed him. I would have."

"Did they find anything that would suggest he had withheld a copy of the schematic for the Rosy Transmitter or a copy of Doug's research notes?"

"Not exactly. We don't *know* if he did or didn't. We don't know if he did and the killer got them. We don't know if he didn't and the killer killed him, trying to get something Johnson didn't have. But I have my suspicions. Let me give you the thumbnail on what else I've found." He leaned back in his chair. Freda was amazing. "The day after we hit his house and confiscated all that worthless stuff, he called the Chinese, Russian, and Israeli consulates in San Francisco. All three called back later the same day. There were no further communications between them—at least not through his cell or landlines."

"Are you suggesting our visit to his home somehow precipitated his sale of the plans to the three countries?"

She shrugged. "Nope, I'm not. The only person who *does* know is dead. I'm just giving you the facts. The next day at 11:28 A.M., the San Francisco PD plate reader at the US 101 ramp at Market Street picked up his license plate and the reader in front of the Chinese consulate saw it fifteen minutes later. He was in front of the Russian consulate ninety minutes after that and in front of the Israeli's an hour and a half later. In all three consulates, calls to their capitals took place after he left them. Since the calls were from non-US citizens, the NSA recorded them, but they were encrypted. The NSA said they could decrypt them, but we would have to pay for it."

"Sounds like them." Courapo shook his head. "So much for interagency cooperation."

"Three cars followed him all the way back to Palo Alto. They were registered to people and organizations on our watch list, otherwise I wouldn't have noticed them. Those people and companies were associated with the Chinese, Russians, and Israelis, respectively. Once I figured out who belonged to those plates, I did an area search and traced where they'd been. Those same cars showed up at Johnson's house over the next three days while Johnson was in class. They stayed about an hour and then returned to San Francisco."

"It would have been them searching his house," the agent thought out loud.

"Yeah, that's what I figured. They returned about a week later, but they only stayed about ten minutes. Johnson should have been home. His car went by an hour before the first consulate showed up, which coincided with the end of his last class for the day."

"So, representatives of all three consulates showed up at his house on the same evening?"

"Yep. But here's something really interesting. The next day, he went to a FedEx Office and got something copied—three times actually. We found the receipt in his personal effects—Ninety-eight pages of something. I talked to the store and got the actual guy who did the copying; he said it was notes with a lot of scribbles and a smudged diagram that might have been a schematic. I didn't have a copy of the real thing from JPL, so I didn't think it would do any good to grill him. He told me, and I quote, 'It looked like physics professor shit.' I think a lot of grad students and professors use them to copy their notes."

"The hard drive in the copy machine." Freda didn't understand. "All commercial copiers scan whatever they're copying to an internal hard drive and print it from there. Most of them have space on their hard drive for weeks of data—whatever he copied might still be on the disc. Call them now and tell them to stop using that machine."

She walked back to her desk and made the phone call. When she returned to Courapo's office, she said, "They said they would, but it would be a huge inconvenience, and, if we were more than a couple of hours, they're going to need a warrant. I told them, if we had to issue a warrant, we would impound both machines. They were a lot more willing to work with me after that—they only have two high-capacity copiers and one is down. They wanted to know how long before they could use the one that was working, so I told them later today. They said they would squeak by on their low capacity backup copier."

He picked up the phone and dialed a number. "Bernie, go to the FedEx Office on 249 S California Ave in Palo Alto, STAT. Copy the hard drives on *both* copiers. All of it, not just what the directory points to. I want every sector of every cylinder. Make sure you take enough capacity." He put the phone back in the cradle. "I wonder where Johnson had the notes hidden. *We* searched his house *twice*."

She shrugged. "After he made the copies, he hired a courier to deliver three packages. Guess where."

"Gee, let me guess—the three consulates?"

The Beginning of the End

"He shoots. He scores!" She laughed. "All three consulates sent an encrypted email within an hour of receipt containing a large attachment to their homeland capitals. All three consulates dispatched a diplomatic courier carrying a diplomatic pouch the next day for their homelands."

"So, Johnson sold the Rosy schematic and research notes to the Chinese, Russians, and Israelis. Any idea what happened to the originals?"

"I expect whoever killed him got them."

"How about on the night of his death? Did the plate readers run by the stakeout teams turn up anything?"

"Yeah. I got to it today. I believe the perp was driving a rental car. It wasn't until I checked with Enterprise that his name popped up with skyrockets and flags waving. You're not going to like it."

Courapo sighed. "Let me have it."

"The car was rented by Ibrahim Sualla, a Lebanese adjunct professor teaching at Stanford on a professor exchange program. He drove by the stakeout team at 11:33 P.M. They have no record of when he left or if he even stopped, but if he did stop, he didn't go by the team on his way out. And get this: the reason he was on the watch list is because his father-in-law is a Hezbollah commander in Gaza. The professor has since returned to Lebanon."

"How did he bypass the no-fly list?"

"The state department approved his travel. Something about a peaceful exchange of ideas between friends."

"Friends with Hezbollah? What were they thinking? No one could be that stupid! Did you contact TSA? Do they still have the X-ray of his carry-ons and baggage?"

"Yes and yes. Here are the pictures."

He picked up the grainy photos. A stack of papers about an inch thick was in the backpack of the professor's carry-on. "Any trace of him after he got to Lebanon?"

"Nope. He dropped off the grid."

"Which means Iran now has Rosy. Thank you, Freda—terrific job. If you would excuse me, I need to make a couple of phone calls."

"There's one more thing."

"What's that?"

"Johnson opened an account in the Cayman Islands the week before he died. I found the registration hard copy in his documents. The bank refused to give us any information, so NSA hacked into them for me. On the day before he hired the courier to deliver the packages, three separate deposits were wired into the account for ten million dollars each. The deposits were made by companies with no affiliation to any of the governments in question. A withdrawal cleaned out the balance the day after the Lebanese professor landed. It went to an Iranian children's charity in Switzerland and then disappeared an hour later as a cash withdrawal."

"Send the names of all of the depositing companies and the Iranian charity to the Office of Foreign Assets Control in the treasury department. Tell OFAC to put them on the Specially Designated Nationals List as organizations funding terrorism and tag them with an entry to call me if anyone questions their placement on the list. While you're at it, tell OFAC to put the Lebanese professor ... what was his name?"

"Ibrahim Sualla."

"Yeah, him. Tell OFAC to put him on the list, too. The least we can do for the bastard is to freeze his personal bank accounts. Did you search his quarters?"

"Nope, not yet. I just made the connection this morning."

"And there's been no trace of Doug since he escaped from JPL?"

"Everyone understands that if he surfaces, you should be told immediately. We grilled the interviewer at the radio station this morning, but he was not particularly helpful. His father is a hotshot lawyer in Berkeley, and he showed up after fifteen minutes with a federal court order releasing his son."

Courapo shook his head in frustration. "Well, get the team going on searching the Lebanese professor's quarters. Like I expect to find anything."

"Will do." She got up and walked back to her desk.

... ...

The Beginning of the End

After Bradley Smythe posted it, the YouTube audio session of the KALX interview with Doug went viral. There were over a million hits within three days, and the video began appearing on anarchy websites all over the world. It was translated into at least thirty different languages, and Al Jazeera posted an Arabic version that had so many hits the traffic brought down their website for a few minutes. The number of downloads of Doug's Rosy Detector plans and code set records at every one of the sites on which Doug had posted them. Suddenly, the governments experimenting with Rosy Transmitters had to be much more careful—the whole world was listening.

... ...

Dr. Lowell steepled his hands in front of his face. "Do you have any idea might be sabotaging the transmitters?" He was talking to the floor supervisor in the assembly plant.

"No, I don't, but it has to stop or we're not going to make our commitments."

"Are the new cameras installed?"

"Yes."

"Where no one would notice them?"

"I think so. One is behind a one-way mirror. The other is inside an emergency first aid locker, aimed out through the glass."

"Let's see what they show up. Don't make any announcements that would tip off the person doing this."

Chapter 38—Gold!

June 25

"What the hell are they building on Wysnewski's farm?" Amos Wilson wondered out loud as he watched truck after truck turn up the driveway.

"I don't know, dear," his wife responded without stopping her knitting.

"Of course you don't," he snapped, irritated. He went back to watching the nonstop passage of loaded trucks going in and empty ones coming out.

The first thing they had done to Wysnewski's driveway was to make it into two lanes. The construction crews had spread at least two hundred truckloads of gravel on that dirt road—six-inch rock first, then three-inch, and then three-quarter-inch. They had smoothed and rolled each layer so it was flat and hard and finished the driveway with two inches of asphalt. It had to be the stoutest driveway in the county—you could land a 737 on it!

The trucks were mostly cargo boxes—the kind that came from container ships. Sometimes they pulled flatbeds with the contents tarped so securely that he couldn't figure out what they were carrying. He was dying of curiosity. What they hell could they be building, and why was the government building it here?

He had walked over to say hi, hoping he could see what was going on. Two unsmiling guards with badges met him at the beginning of the driveway and told him he couldn't go any farther. Both guards wore wearing body armor and carried a pistol on their belt and an automatic rifle in the crook of their arm. Only one guard spoke; the second guard stayed on the other side of the driveway behind a concrete barricade. Neither guard pointed their rifles at him, but he had no doubt they would have been if he had not turned around and walked back to his house.

Before the driveway was completed, another crew had started erecting a double row of twenty feet high chain link fence, topped with razor wire. Every fifty feet was a sign announcing "Federal Property—No Trespassing—Deadly Force is Authorized."

Amos got out his binoculars. The trucks were not even stopping at the farmhouse—the crews had extended the driveway over the hill behind the house and the trucks disappeared into the forested bowl on the other side. Several times a day, the top of a huge crane appeared over the ridgeline, but what it was lifting was hidden by the hill.

"What the hell are they building over there?" he muttered again in frustration.

His wife didn't answer. She rolled her eyes and began the next row, her knitting needles clicking softly together.

... ...

"No construction permits have been issued to Wysnewski's farm," the county clerk told him the next day.

"Well, the feds are building something there. Must have been a thousand trucks gone up that driveway in the past two weeks."

"Maybe Stanton can go check on it," she said, chuckling. "No one would know better'n you that you can't build nothin' without the county gettin' their fee."

The county's Building and Planning department had caught Amos putting an addition on his house without the required permits. He'd had to hire an architect and engineer after the fact to create plans for the addition, and then pay a fine on top of the basic fee. His face turned red, but he kept quiet.

The clerk checked another report. "The property is still titled in Wysnewski's name. Whoever bought it never registered the deed change. Why do you think the government bought it?"

"Gee, I don't know—maybe because of the big black and white signs they put up saying, 'Federal Property, Keep the Fuck Out!'" He smirked. "None of this makes any sense."

"If it *is* the federal government, there's not much the county can do about it. We have to follow their rules, but they don't pay any attention to ours. We can't even tax a federal installation." She paused. "Anything else I can help you with, Amos?" She tried to hide her grin. "Do you need a building permit for anything?"

"No," he said curtly. "Thanks." He turned on his heel and walked out of the county admin building. "I think Melody might need some exercise." He was talking about his fat, old mare who spent most of her time these days munching on the belly-high grass in her pasture. "She used to love goin' up in them hills. Bet I can see what's cookin' from the top a that ridge."

By the time he got back to his farm, it was two o'clock. He saddled Melody and rode out to the edge of his property, where it met Wysnewski's property line over a mile from his farmhouse. The old logging road was still there—a little overgrown, but still passable. No fence or "No Trespassing" signs were in sight. The road apparently hadn't been used in years and they encountered some washed out places. Melody went around them easily. It was a beautiful day and Amos enjoyed his ride immensely. His mare seemed to like being out of her pasture, as well. They went up through the hills, following the logging road, as a hawk floated high above them, riding the thermals coming up from the valley.

Suddenly, there was a muffled boom. "That sounded like dynamite! Who the hell's blastin' and what the hell *are* they blastin'?" He cleared the ridgeline and peered down into the bowl behind Wysnewski's farmhouse. Even in his wildest imaginings, he was not ready for what he saw.

They were mining a hole into the side of the mountain. Massive piles of rock filled the bowl. A train carrying twenty carloads of rock had just come out of the entrance. As he watched, each an operator dumped each car into a waiting truck that carried its load up a road to the top of the bowl where it dumped the rock and returned for another load. "They found somethin' in there!" He crowed triumphantly. "Somethin' valuable—has to be. There's no other reason to blast a cave outta the guts of that mountain—only way to justify all them people and supplies."

He stayed for another hour, took some pictures, and then decided it was time to get back before the sun went behind the big mountains to the west. Just then, a man in camouflage clothing and paint on his face stepped out from behind a tree with his automatic rifle pointed at Amos's chest.

"Get off the horse, Mr. Wilson," the man commanded. "Slowly."

... ...

"Mr. Wilson," the FBI agent asked again, "why were you up on that ridge?" The agent had been grilling Amos nonstop for the last three hours. The interview room was over eighty degrees, the smell of stress and sweat thick in the air.

"I was on a ride," the old man said obstinately. "There was no signs on that damned logging road. I been up that road hundreds a times in the past fifty years—Wysnewski and me used to hunt up there all the time."

"Why did you take all those pictures of the excavation?"

"Ain't no law against taking pictures. Leastways none I ever heard of. What did ya find in that mountain? Gold?"

"That's not what's going on, Mr. Wilson. This is a highly secret project of the federal government. You were trespassing—you knew you were trespassing. We have pictures of you reading the signs on the fencing erected across the front of the property and of you watching the trucks through your binoculars. We also have a recording of you trying to walk past the front gate. We think we have a pretty strong case to charge you with espionage."

"*ESPIONAGE?*" Amos screamed. "*ME?* I'm a goddamned *vet*! I served in Vietnam in the 101st Division! I was in Pleiku during Tet. I got the frigging Silver Star and two Purple Hearts defending this goddamned country! I buried my son in the cemetery behind our house—he got killed in Iraq! My father fought in WWII *and* Korea, and *both* my grandfathers served in WWI. You got a lotta goddamned balls callin' me a spy. Ain't nobody more red, white, and blue than Amos Wilson."

"Why were you up on that ridge, Mr. Wilson?"

"I want a goddamned lawyer."

"If we declare you an enemy combatant, you will be jailed without access to a lawyer for as long as we like. You won't see your wife, your remaining son, his children, or your friends. You will be held in solitary confinement—no books, no movies, no visitors—nothing but a six-by-twelve cell, twenty-three hours a day. The CIA will question you, and you really don't want those guys questioning you. So, why were you up on that ridge?"

Amos took a minute to consider his options. He had not told his wife where he was going—no one knew he had gone up that frigging logging road. No one knew he was here, being held in captivity by these assholes. If he never returned to his house, they wouldn't be able to even guess where to start searching. He was up the smelly creek, the paddle was gone, and the canoe was sinking fast. He took a deep breath and swallowed his pride.

"I was curious."

"Curious of what?"

"Of what you were building, moron!" he said vehemently. "Wysnewski and his family lived on that farm as long as my family lived on mine—both of us got at least four generations a roots going down into that dirt. When you started the truck brigade and that dynamite blasting, of course I was curious. This is quiet farmland—the most excitin' thing we got going around here is watching a bull mount a cow. On a really wild Saturday night we go down to the Grange to play bingo. I'll bet I'm not the only one wondering what you're doing."

The agent got up and left the room. He came back an hour later. "Mr. Wilson, you are free to go. We are building a research lab to try to figure out why the women of the world can't get pregnant. The scientists must do their research in sterile conditions, which is why we're putting it inside the mountain. This information is top secret, and we are depending on you to keep it that way. Can we count on you?"

"I'm an American from my hair to my toenails," Amos told the agent. "You can count on me."

"Don't go up on that ridge again."

"I believe I won't."

The agent opened the door. "Agent Murphy will return you and your horse to your ranch."

The Beginning of the End

After Amos was gone, the agent who'd been watching the interview through the mirrored wall came into the interview room and sat down. "Do you think he bought it?"

"Yeah," the agent laughed. "That bit about keeping him in isolation and having the CIA question him—it always works."

"How long do you think it will take before he spreads the story to everyone else?"

"If I had to guess, maybe an hour. Are the wiretaps in place?"

"Yep. This should take a lot of the heat off the security personnel."

Chapter 39 – I Want Some Answers

June 26

"What do you mean no one stopped him?" President Klavel screamed. "He waltzed onto a plane and flew away with the plans to the most dangerous technology ever to appear on the face of this planet?"

"He wasn't on the no-fly list," the secretary of homeland security said. "There was nothing suspicious in either his carry-on or checked baggage."

The president glared around the secure, bombproof conference room a hundred feet below the White House, his face red with frustration. His National Security Council tried to avoid meeting his eyes. He took a breath and tried to calm down. "And why was a Lebanese national, whose father-in-law is a Hezbollah commander in Gaza, not on the no-fly list? Why was the son-of-a-bitch in this country to begin with?"

"Because he was part of an exchange of university professors," the secretary of state spoke up. "We were able to get a CIA-trained professor into the University of Applied Science and Technology in Tehran under the same program."

"Does anyone have any idea how he found out about Rosy?"

"A mole?" the director of central intelligence of the CIA suggested. "Hundreds, maybe thousands, of people know about Rosy around this country. DOD, CIA, NSA, FBI, and NASA all have active programs developing the technology."

The director of the NSA spoke up. "The original email Doug Medder sent Dr. Langly was unencrypted. We examine all transmissions going into and out of JPL, as we do on all federal reservations. I had my people remove Medder's email from every server it had touched to stop any possibility of another Snowden episode, but anyone watching the personal emails of JPL staff could have opened it, read it, and made a copy. I'm sure many countries hack into our Verizon, AT&T, and Sprint servers, just like we do to theirs."

"If they'd received the plans in an email, why the hell would they need to steal them?" National Security Advisor Dick Goldblum smirked.

"Maybe they didn't read *that* email," the DCI proposed. "Maybe they read another one that just talked about what Rosy could do—or maybe they intercepted an email from one of the consulates Johnson had contacted. The email could easily have had all the pertinent data, including his name, but none of the details. We record all *their* emails and decrypt them as computer time becomes available. I'm sure other countries do the same."

"He might have gotten wind of the kids' project through the Stanford grapevine and connected the dots," Dick suggested. "It might have been a fishing trip that paid off."

"Douglas Medder escaped from JPL and has not been apprehended yet," the secretary of state said. "He could have given it to them."

The DCI shook his head indulgently. "If Medder gave it to them, why would they kill Johnson and compromise an agent already in the United States?"

"Do we have any idea where the goddamned Iranians took the plans?" President Klavel asked the room. "Where they are doing their development?"

"I'll have our Iranian assets try to find out," the DCI promised.

"How about the goddamned Russians, Chinese, and Israelis? Where are they working on Rosy? What have they done with it?" There was silence. No one knew what those countries had developed or were developing. The NSA had not yet picked up anything suspicious in phone or email traffic.

"What about Medder's goddamned detector? What are you doing with that?"

"It works great in the lab," the DCI said. "JPL is about to launch our pickups."

After thirty seconds, President Klavel stood. "You guys have some work to do. We will reconvene tomorrow." He pounded on the table with his fist in time with the next four words. "I want some answers!"

Chapter 40 – Feeding Frenzy

June 27

"Why didn't you tell me you were pregnant?" Kevin asked Lily.

"I didn't know how you felt about babies." She crossed her arms and hunched her shoulders defensively. She had known this conversation would happen since she announced her pregnancy to the world at the fence. All her carefully thought-out responses evaporated—time for the truth. "I started to tell you a hundred times, but I chickened out."

JPL had kept them separated since his nose was broken a week ago. The bandage across the bridge of his nose didn't come close to covering the massive bruise that filled the center of his face. It was the tissues around his eyes that were most shocking, however; the damaged skin was vivid with yellows, greens, and reds. Lily and Kevin sat together outside the Ninth District Court in downtown Los Angeles.

"For the record, I love babies," he said, holding her hand. "Beyond a random daydream here and there, I've never thought about having one of my own. I'd always believed the world was so screwed up I didn't think I wanted to bring another child into it. Are you sure you're pregnant?"

"Yes, Kevin, I'm sure." She rolled her eyes. "My conception date is the one time we had sex without a condom. I went to my first OB appointment over a month ago."

He was quiet for a while. The corridor outside the courtroom was silent. The FBI had smuggled them into the courthouse via the underground garage, bypassing the noisy demonstration in the street demanding the students' release. The judge hearing both sides of the case had prohibited anyone, beyond the parties directly involved in this hearing, from entering the courthouse.

"Remember what you said before we went into your room, before we made love?" he asked her

"No. That night is a blur."

"You said, 'Maybe we'll get lucky.'"

"When I said that, I was hoping I *wouldn't* get pregnant."

"I understand, but I think a higher power intervened. I think we did get lucky … because you are one of the last women on the planet to get pregnant. This stuff doesn't happen by accident."

She reached out to him, put her hand gently on his cheek. "I love you."

"I love you, too," he pulled her into his arms. "We'll get through this together."

"Hi, Kevin. Hi, Lily." A middle-aged woman in an expensive suit walked up to them and sat down. The woman sensed she was entering the middle of an emotional moment for the two of them and gave them some time to compose themselves. "My name is Anabel Stuart. I am a lawyer for the ACLU. Do you know what is happening today?"

"No idea," he said. Lily shook her head.

"I am the person who petitioned the court to issue the writ of Habeas Corpus. Our constitution guarantees you cannot be detained indefinitely without being charged with a crime and tried by a jury of your peers.

Today, the judge will hear preliminary arguments about whether or not the government can continue to incarcerate you at JPL. Whatever happens today, one of the parties—either the government or the ACLU—will appeal. It will probably end up at the Supreme Court. That could take years, but we will try to have you released while the appeals go forward. The government will resist because it is their contention that the knowledge you have is so dangerous to the safety of the United States that they cannot allow you out of protective custody."

"Is that what they call JPL?" he laughed bitterly. "Protective custody?" Ms. Stuart nodded. "I didn't feel particularly protected when my nose was being smashed."

"I will be sure to point that out. The government is getting a lot of heat from all over the world to release you."

"Really?" Lily was dumbfounded. "Why would they care about us?" Dr. Lowell had pulled all their off-the-air TV access ever since they'd arrived at JPL, except for special events like the president's announcement of humanity's infertility.

"You two have been thrown into international fame along with your Rosy Transmitter. Countries that don't like the US, and there are a lot of them, are having a field day with the picture of a bleeding Kevin reaching out to the cameras on the other side of the chain link fence." On her phone, she brought up the now-famous picture of Kevin right after his nose had been broken. "They are saying: 'The government of the US is a hypocrite who tells everyone else to respect human rights when this is how they treat their own citizens.'

"The fact that Lily started out as a Chinese national who was given political asylum in the US has turned out to be as big a deal as Kevin being a natural US citizen. China has offered you and your families full amnesty, tuition-free completion of your PhDs at the university of your choice, and guaranteed positions on their space station team. Russia, Israel, and Iran made similar offers to both of you yesterday. This morning, countries from all over the world have followed their lead and offered you citizenship, money, education, and research positions. It's like a feeding frenzy and no one is missing a chance to take a bite out of the exposed underbelly of the US."

"My *family*?" Lily asked, her voice cracking as the implications of what Ms. Stuart had said sank in. "My family in China is alive?"

"We think so. The Chinese news network, Xinhua, did an interview with your mother yesterday and Fox News ran a subtitled version last night on prime time. Your mother said, 'Be strong, Lily!'"

"That was one of her favorite phrases," she said, her chin quivering. Kevin put his arm around her; she turned her head into his shoulder and began to cry. "I thought she was dead," she said between sobs. "I thought they'd killed my whole family."

"Give me a minute." Ms. Stuart pulled out her cell phone again and started typing into it. A moment later, she held it up for Lily. "Is this your mother?" The Fox News clip playing the interview appeared.

Lily gasped and touched the screen. "My mother! Yes, that *is* my mother." She watched the video three times, clutching a tissue the lawyer gave her, now soaked with tears.

"Obviously, the US government doesn't want either of you to go to any of those countries. They will resist strongly."

"You said Rosy was out of the box now," Kevin said. "What did you mean?"

"Your friend, Douglas Medder, posted a full description of its capabilities and what the US government has done with it on the WikiLeaks website. The whole world is up in arms about the US having the means to send any of its bombs, from a hand grenade to a nuke, anywhere, at any time without the slightest warning, and the idea that the US can listen to anyone without any possibility of detection has got every government scrambling to find a way to block it. North Korea announced it has had a Rosy Transmitter in development for over a year."

Lily suddenly clutched Kevin's arm. "Dr. Johnson! He has a full set of our research notes. He even has a copy of my original schematic."

The dots connected. "Dr. Albee Johnson?"

"Yes."

"He was murdered two weeks ago. The FBI took over the investigation." Both students were quiet, remembering their advisor and hoping they weren't responsible for his death. Ms. Stuart scribbled a note. "Did you tell the FBI he had your notes and schematic?"

"Yes, we did—on the first day of our captivity," Kevin said.

"Did the WikiLeaks posting include the schematic and research notes?" Lily asked.

"No, just a description of what the US government did with your idea. How they turned what you wanted to use it for—instantaneous communications and transportation—into a weapon of mass destruction. But Doug did include the plans for a Rosy Detector."

Both Kevin and Lily stared at her, dumbfounded. "A way to detect a Rosy wormhole?" they asked together.

The Beginning of the End

"Yes. Every time someone opens a wormhole, it announces the coordinates of both ends of the wormhole. According to *The New York Times* this morning, eight other countries around the world are opening wormholes. They expect the number to increase quickly."

"Rosy broke free, just like Doug said it would," Kevin whispered.

Lily was incensed. "Then why are we being kept at JPL? There's nothing to keep secret. Rosy's out of the bag!"

"I will ask that question also."

"Are the Iraqis going to invade us?" Lily asked.

"What do you mean?" Ms. Stuart was puzzled by her question.

"Well, we invaded them because President Bush had 'confirmed intelligence' that Saddam Hussein possessed weapons of mass destruction, even though they didn't have a one. Seems like it would be fair if they invaded us for our creation of yet another instance of what we invaded them for."

"I don't think it works that way."

"It would if we were the good guys," she said quietly.

"If we were the good guys, you two wouldn't be under lock and key."

... ...

Outside the admin building, the marines were on full alert. A noisy demonstration was in progress at the front gate. Demonstrations took place at the entrance to JPL every day, but this one was especially angry. People chanted and carried signs, and the LAPD had already arrested five people for chaining themselves to the gate.

The ex-senator from Wisconsin who'd been so vocal in his opposition of the USA PATRIOT Act while he was in office was in the process of making a fiery speech. He stressed the brilliance of our forefathers, who gave us the protections the fourth, fifth, and sixth amendments. He said it was those amendments that set the United States apart from the despotic governments of the world.

"If the US government can lock up Kevin and Lily for being young and smart, then it is no better than Iran, North Korea, and Hitler's Germany. Those kids haven't broken a single law, yet our government is holding them in captivity *because* they were *brilliant*! What's next? Will they lock up people because they are stupid? Washington will be a ghost town if we do that. We should be giving those kids a medal instead of locking them in their rooms behind a cordon of armed marines!"

Every news channel in the country and many overseas carried the speech; even Iran and North Korea aired it, editing out the references to their countries. Those same feeds also had images of heavily armed SWAT officers arresting chained protestors and dragging them into LAPD transportation vans. The ex-senator was campaigning to regain his senate seat by promising to submit a bill stripping the PATRIOT Act of its powers to hold American citizens without charge or trial. He was experiencing an eighty-seven percent approval rating, and the election pundits unanimously predicted him to be the landslide winner.

President Klavel was getting pressure from his stoutest supporters to release the students or try them for a crime. Even *The New York Times* and *The Washington Post*, bastions of support for the president, were openly critical of the government's policy toward the two students. The *San Francisco Chronicle* ran a political cartoon showing Klavel grinding the Constitution into dust under his feet while he put yet another lock on the gate to JPL. Behind him, Lily held a bleeding Kevin to her chest, surrounded by a squad of bayonet-wielding marines.

... ...

"What about Medder's Rosy Detector device?" President Klavel was meeting again with his National Security Council. "How did your research on it turn out?" As usual, they had gathered in the secure bunker under the White House.

"It works better than we had hoped," General Angle said. "The farther apart we put the pickups, the more accurate it becomes. We have already implemented a very precise detection system utilizing satellites launched from JPL's Rosy Transmitter."

"Is there any way to block it? To make our portals invisible?"

"Not that we've found. The frequencies used by the transmitters are so specific, there isn't much of a fudge factor. We have to use those frequencies, and when we do, the pickups hear them."

"Damn!"

"Well, that's bad *and* good," his national science advisor spoke up. "The bad part is they can detect our transmissions. The good part is we also can detect theirs, so there is no change in the balance of power between our adversaries and us. It's true we can't use Rosy as a stealth weapons delivery system anymore, but we can still use it as an instantaneous attack retaliation system. We have already begun building it. If anyone sends something at us or our allies, we can respond in kind on a moment's notice.

"Communication portals can be made so small that detection is very difficult. While someone might be able to say we opened a portal from here to there, they wouldn't have any idea what was sent through. We still benefit from Rosy, and we can also use it as the students intended: for moving mass from one place to another for almost free. We could, for example, use it to build a US-only space station or, as Dr. Lowell at JPL wants, to build a starship to find an uninfected planet to rebuild humanity."

The director of the NSA spoke up. "We know who else has gotten Rosy."

The president sighed, waiting to hear how far the technology had spread.

"As of this morning, Israel, China, Russia, Lebanon, Libya, Indonesia, Afghanistan, India, Pakistan, and Iran. The last three are new as of this morning. We expect those numbers to expand significantly in the near future."

"No North Korea?"

"No, sir, not yet. There is one thing we don't quite understand."

"What's that?" The president readied himself for another surprise. Surprises in this meeting were hardly ever good.

"Our listening stations have turned up something quite unexpected. Every time someone opens a wormhole on Earth, another wormhole opens at three separate places on the moon, only those wormholes don't have a matching ending location. No one can figure out why that's happening. We want to investigate one of the sites originating the signal."

"Really!" This wasn't the type of surprise he'd been expecting. "What do you think they are? Who could have put them there?"

"We don't know," his national security advisor said. "And that's exactly why we want to retrieve one."

"What will it cost?"

"NASA says they could have an exploration module ready in a month. It would carry their backup Martian Opportunity lander, capable of minor excavation and retrieval. We would send it into orbit around the moon via Rosy transmission and it would deploy the lander. Opportunity would find whatever's creating the transmissions and, if possible, bring it back to Earth through another Rosy transmission. They say they can do that for about twenty million dollars."

"Do you think it's worth it?"

"Well, we know we didn't put them there, and if we didn't, and then someone else did. No one else on Earth had this technology six months ago—we think these might be the devices that tipped off the aliens when the students opened their first wormhole. This might be our first chance to examine alien technology."

"Did the interviews with them reveal anything about the starship and its technology? Could it have put the devices on the moon?"

"The students know nothing about the rest of the starship," the director of the FBI said. "They were interviewed extensively. The only places they saw were the room the aliens kept them in and the corridor between that room and the starship lander. There was nothing resembling armaments or what the ship was capable of in those places."

Klavel thought about it for a moment. "Absolutely. Tell NASA to go get it. Give them two weeks—that way, they might bring it back in a month."

Chapter 41 – Saved by the Donut

July 4

"Doug?" A little part inside of him melted when she said his name. The voice at the end of the line was Clara's—the voice that filled his dreams at night.

"Hi, Clara," he said, almost unable to form the words. He took a deep breath and then continued, forcing a calm upon himself he sure didn't feel. They didn't have much time. "How are you? Are you safe? I was so worried."

"*You* were worried!" she said in disbelief. "You were the one who disappeared! I saw on the news that NASA had detained you in Los Angeles. Was that why you didn't answer any of my phone calls? What did you do, Doug? Did you break the law?"

"It's a long story. I didn't break the law, but I can't talk about it now. We have about thirty seconds until I have to hang up."

"Doug, are you in trouble? Why did I have to call this number at exactly 5 P.M.? I tried other times, but your phone must have been off."

"I can't talk about that now. Do you remember where we always said we wanted to live?"

"Yes, it's—"

"Don't say it. The government has tapped your line and this one also now. I will meet you there in one week. Be sure to travel there the way we said we wanted to. They will try to follow you." He ended the call on the GoPhone he had bought with cash at the 7-Eleven in Carmel, California.

"Come on, boy," he called to the stray dog he had temporarily befriended. He pulled out a strip of duct tape from the roll he'd bought with the phone and taped the phone to the dog's collar. Next, he pulled out a bag of cheeseburgers, took them out of their wrappers, and tossed them on the ground.

The dog was ecstatic, gobbling the burgers as Doug went around the corner. He ditched the hat, sunglasses, shoes, and hoodie he'd bought at The Salvation Army store into the dumpster behind a motel and replaced them with his old clothes from his backpack. Mona had taught him how to cover his tracks, and he was getting better at it.

He hunched his shoulders like a homeless guy, shuffled into a nearby bar, scanning the people like he was looking for someone. He then went out the back and across the alley, into the rear entrance of a Chinese restaurant, and out the front. He walked the four blocks to Route 1 and found some cardboard in a dumpster behind a QuikMart. He made a sign that said "UW—Seattle" with a black magic marker and stuck out his thumb.

After half an hour, he had no takers. A cop had passed him twice and was coming around for his third drive-by, so Doug shrugged on his backpack and started walking north, holding his sign so the traffic behind him could see it. A clean-cut, muscular guy—maybe twenty-five—in a Volvo station wagon pulled over.

"Hey, I graduated from the University of Washington, too," the driver said through his open passenger window. "Jump in. I'm going up to Kitsap-Bremerton. I have to report for duty at the shipyards there. I'm in the Navy."

Doug grinned. "Goin' to the U District in Seattle. Thanks." He threw his pack in the backseat and got into the passenger seat in the front. "Nice car. What was your major?"

The cop followed them for a couple of blocks and then turned into a Dunkin' Donuts to join three other Carmel police cars waiting for him there.

... ...

An hour later, a black SUV stopped next to an overturned trash can in Carmel. Three dogs were feasting on the garbage inside the can; one had a phone taped to its collar.

"Let me have the rest of that sandwich you didn't finish," Agent Courapo said to the man beside him.

"I was gonna eat that later," the man complained.

"Really?" Courapo cocked his head, raised his eyebrows, and held out his hand.

His companion sighed in resignation. "Okay, take the damned thing." He dug it out from the Subway bag. "It's soggy, anyway."

The other two dogs took off as soon as he got out of the car. The dog with the phone, however, took the proffered sandwich and chowed down, amazed he'd been so lucky twice in one day. The agent cut the tape holding the phone with his pocketknife.

"I've got the cell phone," he told Freda into his encrypted phone. "It was taped to a stray dog's collar. Doug is nowhere in sight. Alert the Highway Patrol that he was sighted in Carmel and we think he is heading north. They should watch for hitchhikers and hikers—one or more. See if they can increase patrols on I-5, I-680, I-580, US 101, Cal Route 1, and Cal Route 152."

"Should I include I-80?"

"Yeah—the part that goes from Oakland to I-5—and tell the NSA to examine every face going over the Golden Gate, Oakland Bay, San Mateo, and Dumbarton Bridges. We want a real-time alert if they get a hit on Doug. When you're done with that, start examining the feeds from the surveillance cameras around Carmel."

"We'll need a warrant to do that, and it would help a lot if we had a current picture of him."

"We already have a warrant—a classified FISA warrant. I'm on my way to the 7-Eleven where he purchased the phone. Assuming they have a security camera, I'll send you the picture from there—use it on the alert to the Highway Patrol. Also check the car rental places in Carmel to see if they've rented a car to anyone fitting his description."

"Yes, sir." She paused on the end of the line. "Sir?"

"What is it?"

"This is Fourth of July weekend—the roads are going to be swamped. Do you think there's a chance we will be able to find him?"

"We have to try, Freda. Maybe we'll get lucky."

Chapter 42 – Give Me a Minute

July 5

Dr. Langly burst into the director's office. "Is it true the Chinese, Russians, Israelis, and Iranians have Rosy?"

Dr. Lowell studied the other man's face. "Please close the door and have a seat."

Dr. Langly's crossed his arms belligerently. "I believe I will remain standing."

The director got up, walked across his office, and closed the door. "Art, you know I can't answer your question." He walked to one of the chairs in front of his desk and sat down. "I can't even acknowledge you asked it."

"You don't have to, Sam. It's true—I can see it in your eyes. Besides *The New York Times* reported this morning that those four and fifteen others are opening wormholes."

"What difference does it make? Do you think Kevin, Lily, your grandchild, when they're born, and all of us at JPL are in any less danger because those countries may have Rosy? If anything, we are in *more* danger now, thanks to Doug. Ever since his interview at Berkeley, everyone knows what Rosy can do and that we have it. Do you think Pakistan, India, Yemen, North Korea, Nationalist China, ISIS, the Taliban, or Al-Qaeda are less of a threat to those kids now? The list is almost endless. Can you name me one country that wouldn't kill to have Rosy technology?" He paused significantly and then added, "Or one country that wouldn't kill to keep another country from getting it?"

"I want the kids to have something like a normal life," Art said, sitting down across from Dr. Lowell. "I don't want my grandchild to grow up in a prison."

"JPL is hardly a prison."

"It certainly isn't a home in the suburbs," Art said obstinately. "No home I know of is surrounded by armed marines and razor wire. There aren't any playgrounds. There aren't any schools. There aren't any other children."

"Lily having her baby here behind those wire fences outside, may be a blessing. Have you been following how many babies are being stolen worldwide?"

The news channels were screaming about baby thefts in every country of the world. A huge underground market had sprung up as a result of the infertility epidemic, supplying "donated" babies to affluent couples who would pay almost anything to have a child of their own. There was nothing like scarcity to increase demand. Couples who had never considered having children of their own were willing to pay a fortune to have one now. Those people had emptied the orphanages of the world—even in the poorest countries like Malawi, Burundi, and the Central African Republic.

Art decided to change tactics. "Then why can't Kevin and Lily have internet and television access? If they knew about how dangerous it was to have a newborn outside, maybe this place wouldn't seem like a jail to them."

"You're right," Dr. Lowell said, relenting. "I will allow that immediately, subject to the knowledge that all communications are monitored. All outgoing emails are read before being sent through our firewall and all incoming emails are read before anyone receives them. No chat rooms, blog sites, or social networking—nothing like Facebook, Instagram, or Twitter. Only approved, read-only sites. No uploads, downloads, or attachments. All channels on cable will be accessible."

"Including the news channels?"

"Yes, including the news."

"They may have to send and receive assignments as attachments."

"Attached incoming assignments will be read and approved. Outgoing assignment attachments will go through the same screening process. No uploads or downloads."

"How about phone calls, Sam? Lily wants to talk to her mother."

Dr. Lowell sighed. "Phone calls are a problem, and a phone call to China is an even bigger problem." He contemplated how to proceed. Finally, he shrugged. "Okay, sure—as long as the call is made from a designated phone somewhere on JPL. The call will be monitored and terminated if anything suspicious is discussed."

"Her mother doesn't speak English. The conversation will be in Mandarin."

"We have people who can listen to and evaluate their conversation in Mandarin."

"How about school? Both Kevin and Lily want to continue their classes. Stanford has offered to allow them to attend remotely from JPL, and they can do the lab work here. They want their computers and materials from their dorm rooms, though. Both were working on their master's theses before Rosy surfaced—all their research is on their hard drives."

"School may not be allowed because of the interaction."

"It's school, Sam, not a DEFCON convention. Can't someone listen to the lectures when they do?"

"We'll try. It may not work, but we'll try. I will have the hard drives in their computers examined and all Rosy-related data will be removed. After the scan is completed, they can have them back. I will make sure they have access to all the unclassified information available in the JPL archives—much of it has never been published. They will also have access to the Library of Congress online files. Those files contain most of the accumulated knowledge of humanity, all indexed and cross-referenced. As far as the rest of the contents of their dorm rooms, they can have it. We've already pulled anything Rosy-related."

Dr. Langly suppressed a wry chuckle. What good would removing the Rosy data do? At least a hundred people knew how to make a Rosy Transmitter now, and that was just in the United States. He remembered Lily drawing the Rosy schematic from memory during their first meeting. How would they erase that?

Dr. Lowell steepled his hands in front of his face. "I would like to ask a favor in return for all of this."

"What favor?"

"I'd like them to give a television interview. I'd like them to say they are here for their own protection—that they want to be here and appreciate the safety we are providing them."

Art stared at the director, wondering how desperate Washington actually was. The demonstrations at the gate were a pain in the tail for everyone working at JPL. From the first day the FBI had brought Kevin and Lily here, many people working at JPL had wondered why they were even being kept on this reservation. Since the ACLU showed up at the front gate, the demonstrations had become a huge thorn in the side of the president. The press was having a field day with embarrassing the government and President Klavel, and his approval ratings had plummeted into the teens.

Langly decided to test the water. "Because they are being kept here, they have no income and no way to earn an income. Both of them have student loans they cannot repay, ongoing tuition, books, and fees."

"Valid points. How does this sound? We will pay all of their expenses at Stanford while they complete their PhDs, we'll pay off their student loans, and we'll give them a salary of, say, a hundred thousand dollars a year, each, retroactive to when they arrived at JPL?"

"That's a very generous offer. I'll see what they say. There's one more issue, as long as we're discussing it. I suspect you will not let them take a job somewhere else after they graduate. What's going to happen in two years, when they have their PhDs?"

"I think I can guarantee a job in their fields."

"With what salary?"

"What do you think is fair? You got sixty thousand when you started at JPL twenty years ago and you graduated from MIT, summa cum laude. How does two hundred thousand a year sound?"

"I didn't invent the most important technology since the wheel, before I left graduate school. I'd be willing to bet almost any technology company in the world would offer them a million dollars a year to work for them. Maybe we should put them up for auction." Dr. Langly smiled like the Cheshire Cat. "What *would* the US government give as an opening bid?"

Dr. Lowell's face screwed up like he had swallowed something spoiled. "I could probably get them a salary of half a million, assuming they would cooperate with press conferences and get back to work at JPL. Let me ask."

The Beginning of the End

"Plus guaranteed annual raises at twice the rate of inflation? We *are* talking about this salary for *each* of them, correct?"

Dr. Lowell sighed and then nodded. Maybe a half a million dollars would be enough to stop the sabotage that he was sure one of the students were doing in his production plant.

"Can they be submitted for the Nobel?"

The director cleared his throat and sat up straight. "You aren't *submitted* for the Nobel—you know that. The Nobel Committee decides who's in the running. There is also the complication that no one can duplicate their research since they can't publish their findings."

"You mean beyond the US and nineteen other governments?"

"None of them are going to admit to having Rosy."

Dr. Langly raised his eyebrows and they stared at each other. Both knew what a political sham the Nobel nomination process was.

"I would think it's a good bet they will be in the running. Besides, having a Nobel would make it a lot easier to justify their salaries."

"When will you know about the offer?"

"Wait outside my office. I'll have an answer in a few minutes."

"I'll need it in writing."

Chapter 43 – Peace Be With You

July 6

"Dr. Farajidana, how are the projects progressing?"

Dr. Farajidana had rarely spoken in person to Ayatollah Masoud Khamenei, supreme leader of Iran, and he was nervous. The meeting took place at the Ministry of Science, Research, and Technology in Tehran; the ayatollah attended electronically from an undisclosed location. "The Rosy Transmitter has proven more successful than we had hoped. We believe we can jam the Americans' transmitters and ours will be unblockable."

"When will it be capable of sending a one-ton payload?"

He checked his notes and took a drink of water—more to assuage his nerves than moisten his dry throat. "We expect the delivery system to be functional by the end of next week."

"Have you been able to determine the aiming coordinates of the targets on your list?"

"We have, Supreme Leader." This was an area in which he was much more comfortable. "Our agents around the world have aided us in identifying and locking coordinates for each of the targets on the list I was given. The mobile transmitter Dr. Dehpour created has helped with this task immensely. Our targeting transmitter is able to lock onto the mobile transmitter when the mobile is at the target. Once we save those settings, we can send anything we want, whenever we want, to those coordinates."

There was a pause. "Have you made any progress in discovering the cause or cure of the infertility that has disrupted the families of so many of Iran's young people?"

"We have identified the virus that caused the infertility, but we have not discovered how it accomplished the infertility of humans and why no other species are involved. We have never seen a virus like this. For one thing, it is huge—ten times larger than HIV. It has a full set of human DNA but doesn't use it for any internal function. This is the first virus we have ever seen which even *has* DNA—all other viruses, including this one, have RNA which modifies the DNA of the host. We have analyzed the human DNA inside and determined it to be Asian."

The ayatollah had expected the long, corrupt arm of the United States to be the cause of the plague. That the DNA was Asian was unsettling. "Do you foresee the possibility of a cure in the future?"

"God, in his wisdom and beauty, may show it to us, but until he does, we will continue to search for a cure. Dr. Sarboulaki is leading our efforts. He has attended the international caucus, which is acting as a clearing house for everyone's discoveries."

"Please announce your identification of the virus that has caused this plague. I would like the world to know that Iran has accomplished what the United States, with all its trillions of dollars, could not."

"It will be so, Supreme Leader."

"And be sure to tell Dr. Sarboulaki I appreciate his dedication."

"I will be proud to do that. Peace be with you, Supreme Leader."

"And with you, Dr. Farajidana."

... ...

Lily was adamant. "There's no deal unless all charges against Doug are dropped—and, if we are nominated for the Nobel, he has to share it with us."

"Lily, this offer is a dream come true," Kevin pointed out. "Do you have any idea what the job market is now? They are going to pay for the rest of our PhDs, pay off our student loans, and give us a job our peers only daydream about. Plus, we would be the youngest recipients of the Nobel ever. Einstein was forty-two when he got his."

"I understand exactly what the offer is; so do you. They are paying us off to get out of the spotlight. Are you telling me you'd even consider doing this without having Doug forgiven? Without him we would still be back in the lab playing with magnets. Without his computer-controlled mirror, Rosy is just a cute parlor trick, and without Doug siccing the ACLU on them to turn up the heat, this offer would never have happened. And you would work on the continued weaponizing of Rosy?"

He sighed, watching the Nobel and the fame associated with it slip away. "Yeah, you're right. I was being greedy. That's one of the things I love about you: you call me on my shit. They'll never go for it—they want to hang Doug out to dry. And did you hear about how someone has been sabotaging the production plant? Many of the transmitters that are going to be used to launch bombs have had little things done to them that made them nonfunctional."

A cold hand grabbed hear heart. "No I haven't heard about any sabotage."

"They are putting in new cameras to see if they can catch the person. Do you really think they will let Doug go?"

Lily pursed her lips, realizing she would have to be much more careful when she "altered" the transmitters. "What choice do they have? Between how they've treated us and with no cure found for the infertility, this could easily cost President Klavel his reelection. It could also shift the balance of power between the republicans and democrats in Congress. He isn't going to let that happen."

She opened the door to let Dr. Langly back in. At Kevin's request, he had been waiting outside while the two considered Dr. Lowell's proposal.

"The only way we will accept the deal is to have all charges against Doug dropped," Kevin said. "And Doug has to share the Nobel with us."

His father was shocked they would turn down the offer of a lifetime to save their friend, but his shock slowly morphed into pride. He was not sure he would have had the same moral strength if he'd been faced with the same decision. He chuckled, imagining the conversation the director would have with his superiors. "I'll tell him."

"And I want a house," Lily added.

It was Kevin's turn to be surprised—they hadn't talked about a house at all. She tried to ignore his reaction. "I'm not going to raise my baby in an 'executive suite.' I'll pay to build the house, but I want one."

……………………………

"Dr. Clive didn't show up again," Dr. Lowell's secretary announced during their daily planning session. "This makes two days in a row."

"Did you call his house? Maybe his wife had a relapse."

"Yes. I left another voicemail, and I called his cell phone. It rolled over right away, like it was off, dead, or in a dead zone."

"Send Security over to his house to knock on his door. There has to be a good reason why he's absent. He's never missed a day before yesterday."

"Dr. Langly is waiting outside to see you."

"I'll bet he is." Dr. Lowell smugly expecting the students falling all over themselves as they accepted his offer. He prepared himself mentally to be their kindly benefactor.

……………………………

"They didn't accept the offer?" Dr. Lowell did not believe what he had heard. "They want to negotiate the most incredible contract that's ever been made in the history of physics for *better terms*?"

"Well ... yes," Dr. Langly said, enjoying the director's discomfiture far too much. "They want all charges against Doug dropped and for him to share the Nobel, and Lily wants a house."

"A house? A frigging house? There aren't any houses on JPL."

Kevin's father knew he had won; the director had never uttered anything close to a curse word before. "Well, she did say she would pay for it. Something about, 'If you're going to keep me here, I want a house for my baby.'"

Dr. Lowell struggled to contain his anger. Those kids must not have understood the offer—what they had just rejected. They would turn down a Nobel Prize in Physics because they couldn't have a *house*? He took a deep breath and then another.

The house was not actually a big deal—the new facility being prepared in Nevada had houses for everyone and it would be ready in six weeks. Dropping all charges against Doug, however, would be a tough sell. President Klavel himself had approved the terms of the offer; any changes would have to go back to him.

"I'll ask."

... ...

"He's gone," JPL's head of security told Dr. Lowell. "A window was broken in the back of the house. His wife's gone, too. Blood with her blood type was all over the bed, along with cut ropes at all four corners. The majority of blood was where her head would have been, and there was dried semen in the middle of the bed."

"You don't think this might have been a rough sex session that got out of hand?" he asked hopefully.

"If you're asking my opinion, I'd say no. We didn't find any toys or cameras. Those always accompany a voluntary rough sex session. If it was just a rapist, he wouldn't have taken the bodies when he was done. No, I'd say, given that Dr. Clive was one of the architects of the Rosy launch mechanism, that he was snatched and they took his wife to give themselves some leverage, in case he got reluctant to share later. I imagine her beating and rape was to make sure he was paying attention—at least that's what I would have done."

Dr. Lowell stared at the man, wondering why he was forced to associate with such people. The whole world knew what was going on at JPL, thanks to Douglas Medder and his interview at Berkeley. After that interview, of course someone would kidnap one of his scientists. One of the bully countries of the world had taken matters into their own hands and grabbed a scientist who could build Rosy.

"Do you have any idea who snatched him?"

"NSA is checking all the people who boarded commercial flights out of L.A. since Dr. Clive came up missing. I'd be willing to bet they didn't leave that way, though—too many footprints. The same thing is true with chartered flights. I suspect Dr. Clive and his wife are on a freighter that left the Port of LA one or two days ago, so I got a list from the harbormaster. If I had to guess, I'd put money on the *Da Nang*, a freighter of Vietnamese registry supposedly on its way back to Vietnam for another load of sweatshop clothes. Someone turned off the ship's AIS transmitter, which shows where it's located, about the time it reached international waters two days ago. The *Da Nang* will probably appear in Haiphong Harbor in a week, unless it changed course after it switched off its AIS."

... ...

"Can't we stop the bastards and search the ship?" President Klavel screamed. The image of the ship from a satellite was on the screen in the briefing room. It was clearly on a course for northeast Asia, maybe Russia, Japan, or the Korean peninsula. "Send in the Seals like we did with that other guy, Captain ..." He snapped his fingers a couple of times trying to remember the guy's name.

"Phillips," his secretary finished.

"Yeah, Captain Phillips."

"What if they aren't on the ship?" his secretary of defense asked. "We risk getting charged with piracy—the Vietnamese will say we're no different from the Somalis, and they won't be found, you know. If we even show up on the horizon, Dr. Clive and his wife will be dead and gone without a trace, feeding the fishes three miles down."

"I just know it's going to North Korea. This is how those bastards operate. See if we can move an asset to the Port of Nampo to observe the ship's arrival."

"It's a little early to begin shuffling assets around the DPRK. We don't *know* the destination. All we do know is the ship is heading toward northeast Asia.

"Can we send a Rosy bomb into it?"

"Not without the whole world knowing we did it."

"Are any of the AAS set up yet?"

Someone at the CIA had dreamt up the Alternative Attack Sites with the idea of exploiting the Rosy tracking system instead of fighting it. They had smuggled into Iran and Chechnya an unmanned, remote-controlled Rosy launch vehicle which could send bombs anywhere in the world when it received an encrypted radio message from the US telling it where to target. Any retaliatory return fire would also damage the launch area instead of the United States.

Each device was equipped with several different types of ordinance along with loading and aiming capabilities that could send one of those bombs anywhere in the world within ten seconds of being remotely activated. As soon as the launch was complete, the device would detonate the rest of the explosives. Until then, it appeared to be a parked trailer in a storage lot with nothing inside that could be traced back to the US—no English manuals, no corporate logos, nothing. They had not been used yet outside of technical testing at the range in Nevada, but fifty others were under construction.

"The AAS in Chechnya is functional. Do you want to use it? If we get caught, it would be considered an act of war. We don't even know if they are on that ship."

"You said you intercepted several encrypted transmissions from the ship."

"That's true, but that in itself is not illegal or even unusual—Vietnam continues to have a certain level of distrust for the good old United States. The *Da Nang* could have received orders to stop for a load of goods at Japan or Russia on the way back to Vietnam. The NSA is trying to decrypt the messages, but they said it could be another day."

"Then we wait," President Klavel said in frustration. "While we're waiting, I want everyone who knows how to build a Rosy Transmitter moved to Nevada—JPL, FBI, CIA, DOD—everybody! All Rosy research will be conducted from the Nevada site, where we can keep it under lock and key. Do it now, before someone else gets snatched."

"Nevada isn't ready yet—it won't be finished for another six weeks."

The Beginning of the End
"Move them, anyway. We can't afford for anyone else to disappear. If we need FEMA trailers for everyone to live in until the construction is done, set it up."

Chapter 44 – Better Than Sex

July 7

The desk sergeant held the poorly-drawn picture that could have been something out of *Creature from the Black Lagoon.*

"I told you it wadn't no damn fish!"

"Mr. Carver, have you had anything to drink today?"

Buddy Carver had been fishing in the South San Francisco Bay most of this life. His father had taught him how—he could identify every fish that lived in the bay. He knew the difference between a fish and a goddamned sea monster, and he'd seen a sea monster. "No. I ain't been drinking!" he said loudly, which was not entirely true. He had not been drinking in the past hour. When he'd seen the head of the monster he had pulled up in his net, he'd gone from passingly drunk to stone-cold sober in about two seconds. He had thrown the net into the bay and almost capsized the boat getting the motor started.

The desk sergeant peered around him at the next two people waiting patiently behind this drunk fisherman. "Mr. Carver, I've taken your report. There's nothing we can do at this time. I'll let Fish and Wildlife know about your sighting and show them your picture. Maybe you should go home and get some rest." The desk sergeant's voice got louder, "Or maybe I'll find you a comfy bed in the back of the station." and louder still with a red face. "Or maybe I need to perform a breathalyzer test on your ass and cite you for piloting a water vehicle while under the influence."

Buddy grabbed his driver's license and stalked out of the station.

... ...

Byteen crawled up through the portal they used to access the bay from Fey Pey's ship. There was no Rosy glow here—just a pressurized room with a hole in the floor that opened into the San

Francisco Bay fifty feet below the surface. He pulled up the sole and juvenile sturgeon he had stolen from the fisherman's net behind him.

"How was the hunting?" Uta asked. It was her turn to guard the portal.

"Better than sitting in here."

"I know that's right. Which one are you going to give to the captain?"

"This one." He held out the sole and snickered, whispering, "A fish for a fish."

Uta laughed out loud, realized she did it, and looked around in panic. No one made jokes about Captain Pey being a fish unless they were very, very careful. He was an air-breathing, aquatic mammal, and calling him a fish could get you gutted and fried.

Byteen decided he had said too much. If Captain Pey found out a native had seen him, no one would be allowed to hunt anymore. He would have to be more careful of the fishermen's nets. He shivered again at how ugly the natives were here.

Uta suspected the source of his anxiety. "You don't have to worry about the captain. He went out for a swim."

"He does that every night, doesn't he?"

"Yeah. I think so. At least, he does it every time I'm on watch."

"I wonder where he goes."

"Maybe he has a girlfriend? Maybe he found another aquatic mammal he can 'play' with."

Byteen hefted the sturgeon; it was twenty kilos at least. "I'll save you some fish. Stop by when you finish your shift."

"Thanks, Byteen." She gave him a seductive smile. "See you then."

Maybe Uta would want some dessert after a dinner like this. He could probably find another movie with lots of natives being mashed.

... ...

Captain Pey waited at the rendezvous point. The idiots were late again. A motorboat approached him at high speed, and he took a breath of air and swam out of the path. It felt good to swim again. He leaped out of the water and twisted around in midair, doing a full airborne flip.

"Look, Mommy!" a twelve-year-old girl in the boat called out. "A dolphin!"

Her mother saw the first jump. "I've never seen that species before." She took a picture of his second and third jump out of the water with her cell phone camera. "I'll check it out when we get home."

... ...

President Klavel's National Security Council was in session in the East Wing of the White House. The head of the NSA was giving a briefing about the decrypted transmissions from the *Da Nang*. "One of the transmissions was a schematic of how to build a Rosy Transmitter. Dr. Clive is or certainly was on board."

The director of intelligence operations of the CIA spoke up. "They won't kill him until they make the transmitter work."

"Is the schematic functional? Would it work?" the president asked.

"Yes. My people tell me it should," the DIO replied.

"What else can he tell them?"

"Well, the schematic he gave them is pretty primitive compared to what we have now. They still need to invent a magnetic mirror and the software to aim it."

"Did Dr. Clive know how to do that?"

"Maybe," Dr. Lowell said over the secure phone line connected to the speaker on the table. "I've checked with the rest of my staff on what he knew. He worked on the transmitter team. That he gave them such a primitive design is a clear statement he was supplying this information under duress. Everyone works pretty closely together here—I'm sure he knew enough about the mirror to guide them through making a first attempt."

"There have been no other encrypted transmissions from the *Da Nang*," the head of the NSA said.

"Blow it up," the president said. "The sooner the better."

The Beginning of the End

"Yes, sir." The secretary of defense rose from his chair. "It will take about fifteen minutes."

Twelve minutes later a faint rose-colored beam, about two feet in diameter, pointed down into the ground from a trailer parking lot outside Grozny, Chechnya. One minute later, a massive explosion ripped apart the storage area, killing three workers and injuring a dozen more.

All over the world, Rosy Detectors began screaming about a large portal transmission between Chechnya and the middle of the Pacific Ocean. No one knew what, if anything, had gone through the portal except for three countries: the United States, North Korean, and Vietnam. The Americans knew because they'd caused it; the Vietnamese and North Koreans knew because only one country in the world had a reason to blow up the *Da Nang*. The cargo ship sank within seconds, taking everyone on board to a wet, cold grave.

President Klavel was ecstatic. He watched the ship sink via a live satellite feed with an excitement that was almost sexual. The AAS worked! The thousand-pound bomb had appeared about a mile over the *Da Nang*. The smart technology inside had oriented on the ship and then flown the bomb down the exhaust stacks like a cruise missile. It exploded *inside* the *Da Nang*'s engine room, splitting the boat open from bow to stern like an M-80 inside a shoebox.

Chapter 45 – Rosyville

July 8

In 1950, President Truman established the 680-square-mile Nevada Test Site for the testing of small capacity nuclear weapons, up to one megaton. It was located about seventy-five miles northwest of Las Vegas, within the bounds of the Nellis Air Force Gunnery and Bombing Range, which was the size of Connecticut. The test site was divided into thirty sections called areas, and most of the nuclear blasts were in the north and east areas of the test site. In 1962, President Kennedy received a telegram from Linus Pauling, one of the famous scientists of the day, about the immorality of duplicating Russia's nuclear testing. President Kennedy agreed and cancelled all above-ground nuclear detonations within the continental United States. The Nevada Test Site was renamed the Nevada National Security Site (NNSS) by President Obama in 2010.

… … … … … … … … …

On April 1, the government broke ground on a secure town for Rosy research at the Nevada National Security Site; they called it SH-29, which stood for Safe Habitat in Area 29. The US had done no nuclear testing in Area 29 because it adjoined US Highway 95 and would have been a security nightmare. It was upwind from the areas where the blasts had occurred and divided from them by a mountain range. For those reasons, it was one of the few areas at NNSS that contained no residual radiation.

The NNSS was already fortified and guarded, with a secure perimeter. SH-29 was supposed to be ready for habitation on September 1. With competing construction schedules and delays in building-supply delivery, however, the occupancy date had slid to September 15. President Klavel's order on July 6 to move everyone to SH-29 had caught the contractors by surprise, and it became a

The Beginning of the End

madhouse of trucks, people, and construction equipment, trying to finish the development amid the tenants trying to settle in. The mailing address was a post office box in Las Vegas, but everyone who lived there began calling the town Rosyville.

... ...

Lily walked around the inside of her new home. While it was not a mansion in Beverly Hills, it was a house with a yard. Well, the "yard" was still dirt with big ditches where the contractors had laid electrical lines and plumbing, but it would have grass and bushes someday. The water worked, the air conditioning worked, and the lights turned on and off. The carpet would be installed next week, along with the kitchen. All the stuff from their dorm rooms was stacked in one of the bedrooms, and Kevin's old Toyota sat in the driveway with a dead battery, a not-too-unusual circumstance for his car. A refrigerator was their only appliance. The cooktop was a two-burner propane camping stove on a card table in the garage.

She decided a walk would be a good idea, wanting to check out the shopping center that was supposed to be here. Her baby bulge was becoming more noticeable, and the only clothes that still fit were her jogging suits. She filled a bottle with some water, put it in her backpack, and slipped on her shoes by the front door.

A workman at the corner was putting up a street sign. "Hydrogen Drive" was painted on it. As she walked toward the shopping mall, she noticed the street names were arranged alphabetically after the elements; the cross streets were named after famous scientists. Argon Drive and Einstein Street was where the shopping mall, school, gas station, and auto repair shop were located. On the other side of Argon Drive, huge beige buildings were in the final stages of fabrication, marking where the industrial area began. Those streets were named after famous soldiers, seamen, and airmen with the cross streets named after astronauts.

Lots of vehicle traffic filled the roads—over five hundred families had moved into Rosyville. Excluding the construction workers, the average education of the residents was the highest in the United States at 7.3 years of college.

The "shopping mall" turned out to be a Post Exchange run by the Army, and until the exchange was ready, a temporary grocery store had been set up with ten tractor-trailers.

"Do you have any fresh oranges?" Lily asked the clerk, amazed someone so young had the security clearance to work at a facility like this. He couldn't be more than eighteen.

"Nope—no fresh anything, except dairy—milk, eggs, and such. The produce won't show up until the grocery section of the PX is ready for it. Got some canned oranges and frozen orange juice. If something is frozen or canned, there's a good chance we got it." The clerk looked left and right and then whispered covertly, "I got some double chocolate Häagen-Dazs bars I smuggled in—five bucks apiece."

She smiled. At another time of her life, she would have bought the whole box. Now, even the thought of ice cream turned her stomach.

"Thanks for the offer, but I can't eat ice cream." She patted her belly. "Frozen orange juice sounds good, though. Do you have two frozen steaks, some barbeque sauce, a couple of cans of green beans, and a box of rice?"

"Basmati or jasmine?"

"Basmati."

"Sure. I'll be right back."

While she was waiting, she watched the crews building the PX across the street.

"Here you go, Ms. Yuan."

Lily studied the young man's face. "Do I know you?"

He blushed. "No, ma'am—I recognized your face from the news feeds on TV. But even if I hadn't, the chip in your ID identified you to the computer. Would you sign here please?"

"Sure." She signed the signature panel. No one used money in Rosyville—all charges were deducted from their payroll.

"How's your baby doing?" he asked, handing her the receipt.

"My baby is fine so far. Do you have children?"

"Nope. My girlfriend and I were so worried about getting pregnant we hardly ever did it. Now that we can't have babies, it's like we're making up for lost time. I can't wait to get off work."

The Beginning of the End

She glanced at his ID badge. "Matt, I'm glad someone got some good out of this. You wouldn't have any clothes in those trailers, would you? This jogging suit is about the only thing I have that still fits."

"Nope—not 'til the main PX opens next month."

"Well, then thanks for the groceries. Bye." She turned away.

"Uh, Ms. Yuan?"

She turned back. "Yes, Matt?"

"I could get something for you in Las Vegas. I mean that's where I live. I could bring it back tomorrow."

She smiled her biggest smile. "That would be *wonderful*! You won't get into trouble for bringing them in, will you?"

"Nah, they don't care about clothes. Now explosives, weapons, or drugs—they would be a different story."

"A couple of jogging suits, then—size 12, I think. Something with an elastic waist band." She rolled her eyes. "If I get too big for that, just shoot me."

"I'll see what I can find. Price guidelines?"

"Nope. I'll pay you for what you find."

"See you tomorrow."

"Thanks, Matt!"

The frozen steaks in her backpack were cold against her; they felt good in the Nevada noonday sun. She drank some water from her bottle and walked over to where construction of the school was in progress. It would be complete for the beginning of the school year in September and was made up of fifteen portable buildings—one building for each grade, plus one for admin, one for kindergarten, and one for daycare—arranged in a long rectangle with a central covered sidewalk connecting them. At the far end of the rectangle, a concrete slab had steel girders bolted to it that extended into the air at least fifty feet, looking like a huge red skeleton. A monstrous crane was setting the roof beams in place. It was supposed to become a gymnasium with a basketball court. At the other end of the school campus, a gaping hole in the ground would be an indoor swimming pool someday.

Chapter 46 – Northbound

July 9

The lights of Coeur d'Alene, Idaho, appeared in the distance as the rusty, blue-green Chevy pickup crested the hill and descended toward the lake. Doug had been traveling for five days, avoiding the police, keeping a low profile, and following the travel plan he created before he'd left. The exit ramp for US 95 was approaching quickly.

"This is where I get off," he told Clarence, the old man who had picked him up in Spokane.

Clarence spit into the cup in his right hand and slipped it into the plastic cup holder stuck into the vent in the dashboard. He pulled the old pickup onto the exit ramp, downshifted, and stopped at the light at the bottom. The man held out his hand to Doug. "I don't get the chance to be God's helper much these days. My wife says it's too dangerous to pick up hitchhikers, but I'm glad I did this time. Good luck, young man. I hope Betsy's there."

Doug shook the man's hand firmly. He had told the old farmer all about Clara—he'd changed her name to be careful—and how she would be waiting for him, how they were going to be married and share their lives together. "Time will tell, Clarence. Thanks for the ride. I appreciate it."

"God be with you, Jimmy."

Doug jumped out and retrieved his backpack from the bed. The light turned green, and Clarence waved, put the truck in gear, pulled across the intersection, and back into the sparse traffic on I-90. Doug ran across US 95 to the shoulder on the northbound lane and started walking north. According to his travel plan, a bus stop was supposed to be next to the highway by a shopping mall about half a mile up the road.

When he got there, the schedule posted in the shelter listed the next bus to Garwood, the end of the northern route, was due in twenty-five minutes. He sat down to wait. The chances of a

The Beginning of the End

hitchhiker getting a ride in town were pretty slim and there were more police; it was better to take the bus to the outskirts and try hitching from there. Maybe he would get lucky and a trucker pulling a load of produce to Canada would pick him up. After sneaking across the border, he would be just a day's walk away.

... ...

The hamlet of Yahk, British Columbia, was not what you would call a bustling metropolis. Clara's cabin was easy to find—cross the river, turn right, take the second street on the right and then first left, and go to the end. Doug approached it cautiously.

The light was on in the living room. A small stream burbled behind the cabin and a horse blew in the barn beside it. His heart did a flip-flop when Clara walked past a window and went into the back, where he assumed the kitchen was. The smell of dinner cooking made his stomach growl. No car was in sight. He walked silently around the cabin twice but found nothing suspicious, so he moved fifty feet back into the woods and waited.

Clara had described this homestead to him so many times that it felt familiar and comfortable, like an old sweater. Her mother's parents had been Canadians, and they'd spent their whole married life together here. Her grandfather had built the cabin and barn when he was a young man, right after they got married, and she'd visited them for whole summers during her childhood.

When her grandmother died, she'd left the property to Clara. Her husband, however, had wanted nothing to do with it—he'd liked the bright lights of a big city. To Doug, this sounded like the place he had always wanted and never found. Who could want more than this—and why? He shook his head, wondering if her husband had found city life and happiness on the other side. One man's Heaven was another man's Hell.

After two hours of uneventful watching, he finally approached the house. Clara answered his knock. "Doug?"

While he had walked and hitchhiked all those miles, he'd wondered how she would greet him, *if* she would greet him—if she would even *be* there. Sitting by the side of the road, hot, dusty, and thirsty, he had replayed his memories of her face, auburn hair, green eyes, and alto voice—how she only came up to his chin when he hugged her. Now here she was, standing in front of him, and all of his carefully rehearsed sentences went out the window. He got lost in her eyes—the eyes that had accompanied him in his mind during his long journey to Canada, evading the police and the FBI. He said the words that filled his heart. "Clara, I love you."

She pulled him into her arms and kissed him He was shocked. This kiss was completely different from the ones they had shared in Palo Alto. This was not a peck on the cheek or kiss of affection—it was a kiss from lover to lover. It was a kiss to remember on a lonely night—one that would make almost any sacrifice worth making. All his waiting, walking, and wondering were suddenly irrelevant. He kissed her back.

… … … … … … … …

"How long have you been here?" he asked later that night as they lay in bed.

"I arrived today. In the phone call, you told me to come like we always said we would. You've told me over and over that, the first time you came up here, you wanted to come on horseback—you wanted to ride the same trails as I had as a kid. I left my truck at the horse trailer parking area at the state park on the US side of the border. From there, it was an easy one-day ride to Yahk. Sophie loved getting out of the trailer after that pull from home, and those trails were so familiar to me, I could have ridden here in my sleep."

"No one followed you?"

"I don't know. I don't think so. As I crested the first hill, about a mile away, I turned around to look back at the parking lot. A black Suburban pulled up next to my truck. It sat there for a few minutes and then the passenger got out and studied the hills with binoculars. The driver pulled a radio-dish thingy from the back seat and pointed it around at the hills. He stopped when it was aimed at me where I was hiding in the trees."

"They planted a bug in your tack," Doug said tensely. "Is it out in the barn?"

"Yes!" The fear in her voice was palpable.

The Beginning of the End

He got a flashlight and walked out to the barn. After going through every bit of tack Clara had brought with them, he found the bug in Sophie's breast plate between the pad and leather. It was the size of a dime. He turned it over in his hand.

"They must have put it there when I stopped to eat at that truck stop. Sophie was going crazy when I came back out—I gave her some oats to calm her down."

"They'll be here soon, following it." Doug pondered what to do, perplexed. The bug had been at Clara's cabin for at least twelve hours. The only reason the Feds hadn't shown up was this was Canada and they needed to obey agreed-upon international protocols, but they must know where Clara stopped. Within another twelve hours, they would show up here. A idea occurred to him and he laughed—if they wanted to follow the bug, he'd let them—and buy them an escape window at the same time. "Do you have some duct tape?"

"I don't know. Let me check." She returned in a couple of minutes with a roll that was mostly used.

"Wait here. This won't take long."

He walked the short distance to the general store in the center of Yahk, where a gasoline tanker was filling the station's tanks. The driver stood nearby, monitoring the filling operation. Another truck was parked behind the store with the refrigeration unit on the trailer running. The lettering on the truck said "Everest Trucking, Toronto, Canada. We deliver anywhere." A picture of a tractor-trailer climbing Mt Everest was painted on the side. Doug taped the bug to the rear bumper of the trailer and smeared the tape with dirt. As he walked back to the cabin, the truck passed him, heading east on Route 3.

Chapter 47 – Marry Me

July 10

The next morning, Clara slid some fried eggs onto the plate in front of him; he was already munching on the bacon and toast. "You haven't told me how you got here—why the FBI arrested you three." Doug didn't say anything. He was watching the morning sun reflecting off the stream next to the cabin as the water flowed over and around the rocks. She thought maybe he didn't hear her, so she reached and touched his arm. "Doug?"

"It began almost seven months ago," he said quietly. "You remember that long weekend between New Year's Day and when winter quarter started—when Lily, Kevin, and I spent all four days working in the physics lab instead of us going up to Bodega Bay, like you and I had planned?"

"I *do* remember that weekend. I was so mad at you."

"Well, that was when we opened our first wormhole."

Clara had read enough about Doug, Lily, and Kevin to know what a wormhole was. He told her the whole story—even the part about the aliens kidnapping them and what the octopus captain had said. He told her about being arrested by the FBI and being held incommunicado at JPL, about being lonely and missing her, about his escape and finding the antigovernment underground at Sunshine Ranch, and about meeting the scientists at UC Berkeley and building the Rosy Detector. "I did an interview with the student radio station at UC Berkeley. I had to tell the world about Rosy, what the US had done to our invention, and how to stop it—don't know if it worked. Maybe I'll find out someday. It took me a week after that to make my way up here."

By the time he had finished explaining, she was crying. He had no idea why.

"Doug," she said slowly, almost unable to speak, "please forgive me."

"Of course." He took her hand. "For what?"

The Beginning of the End

"For aborting our child." He didn't understand. "I was pregnant when you disappeared. I was going to tell you the Saturday they took you. I had it all planned—dinner, candles, soft music. After you were gone, I had nowhere to go—no one to turn to. I made a decision out of anger, thinking you had abandoned me—thinking you'd somehow found out I was pregnant and didn't want it." She struggled to regain enough control to continue. "I had the abortion, and then went home to my parents to try to heal spiritually. Now we can never have the child I threw away."

Doug stood and pulled her into his arms. They clung to each other for several minutes, weeping at how their lives had not turned out as either of them had hoped. He pulled away from her enough to lift her chin and look directly into her eyes. "Marry me, Clara. Marry me now—today. There may not be a tomorrow, and if I die, I want to die with you as my wife."

Chapter 48 – A Couple of Quarts Short

July 12

Paul Bettner, one of the creators of the app Words with Friends, created a free mobile app based on Doug's Rosy Detector Java code and the three pickups he'd built and installed on the roof of Zynga's data center. He added an interface which translated the coordinates of the beginning and ending portals into a country/city name, which made it much easier for people to understand where the ends of the portals actually were. His app could also browse the history database, which Zynga maintained, of previous Rosy transmissions.

When there was no Rosy traffic to report, the free version advertised Zynga's other products and offered free trial downloads. The one-dollar version had no advertising. All money generated from the sales of the app was put into an escrow account to be used for Doug's defense, if he ever went to trial. Zynga posted the apps on the stores at Apple, Amazon, and Barnes and Noble. Downloads at all three stores surpassed all previous download records with the free and paid versions about evenly split. Sales of Zynga's other apps went up by eighteen percent, and their stock value doubled on the New York Stock Exchange.

… … … … … … … … …

"Welcome to Canada," the border agent said to Clara as she pulled up to the booth. "Passport please, and I need your vehicle registration and proof of insurance." The agent was middle-aged, female, and might have been Scandinavian. She eyed Sophie in the horse trailer behind the truck. "And your horse inoculation records also, please."

Clara had ridden Sophie back to her truck via the same trails she'd taken when she'd ridden to Yahk, two days earlier. The sun was going behind the mountains to the west, and she was tired, a little sunburned, and smelled like horse. She handed the documents to the agent.

"Do you have any other pets with you, Ms. York?"

"Nope. Just Sophie, my mare."

"What is your business in Canada?"

"A vacation—sightseeing and horse riding in the Canadian Rockies."

"How long will you be staying?"

"About a month, I figure. I've always wanted to ride through the color in Banff."

The agent studied the papers then passed them back to her. "The color won't start for another month, but you should have a beautiful ride. Please pull your vehicle and trailer into the examination building—you have been selected for a random search." She indicated a large metal structure on the left side of the road.

"Yeah, right!" she muttered, rolling her eyes. "Random, my ass."

The search team was waiting for her. As they went over the truck and trailer from bumper to bumper, she got some entertainment when Sophie let loose a load of horse manure on the floor next to the trailer where they had tied her. She then spread her rear legs, lifted her tail, and added a couple of quarts of urine on top of the manure. The team took out the seats of her truck, removed the door panels, and even pulled apart the bale of hay and bag of feed that were in the tack room in the front.

As the team worked, a Mountie walked up to Clara in his spotless scarlet uniform, complete with the Smokey Bear hat and shiny black knee-high boots. "Ms. York, would you come with me, please?" They entered a small interrogation room with a mirrored wall on one side, a small metal table in the middle, and two hard wooden chairs bolted to the floor. No one else was in the room. The Mountie left.

After an hour of sitting by herself, two men in black suits and sunglasses entered. One took a seat across the table from her; the other stood with his arms crossed, leaning against the wall behind the first. They looked like the men in the Suburban from when she'd left her truck in the horse trailer parking lot.

The person sitting at the table took off his sunglasses. "Ms. York, I am Special Agent Courapo of the FBI. I'd like to ask you some questions."

"Am I under arrest?"

"No, ma'am."

"Can I leave now?"

"Well, yes, you can, but you can't go into Canada unless we approve it."

"What are your questions?"

"Where have you been for the last three days?"

"I rode into the hills. My grandparents lived near here when I was a child; I visited a number of places I went when I spent summers with them."

"Did you have any contact with a tractor-trailer from Toronto?"

"I didn't see another soul."

"Do you know where Douglas Medder is?"

"I haven't seen Doug since he disappeared from Palo Alto six months ago, when he left me pregnant. Would you happen to know where he went?"

Courapo frowned at her, and then at her papers. "You aren't pregnant now. What happened to the baby?"

"I had an abortion, Agent Courapo. I'm a single, white woman earning minimum wage as a legal secretary. When Doug didn't come back, I made a decision. If I could find the people who took Doug away from me, I would scratch their eyes out. Are we done?"

"If Doug contacts you, would you mind letting us know?"

"What did he do? Why do you want him so badly?"

"Harboring a fugitive is a felony, Ms. York. If you are found guilty, you could go to prison for the rest of your life." She stared at him without saying a word. "You may go."

The search team had finished reassembling her truck when she came back to the search area, and she loaded Sophie into the trailer. "What about the horseshit?" one of the members asked her, pointing to the mess on the floor.

The Beginning of the End

"You can give it to Agent Courapo. After that episode in the interrogation room, he must be a couple of quarts short."

Chapter 49 – Parking Tickets

July 13

The next morning, Doug and Clara drove the thirty miles to Creston, BC. That was the nearest place to get a marriage license. "Look for Canyon Road," she said. "The guy at the General Store said the Service BC storefront was on Canyon Road."

"We're *on* Canyon Road. It's the same road as Crowsnest Highway ... There it is, 1404."

She pulled the truck into a parking space across the street and hesitated before opening the door. "Doug are you sure you want to do this? You will have to give them your name, which is probably in every online database in the US and Canada."

He'd been thinking the same thing. "It makes no difference, Clara. I'm in Canada now. I can't go back to the US, so, assuming they are going to arrest me, I'll ask for asylum." He picked up her hand. "Are you having second thoughts?"

"Absolutely not! I love you. I want to be your wife."

"Then let's do this, and damn the torpedoes."

... ...

"Congratulations, you two," the clerk said. "A marriage license is a hundred dollars, Canadian. I'll need the following from both of you: your birth certificate, immigration form, and permanent resident or citizenship card. I need them so I can confirm your full legal names, birth date, and place of birth."

"Both of us are US citizens," Clara said. "Would our passports do?"

"Yep. We don't usually allow them except for people visiting Canada. What made you decide to tie the knot up here?"

Clara smiled at Doug lovingly and squeezed his hand. "When the mood strikes, you don't argue."

The Beginning of the End

"I don't have a passport or driver's license," he told the clerk. He stopped short of saying the FBI had taken his. "I lost them a couple of days ago when I lost my wallet."

"Give me your name and address—let me see what I can find."

"Douglas Medder, 1525 Front Street, Palo Alto, California."

The clerk's eyes grew wide when a pop-up told her he was on the FBI's Ten Most Wanted List. She pressed a button with her knee, calling the police. "I've got it here. You were born on August 13, 1991, in Garberville, California."

"That's me."

"And the picture on your California driver's license matches your smiling face."

A squad car rolled up to a stop outside the storefront. Two policemen got out with pistols drawn and carefully entered the door. *"Everyone freeze!"* they commanded.

"That is Douglas Medder," the clerk said to them, pointing at Doug. "He's wanted by the FBI."

"On the floor now!" the officer ordered, leveling his gun at Doug. "Hands behind your back!" Doug did as directed.

"That woman is with him," the clerk added, pointing at Clara, who lay down beside Doug without being told. She stared into his eyes as the cops zipped plastic handcuffs on both of them. Two more police cars pulled up with their blue lights flashing like mad, and one of the officers began directing the car traffic as people stopped to gawk. A small crowd gathered on the sidewalk as the police led Doug and Clara to different cars.

"Were they trying to rob the Service BC?" a woman asked one of the cops.

"No, ma'am." The cop smirked. "Unpaid parking tickets."

The woman put her head down and hurried away, reminding herself to pay that ticket she'd gotten in Vancouver last year.

Clara tried to turn around, straining against the seatbelt, to get a last glimpse of Doug before they took him away forever. He was looking back at her through the glass in the other police car. "I love you," she mouthed.

"I love you, too," he mouthed back.

Chapter 50 – Waiting

July 14

The lunar lander was able to locate the site of one of the devices transmitting wormholes from the moon in about five feet of dust near the center of Longomontanus, a crater southwest of the moon's most famous landmark, Tycho, in the southern highlands. The area around the device was recently disturbed. After excavation, the device was bigger than JPL had expected, almost exceeding the capacity of the reentry capsule. The lander required several hours before it could successfully secure the device for the trip back to Earth. It Rosied the capsule to a hundred miles above Rosyville. Reentry was non-eventful, and the capsule parachuted into the northern edge of NNSS. A marine contingent retrieved it using the Black Hawk helicopter assigned to Rosyville.

The device, a metal tube about three feet long and six inches in diameter, lay on a lab bench in one of the warehouses. It had a power supply, but no one could figure out how it worked. Every time a wormhole was opened somewhere on Earth, it created a virtual magnetic mirror that sent a signal toward the center of the galaxy. No one understood how it accomplished this. There were no external markings or even any way to disassemble it; from the outside, the tube appeared to be solid and homogeneous.

Dr. Assau assembled a team to examine the device. After a day of scratching their heads and trying every test they could think of, he decided to give Dr. Lowell an update and get some guidance.

"It's not what any of us expected."

"What's its density?" Dr. Lowell asked.

"About like solid aluminum—16,600 cubic centimeters and weighs 45.2 kilograms. We figure most of the weight is from the exterior shell."

"Have you X-rayed it?"

"Yes. We can see the outlines of components but, because of the shell, there's not enough detail to understand what they do."

The Beginning of the End

"What is the shell made of?"

"Pure gold." The director looked up in surprise. "That actually makes a lot of sense. Gold is inert. If you want to protect something for a long time, gold would be the obvious choice."

Lowell got out his cell phone and keyed some numbers into its calculator. "The price of gold is about forty-five dollars a gram. That makes the shell worth about two million dollars. What is the signal it sends through the Rosy portal?"

"Simple FM radio wave burst transmission. We don't understand what it means, but the message is very simple."

"Is the device reactive to any other radio signals?"

"None of the ones we tried. We did the whole frequency range of AM and FM. We even tried feeding back the same signal it sent—no effect."

"Did you try to connect to it with a Rosy transmission?"

"Yes. Other than the device reporting another Rosy transmission, it had no effect."

"How about an MRI or CT scan? Have you tried them yet?"

"We don't have them here—we'd have to go to a hospital in Vegas. Because of the shell, though, we don't think either will be successful."

"Go do it—and take some armed guards with you. The last thing we need is for someone to steal the first alien technology we've ever seen." After Dr. Aussau left, he dialed Kevin's office number.

"Kevin Langly here."

"Kevin, Dr. Lowell. While you were on the starship, did the octopus say anything about wormhole detectors being placed on the moon?"

There was silence on the end—long enough that Dr. Lowell wondered if the connection had been broken.

"No," the reply finally came. "Why do you ask?"

"Just wondering. Thanks."

... ...

"They want all charges dropped against Medder?" President Klavel screamed. "He embarrassed the United States! He divulged national secrets! He resisted arrest! He prevented us from using the most incredible defense technology since ... since I don't know when! How could we just drop all charges?"

"Cool off, Jim," Mitch Donner, his chief of staff, said calmly. "Don't lose your perspective. 'How?' isn't really the question. The question is: Do we want to? He's in Canada—I imagine he's already asked for political asylum. I have no doubt Canada will grant the request because we turned them down when *they* asked for Rosy technology. This has become more of a 'damage control' than a 'punishment' situation."

Mitch licked his lips and continued. "Consider this: He's become a cult hero all over the world for his resistance to Rosy being used as a weapon, and his Rosy Detection software had more downloads in one week than any game in the history of computer downloads. If you pardon him, we can come up looking like we're on his side—that we agree Rosy should be used for peaceful things—not to mention we can begin to heal relations with our friends north of the border. If you choose not to pardon him, we'll never be able to bring him to trial and Canada comes out as the good guys because they didn't back down from the big bully. I don't see anything good coming from *that!*"

"So, the slimy bastard skates? Without any repercussions?"

"This isn't about good or bad, Jim—this is about using what's happened to our advantage. If the decision was up to me, I would give all three of those Stanford kids a medal and hold them up to the younger generation of voters as role models. That age group contains your lowest ratings—getting face time with them in front of the cameras would help you get some votes."

... ...

"Mr. Medder, I am L. Samuel Higgins, the barrister assigned to represent you in court today." They were in a lawyer's conference room at the regional justice center. The room contained four chairs and a beat up table.

"I want to apply for political asylum in Canada."

The Beginning of the End

"I understand that, Mr. Medder. The problem with your application is that you are a US citizen. Canada hasn't had many people from the US ask for asylum since the bulge after President Trump's immigration policies, and we now have strict quotas on immigration. The big problem, however, is that the US has already had discussions with the Canadian government about returning you to them. The discussion is taking place at the highest levels."

"I can give you Rosy, if you give me asylum," Doug said, not believing he was saying the words.

"Rosy?"

"The Rosy Transmitter everyone is talking about. It allows anyone to send anything anywhere. Lily Yuan, Kevin Langly, and I invented it—I'm sure you've heard about Rosy and us on the news."

"I will convey your offer to the court."

"*Don't tell the court!*" Doug said loudly, panicking. "Tell the Prime Minister *in person*, no phone calls or emails. The fewer people who know about Canada having this technology, the better. If you say it over the phone or through the internet, the NSA and God knows who else will hear it, and Canada will be screwed. If you have to tell anyone, tell the Canadian Security Intelligence Service—they'll understand what this is. If the US even thinks I might give this to Canada, I'm a dead man and so is everyone else in this town."

"Let me see what I can do."

"I want Clara to be allowed to remain with me. If she has to return to the US, she will be arrested for helping me."

"I understand. I'll let you know what they say."

"There's one more thing. After I show Canada how to make and use Rosy, I want to be released to lead my life in privacy. The reason I'm here is because the US tried to keep Lily, Kevin, and me locked up illegally to prevent the technology from escaping the US. Clara has a house in Yahk, BC, her grandparents left her—we want to live there."

Mr. Higgins left the conference room, and the deputy escorted Doug back to the court waiting area. This was where all the arrestees scheduled for an appearance today waited until they their moment in court arrived. Doug's assigned time was later that afternoon. The court called the other people for their various infractions as the day progressed. The waiting area slowly emptied, but the clerk never called his name. The sun was setting over the mountains through the small window near the ceiling when the police led Doug back to the police station and put him in a cell. Another day went by with no visitors, other than a trustee who mopped his floor. Three times, he brought Doug food and then picked up the meal tray an hour later.

Chapter 51 – Let's Go

July 16

Both the MRI and CT scans showed the outline of components inside the tube, but again without enough detail; no one had any idea what they did or how they interacted with each other. At one end was an array of metal studs—iron, from what they could determine—just under the surface of the enclosure. Dr. Aussau figured the device used these studs to create the virtual magnetic mirror that aimed at the center of the galaxy without having an actual dish attached to the tube. He came up with a theoretical explanation about how the mirror might be generated by varying the magnetic energy of each stud. As fuzzy as they were, the scans still allowed them to measure the exact thickness of the tube walls.

Dr. Lowell made the decision to open the enclosure in the vacuum room because it was completely sealable. They would leave the air in the room, instead of sucking it out as they did for a satellite test. If any microbes were inside, they would be isolated from the rest of the world. They put two rigorously cleansed Rhesus monkeys into the room with the device; if the monkeys got sick, the whole room would be flooded with three different antiseptics and chlorine gas. The tube would be opened by remote control; a single hole drilled into what appeared to be a small, empty area. They would insert a flexible, nonconductive fiber-optic straw attached to a camera into the hole to examine the inside of the device.

The drilling was completed without incident. A gas flowed from the hole. One of the technicians collected a sample and took it to the mass spectrometer. The gas turned out to be argon, another inert element. Kevin's father used the remote control robot to insert the optics straw through the hole. The display showed the components that had appeared on the various scans, but the examination proved to be nonproductive; he had no room to maneuver the straw.

"Cut it open," the director ordered. "We need to find out what's inside and how it works."

The team studied the scans to find a way to cut through the enclosure with the least possible danger of damaging the components inside. An axis cut around the middle was the safest since the fewest internals would be near the saw, but it would also be relatively futile, since very little of the insides would be exposed. Even though it was the most dangerous, they selected a cut from tip to tip, down the sides of the device. It would divide the tube in half, like clam shells and expose the parts inside, hopefully without damaging them.

The cut took over an hour to make in two phases. The first cut was made down the top surface from tip to tip, and then the device was turned over with the robotic arm, and the second cut was done the same way. To minimize the chance of penetrating into the interior any more than was absolutely necessary, the technician operating the saw made six passes on each side, slowly increasing the depth for each pass. As she ended the last pass of the second cut, the two halves suddenly separated and fell against the jaws of the robotic arm. The saw operator slowly expanded the jaws until the two halves lay next to each other on the table. The team studied the interior of the device with fascination. Some small connectors that might be wires led to the studs used to form the magnetic mirror; they were still attached to the other half of the tube. The major components were exposed, but no one had any idea what they did or how they functioned. The monkeys watched with interest from their cages.

Dr. Lowell congratulated the team. "Okay, everyone. Good job. We let it sit for twenty-four hours. If the monkeys are still alive tomorrow, we'll go in to see what we can figure out."

… … … … … … … … …

A constable escorted Doug to a lawyer conference room, where Mr. Higgins was waiting for him inside. "Mr. Medder, your application for political asylum has been granted by the minister of state himself."

The Beginning of the End

"What about Clara?"

"She has also been given asylum and will be allowed to remain in Canada indefinitely."

"And we have that in writing?"

"Yes, sir—right here. However, the government wants to modify your request a little."

"What did they say?" He sighed, preparing himself for the worst.

"That you live in Calgary and work at the Canadian Aerospace Research Centre there. You will not be kept under lock and key, but both you and Clara will be required to have a locator implant installed. This is for your protection. If someone tries to kidnap either of you, the locator will alert the police as you pass through any mass transit facility or border gate without pre-notification. Your position at the research centre includes a house, a car, and a pretty wonderful salary."

"Can I finish my PhD at the University of Calgary?"

"I'm sure that can be arranged. All you have to do is sign this form. As soon as you do that, I am to put you on the helicopter flying down from Calgary as we speak. It will fly you back, where a group of scientists are eagerly awaiting your arrival."

"And Clara?"

"She was released yesterday. She went back to Yahk to feed her horse."

"The house in Calgary has to have enough land for her horse, and it needs a barn. Could the car be a truck?"

"I'm sure you'll be able to find something suitable. Canada is most grateful for your offer and plans to make your stay something you will enjoy."

"I need to go to Yahk first—I need to marry Clara. Once I'm married, everything else can happen as it will."

"Let me make a phone call."

Higgins returned in half an hour, shaking his head in amusement. Never in this lifetime did he expect to be in a top-secret negotiation between his government and a scientist on the FBI's Ten Most Wanted List. "Clara's house has no phone service—I had to convince the manager of the Yahk General Store to go get her. Clara said she will meet you in Calgary tonight. A marriage license will be issued tomorrow and the ceremony performed. The store manager will feed and care for her horse until she returns. Once you two find a place that meets your needs, she can return to Yahk to retrieve her horse."

Doug reached across the table to the paper. He had already read the document twice while the barrister was gone.

"There's one more thing you should know, Mr. Medder, before you sign that paper."

"What's that?"

"The United States has dropped all charges against you."

He stared at Higgins in disbelief. "Why would they do that?"

"I have no idea, but they have. The announcement was on the news and I also got it from Ottawa. President Klavel himself announced it at a news conference—he said the United States attorney in charge of the investigation had mishandled it and was being sacked. The president personally had to step in to correct the wrong. The three of you—you, Lily, and Kevin—have been invited to the White House to receive the Presidential Medal of Freedom."

Doug gave a single bitter laugh, signed his name to the agreement with Canada, and stood. "He can stick that medal up his ass. Let's go."

Chapter 52 – Go to Work

July 18

The monkeys were alive and well, and the lab animal caretaker retrieved them for feeding and exercise. Dr. Lowell wanted everyone to wear protective hazmat suits—not for the technicians' protection but to prevent the device from getting human contamination. Soon, the room was full of sensitive detection equipment, ready to pick up emissions of any kind. Cameras were poised to record gamma rays, X-rays, heat, magnetic fields, and light throughout the entire spectrum of visible and invisible wavelengths.

"Turn on the Rosy Transmitter," Dr. Lowell ordered. The studs created the magnetic mirror and a small rosy glow came from the component underneath them. The package at the bottom created the energy for the rest of the components. Ten seconds after the initial signal was complete, the entire package went to sleep again.

"Total energy usage was in the order of one tenth of a watt," a tech called out.

"I captured a picture of the mirror," another announced.

Everyone clustered around the display. A perfect, invisible-to-the-naked-eye magnetic mirror had appeared in midair around the end of the device like a hologram. The rest of the team began giving the statuses on their displays.

"No gamma or alpha radiation was produced."

"No X-rays were produced."

"No heat was produced."

"No visible light was produced."

"No sound was produced."

Dr. Lowell got very quiet. "I want to make this very clear: No one is to do anything to this device that will make it nonfunctional. Do not cut any connectors and do not remove any components. I want you to study it working and glean all you can. When we have exhausted all possible avenues of research on the working unit, I will decide when we initiate disassembly. Am I clear?" Everyone nodded. "Then go to work. I want to know what makes it tick. Find out how it is powered, how it creates that wonderful mirror, how it is programmed, how it detects a wormhole, and how those conductors work. We will meet daily over lunch beginning tomorrow."

Chapter 53 – Tools

July 22

"Do you, Douglas, take Clara to be your wife, to love her and care for her until death?" The aging justice of the peace had agreed to perform the ceremony when they'd brought him the marriage license. His backyard was a small outdoor chapel surrounded by rolling hills of wheat, with the snow-capped Canadian Rockies in the distance. A pair of robins hopped across the yard, searching for breakfast.

Doug smiled at Clara. "I do."

"Do you, Clara, take Douglas to be your husband, to love him and care for him until death?"

She smiled back at Doug. "I do."

"Then, by the powers granted to me by the province of Alberta, I declare you husband and wife. Congratulations!"

They kissed softly.

"I love you," he whispered into her ear.

She gave him a fierce hug. "I know. I love you, too," she whispered back.

They had found a farm for sale about ten miles from the Aerospace Centre. The property had a house, barn, garage, and fifty acres of rolling pastureland with a stream running through the middle of the pasture. Sophie was in heaven; within an hour, she had discovered the horses next door and was grazing near the fence line. The Centre had bought the farm for them along with a new, bright red Ford F250 four-wheel drive pickup.

Doug had met with the team and showed them how Rosy worked; the first meeting was serious déjà vu for him. Like the meeting with the staff at JPL, the scientists went from disbelieving to amazed to incredibly excited. They had knocked together a small transmitter and made it work. Now the team was going through their development research and construction to make it better, just like the JPL scientists had done, and didn't really need him around beyond asking a few questions. In a week, he was scheduled to begin working with the magnetic mirror team to explain the Java code that controlled the mirror and how the interface functioned.

Clara set lunch out for them on the beat-up table in the kitchen. Neither had owned any furniture, so she'd packed everything from her grandparents' house in Yahk and brought the contents to Calgary. Every time she used something that had a memory of her grandmother attached to it, she got a warm feeling inside.

She sat down at the table but couldn't sit still, got up, walked around the kitchen, sat down again, and then stood up and walked around some more. She would begin to say something, but stopped before two words were out, like she was dying to tell him whatever it was but also trying to keep it a secret. Finally she managed, "Did you talk to the University of Calgary about transferring your credits up here from Stanford?"

Doug didn't know what was going on, but he decided to play along. "Yep—I got my transcript yesterday. The physics department at U of C said 'No problem.' I get to start halfway through my second year. Their curriculum is very close to Stanford's. I was assigned an advisor—Dr. Sandy Welborn. She's pretty different from Dr. Johnson, but, get this: she knew him!"

Clara rolled her eyes. "What did she think?"

"Well, she was diplomatic. They met at a conference in Vegas and he was hitting on one hooker after another at the hotel bar. Even they were turning him down." Clara shook her head, enjoying the image of Dr. Johnson getting shot down by hookers. She had never liked him the few times she had met him—he talked to her chest.

"He finally walked over to Sandy. He offered to buy her a drink. She shook his hand and explained that she was also attending the conference. They spent the rest of the night, until the bar closed, talking about how to teach undergraduate students a love of physics. They ended up becoming friends and had corresponded ever since. She didn't know he was killed."

"Did she ask why you transferred up here from Stanford?"

"Well, kind of. I told her I got a job offer at the Centre and I was tired of being a poor student. She laughed at that."

The Beginning of the End

"Have you seen the news today?" Clara was about to burst with excitement.

"Nope. I didn't even turn on the radio in the truck." He still had no idea what was going on.

"Doug, the candidates for the Nobel Prize in Physics were announced today. Lily, Kevin, and you are up for it. There are five different groups in the running. The decision will be made in September."

"I won't accept it. Rosy has been turned into something I am ashamed of. That I gave it to Canada knowing how the United States had already perverted it will stain my soul until I die. My only hope is I can persuade them to use Rosy for peaceful things and not as a weapon."

"There's more, if you want to hear it." She reached for his hand across the table.

"More? What can be more than that?"

"For the first time since the Nobel Prizes have been awarded, one person is up for two different awards."

"Who?"

"You. You have also been nominated for the Nobel Peace Prize for your Rosy Detector. The committee agrees with you about having to control Rosy and, against all odds, you've given the world the tools to do it. And you gave it to everyone simply because the world needed it, without a thought for your own profit or well-being. They are holding you up as the poster child for scientists all over the world. They are saying, 'This is how it should be done. Science is for peace, not war.'"

"I was just one member of the team who invented it."

"They interviewed the other guys you worked with at Berkeley-it's all over the news. Drs. Livingston, Jones, and Nguyen-Tan—said they didn't have a clue how to build it when the four of you started—that it was your idea from the beginning and it was your idea to give it away for free. They whole-heartedly agreed with your nomination."

Chapter 54 – Asian DNA

July 25

The team had identified all the components in the alien lunar device. The small bundle at the base was the power supply and the connectors seemed to be room-temperature superconductors. There was no detectable loss when they transmitted energy from the power supply to the other components. The computer still baffled the team. It picked up the signal from the antenna array (the studs at the top), performed the signal analysis, and then used those same studs to create a magnetic mirror to send a record of the transmission to the center of the galaxy. The power supply generated no heat, no radiation, and no byproducts and it created energy on demand. No one could figure out how it worked.

"Pull it apart," Dr. Lowell told the group. "Do as little damage to the components as you can, and be especially careful with the power supply. If it's a battery, it's the most efficient battery I've ever seen. If it's a power generator, we have nothing even close. Send the recorded transmissions to the NSA—they may be able to decode them."

… … … … … … … … …

Lily began the twentieth week of her pregnancy. Kevin had accompanied Lily to every exam since she announced her pregnancy at the gate, and now this was the halfway point.

Dr. Simmons, the on-site doctor at Rosyville, had disqualified himself from providing OB care for her, as he hadn't received any obstetrics training since he'd left medical school forty years earlier. Dr. Lowell didn't want to hire an obstetrician for four months for one patient with the expectation of more pregnancies being almost nil. The process of finding an OB in Las Vegas with a security clearance would have taken months he didn't have, so he agreed to pay for Dr. Plumber's travel expenses plus a day of her time, so she could travel to Nevada. That meant the appointments had to be on Saturdays, since she had to fly from Burbank to Las Vegas, rent a car, drive to Rosyville, and then go back to Burbank, when she was done. Dr. Simmons allowed her to use the Rosyville medical facilities for Lily's examinations.

There was a knock on the door. Dr. Plumber walked in and put her bag on the counter. "Hi, Lily. Hi, Kevin." The marine set her portable ultrasound equipment next to her bag and left.

"Hi, Doc. Was security out here easier than it was at JPL?"

"It is what it is. Security? You'd think I was on a terrorist list from the way they examined my rental car and the ultrasound." She left out the part about the strip search, knowing Lily was not responsible. "So, how's my most famous patient today? Has the baby started moving yet?"

"I don't know. Sometimes I think I feel something, but then I'm not sure."

"Well, most women begin to feel some movement by the fifth month. It will start as a kind of flutter. If you haven't felt it yet, you should expect to feel something within a week or two. You are Rh negative and Kevin is Rh positive, so I'll need a blood sample to make sure your blood isn't fighting your baby's. Let's start with your heartbeat."

She listened to Lily's heartbeat and then the baby's. She took Lily's temperature, blood pressure, and collected urine and blood samples. "How are you feeling? Still running?"

"Yes, every morning. A group of female marines lets me run with them. I think they adopted the baby and me as a mascot. I feel great."

"Well, you are healthy. Your body is adapting to pregnancy perfectly. Let's do the ultrasound."

This was Lily's favorite part of every exam. After a moment of Dr. Plumber fiddling with the pickup, the heartbeat of the baby came through loud and clear. "Everything is normal. Your baby is healthy and growing. Do you want to know the baby's gender?"

Lily picked up Kevin's hand and nodded. He nodded, too. "Yes, we do."

"This isn't one hundred percent, but I would bet on a girl. Sometimes the penis is hidden. The next exam will be a lot more certain. Have you decided on a name yet?"

"She will be named Lan." She pronounced the vowel, like *ah*. "That is my mother's name. It means *orchid*." As she said her mother's name, she felt her very first clear flutter from the fetus growing inside her. She gasped and put her hand over her lower abdomen.

"Have you been able to contact your mother?" Lily's situation was common knowledge to most of the population of the US. The grocery store tabloids ran weekly stories about Lily and her escape from China to the US.

"Not yet. We've gotten permission from China to speak with her. I'm hoping the call will be set up by this time next week."

Dr. Plumber considered how to say what she had kept inside until now. She glanced again at the closed examination room door and then walked to the sink and turned on the water. She stepped to Lily's side, picked up her hand, and began talking very quietly. "There are many Americans who hate what our government has done to you and Kevin. Their behavior is a violation of so many things we believe in. You have done nothing wrong—you aren't terrorists or spies, and you don't support some foreign government that wants to destroy us. You two were just living the American dream—going to school, obeying the laws, and trying to better your lives."

Lily sighed. "We can't do much about the situation, but the government has agreed to hire both of us as consultants, let us finish our degrees, and give us full-time jobs after we graduate. So I guess we aren't being held against our will any longer"—she gave the doctor a big smile—"and I get preggie care from the best doc on the West Coast."

Dr. Plumber turned off the water. "That's great news! When did this all happen?"

"Dr. Lowell got it approved last week. The press release should be going out today. I had an interview with Christiane Amanpour two days ago that will air on CNN Wednesday. I wanted Julie Chen, but she was busy."

The Beginning of the End

"I'll be sure to watch it. We're done with the exam, Lily. You can get dressed. Have you thought about whether you're going to have a chip put into your child?"

"A chip?" Kevin was kind of put off. "Like vets put in a dog?"

"Yep, just like that and for the same reasons. A lot of babies are getting stolen these days. A chip is insurance that, if Lan gets abducted, you might get her back someday. I am recommending this for all my patients."

They had seen the news reports of the stolen babies. Lily looked at Kevin and then at Dr. Plumber. "I guess we need to talk before we decide."

"Let me know. I can install the chip after her birth at any visit."

"How is your practice doing?" Kevin asked while Lily got dressed. "How are you coping with the decline of pregnant women?"

"Oh, we're doing all right. Only half of my patients are actually pregnant. Believe it or not, we're still getting some new pregnancies coming in."

That got Lily's attention. "Do you mean some people weren't infected?"

"Wouldn't that be wonderful! No, these pregnancies are in vitro from previously fertilized embryos. People who harvested eggs and sperm before March 15 to create frozen embryos are deciding to get pregnant. There's a big controversy about who owns the embryos. The donors say they do and the government says they are a national resource needed in research for a cure. Everyone expects it to go to the Supreme Court."

Lily shook her head, amazed that she could still be amazed.

"As far as The Baby Center is concerned, we're slowly changing from obstetrics to gynecology and we're changing our name to The Pasadena Women's Center. A lot of the women we helped have babies enjoyed the experience and are thrilled we can now provide continuing healthcare. We've had to add staff.

"Some of the clinics aren't having such a smooth transition, though. At least five OB/GYN clinics in North Los Angeles have closed. The big change is at the medical schools—they are marketing alternative specialty education to the docs and nurses who haven't done anything but obstetrics since they graduated. All the schools have dropped OB education because almost no one choose that as a career path, and they helped the students in those programs to switch majors. Because so many OB nurses and docs are jumping ship to begin their retraining, there's a shortage of available, trained OB personnel. Some of the hospitals have quit offering OB services, turning over their OB patients to another hospital nearby. It's become quite a traffic jam at the remaining birth centers."

"Will the same thing happen to pediatricians and pediatric training?" Lily asked, wondering about getting healthcare for her baby.

"It will unless someone can find a cure for the virus that caused this. I guess you heard about the Iranians."

Kevin and Lily didn't understand.

"What did they do this time?" Kevin asked.

"The Iranians found the virus that caused the infertility. The US research industry is heartily embarrassed they found it before we did. The virus is unlike any other seen before. It's huge and has DNA—no other virus has DNA. Scientists all over the world are examining it, trying to figure out how to kill it and reverse its effects. No one knows where it came from or how it works. The DNA inside is human and Asian, but no one can figure that out, either. The rumor is that this was a biological experiment in China gone wrong."

"Asian DNA?" Lily gasped. "It had Asian DNA? Male or female?"

"I don't know. Why do you ask?"

"I can't tell you," she said, her face pale and sweaty, like she wanted to puke.

Dr. Plumber knew something was wrong, but had no idea what. "I'll try to find out if the DNA is male or female—and I'll see you again in a month." She checked her iPad. "How about August 29?" She wrote the date on one of her business cards and handed it to Kevin, since Lily was staring at the wall, not reacting to anything she said. "Beginning with your next visit, we shift to exams every two weeks." Dr. Plumber knocked on the door of the exam room, and the marine opened it and let her out. He picked up her ultrasound unit before following her.

When the door closed, Kevin awkwardly tried to take Lily into his arms while she sat on the exam table. "Just because it's Asian doesn't mean it's yours, Lily. So what if it is? You didn't volunteer to be the DNA donor to end humanity."

Lily didn't answer. She didn't even hear what Kevin said. She put her arms around her stomach and rocked back and forth, wide-eyed.

Chapter 55 – Profiles

August 1

Dr. Holland Brost, the clinic director and resident physician, stood to greet the couple entering his office. "Mr. and Mrs. Rabinowitz, welcome back to Safe Haven Fertility Clinic. What can I do for you today?"

After they had taken their seats in the plush chairs in front of Holland's magnificent cherry desk, Mr. Rabinowitz cleared his throat. "We want to use some of the fertilized embryos you collected from us and froze before the virus hit. Mrs. Rabinowitz wants to get pregnant."

"Well, that's why you saved them, wasn't it?" Brost said amicably. He turned to his computer and entered their names into a query menu. He studied the screen and then typed some more. The beginning of a frown started to pull the sides of his mouth down. "There is a problem. Your embryos aren't here, anymore."

Mrs. Rabinowitz was confused. "Well, where are they? You said they would be safe."

"The government took them," he said with resignation. "All sperm and egg banks across the country were required to submit a list of their depositors and their DNA background screening. The government decided which ones they wanted for their fertility research."

The further Brost went into his explanation, the redder Mr. Rabinowitz's face grew. An artery in his temple pulsed like mad. "Our embryos were used for research?" he bellowed. "Our children were sent to the government to be guinea pigs? How could they do that? Those were our property! Why did you let them?"

"We had no choice. Congress passed a law in June called the Future of America Act. It required our cooperation. They needed and still need eggs, sperm, and embryos for their ongoing attempts to find a cure for the virus. Every week, the embryo banks across

America receive more demands for our remaining inventory. We weren't even allowed to tell you this had happened."

"Dr. Brost, do you like this office?" Mr. Rabinowitz asked quietly.

He glanced around it. "Yes."

"Well, I'm going to own it by the time I'm through with you. I hope you have a good lawyer, because I'm a great lawyer. You'd better give them a call." Mr. Rabinowitz stood and held out his hand to his wife. "Rachel, let's go."

"The Future of America Act also relieves us of all liability. There have already been three emergency appeals to the Supreme Court, which refuses to hear them. Would you please sit down, so we can discuss alternatives?"

"What possible alternatives can you suggest?" Mrs. Rabinowitz asked, ignoring her husband's gestures to keep quiet.

"We have been able to hide a small number of fertilized embryos from the government, for the time being. Many have the same basic gene pool as yours. These are left over from successful pregnancy attempts—people who did the same as you when you stored twenty of them. They ended up not needing them all to become pregnant, and for a number of reasons, they didn't want us to kill what, to them, were their living children."

All three went silent for a minute while the implications sank in.

Finally Rachel reached up to her husband and took his hand. "Sit down, Wilson. I want to get pregnant, and your huff and puff isn't doing *anyone* any good. If we go to court, there won't be any embryos left by the time you're done." Mr. Rabinowitz sat on the edge of the chair with his teeth clamped together so tightly that the muscles in his cheeks rippled. "Where are the profiles of the donors? Do you have any from Jewish parents?"

... ...

Dr. Lowell was startled. "Are you trying to tell me that little ball at the bottom of the lunar device enclosure is a cold fusion reactor?"

"No, Sam, I'm not," Dr. Aussau said with an enigmatic smile so big that his face positively glowed. "What I've found is even better than cold fusion. I've been trying to create a cold fusion reactor my whole professional life, and now this drops into my lap. Once I figured out what it was and how it worked, I created a duplicate and made that work. This is the answer to the world's energy problem. It produces massive amounts of energy with no pollution of any kind, no radiation, no heat, no carbon—no byproducts at all. It doesn't need super-cooling or rare earth elements." He paused. "Well, the circuit does use a variant of a Rosy Transmitter, but the aura isn't focused by a magnetic mirror and the coils and those superconductor cables from inside the moon device don't require liquid nitrogen cooling."

"Tell me how you figured it out, Birne."

"I was working on the power supply in the moon device. That battery is amazing, by the way. Eventually, the battery went dead. The device had to have a way to keep the battery charged. I remembered we released some argon gas when we first opened the device up, so I bathed the power supply in argon gas—still nothing. I hadn't eaten all day, so I went out for some food. When I got to the parking lot, the kid who had been washing the windows of the building was sitting in his car with a dead battery. He asked me for a jump. When we hooked his car up to my battery it started, but the motor died after we removed his jumper cables. He said the battery had to have enough charge to excite the alternator before the alternator could produce enough energy to keep the car running.

"I threw him my keys and ran back into the lab. I created a bridge from the lab test bench to jumpstart the power supply and flooded the device with argon. The metal powders inside the power supply began a Rosy resonation. As soon as the resonation began, the power supply began producing energy and recharged the battery. The power supply wouldn't work without voltage from the battery to start the powders between the anode and cathode resonating and, even with the battery exciting the powders, the argon atmosphere had to be present before any energy was produced. Once the powders started resonating, the power supply began generating energy within a couple of milliseconds. The voltage it was producing matched the exciter voltage—18.6 volts. That recharged the battery. Without the argon, nothing worked and the battery went dead."

"And nothing is consumed by the energy generation?"

"Not that I can tell. I built a duplicate with some of those wonderful cables from the moon device. I weighed each component to a ten-thousandth of a gram. I ran a hundred-watt light bulb for eight hours. When I was done, I weighed each component again—there was no change. Once the resonance begins, the voltage it produces matches the voltage applied to the exciter circuit. From that point, if the load increases and drops the voltage, the amperage increases until the voltage matches the exciter circuit again. It's like the components are catalysts for tapping into energy from somewhere else."

"Somewhere else? And nothing gets consumed? It's not magic, Birne. Where the hell does the energy come from?"

"With the Rosy transmissions we've done so far, both ends of the portal are in this universe. I'm not sure where the energy comes from, but I'm going to hazard a guess: dark energy. I believe this power supply opens up a portal, but the other end is not in this universe, or at least not in the part we can see. I think we have found a way to tap into the dark energy that makes up seventy-two percent of the mass of the universe. This portal is like an energy spigot on an energy well that will never run dry."

He paused and licked his lips. "When I connected the bridge from the test bench, it was like connecting my car's battery to the alternator in that kid's car. An alternator won't produce energy without an initial charge of the alternator's electromagnets by the battery. The more load applied to the output, the more output amperage is produced to raise the voltage to match the exciter voltage. Turn off the exciter circuit and the generation stops. The key to controlling the output is in the regulation of the exciter circuit and the load. The first power supply I built didn't have a regulator on either end—it self-destructed."

"Is that when the fire alarms went off yesterday?"

Dr. Aussau was still a little embarrassed about the incident. "I asked the fire department to say they were doing a test of the alarm system."

Dr. Lowell commanded his heartbeat to slow down. Like most of the scientists on his staff, his heart ignored him, also. Cold fusion was the Holy Grail of physics. Everyone knew it could be done, but no one had made it work. This reactor, if that was the right word, was as far beyond cold fusion as cold fusion was beyond modern fission reactors. That the discovery was made by his team, under his control, was the plum of all plums.

"How soon do you think you could have a working model ready—one we could put into a satellite?"

Birne hadn't thought that far. "The problem is the construction of the cables. They are made from some weird silicon-based fiber. I called a friend of mine at Hexcel Corp in Delaware—we went to graduate school together and he wants me to send him one. He said he could probably make some in his lab by the end of the week. If they work, we'll need to put a contract in place with Hexcel. I'll need some help with the regulators, too. What I've created so far is pretty primitive."

"Use Dr. Caldwell, and someone needs to examine the battery while you're doing that. Who should I get?"

Birne sighed. He wanted to do that, also, but there just wasn't enough time. "Dr. Kincaid. He had a lot of experience with batteries at Tesla. He has a dual PhD in physics and chemistry."

"How about the computer?" the director asked. "Has anyone made any progress on figuring it out?"

"Not that I know of. We aren't computer scientists—we're physicists. Maybe you should ship it to Intel or AMD to see what they can make of it."

"I'll think about it. Did the NSA figure out what was in the message?"

"No. They said there wasn't enough content to crack the encryption, if the message was even encrypted. It may be just a message in a language we don't understand. The only thing that causes any change in the content is when someone opens a huge wormhole off planet, like when launching a satellite. How long a wormhole is open or if it goes between points on-planet seems to be irrelevant."

The Beginning of the End

Both of them were silent for a moment while they considered the implications of an unlimited, non-polluting, essentially free energy source: clean water everywhere, clean air, and cheap, plentiful food. Places where no one could live were suddenly viable.

Dr. Lowell broke their reverie first. "If we're done, I have some phone calls to make. And, Birne, you look like hell. Go get some sleep."

Dr. Aussau stood too quickly and reached out to his chair to regain his balance. Free energy! And his name would be associated with the discovery! Sleep did sound good, though. He realized he had just worked for two days straight.

Chapter 56 – Mom

August 8

"Mother?"

"Li Li? Is that you?"

Lily almost couldn't speak around the lump in her throat that appeared instantly when her mother's voice came through the phone. No one had called her by her birth name since she'd left China. Li Li meant *beautiful*. When she arrived on American soil, she had chosen an American name as close to her Chinese name as possible.

"Yes, Mama, it's me." Both of them paused. "Mama, I'm pregnant."

"They told me. You'll be a good mother. Do you know if your baby is a boy or girl?"

"It's a girl, Mama. Can I use your name? I want to name her Lan."

There was another pause while that sunk in. "Lan is my grandmother's name, too. You teach her to be strong like you." Lily could hear the tears in her mother's voice. It was an emotional moment for both of them.

"I will, Mama. How is Daddy?"

"I haven't seen him since the day after you left us. He may be—"

The line went dead. The operator came on. "The call was ended by China, Lily. I'm sorry." Lily didn't want to hang up because then the call would truly be over. "I recorded the conversation like you asked. I'll send the recording to your email account."

"Thank you, Lisa." She put the phone in the cradle and walked outside the admin building, kicking herself mentally. She should have known China wouldn't allow any talk about what had happened to her parents after she fled in the middle of the night.

All the questions she had meant to ask were still unasked. What should she do if Lan got sick? How would she know if Lan *was* sick? How should she handle Lan's first tooth? What if she got constipated? What should she eat to help with her milk production? When should she start her on solid foods? Should she read to her from the beginning?

The shade outside the building provided the quiet she needed. Lily leaned her back against the wall and began to cry. She had never felt so alone, even when she had left everything behind and was flying to the United States on the plane from Kathmandu.

"You look like you could use a friend." Matt took a break from washing the windows of the admin building, sat down next to her, and handed her a paper towel.

She blew her nose and tried to smile. "Hi, Matt. Thanks."

"You want to talk about it, or just listen to the wind?"

Lily was quiet for a minute. "I just talked to my mother in China. They cut the call after I asked about my father. Until a couple of months ago, I thought they were both dead."

"Wow... and I was bitchin' because I was hot." They were both silent for a while. Matt figured she needed cheering up. "Hey, at least you got to talk to her! She's not dead. That's gotta count for something!"

"Yeah." She tried to smile. "At least I know that, but I wanted my mother to be part of her childhood. I have so many questions about how to raise the baby, and now there's no one to ask." Lily started to cry again.

"I have an idea. I mean, tell me if you think I'm crazy, but you need a mom and I've got a great mom. I'm sure she would answer any questions you have about raisin' babies. She raised seven of us."

"You have six brothers and sisters?" She was amazed. China had only allowed one baby per household while she lived there.

"Yep—three of each. Two of my sisters still live at home."

"I would love to talk to her, Matt. Do you think she'd mind?"

"Nah, there's nothing she likes to talk about more than babies. Now that most of us have left home, she's complaining about the place being too quiet. My older brother is the only one who's started a family of his own, and he lives in Tahoe. Now none of the rest of us will be able to have babies. Mom would turn inside out to get some baby noises back in the house."

"Thanks, Matt." She leaned over and gave him a peck on the cheek.

He blushed and got up to continue washing the windows. "I'll ask her tonight. Come find me tomorrow and I'll let you know what she says. I'll be washing windows at the PX—it's supposed to open this weekend."

"I'll see you tomorrow. Thanks again." Lily got up and began the walk back to the research center. She hadn't had time to find Kevin when the alert came for her mother's phone call; he would want to know what happened. She still needed to finish the equations on that new mirror design she was working on, as well.

… … … … … … … …

"I know how to do it!" Doug shouted. He stepped out of the shower and walked, naked, into his study, leaving a trail of water droplets behind him on the floor. He plopped down in front of his laptop and began typing.

Clara came in while he was working and set her cup of coffee on the desk. "Know how to do what?" She began drying his back with a towel.

"How to build a reliable mass transit system!"

"Doug, mass transit systems have been running for a hundred years—every major city has one."

He laughed. "Not that type of mass transit. This one moves things, not people, from one site to another using a Rosy portal. I mean after this works, people will be next. This will change the entire transportation industry. We won't need long-haul trucks, cargo planes, freighter ships, or trains—Rosy will do all long distance transports. Local distribution will still be transported as it's done now, but once we can put local ones in place, even local deliveries will be done by Rosy portals.

"The big problem was aiming the transmission—getting the sending site lined up with the receiving site. If they're out of alignment even a little, you send the payload into the middle of a wall or ten feet in the air. All we have to do is point three lasers from the sending site to the receiving site, and the computers at both sites adjust their sending and receiving bays to align with each other. The sending site adjusts its voltage to get the exact distance, and when they line up, you send. This requires a three-dimensional laser pickup ..." Doug stopped talking, completely absorbed in the epiphany that had blossomed in the shower.

Clara thought about what Doug was designing. When people were settling North America, travel had been slow from one place to another. You either walked, rode a horse, or sat in a wagon, and a trip took days, weeks, or even years, depending on where you were going and how you were getting there. While you were traveling, you were part of what you were passing through. When the clouds rained, you got wet. When the temperature changed, you got cold or hot.

Then trains had come. They were a lot less work, a lot faster, and you could see what you were passing through instead of being part of it. When the rain pounded down, the water hit the window and you stayed dry. The train cars had heaters to keep the passengers warm.

When cars and trucks replaced horses, travel was fast, dry, and warm or cool with air conditioning, but you didn't smell the sage or see a lizard run for cover when you disturbed its nap.

After that, airplanes were invented. You looked down on what you were flying over, not knowing if the mountains and valleys were hot or cold. You could see the wake of a motorboat on Lake Mead, but you couldn't feel the wind in your face or the sun on your back.

Now, Rosy would allow people to move almost instantly from one place on Earth to another. You wouldn't see what you had passed—there was no chance to see the Canadian Rockies, the magnificent shoreline of Vietnam, the barren desolation of Cape Horn, or the multicolor mural of the Great Barrier Reef.

Clara took a sip of coffee, closed her eyes, and watched as humanity turned yet another corner on its march away from their roots.

Chapter 57 – Gliese 581d

August 19

The polls for the presidential election in November showed President Klavel near the bottom of the field. A senator from New York was leading his nearest competitor in the herd by five percent. He promised to double the spending on finding a cure for the infertility virus, return all unused embryos to the original donors, and to change the USA PATRIOT Act so US citizens could not be held without being formally charged and sent to trial. Even Klavel's stoutest supporters were distancing themselves from the president. The only person lower than him in the polls was an independent oil billionaire candidate from North Dakota who wanted to isolate the United States from the rest of the world and live without goods from anywhere else. He called his campaign the Buy American party.

President Klavel called the head of the CDC. "Sridhar, what can you tell me? I need a breakthrough."

"No closer to finding a cure for this virus are we today than a month ago." Dr. Hehsa cleared his throat, realizing he was speaking in Hinglish: Hindi phrasing with English words. He did this when he was nervous. He began again. "We know what isn't working in the reproductive process. We know when it was changed, but we have no idea why it isn't working now. When we try to change the chemistry back, the gamete dies. The virus was the delivery system; the DNA inside the virus is simply a blueprint for identifying which species to infect. As far as we can tell, the DNA in the virus is not involved in altering the fertilization at all. We have inserted the DNA of a frog into the virus and had the same infertilization result in the frogs. The virus, apparently, can break the conception process of any selected species. We have used this technique to create infected lab animals on which we can test possible cures. This, however, has not yet yielded any hopeful research to reverse the infection of humanity. One possible benefit of this may be to use this virus to eliminate the mosquito that carries malaria."

This was not what the president wanted to hear. He tried to hide his disappointment. "Okay, Sridhar. Keep trying. Is there anything you need? More people? More money? Anything at all?"

After living with budget cuts and austerity for most of his career at the CDC, Sridhar was still unused to having a blank check. "The problem isn't money or people—the problem is learning how to undo a change to a system we never fully understood. We know how it used to work but not what made the chemicals interact like they did. It's like the difference between knowing how to drive a car and knowing how to make one. We were never able to duplicate the process on models of our own."

... ...

"Why can't we start building it now?" Dr. Lowell asked Dick Goldblum, President Klavel's National Security Advisor, through the secure-voice Rosy device that had been delivered last week.

"You can and you should, Sam. You have a budget of fifty million dollars."

"Fifty million dollars to send robotic satellites to ten different solar systems?" The director was appalled. "We couldn't launch a resupply rocket to the International Space Station for that much."

"And now you don't have to, do you? Rosy changed all that."

"I'll see what we can cobble together," Sam grumbled. "It won't be pretty."

"When do you think you'll be ready for the first deployment?"

"Let me meet with my teams and get back to you."

"Tomorrow. I want a sketch on how it might work by tomorrow."

"I'll let you know." The line went dead.

Sam looked up at the picture of the alien starship. The print shop in Rosyville had printed the Hubble photograph on three-foot by three-foot photographic paper, and he had framed and hung the picture on the wall behind his desk. It was the only decoration in his office. It had become his favorite place to stare and think.

He had twenty-four hours to design a robotic Rosy satellite that would jump to one of ten likely solar systems, determine if that system contained any planets capable of supporting human life, and send the results, along with high-def pictures and scans, back to Earth via Rosy communication channel. At least they had a picture of what worked for the aliens hanging on his wall—that was a huge step in the right direction. He'd created a list of ten candidate stars; at the top of the list was Gliese 581d, twenty lightyears away.

He pressed the intercom button to speak to his secretary. "Katie?"

She responded immediately. "Yes, Dr. Lowell?"

"Set up a meeting with the heads of all departments, ASAP. We're going to the stars."

"Is that what you want me to put in the subject line?"

"No, of course not. Put, 'Meeting to discuss top priority robotic satellite to explore nearby solar systems.' Required attendance. Have it start one hour from now." He glanced at the picture of the alien starship and then added, "Include Lily and Kevin."

"Drs. Particum and Swartz are at Fort Meade," she said, after checking their schedules.

"Tell them to phone in on the secure link—I want everyone's ideas—and call anyone who doesn't accept within half an hour. Tell them to drop what they're doing and be there."

··· ··· ··· ··· ··· ··· ··· ··· ···

Lily and Kevin sat in the back of the conference room as the department heads drifted in. As usual, Dr. Lowell entered as the clock reached the scheduled starting time for the meeting. "Hi, everyone." He sat down at the head of the table. "We have a new project that puts everything else we've got going on hold." He paused for effect. "We have to find a new home for humanity."

The Beginning of the End

There was a collective gasp from the people around the table.

"The president and his advisors have decided we can't afford to wait until a cure for the virus floats to the surface. No one is even sure one can be found. So, he has asked us to find a planet that can support human life. Assuming we can find such a place, we will create a colony there and populate it with uninfected humans."

"Where will we find uninfected humans?" Dr. Linn was curious. "I thought everyone worldwide was infected."

"The source of the people is unimportant. We need to find them a home."

"How we power it?" Dr. Wei asked. "Do we assume star in each local system provide enough energy for solar panels?"

"Would you like to answer that, Birne?"

"We will use the first application of a dark energy generator," he told the group smugly. "The alien artifact we recovered from the moon showed me how. I've already built a working copy."

Everyone in the room looked at him in shock. Dr. Lowell jumped into the silence. "That's right, people, Birne has cracked the dark energy secret, and we are going to use the first ever implementation of a dark energy generator in these satellites, so, you don't have to worry about power. Let's go to work. Remember these initial explorations are not supposed to be all encompassing—they are just going to let us decide which worlds need to be explored further. The satellites are one-way; we need to get them there so they can send us back the data. They don't have to return."

The rest of the meeting was spent roughing out how such a satellite would function, send and receive communications, what it would search for, and where it would be sent. Lowell assigned individual parts of the project to each department head.

As they finished the meeting and everyone got up, Lily spoke for the first time. "Have any of you thought about how this is going to be received by the aliens who planted this virus?" No one understood what she was getting at except Kevin. "They have selected humanity for extinction. We can't get along with ourselves, let alone with the other intelligent species already spreading through the galaxy. Do you think they will let us hop away to another planet and continue our warring ways? If you do this, they will come back, but they won't be dropping viruses, this time. They'll be dropping bombs—bombs that make our nukes look like firecrackers. Humanity isn't ready to start spreading into the stars. They won't let it happen."

The director sat down again. "Lily, no one has found where the virus came from. Are you saying they did this to us—that the aliens planted it?"

"That is exactly what I'm saying, Dr. Lowell."

"How do you know that? What haven't you told us?"

"When we were in the starship, we told the captain everything about what Kevin, Doug, and I found in our research. He was interested, more than anything else, in the fact that we'd *accidentally* launched our transmitter into space. He asked if we understood the ramifications of the transmitter going through the wormhole it created; I realized this would allow us to create a starship that could explore the galaxy and told him. We overheard him say, and I quote, 'That will, most probably, not be allowed.' The virus showed up six weeks later."

"That's not exactly a smoking gun," he pointed out. "We have no provable link between the aliens and the virus."

Lily sighed, knowing she would regret the words she was about to say. Kevin reached out to her hand. "Are you sure you want to do this?"

She nodded, took a deep breath. "It's my DNA in the virus."

Chapter 58 – Nondisclosure

August 29

Lily was busy on another project. Kevin was invited to participate in the design of the mission, but no one expected him to contribute anything. He had been idly listening to the banter about how to aim the satellites at their respective solar systems. He began to daydream of exploring the mountains to the east of JPL visible through the conference room window. One of the astrophysicists was doing a presentation on how he proposed to aim the satellites. His technique was to send them as close as possible on the first jump. Kevin snorted.

"You have something add, Kevin?" Dr. Wei asked, saying her words slowly, like she was talking to an idiot.

"I remember when the dean of men at Purdue took all the freshmen in my class who couldn't decide if they were going to be engineers or mathematicians to the football field. He lined them up on one side and all the cheerleaders on the other side. After the students were in place, he said, "Walk half the distance to the cheerleaders.""

"There point this monologue?" Wei asked, clearly upset that he had taken over her meeting with what seemed to be a stupid college jock story.

He ignored her and continued. "So, after they walked half the way to the cheerleaders, the dean told them to go half the remaining distance. They did. For the third time, the dean said to walk half the remaining distance to the cheerleaders. After the third iteration of splitting the distance, a few of the students walked off the field in disgust. The dean stopped them and declared the students who left to be mathematicians. The rest he told were going to become engineers." He got a roomful of confused expressions. No one understood. "The mathematicians knew they would never get there, but the engineers knew they would get close enough.""

A few of the people laughed nervously as they looked at Dr. Wei. She was furious but couldn't think of a way to respond without sounding like a bitch.

"The point is you don't have to go all the way to the target solar system on the first jump. Rosy can make as many jumps as you need. We have gobs of energy from that spiffy, new dark energy generator Dr. Aussau created. Jump halfway, to a point that is obviously safe, and then jump half the remaining distance to a point just as safe. As you approach closer and closer, obstacles you can't see from here will become apparent and you can avoid them. There's no telling what's changed in the twenty years the light took to travel here from Gliese—the sun might have gone supernova or the planet might have taken a hit by a comet."

"That's effing brilliant!" one of the scientists said quietly. "All we have to do is put a better scan and targeting analysis into the computer. We already have all the sensors built in. Do a quick scan, select the best route for the next jump, and off we go. Much better solution."

Wei was furious. She gave both of them a scathing look and walked out of the room.

Kevin watched her leave with satisfaction. His story had worked as planned. "Cool! Now we can get somethin' done!"

... ...

Lily walked into Dr. Lowell's office and sat across from him at his desk. "I need to make a shopping trip for baby stuff. I want to start getting her nursery ready."

The director sighed. "Can't you find what you need at the PX?"

"They don't even have baby food at the PX. The youngest kid in Rosyville is four."

"How about online? Surely you can order what you need online."

"Look, Dr. Lowell, if I don't get out of here for a shopping trip, we won't need to worry about the goddammed terrorists—I will go insane and take you with me!" She ended the sentence shrilly, wild-eyed and red-faced.

He stared at her for a moment without saying a word. "There might be a way this could work." He had never been married or dealt with a pregnant woman with nesting hormones swirling around inside her. "I could assign some MPs to accompany you in civilian clothes. Could you go tomorrow, first thing? Fewer people in the stores and on the highway. Drive down to Vegas, be waiting when the stores open, buy what you need, and be back by noon."

"Tomorrow is fine. Thanks." She got up to leave his office, satisfied her rehearsals had achieved their desired result.

"Kevin stays here."

"You are such an ass," she said coldly.

... ...

Dr. Plumber arrived right on time, as usual. The exam was uneventful. Lily's baby was healthy, growing, and perfectly normal.

"Where's Kevin? He's usually with you."

"He's working with one of the design teams here, and he's got to register for classes by the end of the day. Stanford is allowing both of us to continue our studies from here. I registered last week. Kevin seems to wait until the last minute for some things."

"Rosyville's new ultrasound is working perfectly. I like the new pickup very much—I'm going to order one for mine."

"Now you don't have to bring your portable unit with you." She was grateful Dr. Plumber had agreed to continue being her OB through the delivery, even though the exams required her to take a day out of her weekends.

"Remember we're shifting to every two weeks for the rest of your pregnancy. Your next appointment is on September 12. Will that work for you?"

"Oh, I don't know—let me check my busy schedule." She pulled up the palm of her hand and studied it. "Well, we're in luck. That whole day is wide open. Dr. Lowell told me not to work my entire third trimester. I think he's trying to make up for the way he treated us at JPL."

"Are you still running in the mornings?"

"Yep, but not as fast or as far as I did a couple of months ago. The marines who run with me go on ahead. I bring up the rear."

"You might think about transitioning to walking instead of running."

"Yeah, it's time. My pelvis is pretty sore by the time I'm done."

"University Medical Center in Las Vegas has agreed to let me deliver your baby there. When you go into labor, Dr. Lowell will transport you to the medical center via the medevac helicopter they keep on base. I will meet you there as soon as I can. I have to fly to Las Vegas from Burbank—luckily the airlines offer about a hundred flights a day."

"The casinos sure make it easy for people to lose their money."

"They do, indeed." Instead of chuckling at Lily's jokes like she usually did, however, Dr. Plumber picked up Lily's hand. "I checked on the DNA in the virus. It *was* from a female. Because you were so upset when I told you it was Asian, I submitted your DNA to be compared to it. I did it to prove to you the virus did not have your DNA. I got the results back yesterday."

Lily smiled sadly at the doctor. "They are the same, aren't they?"

"Yes, they are. Would you like to tell me why?"

"Sure." She gave a deep sigh took a minute to compose her thoughts, and then began. "It was right before Christmas Break last year at Stanford, when I had the dream that led to us inventing Rosy ..."

... ...

Dr. Plumber wasn't sure what to think, wishing she could find another explanation. "That's the most incredible story I've ever heard."

"You should have lived through it."

The Beginning of the End

"So, you think humanity was judged and found not ready for expansion into the rest of the galaxy? That the virus was released to kill our species before we spread?"

"Yep. We didn't make the cut."

"I remember seeing that issue of the *National Enquirer*. One of my patients was reading it when I started her appointment. We both laughed about the screwy Bay Area."

"Maybe their other stories have some basis in fact, as well," Lily suggested, a mischievous grin appearing on her face. "Maybe sasquatch really do exist. Maybe Elvis really is alive and living in a rest home in Minneapolis."

Dr. Plumber rolled her eyes. "I deleted the results from the DNA comparison. I didn't want anyone in the office stumbling upon them. Who knows what people would say without knowing the whole story?"

"Thanks for doing that."

"See you in two weeks."

… … … … … … … …

"Dr. Lowell, I'm worried about Lily." Dr. Plumber had walked to his office after the examination.

"Why? What happened?"

"On a previous visit, she became very upset when she learned the DNA in the Baby Stopper Virus was Asian. Because of that, I submitted her DNA for a comparison analysis. My intent was to prove it was not her DNA, but hers was an exact match. During the examination today, I told her about the results and asked her to explain. She gave me a story that was psychotic. She obviously believed it. Aliens! Species elimination! The only parts that were true were that it was her DNA in the virus and they invented the Rosy Transmitter."

"What do you think we should do?"

"Hospitalize her—she may be a danger to herself and her baby. We need to find out who engineered the virus. This smacks of bioterrorism." Her expression grew serious. "Does Lily have any background in biochemistry?"

He considered how to proceed. "Dr. Plumber, have you ever seen this picture before?" He indicated the picture on the wall behind his desk of the alien spaceship Hubble had taken.

"No, I haven't. It looks like something from *Star Wars.*"

"Well, I guess you're right. It could be, but it's not. This is a picture of the alien starship that kidnapped Lily, Kevin, and Doug. It was taken on March 13 of this year by Hubble—about the time they released the virus. Everything Lily told you is true. Now that you know, I am going to have to ask you to sign a nondisclosure agreement."

She was shocked. "You mean the source of the infection was that alien spaceship? They infected us because Lily invented the Rosy Transmitter?"

"It's a little more complicated than that, but I guess that's close enough."

"Why haven't you told everybody?"

"President Klavel decided the world wasn't ready to hear about aliens as real, living, breathing beings. He thought we would have mass panic."

"What if I don't sign the nondisclosure?"

"I'll have you arrested."

"You mean like you did to Lily, Kevin, and Douglas Medder?"

"Yep, just like that."

She stared at him. He stared back at her without blinking, stone faced. "Where's your paper? I'll sign it, but I may not be back. I've gotta think about this."

Chapter 59 – Field Goal

August 30

It was only the end of August, but the Labor Day sales were in full swing in Las Vegas. Walmart and Sam's Club announced they were running a closeout sale on baby clothes sizes zero to twelve months, cribs, bassinets, and infant car seats. Diapers sizes newborn to one, were also on sale, along with infant toys. Costco and Kmart followed suit. Lily had talked the MPs into taking two Suburbans.

"If this is the one trip Dr. Lowell allows me, I plan on bringing a lot of stuff back." One of the MPs started laughing and Lily laughed too. "Don't get between a pregnant woman and her credit cards!"

Matt's mom was able to meet Lily in the parking lot at Costco. She walked up to the first black Suburban and knocked on the window. "Lily?"

Lily got out. "Dott?"

"Hi, Lily. I figured that had to be you. In this heat, there aren't too many parked, black SUVs with the motor running and the windows up." Dott gave her a big hug. Lily liked her instantly.

Matt had not described his mom; she didn't know what to expect. Dott was about the same height as her, but while Lily was slim and energetic, Dott was round and energetic. Her blonde hair was about half white and she laughed a lot.

"I threw out all my baby stuff years ago—I had saved it until my last move. I decided I wasn't a storage center and wasn't going to move it again, so out the door it went. Goodwill and The Salvation Army aren't even accepting baby items anymore. I guess everyone had the same idea, since the Baby Stopper Virus hit."

Lily had been living with scientists for six months. Their idea of fun was to drink two beers and watch sci-fi B-movies. Dott, on the other hand, liked to talk, and Lily was thoroughly enjoying her nonstop, nonscientific, female chatter. After they had bought what seemed to be most of Costco's remaining baby inventory, they did the same at Sam's Club, Kmart, and Walmart.

She filled the carts the MPs pushed around behind her; in between all the big things, she crammed every baby toy and baby help-thing she could find. Everything was on sale, as the stores cleared their baby aisles so they could stock items that were going to sell in six months. Lily bought three sizes of baby car seats, even though she wasn't sure she would ever use them—she never drove anywhere at Rosyville.

"Get the Diaper Genie," Dott said at Walmart. "Trust me on this—and buy two refill boxes." They needed another cart for the boxes of diapers.

At three o'clock, she was hungry; she spotted a TGI Fridays across the parking lot. After her purchases were safely stowed in the Suburbans, she asked the MP's, "You guys have time for a late lunch over there? It's on me."

The sergeant glanced at the other four, and they nodded hopefully. "Yes, ma'am—but you might neglect to pass this on to Dr. Lowell. He wanted us to return by noon."

"Lunch? What lunch? What restaurant?"

Ten minutes later everyone had settled into two adjacent booths. Lily watched everyone else in the dining room laughing, talking, and eating and realized how much she had missed mingling with people—ordinary working people.

A young woman approached her table. The MP's started to stand, but Lily waved them down.

"Excuse me, ma'am."

"Hi. What can I do for you?" Lily asked.

"You're pregnant, right?"

She rubbed her swollen stomach and chuckled. "Yep, I sure am."

"You must have gotten pregnant right before the Baby Stopper Virus. My husband and I were married in April. We wanted to have kids right away, but now I guess we never will. Can I ask you something personal?"

"Sure," she answered, unsure of where this was going.

"May I touch your stomach? I wanted a baby so much—I just wanted to feel what being pregnant felt like. This is probably as close as I'll ever get."

The Beginning of the End

Lily took the woman's hand and placed it on her stomach. Lan chose that moment to kick a soccer ball. The woman's eyes got huge.

"Did it just kick?"

"I think that was a field goal."

"Thank you. Thank you so much." A tear slid down her cheek as she turned away and returned to her table where a young man sat, watching every move.

"That was amazing," Dott whispered.

Lily didn't answer. She was trying hard not to think about being the source of the DNA for the virus.

An hour later, they walked out to the Suburbans. Dott reached inside her car—an old, beat-up Honda Civic—and pulled out a brand-new diaper bag. She handed it to Lily. "Here is your own world famous Dott's New Mom Starter Kit. It has all the stuff I didn't buy for my first baby and ended up needing. She ticked off things on her fingers. "Baby sunscreen, a sun hat, a medicine dispenser, baby Tylenol, a nipple guard, industrial-sized menstrual pads, baby wash, lanolin, nipple cream, Aquaphor, Vaseline, Q-tips, a fingernail clipper, a hair brush, breast pads, baby lotion, disposable changing pads, and a copy of *The Sh!t No One Tells You*. I know you'll find other things you need, but this should help."

Lily was flabbergasted. She held the package to her chest without knowing what to say. It was the most incredible gift she had ever received. "Thank you, Dott. This is amazing. Thank you so much." She gave her a big hug.

"When you have her, let me know," Dott whispered into her ear. "I want to hold the world's last baby."

Chapter 60 – The Leak

September 12

Pasadena Health Center, the last open Planned Parenthood storefront in LA County, decided to close their doors. Nationwide, Planned Parenthood had provided birth control, reproductive health services, adoption services, and abortion services since the Supreme Court made abortion legal in the famous Row v. Wade decision of 1973. Planned Parenthood had tried to stay alive by changing from a focus on birth control to low-cost reproductive health care and the prevention and treatment of sexually-transmitted diseases. They also began helping people who wanted to be parents to find either a fertilized gamete or a child in need of adoption. None of those services, however, did much for the corporation beyond postponing the inevitable.

It was the abortion services Planned Parenthood provided that had caused so much friction between them and the Christian Coalition led by the Baptists and evangelical Christians. Abortion clinics nationwide had been the target of violent, dangerous, and damaging demonstrations by members of the Christian Coalition for forty years. When the First Baptist Church of Pasadena found out the Pasadena Health Center was closing its doors for good, some church members wanted to have one last noisy, rub-your-noses-in-it demonstration.

When the pastor found out about their plans, he forbade it. "We haven't won our battle against Planned Parenthood's abortions," he told his congregation sternly. "All of us, including Planned Parenthood, have lost the war. You want to celebrate their demise; I want to mourn them. They are just another casualty of the Baby Stopper Virus that has claimed our future. I would rather they stayed alive and thrived in their ungodly business, if that meant the return of babies to the rest of us."

… … … … … … … … …

PAG Pharmatech in Shenzhen, China, completed the retooling of their closed-down prenatal vitamin plant into production of a second line of organic sport vitamins.

... ...

Wallach Surgical Devices dropped their line of fetal dopplers, endometrial cell samplers, NST archiving software, and fetal monitors from their mail-out and online catalogs. In the same letter and email, they announced a new line of arthroscopic cameras and surgical devices

... ...

The container went through the Rosy send without incident. It arrived in the receiver dock with a metallic clang that sounded like a garbage truck emptying a dumpster. Doug opened the door at the end of the pod. What had been an empty, cavernous room was now full of forty tons of cargo container. Inside the container were rocks.

The supervisor activated the unload mechanism. There was the noise of a motor whirring and then a bang. A technician scooted under the landing mechanism and announced a cable had sheared off. He called for a welding unit and mask; ten minutes later, he crawled back out. Doug pressed the unload activation switch. The container slid smoothly out into the warehouse in Calgary the Canadian government had rented for them to use. This transmission had moved the container one hundred feet; they could just as easily have sent it to Halifax.

Send and receive facilities were being planned for ninety-eight sites around Canada with more being added daily. This would cause a massive reduction in Canada's carbon emissions and fossil-fuel energy use. It would also allow settling of huge areas of the country that were currently unlivable because of Canada's brutal winters and harsh terrain. Now goods could be reliably sent anywhere all year round, whether it was in the middle of a hurricane, or a sunny day.

Phase two was a people-mover network. Canada's two largest airlines, Air Canada and WestJet, would operate it since commercial air flight would be the big loser once the people-mover network was up and running. The send and receive sites would be installed at the various airports throughout Canada. The anticipated cost per seat was about ten percent of what a corresponding airplane seat presently cost, with the funds used to pay for the maintenance of the sites and the people to run and secure them.

The Canadian government was not comfortable with moving this quickly. The Department of Finance was trying to adjust its regulations to create a reasonable way to tax the transmissions. The reduction of income from the fuel taxes as fewer and fewer planes, trucks, and trains moved across Canada would have to be recovered from somewhere else. They were also taking into account the people who would be put out of a job by the Rosy transmission services—transportation personnel; oil supply personnel; truck and aircraft manufacturers; trains, truck, and aircraft parts manufacturers; trains, truck, and aircraft maintenance people. The list was growing every day as the repercussions sank in. Rosy would be eliminating huge parts of the transportation industry.

Phase three was when Canada would start using Rosy to begin shipping internationally. Cargo ships were one of the biggest carbon polluters in the world, and Rosy would almost completely replace them. The whole cargo shipping industry would collapse or at least shrink to almost nothing, along with the ports, longshoremen, shipbuilders, chandlers, crews, captains, shipyards, and pirates. Countries with canal fees, like Panama and Egypt, would have to find another way to generate the income.

Other Canadian ministries were also finding peaceful ways they could use Rosy. The mail distribution industry would change forever. Everything would become cheaper, since the costs of transporting the goods would be cheaper. However, that would mean yet more taxes not collected from the existing tax base. In its place, the burgeoning Rosy freight mover industry was forecast to replace those funds.

The Beginning of the End

Canada's Department of National Defence had required Doug's team to put safeguards in place that would prevent anyone from sending to an unauthorized site. The device would self-destruct and become entirely nonfunctional if any alteration was attempted or someone moved the device to a new location. Of course, there had to be a way to add new sites and move the devices, and that required specially linked encrypted Rosy radios.

… … … … … … … … …

Lily waited in the examination room for Dr. Plumber to show up. This was unusual—Dr. Plumber was never late. "Her flight must have been delayed," she grumbled. She waited another fifteen minutes, got dressed, and walked out to the nurse's desk. Dr. Simmons was coming out of the clinic break room.

"Did Dr. Plumber call? Is there some reason she didn't come today? We had an exam appointment scheduled."

"She was pretty upset when she left after her last visit," Dr. Simmons said, trying to be diplomatic. "She made some rather forceful comments about Dr. Lowell's parents."

Lily was in disbelief for a moment, and then the dam broke. "You've got to be kidding me! What's he done *now*?" She turned on her heel and stalked out the door before turning toward the admin building.

Sam was waiting for her—Dr. Simmons had thought a warning phone call was a good idea. "I had her sign a nondisclosure after you told her about the aliens and how you suspected they were the source of the Baby Stopper Virus."

"And you used your usual tactful way of asking her, didn't you?" she asked angrily. "Something like, 'Sign this or you'll go to jail.'"

"She wanted to commit you, Lily. She thought you were psychotic."

"And now I'm two months from delivery and don't have a doc! *Thanks*! What the hell am I supposed to do *now*?"

His phone rang, and he picked it up. "Hello. This is Dr. Lowell." He listened for a few moments and then said, "Thanks. I'll tell her." He put the phone back in its cradle. "That was Doctor

Simmons. Dr. Plumber is at the clinic. She's waiting to speak with you."

Five minutes later, Lily walked back into the clinic. Dr. Plumber got up from where she sat in the waiting room. "Hi, Lily. Let's go into the exam room. We need to talk."

Lily sat on the examination table as Dr. Plumber closed the door behind them. "I apologize for being late. When I left here last time, I was pretty angry."

"Dr. Lowell is such a jerk."

"That isn't the word I would have chosen," she said, remembering the scene she had made as she left the last time. "In fact, that *wasn't* the word I chose."

"But you came back. I'm so glad."

"I had to do some soul-searching. Your story was a little hard to swallow. Once Dr. Lowell confirmed everything you told me, I was faced with a conundrum: Should I continue to give healthcare to the person who indirectly caused the demise of humanity in general and my baby delivery business in particular, or should I renege on my vows as a doctor? I played back our conversations, though, and realized you really didn't have anything to do with what happened—you were just a pawn in a much bigger conflict. Do you have any idea who or what planted that dream in you?"

"None at all. I've studied that dream from beginning to end a thousand times. There is nothing that can be used to identify where it came from or who did it."

"I considered what I would have done if, say, I'd had a dream that showed me a way to kill cancer or aging or any manner of chronic health problems that plague humanity. I would have pursued it with every fiber of my body, just like you did—and I'd be in the same boat as you are, if that solution had led to the same place."

"So, you're still going to be my doc through the delivery?"

"Yes, I am. But we have a bigger problem that surfaced today." Dr. Plumber pulled out her cell phone and opened a Reuter's news clip she had received. In the headline, it said "The Source of the Baby Stopper Virus Is Found!" Lily's picture was underneath the headline. The text of the article said Lily's DNA was an exact match to the DNA in the virus and it implied she was somehow responsible.

"My *ex*-office manager leaked the results of the DNA test I submitted. Now the whole world is up in arms about why it's your DNA and what your link is to the virus. Some blogs are even saying you created it to get back at China for killing your parents."

"My parents aren't *dead!*" Lily said, standing up. "At least, my mother isn't. How would I even create a virus? I'm a physics student—the only viruses I know anything about are the kind that infect computers!"

Chapter 61 – Americans

October 1

Pasadena High School ended the last baby training section of their health education class as the students turned in their crying, wetting baby simulators. Unlike the end of previous classes, it was a quiet, somber moment. There was no joking around among the students about how the simulators had kept them up at night. Many students' eyes, both male and female, were wet as they surrendered the dolls to their instructor for the last time, knowing they would never be able to use to training they had just received.

… … … … … … … … …

"What is the status of the SHIPS?" President Klavel asked his National Security Council. "It's been four months since we started building them." His council was meeting in the secure bunker under the White House. Construction of the three Sterile Heritage Protection Sites (SHIPS) were well underway. This was where the uninfected human fetuses would be born and raised, in case no one found a cure for the Baby Stopper Virus. One was in Montana, another in Nevada, the third in West Virginia. All three were in geologically stable regions.

Dick Goldblum, his national security advisor, spoke up. "The excavation is complete. They are sealed and sterilized. The solar panels and wind towers are in place and in the process of being connected to the caves. The water supply and waste elimination systems have been laid out and are under construction."

"What is the target date for a full system test?"

"West Virginia is closest. If everything goes as planned, we expect it to be complete by Christmas. After that, Montana in February and Nevada in March. The hydroponic and ventilation systems are taking the most time; those estimates may change if weather gets in the way. Montana is renowned for its crippling snowstorms at that time of year."

"How are the surrogates growing?" The president was referring to the babies grown from B15 embryos, eggs, and sperm collected by fertility centers and sperm banks. Those embryos were growing in surrogate chimpanzee mothers. No infected human mother had yet birthed an uninfected baby. Chimps, however, had immunity to the virus and therefore had not passed it to the fetuses up to this point.

"The surrogates are healthy and about halfway through their gestation," Dr. Hehsa told him over the secure web camera in his office at the CDC. "There is no infection at this time. They will be born between February 11 and April 13. If their target SHIPS is not complete, they will be cared for in the temporary sterile facilities that have been constructed beside them. The uninfected submariners will be providing most of the care. We have identified 453 sailors; all but four have volunteered to do this. We also have eighteen females who were on assignment in the submarines. Fourteen are pregnant, as well."

The president did a quick calculation on his cell phone. "That's about one hundred and fifty caretaker personnel per installation. Will they be able to care for a thousand babies?"

"That shouldn't be a problem," the secretary of defense said. "Most OB wards have a higher ratio of newborns to nurses than that. They won't start with one thousand, though—one thousand is the projected sustainable population the SHIPS will reach after about fifty years. Each will begin with something around three hundred. That works out to be about six babies per sailor, considering they will have to run three shifts."

"How about the artificial womb the Chinese were making? Did it ever work?"

"We don't know," Hehsa answered. "They said the first fetuses died after seventeen weeks, but they have given no further updates. We don't know if it's because they are embarrassed at their failure or because it worked and they don't want to share it. None of my contacts there will return my calls."

General (retired) Rolland Angle, the head of the NSA, spoke up. "We've been monitoring China's phone and internet traffic, of course, but there is no mention of it. We think they are using their secure Rosy communications to talk about all aspects of their habitats. Our satellite Rosy tracker system sees minor Rosy transmissions from their SHIPS sites to Beijing. They are consistent with communication portals, but we can't intercept them or study their contents."

David Bartow, the director of central intelligence of the CIA, added, "None of our Chinese assets have been able to find out anything. The Chinese government is keeping security on the whole project as tight as a drum. That makes me think it *is* working and they don't want to share."

"So, are we building one of our own? The goddamned Chinese don't have anything on us—we trained mostta those bastards."

Dr. Hehsa spoke up. "Our own artificial womb is going through final testing at the end of this month. It should be functional and in production by the first of December."

Klavel was still angry about the Rosy technology escaping from the US and even angrier about losing their anonymous delivery system. He took a breath to calm down. "How will the children inside be educated and receive health care?"

"We have installed computerized instruction courses for every course of study our team has decided they will need. We also aren't going away anytime soon, Mr. President—if we've forgotten any training or needs as the population inside matures, we will provide it. Each SHIPS has at least three medics and one MD from the submarine staff. The officers will be in charge and run the SHIPS as ships. Military discipline will be maintained."

"How about the Baby Stopper Virus? Are you sure it will die off when the last of the infected people die?"

"We believe so. It only grows in its target organism. If it has nowhere to grow, we believe it will die, like the smallpox virus did in the twentieth century. This virus only infects humans—all our research indicates it will die without a human vector to keep it alive. However, we also believe the demise of the virus will take at least one hundred years after the last infected person dies—maybe even two hundred. We just don't know."

The Beginning of the End

"So, we're talking one hundred years until the last infected person dies a natural death, and then the people in the SHIPS will have to live, breed, and stay alive as a gene pool for another two hundred years before they can emerge and begin to repopulate the world. Three hundred years inside a cave? Can the SHIPS do that—keep them alive and healthy for three hundred years?"

"Yes, sir," Dick Goldblum spoke up. "Their design lifetime is four hundred years. We chose every component for reliability and durability. Each one has forty exact replacements split between the storage bunkers outside and the caves within each facility. The manufacturers sterilized and sealed the replacements in containers that will outlive the SHIPS. The people inside will have sterile suits to wear if they need to go outside to access replacement parts in the storage bunkers or perform maintenance on the facilities."

The president finally asked his most important question—the one his major campaign contributors had been whining about for months. "How can we be sure these surrogates are gonna be Americans with American values and American beliefs?"

The rest of the people in the room stared at him without comprehension. After a full minute of silence, Dr. Hehsa spoke up. "Are you asking if they will be human, or are you asking if they will be Caucasian and Christian?"

President Klavel looked around the room at the white, yellow, brown, and black people staring at him in disbelief and realized he had crossed a line. He decided a serious back-pedal was in order. "Human would be nice," he said, trying to laugh. Even to his ears, however, it sounded rather forced. "What I meant was: how will they learn about the American Constitution and the Declaration of Independence—about democracy, the American spirit, and American fortitude?"

"To answer your *original* question," Hehsa said coolly, "we made no attempt to screen the donor gametes and embryos, other than to try to keep genetic diseases out of the mix. I'm sure the population of growing fetuses contains all races present in our society. As far as their education in social values, religion, or civics, that is a little out of my area of expertise."

After an extended silence with no one meeting his eyes, the president cleared his throat and continued. "Have we found where other countries' SHIPS are being built?"

"Yes, sir," Admiral Swank said. "We have identified thirty-seven habitats under construction. That number may increase if the likelihood of finding a cure for the virus diminishes any further. I'm sure they know of ours, as well."

"What countries are they located in?"

He checked a notepad in front of him. "India, Russia, Japan, Iran, China, England, France, Germany, Italy, Israel, Saudi Arabia, Australia, South Africa, Brazil, and Venezuela."

"Venezuela? Really?"

"Yes, sir," the admiral said without emotion. "Of the fifteen countries building a SHIPS, China and Israel are ahead of us both in quality and quantity. Their habitats appear to be secure enough to withstand a direct nuclear strike. Both China and Israel have four habitats nearing completion."

"I want the coordinates of each of the thirty-seven SHIPS programmed into our launch computers at NORAD headquarters. If anyone decides they want to be the only game in town, we won't allow it."

President Klavel put his hands on the table. "I think this meeting is done. Good job, everyone. I need to see Admiral Swank and General Angle. The rest of you can get back to work." After the other members of the council filed out, the president turned to the two remaining men. "Now tell me about our hidden SHIPS. How are they progressing? I have about an hour until I have to be at a fundraiser in Glen Burnie."

Chapter 62 – I'll See What I Can Find

October 7

Worldwide, Rosy detectors began picking up many large wormholes originating from various parts of China to an orbit 22,000 miles out into space. Hubble sent back pictures of the supplies floating in huge net warehouses centered above the equator over Malaysia.

The area 22,000 miles out from Earth is called the geosynchronous point. The speed of satellites in this orbit is identical to the speed of the rotation of Earth, so this is where companies like AT&T, DISH, and Hughes put that communications satellites that provided weather, GPS, television, and internet service to the world. From Earth, the satellites appeared stationary. Using this orbit allowed the items China had sent to remain over Malaysia, in plain view from all regions of China.

… … … … … … … … …

"What are they building?" President Klavel asked Dr. Lowell.

"I have no way of knowing, Mr. President. If I were to hazard a guess, though, I would say a starship."

"How can those bastards be building a starship? *We* aren't even building a starship!"

"Would you like us to start building one?"

"And send it where? You haven't gotten those planet finders complete yet. When are they going to be launched?"

"They should be ready in about one more week. Preliminary trials have gone better than expected. Based on the assumption they will find somewhere habitable for humans, though, we wouldn't be able to go there for at least another six months while we build a vehicle to get there. I'd be willing to bet the Chinese are building their own planet finders. Wouldn't it be something if we both chose the same place to send our people?"

"Congress is giving me a ration of shit about how much money we're spending. I can't get the money for a starship without raping some other program. Can you use the rest of your budget to start building one?"

"You mean the budget we were allocated to explore Mars that we used to build Rosyville?" Dr. Lowell smiled to himself. All he did was ask for the money—he didn't care where it came from.

"I'll see what I can find," the president grumbled. "Goddamned Chinese!"

Chapter 63 – Hammer Time

October 13

The ten satellites were ready to launch. Each was named after a famous explorer, but there was some controversy about using the names of Hernan Cortes and Christopher Columbus. Cortes had explored, conquered, and pillaged Central and South America, murdering tens of thousands of indigenous people along the way. Many of the residents of Rosyville grumbled about using such a bloody name for one of the satellites. Christopher Columbus had made slaves of the natives he encountered and cared nothing about their welfare—and he was also not the first person to discover or colonize North America. Dr. Lowell put it to a vote.

There were four questions on the ballot:

Should one of the satellites be named "Hernan Cortes"? (Yes or No)
If "Hernan Cortes" should not be used, what name should be? (Fill in the blank)

Should one of the satellites be named "Christopher Columbus"? (Yes or No)
If "Christopher Columbus" should not be used, what name should be? (Fill in the blank)

The entire population of Rosyville took part in the vote. They chose overwhelmingly (91%) not to use Cortes's name. The most popular alternative turned out to be Sacagawea (34%), the woman who led Lewis and Clark to the Pacific Northwest. Alfred E. Neuman, mascot of *MAD Magazine*, was a close second at (28%) followed by Bart Simpson (17%). The Columbus decision was much closer—53% voted not to use his name. Leif Erikson was voted his replacement with an astonishing 87% of the vote. His nearest competitor was Zheng He (10%), a Chinese explorer who purportedly published a fairly detailed map of the west coast of North and South America in 1418.

… … … … … … … … …

The new power supplies were functioning flawlessly. Not having to worry about solar panels and the associated mechanisms to unfurl and aim them had saved huge amounts of development resources. Instead, those people were used in the propulsion, scan analysis, and communication facets of the satellites.

For the first time, Kevin was an important part of a JPL design team. Dr. Lowell had replaced Dr. Wei with Dr. Donald Doogan, or DD as everyone called him. He was the first NASA scientist Kevin had met who laughed at his own mistakes. "If you don't make mistakes, you aren't trying hard enough!" he told Kevin on his first day as manager of the project. "Making mistakes is good. Having them go into production is bad. That's why we test."

Kevin smiled when he said that. "Doug would always make us test each new idea we came up with while we were making Rosy work."

"I wish I could have known him better before he left," DD said wistfully. "Did you ever find out where he ended up?"

"Nope. I asked Dr. Lowell, but if he knew, he wouldn't say."

"I'll bet he's still embarrassed Doug escaped on his watch."

"If he hadn't kept us on such a short leash," Kevin said spitefully, "Doug would still be here."

"If he hadn't done that, you might be working for the North Koreans."

"I guess it's a little different from your perspective. The way we were 'recruited' pretty much sucked." He grew quiet as he remembered how all three of them had chafed at being arrested, and then held prisoner at JPL.

"Compared to the people who snatched Dr. Clive, the FBI treated you guys like rock stars. You heard the details of what Security found when they broke into Clive's house, didn't you?"

"No. No one tells us anything."

The Beginning of the End

DD filled him in on the torture of Dr. Clive's wife and the beating Clive must have endured. Kevin was white by the time Doogan was finished.

"They did that to get Rosy?" he asked in disbelief. "No wonder the aliens decided to end humanity."

"You may be judging Dr. Lowell a little too harshly. A lot of us told Sam to back off on you guys. We thought JPL could give you a lot more freedom and still keep you protected. I don't think he was given much latitude, though—the people in Washington were running the show."

Kevin cocked his head at that statement. Until that moment, he had blamed their treatment solely on Dr. Lowell. He was not sure he was ready to believe the man had just been following orders or that he would have done things differently if their treatment had been solely up to him.

Kevin decided he liked DD, and he *really* liked DD's management style. The team had worked twelve-hour shifts for the last month. Doogan kept everyone focused, happy, and working together, and he had done it without overtly doing anything. In reviewing the past month, he had witnessed countless examples of Doogan's low-key approach to leading the team and keeping them marching toward their common goal—friendly encouragement, a statement of appreciation when everyone else could hear, arranging for his wife to babysit on a moment's notice, and soothing the feathers after the inevitable conflicts between team members. There was no time to do anything but eat, sleep, and work, but he had not had this much fun since he and his friends invented Rosy.

Lily came to visit him with lunch, and they sat down in the break room. She had brought a green chicken curry over quinoa—his favorite meal.

"I wish Doug was here to help with the Java," he said between bites. "Mine will work, but he could do the same thing better and in half the time." He was working on the jump target selection software and he told her all about how he was approaching the problem.

"How are you going to test it for real?" Lily asked after she understood his regression algorithm. "Simulations only go so far."

"Remember that balloon satellite we sent a million miles out—the first Rosy send from JPL?"

"Of course. I got Dr. Lowell to give me a print of the Hubble picture of it appearing."

"We're going to send a test satellite to it."

"Where is it now—it must have drifted thousands, maybe tens of thousands, of miles from where it was sent."

"Exactly. The satellite will have to find it and then tell us about what it found."

"Excellent! When are you sending it to start its search?"

"We're waiting on the propulsion team to finish their interface to the computer. They're saying it will be done in two days."

Meals were the only chance Lily got to see Kevin, besides when he passed out from exhaustion in their bed. She missed the mental interaction she'd had with the rest of the Rosy research teams. Mostly, however, she had mixed feelings about the exploration satellite project. Part of her was dying to roll up her sleeves and jump, heart and soul, into the coolest project ever. Another part of her was positive the aliens would never allow it and knew the hammer was about to fall.

Chapter 64 – Change

October 15

Dr. Lowell stood behind a lectern with the NASA logo on the front to address all workers in Rosyville in the auditorium of the high school. "I appreciate the number of volunteers who have come forward to work on the starship. The design you created, without knowing whether we would get funding to build it, has shaved many months off our construction schedule. I especially want to thank the three universities whose engineering departments led this design effort over the past six months: California Institute of Technology, Massachusetts Institute of Technology, and Purdue University. Without their help, we wouldn't have had a chance of beating the Chinese, Israelis, and Russians as the first humans to leave this solar system. Representatives from those three schools are here today. Please stand."

He had invited the chancellors of the three universities and the heads of their respective engineering departments to this kickoff celebration. Four men and two women stood and waved, and the crowd clapped enthusiastically. The residents of Rosyville who had attended those schools applauded wildly and chanted their school fight songs.

The director waited for the commotion to settle down before he continued. "The first deliveries of the materials will begin arriving tomorrow and will continue for many months. We will need to send them into orbit and create great, floating warehouse areas to contain them until the construction crews need them. I want to caution you about volunteering too quickly. Working in space is a dangerous business. Please talk about this with your families before you commit to working on the starship. Think about what it would mean if, God forbid, there was an accident and you didn't come back."

Ninety-six percent of the employees at Rosyville had volunteered—even the old men and women way past their physical prime. Mechanics, mathematicians, secretaries, scientists, clerks, cooks, engineers—almost everyone working for NASA secretly (and some not so secretly) wanted to go into space, to see Earth from the inside of a spacesuit instead of from a picture or computer monitor. They shared a common dream: to feel weightlessness for themselves, watch stars that didn't blink, and witness firsthand the experience of floating in free space above the magnificent planet they called home.

This was not going to be a walk in the park, though. This construction project would mean months away from families—months of hard work in cramped quarters, and being in daily danger while the ship took form. Some of the volunteers would probably not be coming back alive.

Dr. Lowell had removed many people from the list he felt were not up to it, including most of his senior scientists and engineers. However, the people who did go left huge holes in the staff required to run Rosyville and provide the logistical support the people in space were going to need. Rosyville's human resources department was already recruiting people to replace the young men and women accepted for the off-planet construction effort.

… … … … … … … … …

"Would you welcome, please, the next president of the United States, Senator George Robbins from New York State." The national head of the ACLU led the audience in a standing ovation for their endorsed candidate for president.

The senator walked to the podium and raised his hands over his head in his signature greeting. He was handsome, clean shaven, and athletic. The spotlights glinted off his close-cropped, curly black hair and perfectly-cut suit. He radiated confidence and health. The audience went wild. For a full minute, he stood there, basking in the adulation and applause. Finally, he lowered his hands and the audience went silent.

"We have a problem," he began. "Our leadership has lost their way. We are spending more time watching our own people than we are trying to figure out why those people are doing things that need to be watched. Our country was built on honest dissent and the expression of it—the right to dissent was written into our Constitution! Dissent isn't a crime. It should cause our leaders to question what they are doing instead of trying to arrest the people who disagree with it.

"People around the world hate us—and apparently we hate them, because we keep dropping more bombs and sending our young people to die for reasons no one understands. There's nothing down that road but more war, more death, and more hatred. There is a better way, and I'm going to show our country how to use it."

The audience stood again, applauding. When they stopped, Senator Robbins continued. "Our women have stopped conceiving. President Klavel seems more interested in arresting the scientists who have given us the greatest technology since the wheel than he is in making sure we have a future to use it. There has to be a cure, and I will make sure we find it." He received another round of standing ovation.

"We need a change—a change to our foreign policy, a change to our internal policy, and a change in who decides what that policy is. We need a change, and I intend to give it to you." The audience was on its feet again.

"The world is full of people who hate. No one hates when they are born—they learn to hate when they are hungry; when they witness their parents', brothers', and sisters' murder; when they can't get a glass of clean water; when their children die of a disease that can be cured with a medicine they can't afford; and when they can't pay for the education that would allow them to improve their lives. *We can do better!*" Another ovation filled the room. "And we will start in January, when I assume the presidency!" He raised his arms again. The applause lasted a full two minutes.

He stepped back up to the microphone. "We need to stop telling our fellow Americans what to think." The audience began clapping again, but the senator kept on with his next point. The applause got louder with each observation. "Having different viewpoints is one of the cornerstones of a successful democracy. We need to stop arresting people for their own good. We need to stop having one set of values for American citizens and another set for everyone else. How can we say everyone should live by our values when our values include incarcerating enemy combatants without a trial for over fifteen years? If our government thinks people have broken the law, let those people be brought to a trial by their peers to decide if they are guilty or innocent!"

He had one more plank in his platform to hammer home. "My last promise to you is to reform Congress. They are out of control. They no longer work for you—they work for themselves. They have spent us into a debt that boggles the imagination. This must change! When I am elected, I will ask the people of the United States, not the Congress, to pass six constitutional amendments. This is not an empty campaign promise—we *will* make this happen:

1) Let Congress pass no law that does not apply to them as well.
2) Let Congress pass no law that only applies to them.
3) Allow no person to serve in Congress for more than twelve years.
4) Require all pay and benefit increases for members of Congress to be approved by a general vote of the population, never by Congress itself.
5) Give the president the authority to do line-item vetoes that will stop Congress from adding pork barrel earmarks to unrelated bills.
6) Remove all laws retroactively that allow special privileges to members of Congress. We don't have royalty in the United States—all laws should be applied equally to all citizens.

Senator Robbins held up his hands. His pretty wife, dressed in a flawless cream suit, walked over and stood beside him, raising her hands like his before she clasped his left hand in her right one. They stood there together, smiling and waving, as the audience cheered and clapped for a full five minutes. Even people who, after President Obama, swore they would never vote for another black man were changing their minds. It was not the color, it was the man, and the senator was the opposite of everything they hated about President Klavel and the status quo in Washington. They needed a second chance, and this was the guy who would get them one.

Chapter 65 – The Scene of the Crime

November 1

The last Lamaze class in Los Angeles County finished. Five couples attended it, the lowest number of attendees since it was first offered in 1965. After the class, most of the discussion was not about *having* the babies, but about *where* the couples were having the babies, since almost all the hospitals had shut down their OB wards. Most of the couples were electing to go to birth centers instead of hospitals; many of the centers were remaining open into the near future to support the small number of women who'd been successfully implanted by their own or a surrogate frozen B15 embryo.

The centers were run by midwives who had done this for most of their adult lives and had no other options for a professional career; many had a lineage of midwifery running back to before the Civil War. Hospitals and birthing centers had traditionally been sparring partners, competing for the same clientele. Now, however, several area hospitals had decided to officially associate themselves with nearby birth centers to allow them to take over nonemergency delivery services while the hospitals provided emergency backup for problem deliveries.

... ...

Release 1.3 of Zynga's Rosy Detector app appeared on the market, and Zynga offered free upgrades to all previous installations. This release allowed the user to set a portal-size threshold for transmissions to appear on their application. It also allowed the exclusion of certain sites. With more wormholes being put into use all over the world every day, the sheer volume of them was overwhelming.

... ...

The Beginning of the End

Canada's freight mover network was about half implemented. Their wormholes were huge. Many countries from around the world were begging Canada to show them how it was done and offered huge amounts of money to buy the patented hardware from Canada so their countries could put it in place also. A whole new industry had sprung up and was growing faster than anyone had imagined.

The Canadian government licensed the manufacture of the hardware to several trusted Canadian firms, where tight security was the norm. As usual, the Americans dragged their feet at taking advantage of new technology another country created. The Teamsters, Longshoremen, Auto Workers, the Steelworkers Unions were twisting every arm in Congress to whom they had contributed money; they wanted Congress to outlaw Rosy transportation.

… … … … … … … … …

Wormholes were appearing every day in new countries as Rosy technology spread, whether legally licensed or purchased on the black market. The CIA and Department of Defense were very concerned about the Terrible 10—the ten countries in the world that most hated the United States. Based on Rosy transmissions, all ten—Serbia, Yemen, Iraq, Iran, Egypt, Lebanon, Algeria, the Palestinian Territories, Pakistan, and North Korea—had acquired the technology and were developing it. Even more troubling were the semiautonomous tribal areas in Syria, Sudan, Pakistan, Afghanistan, Mali, Algeria, and Mauritania—areas rife with Al-Qaeda, Boko Haram, and Islamic State remnant operations. Wormholes were recently seen originating from those areas, as well.

… … … … … … … … …

Lily was having trouble sleeping. A wicked backache had kept her up for most of the night. She rolled over and checked the clock for the hundredth time. 02:38 AM was on the display.

Walking around the house didn't help, going to the bathroom didn't help, a cup of warm milk didn't help, and Kevin's oblivious snoring just aggravated her irritation. She gave up trying to sleep and pulled on her jogging suit. The baby seemed to be lower in her abdomen as she tied the drawstring around her waist.

Maybe a walk around the block will help, she thought as she slipped into her jogging shoes. Her stomach was very tight. *I'm not due for another two weeks—these must be those Braxton-Hicks contractions I've read about.* As she stepped outside her house, the cool air greeted her like a caress. While living in the desert north of Las Vegas, she had grown used to the hot days and cool nights. With winter closing in, the hot days became warm and the cool nights were chilly. The weather reminded her of her childhood home in China. She turned the corner at the end of the block and knew something was wrong. Her jogging suit was soaked to the knees.

How strange. It can't be urine. She had used the bathroom before she left the house. Then she realized what had happened. *That's not pee. My water has broken!* A cold hand grabbed her heart. *This is happening!* Her first real contraction hit as she reopened the front door and sank to the floor. *Okay, breathe. This will pass.* She pulled out her cell phone and noted the time in a new memo. The contraction subsided.

"Kevin!" she screamed. "Kevin, wake up. I need you."

He came bounding down the stairs naked and found Lily on the floor of the doorway. "What's going on?" he asked in a panic. "Why are you on the floor? Did you fall?"

Her irritation flashed through her like a lightning bolt. "If you'd shut up for a minute, I'll tell you!" She tried to calm down. "I'm in labor. Dr. Lowell left yesterday—call Dr. Doogan and tell him to fire-up the medevac chopper. Then call Dr. Plumber. Tell her my water's broken and we're going to University Medical Center— we'll meet her there. And you might get dressed while you're upstairs."

The medic team pulled up in front of their house in the ambulance with more lights flashing than a sideshow at a carnival.

The Beginning of the End

Neighbors peeked out their windows and then came outside. The ambulance attendants wheeled Lily out on a gurney.

"Is it time?" Mrs. McGrew wanted to know.

"Lord, I hope so! I am so ready to not to be pregnant." Another contraction came. She pulled out her cell phone and recorded the start time.

Kevin came running out of the house, pulling on his shirt. The door slammed behind him.

"Can we just *go*!" she asked the driver, struggling to control her temper.

"Yep. We sure can, Lily. Do you have everything you need from the house?"

Kevin's hands were empty—he had not grabbed her birthing bag. That suitcase was crammed to the bursting point with everything she had even a remote possibility of needing. "Kevin," she called out as he got to the ambulance, "the suitcase! Get the suitcase!"

He ran back to the front door; it had locked when it slammed shut. He shook the handle. "DAMMIT!" His keys were on the dresser in the bedroom.

"The pot, Kevin!" Lily shouted. "Look under the pot!"

He reached under the flowerpot by the front door and retrieved the emergency key Lily had insisted, over all of his objections, he put there. He opened the door, sprinted up the stairs, grabbed the suitcase and his keys, and then ran down the stairs two at a time. On the last step, he twisted his ankle and went down with a crash. The suitcase flew up in the air before landing across his shoulders and slamming his head into the floor. Everything went black.

… … … … … … … … …

Kevin awoke with a start. *Lily!* He sat up—a heart monitor beside his bed and IV bag going into his arm—this was a hospital room. He was wearing a hospital gown and nothing else. He touched his head—a bandage—and found another around his ankle. He got out of the bed pulling his IV stand beside him and hobbled down the hallway to the nurses' station, about twenty yards away. Two nurses sat at their computers, keying in some data.

"Excuse me. Where am I?"

"University Medical Center, Mr. Langly," the nurse said. "You were brought in by the medevac helicopter from NNSS. They said you had sustained a head injury. We put you through an MRI, but you had no damage to your head or neck, other than a mild concussion. You also have a sprained ankle. We thought it was broken, but the MRI showed it's not. If you'll sit down in the wheelchair over there, I'll take you up to your wife. She's in our OB ward, recovering from having her baby."

The story of the circumstances around Kevin's accident had quickly made the rounds at the hospital. The nurse forced herself not to laugh as she told him what his treatment had been; her companion, an older nurse, smirked but remained silent. He was about to tell her how stupid it would be to have her push him, a healthy young man, around the hospital in a wheelchair, but the world started to spin as he got the words ready to say.

Instead of the smart-ass remark he had planned, he simply said, "Okay," walked slowly to the chair across the hall, and sat down.

She around walked behind the wheelchair, removed the IV drip from his arm, released the brakes, and pushed him to the elevator. About then, the words she had said sank into his overloaded brain. *Recovering from having her baby?* "How long was I unconscious?"

"About six hours."

"And Lily's had the baby already?"

"Yes, she has. You are the proud father of a baby girl with a full head of black hair. Both of them are fine."

The elevator doors opened; a woman and young boy were inside. The nurse guided the wheelchair in and pressed the button labeled 3. The boy next to him was maybe six years old, and he stared at Kevin with huge brown eyes. "What happened to you, mister?"

"I fell running down the stairs," Kevin said. "This is what happens when you don't listen to your mom."

The Beginning of the End

The little boy's eyes got even bigger, and he looked up at his mom. She raised an eyebrow. "You see? I told you." She smiled at Kevin, winked, and mouthed, "Thank you."

After the elevator doors opened, the nurse used an access card to unlock the swinging doors to the OB ward. The only sounds were muted voices as they passed one room after another, most of them empty. They rolled down the hallway to room 341. Kevin's father stood up when the nurse pushed his chair into the room, and a woman followed behind him.

Art bent over and hugged Kevin awkwardly. "You had me worried, Son. The nurse said you would recover."

The woman introduced herself in a whisper. "Hi. I'm Dott, Matt's mom." She leaned over and hugged him as well. "Both of them are asleep. Would you like see Lan?"

He nodded, and she pushed him over to the bassinet next to Lily's bed. Lan was wrapped in a birth blanket. All that was visible was some black hair sticking out from under her warming cap and a wrinkled face that was vaguely Asian. Dott picked her up and put her into his arms. He had never held a baby before—he was the youngest child in his family—and he held her like she would break if he even breathed. She chose that moment to wake up, and suddenly the eyes of the most wonderful little girl in the world captured his soul. He stroked her face with his hand.

"Isn't she beautiful?" Lily asked.

"*Beautiful* isn't a beautiful enough word," he whispered back.

Lan heard Lily's voice and tried to turn her head toward it, then she realized she was hungry and let out a wail. Kevin had no idea what he had done to cause her to cry. He turned to Lily and then Dott in panic.

Dott took Lan out of his arms. "Let's check her diaper, and then I'm willing to bet she wants some of Mom's supercharged breast milk."

Two minutes later, Lan was suckling greedily on Lily's breast. Kevin watched in wonder. He had a lot to learn about babies; his education had begun.

"She hasn't latched on completely, Lily," Dott said. "Try holding her more to your side. That's right—feel the difference?"

Lily nodded. "Now, massage your breast a little to encourage your milk to flow. When it lets down, you'll know." Lan gagged a little and then coughed.

"Was that it? It felt like an itchy tickle."

"Yep. You'll need some fenugreek capsules—they boost your milk production and improve the milk you produce. You can buy them at any nutritional supplement store or online."

"How are you feeling, sweetheart?" Kevin asked. "How was the delivery?"

She gave him a tired smile. "The delivery was fine. I was in hard labor for about two hours. It could have been much worse. The epidural helped a lot—Dott arrived as the anesthesiologist put it in. Dr. Plumber got here from the airport as Lan's head crowned and barely had time to put her gown on before it was a done deal. Are you okay? They told me you didn't break anything and were expected to recover."

Dr. Plumber walked in before he could answer. "Hi, Kevin. Welcome to the party. How're you doing? Did the ER fix you up?" All three women's heads turned like a radar battery toward him sitting in the wheelchair.

He smiled wryly. "I have a massive trauma to my pride—it may take years to cure. My head, on the other hand, is fine. Apparently, it's harder than both the suitcase and the floor. My sprained ankle and concussion don't hurt nearly as much as missing my daughter's birth, though."

Lily chuckled at that. "I don't think she cared much one way or the other, Kevin. Thank God Dott was here."

"Thank you for coming," Kevin told Matt's mother, reaching out for her hand.

"I'm glad you're all right, Kevin. We were worried about you. Don't do that again, okay?"

"Yeah, okay." He leaned over to take Lily's hand. "For the next one, I'll be right by your side."

She squeezed his hand and then stroked Lan's face. She had fallen asleep while nursing. "From your mouth to God's ears, Kevin," she whispered.

The Beginning of the End

... ...

The encrypted interspace radio crackled to life. "Grock Species Mining Ship, GSMS-77, this is Grock Central. Acknowledge."

Lieutenant Nussi responded, "Grock Central, this is GSMS-77."

"Grock Central has received a wormhole activity consistent with the building of a starship from the Grock-inoculated planet circling star EB-31-21-98. Return to that planet. Determine if the species there is building a starship. As soon as the determination is finished, contact Grock Central on this channel with your findings. Repeat back the message. It has also been sent to your message queue." The lieutenant repeated the message. "That is the correct message. Please identify yourself."

"This is GSMS-77, Lieutenant Nola Nussi, communications officer, employee number 234-447-844. I acknowledge message receipt." The channel went dead.

Nola rolled her eyes. Captain Xanny wanted nothing more to do with that planet—he had made his feelings pretty clear to the whole ship when they left five months ago.

She opened a channel to his quarters and gave him the bad news. "This is *bullshit!*" the captain shouted. "Let someone else do it! I've got a living to make, and I can't do it playing babysitter to those goddamned dying primates on their goddamned planet! I'll be right there."

By the time he got to the bridge, he had cooled off a little. He called Grock Central and got the same instructions. He called his immediate superior, and then his superior's superior. The orders stood. There was no other Grock Corporation ship within five hundred lightyears of the planet. Everyone else was mining the other side of the galaxy, which was exactly why GSMS-77 was over here.

"Damn, damn, double damn!" Xanny ranted. Commander Chirra, his second-in-command, was about to explode with what he was sure was held-in laughter that only another octopus would have noticed. "Well, what are you waiting for, Yidee? Take us back to that damned planet. We have to return to the scene of the crime."

Chapter 67 – The Coming Storm

November 2

"Grock Central, this is GSMS-77."

"This is Grock Central."

"This is Captain Xanny. Please secure this communication channel."

A moment of static came over the line, and then, "Channel is secure."

"The Grock-inoculated planet circling star EB-31-21-98 is indeed building starships. Four starships are under construction in geosynchronous orbits above the planet. They have also sent forty-two drones to nearby solar systems. We retrieved one and determined it's a scan-and-tell drone. It was searching for habitable worlds. The amazing thing is this drone had some twists I've never seen before—things that would have been very marketable if this species had been admitted to the Ur."

There was a moment of silence from Central, and then the radio came to life. "GSMS-77, continue to monitor the situation. We will notify you when we decide upon a course of action. Please send us all the data you have collected."

The linked light on the communication display went out.

"Lieutenant Nussi, encrypt and send to Central all the scans and pictures we've acquired since we arrived."

"Yes, sir."

"And don't forget the hologram of the disassembly and analysis of the drone."

... ...

"Grock Species Mining Ship, GSMS-77, this is Grock Central. Acknowledge."

Xanny indicated to Lieutenant Nussi he would respond. "Grock Central, this is Captain Xanny of GSMS-77."

The Beginning of the End

"Captain Xanny, you are to send the under-construction starships into that solar system's star, including the fission reactors three of them have in place. You will announce to the species that the GSCB has quarantined them and will not allow them to leave their planet. We have dispatched a team to take over the quarantine duties from you. Until they arrive, if you receive hostile fire, you may respond to protect your ship and crew. We caution you not to destroy the planet or make it uninhabitable."

"When is the team expected to arrive?"

"Estimated time of arrival is ten days from now."

Xanny sighed. Another ten days, and he had to do all the dirty work. "Grock Central, I acknowledge your instructions."

"This message has also been sent to your secure message queue."

The linked light on the communication display went out. He pressed the intraship communication button. "This is the captain. Grock Central has instructed me to destroy their starships and to put a quarantine watch around their planet. They are sending a team to relieve us in ten days. Until then, I am placing this ship on full combat status. All posts will be attended at all times in rotating shifts. Raise the shields and keep their moon between them and us. I do not expect this species to allow us to destroy their lifeboats without attempting to respond in kind—they are primates, after all. We may defend ourselves, but do not, under any circumstances, do permanent damage to this planet. Sergeant-at-Arms, please attend me."

Xanny wasn't sure about enforcing a quarantine around this planet. This was too much like the old days, when he was an unlicensed miner—only then it was him hiding from the quarantine instead of enforcing it while a dying species went through its death throes. As he waited for his sergeant-at-arms to arrive, he considered what form his notification to the species should take. He discarded using the hologram head in favor of his natural body. The shock effect of being an octopus would carry enough weight to make the message more believable.

"You wanted to see me, sir." Lieutenant Fela Fibari sat down next to the captain.

She was feline with gray and black stripes, about fifty kilograms, and one-and-a-half meters from her whiskers to the tip of her tail. Half of her left ear was gone and an old scar made up of three parallel scars began on her right shoulder, continued diagonally across her back, and ended on her left flank. She moved as easily on two legs as she did on four legs, with a peace and grace that belied the ferociousness that had earned her the position of ship sergeant-at-arms.

Xanny and Fela had been companions for most of their lives. She'd gotten the scar on her back from a cave lion attacking the two of them as they were exploring a potential mining claim. Her intervention was the only reason Xanny was still alive. He had killed the lion and nursed her back to health for two weeks in the cave while they'd waited for help to come.

"Hi, Fela. We have a problem." He filled her in on what Central had told them to do.

"So, what type of armaments do these primates have?"

"Nuclear fission and fusion devices, chemical explosives. From our technology scans, I would say they don't have proton devices and are just beginning to find out about Hore transmissions. I haven't seen anything resembling a Hore evacuation device."

"Thank the goddess for that. It sounds like we'll be able to protect ourselves by hiding and using basic shields."

"That was my thought, too."

"Has anyone told the GSCB what's going on?"

"Not my problem," he said to her, enjoying that he could pass the buck for once. "I told Grock—now they can tell whomever they want. Prepare Hore evacuations of their starship sites into their sun. Get their coordinates and worksite dimensions from Analysis. I want to explain to this species what's going on in one hour. Do you think you can have the devices prepared for launch in two?"

"Yes, sir. I will have them ready."

"Thank you, Fela. I want to launch them from the other side of the planet, in case they have created a Hore-locater system. After the launch, move the ship back behind their moon—and use

The Beginning of the End

shielded jumps. If they have one, let's hope their Hore detection isn't sophisticated enough to see the end of the portal through the shielding."

"Understood. And I was just saying it was pretty boring around here."

"Sometimes boring is good."

"And sometimes it's just boring." Lieutenant Fibari padded out of the bridge toward the armaments bay.

Xanny's communication light came on. "Captain Xanny?"

"Yes."

"This is Tech 4th class, Klava, in Analysis."

"What do you want, Klava? I'm a little busy."

"I've begun picking up some Hore energy portals from a site on this planet. You asked me to tell you if that happened."

"Hore energy portals? Are you *sure*?" Excitement exploded inside the captain.

"Yes, sir. I have the coordinates of the site they are emanating from, if you're interested."

"I would like those coordinates immediately, Klava. Please send them to me."

While he waited, Xanny stared at the hologram of Earth. There had been no unidentified departures since the dream plant. The people who planted the dream had to still be on Earth, hiding someplace down there. He hoped they were the ones who opened the Hore energy portal.

"Maybe that son of a monkrus has finally made a mistake— the person who planted the dream that killed a species. Now him, I would like to meet. Me and him—alone."

... ...

"Citizens of Earth." The image and voice of Captain Xanny appeared on every television set and radio getting its feed from a satellite. The people in each country heard his words in their own language.

"I am captain of the starship GSMS-77. You are building four starships to escape the infertility that has stricken your species. Escape will not be allowed. Your species has been selected for elimination by the Galactic Species Control Board. This was decided because you have discovered how to make wormholes that would allow you to spread through the galaxy. This discovery triggered an evaluation of your species by the GSCB to determine if you meet the criteria for admission to the Ur, the government of this galaxy.

"You have failed to meet the five required criteria. You are still warring among yourselves. You have not regulated capitalism. You have not overcome pollution. You have not overcome overpopulation. You have not overcome resource depletion. The law allows no appeal. Your barely-restrained capitalism would have been allowed, if it had been changed to a more restrained form. Your overpopulation, pollution, and resource depletion also could have been changed to follow our guidelines. The deciding factor was the constant violence you perpetrate among yourselves. We cannot allow a savage species with no social conscience to spread to the peaceful trading partners in this galaxy.

"You have one hour to retrieve your personnel from the starships. After that, the starships will be destroyed."

… … … … … … … … …

"Why does this always happen when I'm on shift?" Byteen groaned and then pressed the comm button. "Captain Pey, please come to the bridge."

They had been here on this planet for almost eleven months, sitting at the bottom of South San Francisco Bay. One more month and they could have left! He could have begun spending the money they were promised for the plant of that dream.

Fey Pey floated onto the bridge. "What's happening, Byteen?"

He played back Captain Xanny's announcement. "That son of a monkrus came back?" Captain Pey yelled at the screen, making a rude gesture. "I should've put a laser up his ass two hundred years ago when I had the chance—and now he's going to put up an Ur-sanctioned *quarantine!* We'll never slide through that without getting caught." He glared at the screen again and then left, muttering evil half-phrases and making runes in the air.

The Beginning of the End

Byteen knew the rules about making a pirate's curse—it wasn't a bona fide curse unless the curser spit. He watched for him to spit, but who could tell? He was a goddamned fish surrounded by three inches of water!

... ...

"The starship is gone." Dr. Doogan announced tersely to the emergency command center that had been set up to retrieve the workers as they escaped from the construction site.

Dr. Lowell was incredulous. "What do you mean *gone*, DD? Not blown up? *GONE?*"

Doogan was having trouble believing it also, and he had watched it happen. "I mean gone without a trace—vamoose, nada, missing, not there. Here one moment, gone the next."

"Where the hell did it go?"

"If I knew that, I wouldn't be here—I'd be getting it back."

"How could all the materials to build a starship disappear? It was strung out over a couple of cubic kilometers!"

"The Russian, Chinese, and Israeli starships are gone, also. As far as we can tell, not even a washer is left in orbit. They were a lot further along—their construction sites were a lot bigger than ours."

"Did everyone get down?"

"Ours did. We recovered the last of the evacuees a couple of minutes ago. It was raining parachutes all over the NNSS. Two broken legs, a broken arm, and three sprained backs. All the injured are loaded into the medevac chopper, ready to go down to University Medical Center. Good thing they gave us a Black Hawk."

"Two thousand people with no formal parachute training dropping into the desert and only six injuries—and none of them fatal? That's *wonderful!* I expected hundreds of injuries and even some deaths. Thank God you put those escape pods in place."

"Just another peaceful use of wormhole technology." DD chuckled. "A lot of the younger workers want to do it again. They had a ball dropping into the air ten thousand feet above Rosyville and floating down to the ground. One of the broken arms happened on the way down—two of them started a dogfight, like they were flying jet fighters. If we ever do this again, we'll have to make parachute familiarization part of the pre-space training."

The intercom buzzed. "Dr. Lowell, the president is on the line."

"Everyone please leave," the director told the people in the command center. "This won't be pretty." He waited until the room had cleared and then picked up the phone. "Hello, Mr. President. What can I do for you?"

"Where did it go?" President Klavel asked, his voice dripping with malice.

"We don't know. The other three are, gone as well."

"I know. I just got off the phone with Dimitri. He wants to launch at the aliens."

"What are they going to shoot at? We don't know where they are."

"That's the only reason they didn't push the launch button yet. I have an email in front of me the NSA just sent over—I'd like to read it to you. 'Four small Rosy transmissions originated from a million kilometers out in space, approximately where we see the center of the constellation of Leo. One transmission went into the middle of each starship construction site about ten seconds before everything disappeared. In all four sites, the starships and surrounding supplies started moving toward the sun, and then the largest Rosy wormholes ever recorded opened on all four starship sites. We didn't pick up an exit portal, though. We don't know for sure where the starships, people, and all the supplies went. We suspect they sent everything into the sun, which we think would explain why we did not detect an exit portal. We have searched the sky where the Rosy transmissions originated, but there's nothing there now.'"

Dr. Lowell could hear the president's teeth grinding together; it was not a happy sound. Sam decided he would try to calm him down. "Mr. President, I would consider carefully your response. We can't make the device they used to destroy the starships. While its power was amazing, it did what it did without massive destruction or any collateral damage. I would assume this

The Beginning of the End

is one of the more benign weapons in their inventory. This might not be the time to 'respond in kind.'"

… … … … … … … … …

"The presentations are cancelled," Doug announced to Clara. The Canadian government had allowed them to go to Stockholm for the Nobel Peace Prize presentation ceremony. A contingent of the Canadian Special Operations Regiment, the Canadian equivalent of the US Special Forces, accompanied them to protect against would-be kidnappers and assassins.

All three students had turned down the Presidential Medal of Freedom. Doug had also turned down the Nobel Prize for Physics while Lily and Kevin had accepted it. Lily couldn't travel since she was in the ninth month of her pregnancy and Kevin had decided to remain with her, so they had recorded their acceptance speeches a week ago.

"I guess I don't blame the Nobel committee," she said, looking out the window of their hotel room on the snow-covered streets of Stockholm. "No one knows what to do about the octopus's message. Only six hours have passed since it appeared on TV, and riots are happening all over the world—even in China, and it's after midnight there. A lot of world leaders were here to attend the awards. Without exception, they are returning home to deal with this emergency. China and Russia didn't remove their people; almost five thousand workers vanished with those ships."

He joined her at the window, watching the snowflakes swirl in the lights outside their hotel. "The Dalai Lama has called on everyone to greet this message with peace and prayer. He says he agrees with the aliens, and that this is what the world needs—to draw together in peace and leave our warlike ways behind us."

"Is anyone listening to him?"

"Probably not—they never do. He's said the same thing many times before, without the part about the aliens. Too bad they cancelled the award ceremony—you could have said the same thing or even invited the Dalai Lama to speak with you. Have any other religious leaders responded?"

"Well, the Pope says this was all foretold in Revelation and that we should embrace Catholicism and Jesus as the way to spiritual salvation—that none of this matters in the grander scheme of spiritual life. For the first time in my memory, the television evangelists appear united, saying this is what we deserve for being unrepentant sinners, and that Captain Xanny is simply Satan coming to collect his due. The Buddhists are having a day-long, worldwide meditation to find the way. The Ayatollah has put blame for the whole thing on the US, its allies, and their constant warfare on the rest of the world."

"Did the Ayatollah mention 9-11, Iran's war with Iraq, or their murder of raped women for tempting the men who raped them?" she asked bitterly. "Did he mention the Ayatollah's promise of paradise for suicide bombers, his use of poisonous gas, the terrorist training camps he supports in Iran and Pakistan, or his nuclear weapons development in that speech?"

"Nope, of course not—but he's not the one I'm scared of in all this."

"Who's scarier than the Ayatollah?" Clara asked in amazement.

"The leaders of the US, Russia, and China, that's who," he said softly. "They don't like gettin' pushed around, and that is exactly what the octopus has done. I think they will take this as an act of war against humanity. I expect them to retaliate."

She shook her head "How could they even contemplate that? The aliens made four whole starships disappear without a trace—all the supplies and all the people gone in a couple of seconds. If they can do that, what else can they do?"

Doug didn't answer. He knew the storm was coming. This was just the opening volley. The killer ape from which humanity had risen, finally had an eight-legged poster child on which to blame all the woes of the past eight months, and his name was Captain Xanny.

Chapter 68 – Election Day

November 07

Dr. Birne Aussau stood in front of the scientists, technicians, workers, and their families from Rosyville. People packed the gymnasium to the top row of the bleachers. A group of bored reporters sat in front; they had been invited to what they were sure would be another NASA announcement about the disappearing starships or the aliens. Birne was standing on a stage that had been erected at one end of the basketball court. Outside, the temperature was pushing into the high eighties. Inside, however, was cool from the air conditioning and brightly lit by the gym lights.

Many people in the audience—mostly those with roots in China and Russia—had black armbands, in memory of the people who had disappeared when the starships vanished the day before. As usual, all the major news agencies were invited and most networks were carrying a live feed of the announcement to their data centers via satellite links from the trucks outside. With the networks' talking heads doing the election coverage in the United States and the rest of the world trying to understand the implications of Captain Xanny's announcement, the airwaves were swamped. The networks were recording this "routine" NASA announcement for later use.

"What a day this is," Dr. Aussau began. "One we will both celebrate and mourn for the rest of our lives. Mourn for the friends and fellow scientists from Russia and China who will never walk among us again. I can only imagine how much worse it would have been if Dr. Lowell hadn't made everyone return to Rosyville via the evacuation pod deployment when the octopus gave his warning. That we didn't lose a single person of the two thousand workers who were building our starship seems cause for great celebration to me. Please join me in thanking Sam again for his courageous decision." Dr. Lowell waved from the podium, and the audience gave a round of raucous applause with many of the young people whooping it up.

Birne waited for the applause to stop before he continued. "But that's not what we're here to announce. We're here to announce free energy—more energy than humanity could use in a million years. This is energy without pollution, energy without bounds—energy available to everyone and which could allow us to solve all the problems that caused the aliens to sentence us to death. We have made a discovery. Let me tell you about it."

One by one, the reporters realized this was more than a routine announcement. This was something possibly as huge as the octopus showing up on their TV screens. As one body, the reporters sat up and started taking notes.

"Thomas Edison was adamant that direct current, or DC, as it's known, was the more efficient form of electrical energy. DC requires a lower voltage to supply the same power, which results in a safer distribution system. Nikola Tesla was just as adamant that alternating current, or AC, was the form we should be using commercially. DC power transmission is limited to only several miles from the generating station before the voltage drops to an unusable level, while AC is transmitable over thousands of miles with relatively low energy loss. The controversy was effectively ended when George Westinghouse bought the rights to the AC generator from Tesla and built the first hydroelectric generators used by the Niagara Falls power generating station. He sent that power to Buffalo and Pittsburg. That experiment became the blueprint for the power grids and distribution services that are now in place worldwide."

Birne took a breath and wiped his forehead with his handkerchief. "Now we've come full circle. We have created a new form of energy generation that pulls its power from the dark energy that makes up seventy-two percent of the mass of the universe. We call this new generator the Dark Energy Portal. It produces massive amounts of DC power so cheaply that each household will be able to have their own power supply. It produces this energy without creating pollution of any kind—no carbon, heat, moisture, or carcinogens—and without consuming any resources. Today, we will open the door to all the things that were cost-prohibitive by the expensive, resource-depleting, environment-polluting energy production of the past.

"The Dark Energy Portal will cause a transformation of the entire electrical products and energy delivery industries. The household appliances we use and love are based on fifty- and sixty-cycle AC power. Over time, these will all be replaced with devices that accept DC power, eliminating the need and expense of converting the DC power the Dark Energy Portal produces into the AC power our appliances require today. The electrical grid and power generation sites that block our rivers, pollute our air, and block the view of our beautiful country will slowly disappear. Fossil fuel will become something we use in antiques on sunny weekend afternoons. We can send nuclear electricity generation, with all its poisonous byproducts, into the sun—we won't need it, anymore. There will be no more meltdowns. Electric cars won't need heavy batteries made from rare earth elements.

"Dark energy will change everything. People without clean water will have it at their sink and in their fields. Poverty as we know it will end. With clean water, most infectious diseases won't be spread. With clean water, crops will flourish where only dust and famine grow now. Light will shine where darkness fills the land. Air, water, and land pollution will disappear. And with clean water and the end of poverty will come the end of war.

"This is only the beginning. Think about the ways we use energy in our everyday lives. Almost every aspect of our lives will change dramatically, and those changes will only be limited by our imaginations. I wish Thomas Edison had lived to see this day." A ragged applause began and then grew and grew until the entire auditorium resounded with it.

"When this button is pressed," Dr. Aussau shouted, indicating the large red button on the podium in plain sight of everyone, "Rosyville will be the first community on Earth to use our new Dark Energy Portal as its sole energy source. It won't be the last. Dr. Lowell, would you do the honors?"

Sam got up from his chair and walked across the stage. He reached out to the button. The lights blinked and then stayed as radiantly bright as before. The skirting around the stage lit up with the words "Dark Energy—The Power of the Future" walking across the display over and over. The audience of scientists, their families, and reporters jumped to their feet giving a whooping, clapping, standing ovation.

"Rosyville is now running fully on dark energy. Today, we light ourselves. Tomorrow, we light the world. Everybody remember to take time to vote. Our great country must remain strong for us to lead the rest of the world into the light."

The reporters were scribbling like mad. When they realized the speeches were done, they leapt to their feet and began shouting questions.

"How do you build it?"

"How much does it cost to make a kilowatt?"

"Is it portable?"

"Are you going to license the design?"

"Is the US going to sell the generators to the rest of the world?"

"Do any of our allies have this already?"

"Is Defense using it?"

Dr. Lowell smiled. "Please, people, relax. I will answer your questions if you will ask them one at a time." He pointed to a young woman in the middle of the pack. "Melanie, let's start with you. What is your question?"

"How is the generator built?"

"You can find out by buying a copy of *Science* magazine, where we've published the plans and materials needed. That issue is on newsstands today and available for download at their website. They have agreed to allow free downloads of the plans and the article. The only thing that isn't readily available at the present time is the super-conductor copper-silicon-germanium fiber cables, but I'm sure that will change in a year or two. I expect demand to far outpace supply for the near future."

... ...

Lily leaned over to Kevin. "I wonder why Dr. Lowell didn't have this conference a couple of days ago. This might have won President Klavel the election. Everyone's saying he has lost."

The Beginning of the End

"Well, the polls are still open, but I think you answered your own question. I hope he doesn't lose his job by publishing something the US government would love to have a corner on."

She watched the director answering questions about the device, as though he didn't have a care in the world. Lily realized there was a lot more to him than she had thought.

… … … … … … … … …

Voting booths had been open for ten hours on the East Coast. As the pre-election-day polls had shown, President Klavel was a distant third behind George Robbins, the senator from New York, and Sheila Ferdinand, the governor from Washington state. The exit polls all over the country confirmed this. Nationwide, a massive voter revolt was underway. With a couple of exceptions, anyone in national office was being replaced with someone who had never been. The citizens of the US viewed the incumbents as the reason for the aliens eliminating humanity. The old guard was being shown the door; the only people in office who'd succeeded in reelection were the men and women who resisted the America-will-survive-at-all-costs agenda of the president.

By the time the polls closed on the West Coast, there was no doubt who had won. CNN, ABC, NBC, CBS, and FOX all predicted Robbins as the winner.

A somber President Klavel stood in front of the cameras at his election center in Rockville, Maryland. "I acknowledge Senator Robbins has won the election. He is a good man and will make a fine president. My staff and I will help the transition to his presidency in any way we can."

The election-night news channels carried his concession of the presidency to Senator Robbins once or twice, but no one paid it much attention. The big news was the aliens eliminating humanity, the starships disappearing, and dark energy. Every channel played the speeches from Rosyville, and the talking heads had switched from their election night monologues to incredulous, meandering thoughts about the future of electricity and how to convince the aliens to reconsider. Reporters from all over the world were interviewing professors and scientists. Researchers were beginning all-night development sessions to duplicate and hopefully improve upon the design published in *Science*.

... ...

Dr. Lowell's private cell phone rang. The number was blocked. "This is Dr. Lowell."

"Pack your desk."

He recognized the president's gravelly voice and laughed. "I thought you'd never ask, Mr. President." He pressed the disconnect button. Sam had already received five job offers to head corporate research centers with salary packages starting at a high seven digits. Shell, Exxon, BP, Sinopec, and Aramco had not yet called, but he knew they would. All the energy companies and oil exporting countries would be scrambling to find a way to exploit dark energy since that meant the end of Big Oil's stranglehold on the world.

... ...

"Grock Species Mining Ship, GSMS-77, this is Grock Central. Acknowledge."

Lieutenant Nussi responded, "Grock Central, this is GSMS-77."

"Stand by for a priority message."

"Grock Central, we are ready." She pressed her *Captain Alert* button, summoning Captain Xanny to the bridge. Everyone waited for the message in gleeful anticipation. The quarantine team was supposed to arrive momentarily, and that meant they could escape this babysitting drudgery and return to exploring.

The message began. "The quarantine team has been diverted. You will remain on quarantine duty around the Grock-inoculated planet circling star EB-31-21-98 until relieved, which may be several years. GSMS-77 will serve as quarantine headquarters. Make plans for your crew to rotate to their home stations on a six-month cycle. A resupply shipment will arrive with the materials to create a colony on the moon of this planet. Quarantine duty pay is authorized. Annual replenishment services will be provided in the colony. Crew members are authorized to bring a companion to live in the colony, if they desire."

"This is GSMS-77, Lieutenant Nola Nussi, communications officer, employee number 234-447-844. I acknowledge message receipt."

Captain Xanny had floated onto the bridge as the message began. Now he stared at the radio in disbelief. The other officers were silent as he settled heavily into his chair, spent a few minutes considering their situation, and then shrugged—an odd movement for an octopus.

"It could be worse. Quarantine pay is double what we earn while we search for habitable planets, and every year we receive a bonus based on the last year's earnings while we were actively mining. My wife has always wanted to see what we do—now she can learn how boring it really is. And our bodies stay young with annual replenishment."

He turned to Commander Chirra. "Yidee, create a duty roster. We'll need a crew monitoring this planet continuously—do it in three shifts per day. Then make a rotation roster of who goes back to their homes and when they go. Tell the crew they can request a transfer to another ship, if they find this duty not to their liking. As soon as we receive a replacement, they can go. For the crew who decide to stay, they have the option to bring their spouses or companions, if they wish. When the quarters are finished on the moon, their significant other can visit or stay."

"Yes, sir." Commander Chirra turned to his computer station.

... ...

Senator Robbins smiled into the cameras and held up his wife's hand in a victory salute. The audience cheered wildly as the band in the background started playing "Hail to the Chief." He held that position like a statue until the music stopped, and then stepped to the microphone.

"Today, something has happened that has never happened in this great country before. Today, the voters decided we needed a new plan." The audience cheered again. "As a species, we have to change—we have our marching orders. We have to rein in corporate greed, find a way to stop polluting our world, and end unsustainable harvesting of our natural resources. These things have all been said before; now we have the energy to do it. Dark energy couldn't have appeared at a more opportune time. Isn't it amazing how that happens? It's almost like a higher being is operating behind the scenes. If God gives us the tool, we have to pick it up and use it.

Our biggest problem of all is war and violence. Hate continues to fill our world. The galactic government told us we are being eliminated because we can't stop fighting among ourselves. I tell them they have *no idea* what humanity can do when we set our minds to it. This is simply another challenge and humanity understands challenges. In 1962, John Kennedy said we would go to the moon in eight years. Everyone said he was crazy—they said it couldn't be done—and on July 20, 1969, Neil Armstrong made his giant leap for mankind. We did that, and we can do this, too.

"This is our biggest challenge ever. How do we stop fighting among ourselves? How do we deal with people who hate? I don't know the answer to that—yet. The leaders of the world must work this one out, and I am just one of many. America is not going to bully anyone into doing anything. The human beings on this planet we call Earth will find a solution, and we will do it together.

"We have to succeed, because the alternative is to die—all of us. It would be the end to who we are—to our hopes, to our dreams, and to all the beauty we have created since man learned to think and question. Join me as we find a way to end war and then find a way to get the Ur to change its mind. The first thing I'm going to do when I assume office in January is contact the Ur and ask them to help us, instead of killing us—help us find a way to peace. They've been through this before; they have to know what worked and what didn't.

"Mankind doesn't want to be ended. We will find the way through this problem tomorrow as surely as we have found the way through our other problems in the past. This isn't our last stepping stone—this is just our next one.

The Beginning of the End

... ...

"The Hore energy portal wasn't from the dream planter," Lieutenant Fibari told Captain Xanny, "but the portal is real. They are using it to power the town where one of the countries does all their Hore research."

"Yeah, I know. I heard their broadcasts."

"These primates are going pretty fast. They went from discovering Hore portals to going through them in half a year. Now they have Hore energy in less than six more months. No one has ever done that before."

"What do you want me to do? Give 'em a medal?"

"What if they find a way around the virus?"

"How could they? The best minds in the galaxy have tried before—and failed."

"I don't know. I'm just saying, these aren't your average primates."

The captain stared at the hologram again—he was doing that a lot these days. These primates were hard not to admire and even like. If only they would stop waring among themselves.

... ...

Dr. Hehsa studied the cluster of cells in the microscope. The clone was growing normally. The labs of the CDC had finally defeated the problem with the spindle proteins, and the artificial uterus with the new amniotic fluid was performing flawlessly. Another six weeks of successful growth and he would announce it to the world.

The source of an unlimited supply of uninfected human DNA had unveiled itself to him while he was walking his dog at night in a cemetery near the CDC. The graveyards were full of uninfected DNA; that the people were dead didn't bother Sridhar at all. They had intelligence and health profiles on vast numbers of those recently passed people, so his team could be very selective. It was going to take about a year to ramp up production, but by then, they could have thousands or even tens of thousands of clones growing—enough so they could cull the defective embryos and fetuses and still have plenty left. The gestation period was still the same as it had always been for humans: forty weeks. The SHIPS were complete and they were ready to receive the new babies.

By the time these kids were teenagers, there would be plenty of them to populate the covert starships being built in huge, underground bunkers, complete with their own Rosy launch mechanisms.

The probes had begun to send back their data, and two likely candidates within twenty lightyears had emerged. The second iteration of probes would go out in one week, coinciding with a huge round of Rosy portals all over the world. These were going out from fifty to one hundred lightyears, and the probes were much more sophisticated than the first generation. They would jump from system to system until they found one that fit their parameters.

Chapter 69 – Playtime

January 20

"They've opened a wormhole!" Commander Chirra screamed, as he hit the jump button. Emergency jump alarms shrieked all over the ship while GSMS-77 leapt into the rosy glow, and the nuke appeared next to where they had just been behind the moon. Ten seconds later, the fireball expanded into empty space. The entire crew watched from their vantage point, a million kilometers on the other side of Earth.

Captain Xanny floated onto the bridge in a rush. "Any damage, Yidee?"

"Not from the blast. The reports are still coming in about the emergency jump—nothing to the ship that Engineering has found yet, two crew skeletal injuries reported so far, one life threatening, and many less severe lacerations, bumps, and bruises."

"Where did it come from?" The captain's voice was low and threatening.

Chirra checked the coordinates. "A country in the largest continent—*Russia* is its name."

"You want to play?" The captain laughed coldly, staring hard at the hologram of Earth. "We can play, too." He pressed the shipwide comm tab on his antigrav pack. "Sergeant-at-arms, please attend me."

The End of **Book One** of *The End of Children* Series

If you liked this book, please do a review of it on
GoodReads.com
or Amazon.com, if you bought it from them.
It's reviews that sell books and help me fund my next

Fredrick Hudgin

novel.
Thanks - Fred

Book Two: *The Three-Hour War*

Book Three: *The Emissary*

Both titles are available on Amazon in either paper or e-book format.

Author's Notes

Chapter One

I love alternate history. I wrote this while I was trying to figure out how all of humanity could be descended from a single human female, Eve. I couldn't understand why we didn't look like that scene in *Deliverance*. So I asked myself, what if the Adam and Eve story in the *Bible* was a metaphor instead of being literal? What if the Intelligent Creationists and the Darwinists were both wrong and what actually happened was somewhere in the middle? With this chapter, Eve's DNA was simply used to identify who was going to be raised up, not as a contributor to the actual genetic process. That way the genetic diversity of the participants would remain intact and humanity would have a starting gene-pool of tens of thousands instead of just two.

Then I decided this was alternate history and why not make it a little more fun. What if someone else raised up another species at the same time. Claim jumpers like the old west! And have the claim jumpers be Mer people!

Chapter Three

"gone to the six winds" is something I thought up. It's a three dimensional play on sailing on Earth which is done in two dimensions. When sailing on Earth, you can "go to the four winds" (East, South, West, and North). Add the third dimension (up and down) to space travel and it becomes "go to the six winds." My thinking is that spaces travel is much like sailing and professional space travelers and space pirates would consider themselves sailors in a ship, hence the nautical terminology. I used this analogy in book three also. When we get there, you can tell me if it works. This is future fiction, after all. Who knows what the vernacular will actually be then? And if the aliens will use our clichés?

Fredrick Hudgin

I have been writing poetry and short stories since I took a Creative Writing class at Purdue University in 1967. Unfortunately, that was the only class I passed and spent the next three years in the Army, including a tour in Viet Nam. After leaving the Army, I earned a BS in Computer Science from Rutgers and struck off on a career as a computer programmer.

I find that my years of writing poetry have affected how I write prose. My wife is always saying to put more narrative into the story. My poetry side keeps trying to pare it down to the emotional bare bones. What I create is always a compromise between the two.

Short stories and poems of mine have been published in Biker Magazine, two compilations by Poetry.Com, The Salal Review, The Scribbler, That Holiday Feeling—a collection of Christmas short stories, and Not Your Mother's Book on Working for a Living.

My home is in Ariel, Washington, with my wife, two horses, two dogs and three cats.

My website is **fredrickhudgin.com**. All of my books and short stories are described with links to where you can buy them in hardcopy or e-book form. I've also include some of my favorite poems. You can see what is currently under development, sign up for book announcements, or volunteer to be a reader of my books that are under development.

Books by
Fredrick Hudgin
All are available at Amazon.com

Sulfur Springs – Historical Fiction — Set in Lewis county,
Washington

A novel about two women who settle in the Northwest.

Duha (pronounced DooHa) is the daughter of a slave
midwife. Her mother and she are determined to escape the
racism in Independence, Missouri, by migrating to
Washington State in 1895. But her mother dies in Sheridan,
Wyoming, leaving Duha with no money, no job, and no
future beyond working in the brothels. She meets Georgia
Prentice, a nurse in the hospital where her mother dies.
Georgia takes her in and, together, they begin a life together
that spans sixty years and three generations.

They settle in the quiet, idyllic settlement of Sulphur
Springs, Washington, nestled between three volcanoes—Mt
Rainier, Mt Adams, and Mt St Helens. The beautiful fir
covered hills and crystal clear rivers belie the evil growing
there that threatens to swallow Duha's and Georgia's
families. Three generations must join together as a
psychotic rapist/murderer threatens to destroy everything
that they have worked and suffered to create.

Ghost Ride – Fantasy/Action-Thriller — Loose sequel to Sulfur
Springs. David is the great-grandson of Duha. Rhiannon is
the great-granddaughter of Georgia.

A novel about how ghosts share our lives and interact with
us daily

The Beginning of the End

David is a Green Beret medic. At least he was for thirty years until he retired and returned to his parents' home without a clue what to do with the rest of his life.

While he is trying to figure out how to recover from the violence he'd faced in Afghanistan and Iraq, he meets a woman who shows him the way then disappears.

As David rebuilds his parents' home and attempts to start an emergency care clinic in his rural town, he meets the woman's granddaughter. Together they figure out how to bring down the meth lab that has poisoned their rural town, overcome state licensing regulations preventing the clinic from opening, help their friend attempt to beat his cancer, and discover David's roots buried in an Indian sweat lodge.

Ghosts abound in this story of love, betrayal, supernatural guides, and unfaithful parents. The good guys aren't entirely good. The bad guys aren't entirely bad. Nothing is what it seems at first glance in Chambersville as the book leads the reader on a merry Ghost Ride.

School of the Gods – Fantasy

A novel about the balance between good and evil.

The idea for **The School of the Gods** began with a series of "What if…"s. What if we really did have multiple lives? What if God made mistakes and learned from them? What if our spiritual goal was to become a god and it was his job to foster us while we grew? What if we ultimately became the god of our own universe, responsible for fostering our own crop of spirits to godhead? If all that were true, there would have to be a school. I mean, that's what schools do … give us the training to start a new career.

The School of the Gods is not a book about God, religious dogma, or organized religion. Instead, it's a story about Jeremiah—ex-Marine, bar fly, and womanizer. Jeremiah's life of excess leads to an untimely end. There is nothing unusual about his death other than he is the 137,438,953,472nd person to die since the beginning of humanity. That coincidence allows Jeremiah to bypass Judgement and get a free pass into Heaven. It also begins the story.

Jeremiah's entry into the hereafter leads to him becoming the confident of the god of our universe. As Jeremiah begins his path toward godhead, he discovers the answer to many questions about God that have confounded humanity from the beginning of time: why transsexuals exist, the real reason for the ten commandments, why the Great Flood of Noah actually happened, and where the other species that couldn't fit on the boat were kept. Along the way, God, Jeremiah, and three other god-hopefuls throw the forces of evil out of God's Home, create a beer drinker's guide to the universes, and become all-powerful gods of their own universes.

Four Winds – A collection of Poetry

A collection of poetry in two parts: Poems about love, tears, hope, and fears. Poems that are *not* about love, tears, hope, and fears. Some rhyme—some don't. Some are silly—some are serious. They encompass the beginning of my written career through my current efforts. They lay the groundwork for the prose that I have created. If you can't write about things you experience, you probably need to do something else. And like anything else, you get better with practice. I was tempted to put them into chronological order but after so many years of polishing and correcting, who knows what the actual date should be. Or I could have put them in order of my most favorite to my less favorite. But your order would be different because everyone resonates to poems differently. So I decided to make them alphabetical.

Fredrick Hudgin

Green Grass – Fantasy/Adventure

This is my first young reader book. My grandkids kept asking me for one of my books and they were all full of adult words, thoughts, and actions—clearly not appropriate for young readers. So I wrote this one.

I'm sure you've heard the cliché about the grass always being greener. Sometimes it's true—sometimes it's not. It's usually a little more complicated than that.

There are no adult words beyond what I hear tweens use every day. And no sex beyond holding hands, giving hugs, and kissing. While the book contains some violence and death, it is not graphic and I feel it is presented in a way that most young readers would understand without getting disturbed.

However, being a young reader book doesn't mean that the plots and subplots are not interesting. Susannah and her friends are dropped into the middle of a civil war. There are good people and bad people on both sides of the portal. Deciding who is whom becomes a pretty important question to figure out. After the Earthlings get cloned, things really get complicated. Imagine saying "Hi!" to yourself!

So pull up a chair and enter a world of Magic with dragons, mages, and swords. It is called Gleepth. You can only get there once a year, and only for a few minutes. But no one told Susannah that when she stepped into the portal and into a life beyond anything she had ever dreamed. And there was no way back beyond waiting a year for the next window.

A Rainy Night and Other Short Stories – Fiction/Non-fiction

The Beginning of the End

The little girl who greets Frank on **A Rainy Night** told him about her father and uncle who had not come home from Afghanistan. But there was more to the story than she said ... a lot more. Frank had already lost his wife and family. The girl's loss reached out to him until the men appeared.

In **Ashes on the Ocean**, her husband of forty-three years has died. Suddenly she was free of his strict ways. She rebuilds her life, filling the void he left with bright happy things. But she still had one remaining obligation—to get his ashes to the ocean. The temptation was to repay his years of intolerance in kind, but a promise is a promise.

Being Dad is about healing. How do you bury the memories along with your son when he comes home from the war with an honor guard instead of a bear hug?

This collection of short stories are my favorite of the stories I have I written. Some are twisted. Some are fun. Some are sad and some are happy — kind of like life. I hope you enjoy them.

The End of Children Trilogy – Science Fiction

The End of Children has SEX. It has ALIENS WHO WANT TO CRUSH US and ALIENS WHO WANT TO HELP. It has VIRUSES. It has PRESIDENTIAL CORRUPTION. It has GALACTIC WARS. It has KIDNAPPED BABIES. It has INTELLIGENT PORPOISES and they don't hitchhike!

Some kids find out how to open a wormhole, the government weaponizes it, the wormhole detectors on the moon announce the discovery to the rest of the galaxy, and after the aliens make humanity sterile for being too warlike and put us in an airtight quarantine, we have World War III. It takes three hours to decimate almost the governments and military of the world – thank god for Canada! The male leaders of the world have failed us and the galaxy won't talk to us about a second chance.

But it all ends happily. A brave young woman finally convinces the galaxy we have something to contribute by performing *Romeo and Juliette* by herself in a space capsule with two weeks food and no way to return to Earth. Our galaxy gets attacked by another galaxy. We save the emperor of our galaxy, show his generals how to fight after ten thousand years of peace, and kick the other galaxy's ass. The emperor offers us another world. We turn over Earth to the porpoises, emigrate to the new world (named Atlantis), and get admitted to the Ur with the woman as our representative.

OK. I left out a little. It's a big story, told in three volumes, each with over 100,000 words.

This is the story of how it all unfolds.

Book 1 – The Beginning of the End (you've already read this one.)

The Beginning of the End

Book 2 – The Three-Hour War

Book 3 – The Emissary

Made in the USA
Middletown, DE
02 December 2020